LETHAL DOSE

For Libby and Jeff:

STEVEN
SNODGRASS

dear friends and colleague.
Thanks so much.

LETHAL
DOSE

ICAM PUBLISHING COMPANY
Orlando, Florida   Montréal, Canada

LETHAL DOSE

A Novel by Steven Snodgrass

ICAM PUBLISHING COMPANY

Published in the United States and Canada

by ICAM PUBLISHING COMPANY

Printed in Canada

Library of congress Cataloging-in-Publication Data

Snodgrass, Steven

Lethal Dose / by **Steven Snodgrass**

1. title

Library of Congress Catalog Number 96-67650

ISBN 0-9642463-1-7

First edition, first printing.

Jacket illustration by Garth Low

Jacket design by Dufour & Fille Design Inc.

For Mary Lee

Acknowledgments

I would like to especially thank Gary Snodgrass. His guidance has been invaluable. He has been a big brother in every sense . . .

Many thanks also:

To Stephen Byers, who got the ball rolling on this project. I am
    eternally grateful.
To Geraldine and Lloyd, my parents, for really getting the
    ball rolling.
To Alex Woollcott, my attorney, for being so bright.
To Jody Nassr, my editor, for her enthusiasm and diligence.
To Lindsay and Lise Bohannon, for their sincere efforts and
    opportunities provided.
To Don Nassr, for pointing me in the right direction.
To John Nassr, for saying "yes."
To Bob and Paula Henry, I don't have the words . . . we grew
    up together.
To those who read early and are my dear friends; Patsy
    Snodgrass, D. Hugh and Joanne Puckett, Bill and Meg
    Travis, Richard and Wilma Grise, Oles and Camille
    Drobocky, Tim and Jamie Whitaker, Jim and Emelia
    Stephenson, Elva Garland, Pat Trotter, Melissa James, and
    Maxine Neel.

And lastly:
To Jack and Lee, my sons, for being so cool . . .

PROLOGUE

The air was quiet now. The patrol officer was just settling into his car seat and told himself that he was in for a long night.

He surveyed the area. Boldly printed signs and placards lay strewn on the street, sidewalks and across the lawn of the abortion clinic. The officer expected that some demonstrators would be back to collect the signs and, in an effort to get in their last word, try to do a bit of damage to the clinic before finally leaving the site. Some of them were that angry. He had been told by the officer he'd relieved that one of the demonstrators had a sign saying "Kill the Killers!" but was asked to leave the site by others who were appalled by such blatant hypocrisy.

Extreme as that view may have been, it certainly was not unheard of. Such killings had happened before, and they would happen again some day, maybe even here in this supposedly respectable part of Wichita. And abortion was only the beginning of it. The return of the death penalty in several states had inspired countless demonstrations and turned the post office on its head with the deluge of letters of protest addressed to just about every politician and special interest group in the country. And if that weren't controversial enough, some states were in the throes of considering the legalization of euthanasia.

He shuddered at the thought of that one. Euthanasia. It would never be legalized in Kansas. Or . . . would it? God, who could tell anymore? If, by some weird twist of events, such a law was ever passed here, there would be such an outburst of protest that no officer of the law would be safe doing what he was doing just now, guarding the premises of what the protestors had termed a "death factory." People of all sorts would come out for that one, never mind the known lunatics.

And there were lots of those around. One of them showed up here today. He had handcuffed himself to the front doors of the clinic to prevent anyone from entering. The officers on crowd control were finally able to make a move when some demonstrators tore the sticks from their placards, held them like clubs, and stood in a protective semi-circle around the man. As the police moved in to arrest him, swatting their batons at anyone who got in their way, there was a brief but futile attempt by the demonstrators to defend their territory. Some willingly left the scene frustrated and bitter. Others left outraged, hurling insults as well as anything within their reach at the police officers. A few had to be escorted away. It was a scene alright, and it made the six and seven o'clock news. Just what they wanted.

The officer shook his head, shattering the day's images of mayhem and violence. He glanced at his watch and noted that it was two-sixteen in the morning.

That was the last thing he remembered before the front of the abortion clinic ballooned outward in a sudden effusion of heat and light.

There was a deafening noise and, a split-second later, a shock wave so forceful that it abruptly shoved the patrol car nearly a foot from its original position. A wave of debris flew into the side of the car, cracking the windshield and pitting its metal sides. Instinctively, the officer covered his eyes in time to avoid being blinded by the bits of glass, steel and granite that blasted through his window. His face and forearm were not spared the assault.

Oblivious to the blood oozing from the numerous cuts on his face and arm, he grabbed the radio microphone.

"Three-Charlie-Ten! Three-Charlie-Ten! I have a . . ."

Before he completed his call for help, darkness clamped over his eyes like a pair of cold hands and his body collapsed across the front seat of his car.

Chapter One

His name was Michael A. Statton, and he was alive. The monitors – heart, lungs, brain – all testified to that. His mind was still active, and he could even communicate with other living beings, after a fashion, answering direct questions by moving the single muscle in his body still able to respond to his will.

One eye-blink for "yes."

Two for "no."

But beyond that, the uniqueness of what had been Mike Statton ceased to exist, buried somewhere in the maze of tests that had identified the two cancer sites, and the mind-numbing barrage of radiation and chemotherapy with which the doctors had tried to control them. Now the treatments had been discontinued, and Statton's files, medical and personal, had been transferred to Northwest Regional Medical Center where they came at last into the hands of the very first resident physician enrolled in its newest fellowship program.

The doctor now stood looking down at his patient with an expression that might have defied interpretation even by his psychiatrist-wife.

"Good morning, Mr. Statton," Jeff Taylor said. "Do you remember me?"

Statton's features remained slack. He had lost the ability to control them more than a week ago. But the blue eyes were bright and alert as he blinked an affirmative.

The doctor nodded, and allowed himself a brief smile intended to reassure the man on the bed.

But in point of fact, Dr. Jeffrey Anson Taylor, M.D., was almost as much in need of reassurance as his patient. The first few days on any job had always been difficult for him. He had been awake for most of the previous night trying, with only moderate success, to deal with the special bogeys of the procedure he would be pioneering here and now, at this time and place.

The raucous, crudely-threatening demonstration against that very procedure, which he had encountered en route from the staff parking lot to the hospital entrance, had only served to underline his general sense of disquiet.

And now, a bomb –

No!

Jeff froze for a moment, furious with himself as he found his thoughts wandering. He struggled to cope with the rumor that had greeted him on arrival at his cubbyhole office. A bomb, or something very like it, had been mailed to the hospital.

He took a deep breath and forced his thoughts back into focus.

Mike Statton was the first patient on the first day of a brand-new fellowship program. As far as Jeff knew, it was the very first of its kind anywhere in North America. This combination of "firsts" might have given anyone pause and was certainly more than enough for Jeff Taylor.

Not that he was any stranger to the residency process.

He'd had two of them: the first in surgery, cut short by the accident that had, at least in his own view, eliminated him from that field, and the second in anesthesiology which he'd actually completed just before entering the one-year program to qualify in this new field. In both cases, he'd experienced all the predictable accelerations of pulse rate and the heightening of perceptions he'd come to associate with first-day fever.

Yet those beginnings had been different.

For him, any trepidation on the first day of surgical residency had been more than balanced by the sheer exhilaration of knowing that at last, he was where he wanted to be and doing what he wanted most to do.

Beginning his residency in anesthesiology had, if nothing else, held the consolation of familiar surroundings. He was still a part of the team in an operating theater.

Jeff nodded again to the helpless man on the bed and turned to exchange glances with Dr. Hyman Rickoff, the professor of anesthesiology chosen by the hospital and its medical faculty to head the clinical section of the new fellowship program. No need for words between them. Jeff had known the Chief of Service, Dr. Rickoff, casually at first, and later, as senior attending physician in his field of specialty at Northwest Regional.

Entering the room now was yet another familiar face. Gertrude Nordstrum was the sometime chief surgical nurse who now ran the entire floor from her office at the end of the corridor. She brought the final forms that he had to sign before the procedure could move forward.

Jeff accepted the proffered pen and clipboard and scrawled his name without bothering to check the work. In his view – one that was generally held throughout the hospital – Trudy Nordstrum was no more capable of error than she was of displaying strong emotion. Her most unrestained reaction was the occasional suggestion of a smile or frown. He had long since given up trying to get a rise out of her. She was one hell of a nurse, and that was enough.

Even the room in which they were working was familiar. Operating Theater No. 3 had become more familiar to him than his own bedroom during the course of his residencies. The only strangeness now was the minor shock of seeing people in these surroundings without surgical masks. Sterile procedure was not, of course, required in this case. But it was a jolt nonetheless . . . unreal. Almost as unreal, perhaps, as the bomb in the . . . . Jeff silently chastised himself for allowing his thoughts to stray, once again, to the rumored bomb. He forced his attention back to the immediate situation by looking at the other faces in the room.

Less familiar, but not strangers, were two other men to whom Jeff nodded a greeting as he handed the signed documents back to Trudy. The younger, struggling visibly to maintain a facade of composure but not succeeding particularly well, was the patient's eldest child and only son, Mike Statton, Jr. He was a mature businessman who had been party to many of the discussions and conferences that led to this morning's events, and would be present as the representative of the family throughout the procedure.

Jeff was glad it would be him instead of Mrs. Statton or one of the four younger sisters who had come to their father's bedside, one by one, earlier that morning. He wished that Dr. Rickoff and the others who had set up the fellowship program had decided to exclude family members entirely. The next few minutes were not going to be anyone's idea of a treasured memory.

The other man, standing next to Mike Statton Jr., was Marty Bernard, the legal representative detailed by the hospital to safeguard its interests during the birth pangs of a new and predictably controversial specialty. Jeff had met the lawyer only once before. When Dr. Rickoff introduced him and explained his duties to the residents, he recalled having wondered what quirk of fate had led the man to this particular assignment.

Not that it mattered.

Nothing mattered now except to get on with the business of the day. Jeff turned back to look directly at the man on the bed.

"Mr. Statton," he said, consciously sharpening his enunciation so that the words would be heard by everyone in the room and be properly recorded along with his actions on the videotape that had been running since before he entered the room. "Mr. Statton, we have withheld your usual medication this morning so that your mind could be entirely clear and able to understand and answer the questions I will ask. Is that satisfactory, sir?"

One blink. Yes.

"Are you aware that your present condition is not likely to improve, and that the disease for which you're being treated is not curable?"

One blink.

"Are you also aware of the certain result of the procedure about to be performed upon you, and have agreed to it of your own free will?"

One more blink.

Jeff glanced at Marty Bernard, who favored him with a nod. The legal requirements had been satisfied.

"All right then, sir," Jeff said, "in a moment or two you will begin to feel drowsy. Just relax and let it happen."

His lids came down once more over his bright blue eyes and this time they stayed closed.

An intravenous line was already in place, running D-5 lactated Ringer's to keep the vein open. Jeff used a second port in the line to inject the first of the three drugs selected for the procedure. This was sodium thiopental, a barbiturate intended to help a patient drift away into sleep.

Now that the patient's eyes were closed, it was difficult for the doctors to be sure exactly when the final link with consciousness was dissolved. Within less than a minute his irregular breathing had smoothed, and the electro-encephalogram monitor showed the characteristic patterns of profound sleep or unconsciousness. Time for the next step. Keeping an eye on the monitors, Jeff switched the I.V. shunt from sodium thiopental to pancuronium bromide, a paralyzing agent intended to work on the muscles of the chest.

For a little while nothing seemed to happen. But Jeff knew the drug would need a moment or two to do its work. He exercised a mental discipline that he had learned in the first years of his training to hold his attention steady on the matter immediately at hand while suppressing all peripheral considerations, such as emotion and impatience. In this profession, it was important to present an unruffled exterior to the world.

Yet, from the corner of his eye, he could see the patient's son's face, bright with perspiration, and Jeff yearned to turn aside for a moment to offer some word of comfort. Why the hell did he have to be in here, anyway? He would talk to Rickoff about it later.

Finally the pancuronium bromide began to take effect. Statton's breathing became slower and shallower, and then ceased altogether as muscles of the chest and diaphragm lost the power to respond to the urgings of his nervous system. Jeff watched the chest until he could discern no movement whatever. Then he turned to the third and final step in the procedure.

Potassium chloride has various therapeutic uses, but when it is administered intravenously in sufficient concentration, it will stop the heart.

Jeff opened the potassium chloride shunt and shifted his concentration to the electrocardiogram.

Despite the lack of respiration, Statton's heart had continued a strong, regular action in defiance of the overwhelming forces against it. However, potassium chloride contained a mandate that could not be ignored. Abruptly the line on the electrocardiogram went flat, and stayed that way.

Jeff waited.

The body is an amazing mechanism, he thought. Its capacity for survival in the face of the most extreme challenge is sometimes beyond belief. A final paroxysm of effort from lungs or heart, while most unlikely, was not entirely beyond the imagination. Mike Statton had been a strong man, and his hold on life was powerful.

A minute passed, and then another, without incident.

The machines monitoring heart, lung and brain activity continued their message of flatline finality without a hint of disturbance. As a matter of form and from ingrained habit, Jeff bent over to check the patient's chest for any exchange of air. There was none. He straightened, nodding to Dr. Rickoff, who moved quickly to confirm his findings. Immediately, he directed Statton's son from the room.

Rickoff's part was over and so was Jeff Taylor's. The first procedure of the first fellowship program in America's first legally-authorized Department of Euthanasia had been completed, and it was successful. The patient was dead.

Now he could go try to find someone who had a few real facts about the damned bomb.

Chapter Two

Outside the hospital the demonstrators had begun chanting. Their words, dulled to a background rhythm by the walls of the operating room, became fully audible to Jeff as he strode out into the corridor.

"STOP-THE-MUR-DUR! STOP-THE-MUR-DUR!"

He wondered how long they could keep it up. Surely lungs and vocal cords must have their limits. Did they really expect to influence events by such tactics?

The elevator bank was only a step or two away, but Jeff decided to take the stairs. The elevators at Northwest Regional were justly famous for their sluggishness. Besides, he found himself suddenly craving the release of physical exertion. The suspense was too much – he needed to talk to Rickoff.

Brisk as he had been in leaving the room after the Statton procedure was completed, the Chief of Service had been quicker. One moment he was in the room and the next he was gone. But Jeff was sure he knew where Rickoff was headed.

The fifth floor of the old administrative wing, now converted to clinical and technical services, was normally not crowded on a weekday morning.

However, today was far from normal. Jeff was not especially surprised to find two somber-faced men, clad in dark blue protective clothing with the word "Police" stenciled on their backs, still at work with a camera and measuring tape in the tiny anteroom to Rickoff's office. One of them tried to turn him away as soon as he opened the door, but Rickoff intervened and Jeff was admitted to where the final photographs were being taken of a partially-unwrapped package on the secretary/receptionist's desk.

It was a small desk and virtually bare of other paraphernalia because Dr. Rickoff shared the secretary's services with the head of the hospital's computer support unit, and most of her work was done at the other desk. She was not at work this morning, Rickoff explained in quiet, controlled tones as he led Jeff past the desk to a spot where he could observe without interfering in the police technicians' work.

"Got her over in maternity," Rickoff said. "Sedated and recovering."

"Maternity? Why?"

"She fainted, passed out cold, when she opened the package, and she's already told her story, more than once, to the police. So I couldn't think of any reason she should have to tell it again to some damned reporter."

Jeff nodded thoughtfully.

"So for now," Rickoff continued, "we're telling them she's gone home".

Both doctors' attention was now centered on the package that had caused the secretary's collapse.

It was in no way remarkable – a simple cardboard parcel, slightly larger than a shoe box, with Dr. Rickoff's name and the address of the hospital written in ruler-straight block letters on the mailing label. It had arrived along with the usual circulars, bills and oddments of the morning mail, and now lay where the secretary had left it, after she had cut through the transparent tape and raised the lid. The bomb squad had left it that way, after determining that its contents were non-lethal.

Dr. Rickoff's secretary, however, could hardly be faulted for her reaction. The six railroad flares, roughly strapped together with electrician's tape, looked like sticks of dynamite. The battery pack was real enough and the wires were properly connected.

The only part missing was the trigger mechanism – confiscated, perhaps, by the technicians. Rickoff described it for Jeff as the final pictures were taken and the technical crew began to pack up its gear.

"It's like a kind of miniature mousetrap," he said. "The moving part is spring loaded and held in place by pressure of the lid. Open the lid, and the armature snaps down on the opposite side, connecting the electrical leads, as it would if it were a real bomb. This one detonated a small percussion cap – the kind they use in children's toy firearms – to make the appropriate sound effect."

"Jesus!"

"Indeed – and also Mary and Joseph," Rickoff nodded. "And just so no one should miss the point, underneath the little popper-thing, this funny jokester left a note printed like the label that said, 'If you do commit murder today, the next bang will be louder."

Jeff tried to think of a proper response, but couldn't. He stood mute alongside his friend and senior while the police completed their chores, gathered up the faux bomb and departed, closing the outer door behind them.

The two doctors moved into Rickoff's office and slumped into chairs. It was time to discuss the morning's procedure and make plans for the next. But their minds were elsewhere.

"Was there a postmark from its point of origin?" Jeff began, breaking the silence.

Rickoff nodded. "Yes," he said, "somewhere in Kansas. Wichita, I think."

"The police will check that, of course."

"Of course."

And then for a time the two men sat in silence, each occupied with his own thoughts.

* * *

Jeff's mind was in chaos.

The mirrored door to Rickoff's bathroom was ajar, and he struggled to focus on the image of himself as he tried to recapture the sense of pioneering that had exhilarated him en route to the hospital just two hours earlier.

So far as anyone had been able to determine, this morning's exercise had been the first legally-authorized euthanasia procedure ever performed in the United States. And he, Jeff Taylor, M.D., had performed it. The technique had been flawless, the result as predicted. The patient departed life without pain or fear or regret, avoiding months of anguish and indignity and sparing his family the emotional torment of witnessing his suffering. For that, he could feel only a sense of moral and professional vindication, not unmixed with pride at having explored what had been an untested frontier.

He had done the right thing. He had no regrets. Yet . . .

The reflected image seemed for a moment almost to mock. Tall man. Dark hair, blue-gray eyes, fair complexion. Need to get more sun. Spending too much time indoors lately, he thought. Oversized nose. Mouth a bit crooked. About ten pounds underweight. Jeff Taylor, physician, sometime surgeon, sometime anesthesiologist. Euthanasist?

Today he had taken a human life, deliberately and with forethought, and, even without the element of malice, a part of the essential center that was Jeff Taylor informed him that this was murder. Moreover, it was a specific violation of that oath, "I swear by Apollo, physician . . .", taken by all members of his profession since the time when Apollo had still been worshipped as a true god. "I will give no deadly drug . . ."

No one worshipped Apollo any more, or Panacea, or any of the other deities included in that preamble. But the sense of the thing, the moral implication and the strictures, imposed as much for the protection of the physician and the preservation of the profession as for any benefit to the patient, remained valid. Even more to the point, it was the absolute antithesis of what he had set out to do as a doctor.

God knew, he was no Arrowsmith.

The breast-beating idealists that populated most of the current medical fiction had left him cold, as they did most other doctors of his acquaintance. Physicians did not usually become physicians because of an overriding concern for suffering humanity any more than lawyers went to law school out of any fixation on the ideal of justice. In the real world, there was more concern with the tangible rewards of prestige, augmented earning capacity and the enjoyment of professional excellence.

But for him, there was more to it than that.

Jeff was a healer.

Money, prestige, professional stature and all the rest notwithstanding, his whole nature was oriented towards the goal of curing, of restoring other human beings to their full potential, and it was more than a mere intellectual exercise. It was the chief pillar of his world, as much a part of him as his shoe size or parting his hair on the left.

Yet the need for his new specialty could not be denied. Surely no better example could be found than his own first patient.

Mike Statton was a man who had enjoyed his life. Jeff had not met Statton before he became ill, but the elements of joyful vitality had resounded from every word in the brief biography included in his case records.

At sixteen, Statton had used an elder brother's birth certificate to join the army. He served as a combat medic in Korea where he won a Bronze Star and found a direction for civilian life.

When he was discharged in 1954, he had gone to pharmacy school on the GI Bill. He had worked in the prescription department of a supermarket chain until he was able to scrape together the money to go into business for himself, as the owner of a pharmacy located in the lobby of a medical building. Although it hadn't made him rich, it had provided a decent life-style for his growing family, referred to in other parts of the record: barbed hook lodged near the eye, requiring surgical removal, family fishing trip (1965); measles and chicken-pox contracted from younger family members (1968 and 1970); fracture of fourth and fifth metatarsal bones, family visit to Disney World (1977).

In their early fifties, Mike Statton and his wife, Barbara, had taken flying lessons. Both earned their private licenses, and it was during one of the regularly required flight physicals that the first signs of Mike's final illness had appeared. Diagnosis of cancer had been quickly confirmed and surgical intervention was ruled out by the position and nature of the two tumors. Medical management proved ineffective. Within weeks, Mike Statton had begun to lose control of his limbs, and his pain was made endurable only through an ever-increasing dosage of drugs.

Yet, Mike Statton's actual death might have been postponed for months, perhaps even years.

Medical technology, while still unable in many cases to prolong anything that might legitimately be called "life," had undeniably achieved prodigies in extension of human existence. Such cases had become almost a staple of the news media ("Family Marks Father's Twentieth Year in Coma" and "Judge Refuses Order to Remove Life-Support"), and researchers were constantly reporting advances in the field.

But life, Jeff believed, is more than mere existence, and Mike Statton's life had actually ended the day he lost the ability to live it with satisfaction and dignity.

In the end, shortly before he lost the ability to speak, he had asked his son to help him die, and only the chance arrival of a nurse in the hospital room had prevented the enlarged tragedy of a loving and dutiful son being accused of patricide.

Jeff found himself shaking his head as though responding to a question.

No.

Damn it, no! Submitting a father and son – or any other caring and responsible person – to such an ordeal could not be right. There had to be an alternative, and after years of argument and controversy (climaxed by a floor debate that made headlines around the world), the state legislature had finally provided one.

America's first euthanasia statute had been passed into law less than a year earlier, and survived the inevitable legal testing by a split but lopsided vote of the state Supreme Court.

Opponents were still at work on the next step up the judicial ladder. But the U.S. Supreme Court had, thus far, shown a notable disinclination to become involved in the matter, and the trustees of Northwest Regional had therefore found it both logical and expedient this year to establish a regular fellowship program to train doctors in the specialty.

Applications from potential patients had risen from a trickle to a flood, astonishing even the staunchest advocates, as word of the new euthanasia residency spread through the medical world.

"And that cannot be permitted to happen!" Dr. Rickoff's tone was sharp.

The sound of his voice finally managed to penetrate the wall of Jeff's reverie, and he found himself back in the world of euthanasia and bombs in the mail, uneasily aware that the older man had been speaking for some time.

"Sorry," he apologized, rousing himself upright in the chair and dragging a hand through his hair. "I'm afraid this morning's events have really affected me."

Rickoff waved a dismissive hand. "Bomb scares do that to people. But as I was saying, Jeff, we can't let it affect our professional judgment or our personal lives, either."

Jeff started to answer, but hesitated, and Rickoff hurried on, assuming concurrence.

"Show weakness, any kind of vacillation," he said, "and they're on you like a pack of jackals, just like the abortion clinics."

Jeff turned the idea over in his mind. "Wasn't there some kind of violence at one of the abortion clinics just last night?" he inquired. "There was something about it on the radio, as I was driving in."

Rickoff nodded. "Just so. Another bombing, somewhere in the Midwest."

"Was anyone hurt? I missed most of the news item."

"A policeman," Rickoff nodded again. "Minor cuts and bruises, nothing major. But that's my whole point, Jeff. Why do you think they do things like that?"

Jeff shrugged. "To scare us, I guess," he said. "And I have to tell you, if that's what the person who mailed you that *thing* today had in mind, it worked. I'm well and truly impressed!"

Rickoff snorted. "All right. It would give anyone a minute or two of deep thought, I'll grant you that. But you're wrong, you know, about their intention."

"Wrong?"

"Yes. Because they know damned well you can't scare anyone out of the abortion business, or out of our specialty, either."

"Then . . . why?"

"Publicity!" Rickoff almost roared the word, hammering it home with a flat palm in the middle of his desk. "They love the headlines, the eleven o'clock news items. They love the thought of people paying attention to their point of view. The rest doesn't really matter."

"Well . . ."

"Give them what they want, and they'll just want more."

"And to get it . . ."

"And to get it, they always have to escalate. Today, a fake bomb, tomorrow a real one. Today, no one hurt, tomorrow – who knows?"

Jeff sighed, thinking it over. "And you think sitting on this, keeping it out of the papers and off television, would be better?" he asked, not trying to hide his disagreement.

"Couldn't hurt."

Jeff shook his head. "No sale."

Rickoff looked surprised.

"No sale." Jeff elaborated, "There's no way to test the theory. The fake bomb was reported and the press must know all about it by now."

"I told Jerricoe to stonewall it."

"To what?"

"Stonewall it. No answers, no statement, nothing. And that goes for all of us in the Euthanasia Center. Spread the word, will you Jeff? No one talks to the press. No one!"

Jeff sat still for a moment, trying to imagine the reaction of Carl Jerricoe, Northwest Regional's gravel-voiced Public Relations Director. He wished that he might have seen the ex-reporter's face.

But Rickoff was serious, and there would be no reasoning with him, at least for the time being.

"All right," he said, easing himself upright. "It's your Center, you call the shots. I'll tell the others to put a sock in it until further notice."

Rickoff seemed mollified.

"But all the same, Doctor" Jeff continued, timing the words to coincide with the closing of the door behind him, "I think you'd better get in the practice of signing autographs because, unless I'm mistaken, you're about to have your own personal fifteen minutes of international fame!" It was a good exit line and in all probability, true.

Outside Rickoff's office, Jeff had an almost irresistible urge to return. Bombs and bomb threats were a major concern, yes, but somehow, despite the physical evidence of the package and its accompanying note, the whole business seemed unreal to him, like something out of a movie.

Meanwhile, there were very real and immediate questions he needed to discuss with someone. Questions concerning his own attitude and involvement in the euthanasia service. Questions professional and questions personal. Questions that he could not "stonewall."

Punching the button for the elevator, he allowed himself a moment of mental relaxation and found himself staring with baffled fascination at his own left hand.

Chapter Three

At first glance there seemed to be nothing wrong with it.

In the years since the accident, Jeff had consciously developed the habit of carrying his left hand half-closed, with fingers lightly curled as though about to grasp a small object, in order to minimize the appearance of damage. He knew that most casual acquaintances were unaware of any physical defect. But it was there.

Reluctantly, but unable to resist the impulse, Jeff found himself going through the well-rehearsed ritual of sending a specific impulse down the arm to the hand and observing the result. He ordered his fingers to relax, to uncurl themselves and assume a stance of flat alignment, and was rewarded by instant obedience by his middle finger, forefinger and thumb. His other fingers remained curled.

Staring at them now as he entered the elevator and jabbed the first floor button, Jeff was unable to avoid the urge to retrace – for the thousandth or perhaps fifty-thousandth time – the well-remembered stages of astonishment, renewed effort, growing panic, frenzied determination and ultimate resignation with which he had reacted to the first postoperative demonstration of their immobility.

Until then, it had all been a kind of mind game, a detail somehow blurred and unreal amid the sudden input of pain and astonishment that came from the accident itself.

Things like that simply didn't happen to Jeff Taylor.

The door opened at the first floor and he left the elevator, turning as if by instinct in the direction of the surgical lounge.

Surgery.

That was the long and short of it, of course. Surgery was the reason he had come to Northwest Regional in the first place, the focus of the life he had planned for himself since the first time he saw an actual surgical procedure in medical school.

"Heal with steel!"

That single phrase, the surgical residents' in-house motto, had summed up his whole approach to his profession and to life itself. Heal with steel! Do it now! Do it right! Do it!

And it had worked just fine. For awhile.

"Dr. Taylor!"

A woman's voice cut into the sound-resistant universe of self-examination and Jeff was abruptly restored to the real world. He found himself in the entranceway to the surgical lounge confronting a breathless Nurse Trudy Nordstrum.

"Doctor, I . . ."

Something was amiss. Jeff took a deep breath and tried to bring himself up to speed. Something had happened, or had been happening in the lounge when he came through the door. Something he'd missed because of his preoccupation.

Trudy.

Yes. Looking at her now, he realized that he had never seen her in such a state. The breathlessness he had noted was only one symptom; added to it was a slight, but definite, glow of perspiration on her brow, a hint of rosiness in her usually pallid cheeks. Had it been anyone else, Jeff told himself, he would have been sure that he had interrupted one of the slap-snatch-and-tickle sessions that occasionally enlivened the less frenetic hours in the lounge. Certainly the lady showed every evidence of such recent happy exercise.

But . . . Trudy?

Jeff tried to fit the idea to the individual and found himself utterly unable to do it. It just didn't fly. Despite her age at thirty-something, Gertrude Nordstrum had always presented the image of an elderly maiden aunt. She was pleasant enough but simply not personally involved in the physical side of human experience. Trudy was intelligent, efficient, reliable and loyal. But the idea of a sensual, sexual Trudy Nordstrum was almost an oxymoron.

Besides, he reminded himself, it takes two to tango, and the only other person in the lounge was a young man in orderly's whites, busily mopping the linoleum tiles near the sink.

Had he and Trudy been closer together a moment earlier?

Jeff found himself plucking at something – the remnant of an impression lodged in the far corner of memory suggesting a sudden flurry of activity that might have been triggered by the sound of his footsteps outside the door. Or perhaps even by his absentminded ingress. Something. But it wouldn't come clear, and before he could follow the trail farther, the line of thought was broken.

"Doctor – " Trudy began again.

"Look, Trudy," Jeff interrupted in what he later realized was an inept effort to reduce her obvious tension. "Don't sweat it. We're all grown-ups here."

But that was the wrong approach.

Nurse Nordstrum's complexion, faintly glowing only a moment earlier, suddenly filled with the flaming blood of mortification. Her mouth opened as if to speak, but no sound emerged and a moment later she turned and fled through the double doors.

Well, hell.

Jeff stared after her nonplussed, and then stepped into the room. The young orderly was collecting his mop and bucket and started toward the door.

"All done?" Jeff inquired, more for the purpose of breaking the awkward silence.

"Uh . . . yeah."

His smile was ready and boyish, his dark blue eyes clear and candid. Looking more closely, Jeff decided he might be a little older than he had first supposed – mid-twenties or maybe a year or two more.

"You're new," he said.

The orderly nodded and smiled again with the same boyish grin.

"Two weeks," he said, "but I've been up on obstetrics until this morning."

"I'm Jeff Taylor," Jeff said, offering his hand.

"Dave Wallace."

His handshake was warm and firm, but this time Jeff was sure the blue-violet eyes were detached, almost flat, adding a touch of disingenuousness to his expression.

Releasing Jeff's hand, Dave Wallace retrieved the mop and bucket but seemed to have second thoughts before actually moving towards the door.

"Trudy – Nurse Nordstrum – was only telling me about the big scare upstairs," he began. "I wouldn't want you to think . . . I mean, that's all it was."

"The big scare?"

"The bomb," Wallace went on, "the one that came in the mail."

Jeff blinked, changing mental gears. So much for Rickoff's plan.

"I guess the story's all over the hospital by now," Jeff said.

"Pretty much."

"Well . . . welcome to the wonderful world of medical science," Jeff said.

Another smile, cookie-cutter twin to the others. The doors swung shut behind him.

Jeff moved to the counter and poured himself a cup of coffee, resisted the urge to add cream and sugar, and took it with him to the nearest table, wondering whether to laugh or cry. Or just shrug.

What the hell.

No hospital – at least, no hospital he had ever seen – was, or could be, run like a convent. Too much going on. Too much birth and death and success and failure and grief and joy and tears and laughter. Too much life.

It all happened right here.

Still, the events that had changed the whole direction of his own life and career had taken place elsewhere.

*　*　*

He and some college friends had rented a ski chalet in Vail, Colorado, during a two-week break in the surgical residency. After a couple of warm-up runs, Jeff had convinced himself that the downhill technique he'd developed during undergraduate vacations hadn't deserted him. Light had been fading when he pushed off from the top of the slope reserved for expert skiers.

The first couple of turns had gone well enough, but the third was a zinger and, as he approached it, Jeff had realized that he was going too fast. He had tried to slow down while maneuvering to meet the turn, and it had been almost good enough. But not quite.

The last thing he had remembered was an almost dreamlike sense of lift as he went over the edge of an embankment and caught a glimpse of the earth twenty feet below. And then nothing. Not even the impression of time passing, until he'd woken up in the emergency ward at Vail with an I.V. running and his left arm in a splint.

He had discovered that he had lost a significant amount of blood and suffered fractures of the seventh through eleventh ribs on his left side. There was a forty percent pneumothorax, which meant a collapsed lung. And there was a stabbing pain in the region of his pelvis. He hoped it wasn't broken. Pelvic fractures were a bitch.

By comparison, the damage to his arm and hand had seemed negligible.

He'd watched with interest and trepidation, despite all effort to remain objective and treat the situation as a learning experience, while the emergency room doctors dissected the intercostal muscle, punctured the pleura, and inserted a chest tube. Enduring the temporary shortness of breath while holding still for the CAT scan, he privately concurred in the doctor's final decision to ship him back to Northwest Regional by air ambulance as soon as he was stable.

At the time, it had never really occurred to him to wonder why the doctors at Vail hadn't wanted to keep him there. The hospital was highly rated and well accustomed to treating injured skiers. His wasn't the first chest and pelvic traumas they'd ever seen, and nothing he'd heard seemed to indicate any particular problem except for the usual risk to the liver and spleen, common to such cases. He'd assumed it was just some kind of professional courtesy.

But back on his home turf the situation was soon clear.

The chest and pelvic damage had been extensive, but fully reparable. The arm was another matter. At Vail, a surgical team had applied open reduction and fixation to the radius and ulna and had gone in for a look, but backed out when they had seen what had happened to the ulnar nerve. It was severely crushed, almost severed.

At Northwest, an orthopedic team had undertaken the job of repair and reconstruction. But the surgeon in charge, a recognized major leaguer whose expertise Jeff trusted, had been up front with him as soon as the initial work had been completed.

"The arm itself," he had said, "should be all right, given a bit of time and physical therapy. Also, you should regain full use of the thumb, as well as the index and middle fingers, enough to handle most tasks in a normal manner. Damage to the other two digits, however, was more extensive."

Those two fingers, the orthopedist had told him, would be numb and curled tightly against the palm, at least at first. They might respond to physical therapy, but the odds against full restoration of function or control were somewhere between overwhelming and astronomical.

"I'm sorry," he had said. "I wish I had something better to offer, and believe me I know what this means to you as a surgeon. I know how I'd feel, and it scares the hell out of me just thinking about it. But I was sure you'd want the straight word."

Jeff had told him he was right about that and thanked the man for his honesty. He had spent the rest of the day and most of the night trying to get used to the idea of living the rest of his life in a body not totally responsive to his will. By the time he was wheeled into the O.R. the following day, he had made his peace with the basic concept, and even used the next few days to plow through the literature relating to cases similar to his own.

There was a lot of it. So when the surgeons were ready to say they'd done all they could for him, he'd thought he was ready for any kind of shock. But he wasn't.

Intellectual understanding and emotional acceptance are two very different things, and that had been his first experience of outright insubordination on the part of a body whose ready compliance with all demands had always been taken for granted.

The shrunken, almost wispy appearance of his whole body after its long period of idleness had shocked and disgusted him at first. But the knowledge that it would heal, and the visible evidence of that healing – he hardly needed the cane anymore – had kept him going. He could handle it. The muscles would fill out again and the sense of physical power, of positive authority, would return. That was beyond question.

Until he saw his hand.

Looking at his arm had been bad enough. If the other muscles of the body had softened and gone slack, the arm had actually withered. Could it ever come back? The articles he'd read said it could and he was determined to believe them, no matter what.

The hand, though. Jesus . . . his hand!

As the orthopedist had predicted, the thumb and first two fingers moved weakly in accordance with his mental orders and, if neither strong nor nimble in their first free moments, showed every indication of willingness to become so with a little exercise.

But the other two fingers were dead. That was the only word for them, curled and sensitive neither to pain nor repeated efforts to achieve even the smallest motor response. They didn't even twitch.

The orthopedists and one or two others who had come to observe had told him not to be too discouraged. The physical therapists who came later tried to be reassuring, showing him videos of patients who had overcome disabilities far more serious and extensive than his own.

But none of the patients in their case studies had been a surgeon, and surely none had lived their lives by the inflexible precept of "excel or die" that had been Jeff Taylor's chief legacy from the fierce and affectionate grandfather whose rock-ribbed resolution had been the foundation of his whole life.

The Chief of Surgery, however, had been certain that he should complete his residency. "You're still a fine surgeon, Jeff, and you're right-handed. There aren't many procedures that require all five fingers of the left hand, and for those few I'm sure you can find means to compensate, or simply turn them over to someone else."

It was all true. He knew it, and perhaps if his wife had been there to help him sort out his own reactions he might have come to a different conclusion. But at that time he hadn't yet met Jolene, and the voice he heard most clearly was that of the old man whose love had always contained an implicit ingredient of ultimate challenge: "Make sure you're the best, top-of-the-list, at anything you do. If you give it all you've got and you're still not on the highest peak, give it more! Never, never, never accept second place. Be a winner . . . or find another game."

His letter of resignation had been on the Chief's desk the next morning, and he had been on his way. To somewhere.

Driving down the coast with no specific destination in mind, he had rediscovered the peculiar pleasure of driving an automobile under non-stressful conditions. The car was old, but the years had been kind to the nondescript Plymouth sedan, and he found there was a kind of natural rhythm to the act of manipulating its stick shift over hills and through the moderate traffic of coastal tourist towns.

At Point Reyes, he'd left the coast and turned inland with some vague notion of seeing the wine country he'd heard so much about, and stopped at last in a motel just outside Sonoma where he had scrawled the words "skiing instructor" on the line of the registration card reserved for "Occupation."

Skiing instructor.

Some joke.

Physically weary from the long drive, but still unable to control the headlong velocity of his thoughts, he had carried his suitcase to the room, tossed it into a corner without bothering to unpack, draped his jacket over the back of a chair, and sprawled on the bed to stare unseeingly at the ceiling as the shadows of early evening gradually collected there.

Skiing instructor. It was a joke at which only he could ever laugh, if he could get beyond its dark side.

It was a typical Jeff Taylor gesture, differing only in scope and effect from the answer he'd given the Dean of Admissions at St. Louis University School of Medicine. The older man's tone had been openly condescending as he quizzed Jeff about his academic qualifications, expressing reservations about southern educational standards in general, and those of Jeff's native state in particular.

"What makes you think a boy from Kentucky could compete with the kind of students we have here at St. Louis?" the dean had wanted to know.

Jeff had opened his mouth to answer, the words already boiling on his tongue.

His first choice, the medical school on which his sights had been fixed through four years of college, had been full before his application was even processed. If he failed to gain admission here, he would have to resign himself to another year of waiting. But the old bastard was just too much. Just too damned much, entirely.

"I would make a better doctor," he said, leaning forward across the desk and speaking distinctly so that there could be no possible misunderstanding, "than any arrogant, insolent little son-of-a-bitch who ever came out of this place."

And before the astonished man could resettle the rimless glasses that had slipped to the end of his nose during that recitation, Jeff had been out of his office, out of the building . . . and out of luck, so far as getting into med school that year was concerned.

He'd taken it in stride, though, putting in a year of graduate school at Washington University and setting up a combination of early application and academic achievement that propelled him almost effortlessly into the school that had been his first choice the previous year.

Skiing instructor . . .

Got to control impulses like that, boy.

But after a moment, the sheer childish bravado of the phrase was too much for him and he found himself laughing, really laughing for the first time in weeks, at himself and the world and the wallow of self-pity in which he had almost allowed himself to drown.

Bullshit!

Laughter was a first step, and the second was to sit up on the edge of the bed and wipe the dim ceiling clear of the wistful images that had been gathering there. The hell with them and the hell with whining. Shit happens! You can hide in a cheap motel room and blubber about it, or you can get up off your ass and get on with the business of living.

Hyman Rickoff . . .

Yes!

The very last person he'd talked to before limping away from Northwest Regional had been Dr. Hyman Rickoff, one of the head honchos in anesthesiology. What was it he'd said? At the time, he'd been too busy feeling sorry for himself to pay much attention, but somehow the words had been registered and recorded somewhere in the back files of his mind. What?

Oh, yes. There'd been a dropout from among the anesthesiology residents who were due to start the next month. The slot was his, if he wanted it. It wasn't surgery; he'd be on the other side of the operating table. But he'd still be there, in the O.R. Part of the team . . .

As he gathered his belongings, Jeff had tried to remember his response to Rickoff's offer, but it was no go. The words had vanished. And he found himself hoping they had been at least civil because now that he thought of it, the idea wasn't such a bad one, at that.

Anesthesiology was a decent specialty, respectable and respected. Not that he'd ever considered it for himself, of course. From the first, he'd always thought of himself as a surgeon, an R.D. – Real Doctor – somehow anointed in a way that those involved in non-surgical specialties could never be, and entitled to condescend (at least in his heart) to the "gas passers" who spent the days presiding over various levels of controlled unconsciousness.

Nonetheless, by the time the motel door had closed behind him, his mind had been made up. He was even considering a long-distance call to Rickoff, just to make sure of nailing the open slot in the residency program.

That had been the beginning.

At the moment the decision had been made, one kind of life had ended for him and another had begun; one that had in fact led him now to –

"Dr. Taylor?"

The sound of his own name, coming from behind him, dissolved the images of the motel and its stuccoed ceiling and all of the thoughts that he had had back then in a single instant, and Jeff found himself back on the couch in the surgical lounge, still holding a paper cup of coffee long since gone cold.

"Dr. Taylor . . . I think that's your page."

Jeff looked over his shoulder to see the new orderly – Dave Walton? Wallace, yes, that was the name – leaning through the lounge doorway.

Before he could speak, the page came again.

"Thanks," he said, bestirring himself and glancing at his watch. Lord. No wonder he was being paged.

"Nada."

The orderly's head and shoulders disappeared from the doorway and Jeff came to his feet, stifling a yawn and looking for somewhere to dump the neglected coffee. Rickoff's post-mortem seminar on their first euthanasia patient had been scheduled to begin five minutes ago, and of course he would use part of the time to give them the straight facts about the fake bomb that had frightened his secretary. The Chief would be irritated by his tardiness, and Jeff couldn't blame him.

By the time he reached the lounge doors en route to the elevator, he was almost running, and had to execute a neat broken-field sidestep to avoid slamming bodily into the orderly, who had rounded up a train of wheelchairs just outside.

"Sorry!" he said over his shoulder, not breaking stride.

"Nada . . . no problem."

The orderly stopped to watch the doctor run down the hall. He was shot with luck; the elevator door opened just as he arrived at the end of the corridor. Jeff Taylor might have been intrigued by the emotion that animated his watcher's features for a brief moment before being sternly suppressed.

It was the very smallest of smiles.

And it was very cold, indeed.

Chapter Four

Driving home that evening, Jeff hesitated in the act of switching on his car radio. He seldom had time to read a newspaper, so he kept the radio tuned to the city's only twenty-four-hour news station as a matter of policy. A man owed it to himself to know what was going on in the world, even if that knowledge did come in puzzling little sound-bytes that always seemed to raise more questions than they answered. But tonight he found himself reluctant. Listening to the news was one thing. Being a part of it was another.

Carl Jerricoe, the hospital's public relations director, had warned everyone connected with the Euthanasia Center to keep a low profile, at least for awhile. "Until the silly bastards get something else to write about," he had said.

The advice, however, was hardly necessary.

Ever since the Medical Center's quiet announcement of the world's first euthanasia fellowship, Jerricoe's office had been besieged with news media demands for interviews with the doctors involved in the program, the trustees who had approved it, even the patients who might be candidates for the procedure.

What made you decide to kill people instead of curing them, Doctor?

Do you look on yourself as a murderer?

How do you decide who's going to live and who's going
to die?

Does your family think you're doing the right thing?

What will you say to the patients' families afterward?

Print media or electronic, the questions were always the
same: loaded, prurient and virtually mindless.

Against their better judgment, Jeff and the other residents
yielded at last to Jerricoe's plea that they "give the public a few
solid facts for an anchor before their imaginations turn us all
into Boris Karloff." They had taken part in just one open press
conference on the day their program was formally inaugurated,
and it had been a shambles. Seeing himself on television that
night, and hearing his own voice – did he really sound like that?
– Jeff had resolved never, under any circumstances, to allow
himself to be placed in such a position again. And even Jerricoe
had been willing to acknowledge an error in judgment.

"Worse'n I thought," he admitted. "The sharks are smelling
blood here!"

Since that time, the public information office had barred the
door, seldom bothering even to pass along the various
interview requests. But word that the first patient had, in fact,
been accepted for legal euthanasia procedure had somehow
leaked to the outside world, and what had been a slowly
diminishing clamor had become a roar.

To keep it from getting entirely out of hand, it had been
agreed that Jerricoe would issue one statement early in the
week confirming the bare facts of the case (though, of course,
withholding the identity of the patient and any personal
information concerning him with the exception of age and sex)
and another after the procedure had been completed.

That second statement, Jeff knew, had been issued shortly
before noon, and he was curious to see what the reporters had

made of it, especially in light of the inevitable police report on the simulated bomb sent to Rickoff.

The bomb.

Yes. The news media were sure to pick up on the bomb – make it the center of the story – and for once Jeff found himself in agreement. Never mind the fact that it was a fake; the very existence of such a thing was a development he couldn't really come to terms with, despite the plethora of abuse, both written and oral, that had descended upon Northwest Regional since its announcement of the euthanasia residencies.

He'd stopped reading the letters after the first few. But he'd photocopied one of them and shown it to Jolene, whose psychiatric orientation had seized upon the handwriting. It was sprawling and uneven, erupting here and there into block capitals and then bending around a corner to continue in the margins of the page. She identified the missive as the work of a "simple schizoid," meaning that the writer was a demented person, presumably free in society (the letter bore no sign of institutional screening) and now somehow fixated on the euthanasia service as the earthly personification of evil.

"Your very footprints," the author had written, "bear the reek of HELL."

Good to know. Have to watch those footprints.

Jolene said the writer probably wasn't at all dangerous; most people suffering from that particular malady were too busy protecting themselves from imaginary bogeys to work out any coherent strategy of attack. They disturbed their neighbors occasionally by holding animated and public conversations with empty air, or were apt to base a whole program of action upon a perceived but totally unwarranted connection between unrelated phenomena; to denounce space exploration, for instance, on grounds that the earth is obviously flat and all claims of orbital flight therefore spurious. But physical violence was usually beyond them.

"Can't concentrate long enough," she explained.

Jeff's concern, however, was with the idea of being hated at all, regardless of the mental condition of the hater. He wasn't accustomed to the sensation, and he didn't like it.

"Why us?" he'd wanted to know.

Jolene tried to sort it out for him. "Any new idea, anything that anyone does that deviates from established modes of conduct, is bound to generate opposition. It's perfectly normal. People really don't like challenge, no matter what they say. They'd rather stay in their comfortable rut."

"But you said this guy . . ."

"Was out of his tree," Jolene nodded. "Schizophrenic. But that doesn't mean there aren't a lot of people out there who are perfectly sane, and still very much opposed to what you're going to do."

Jeff thought it over and knew she was right. As usual. The schizophrenic diatribe wasn't the only letter of its kind they'd received, and for every one of those there were plenty of others that were sanely composed, neatly typed or handwritten, and still bursting with outrage at the whole idea of doctors deliberately taking human life.

He'd stopped reading those letters. So had the other two doctors enrolled in the fellowship program. But they would have had to be deaf, dumb and blind to miss the wave of protest that swelled and swirled around Carl Jerricoe's announcement that the first actual euthanasia procedure was imminent.

Sign carriers had been marching back and forth outside the medical center for three days, the hate mail had become a flood, and almost everyone involved in the program had been forced to get an unlisted telephone number in order to get a night's sleep.

Hell of a way to spend your spare time.

Still, putting your fingers in your ears was no way to stop the noise, and he really did want to get an idea of what people were saying about the day's events.

When he turned the radio on, though, the news station was burbling out a commercial, followed by a report on rush-hour traffic conditions, followed by another commercial, followed by sports, and by the time he thought they might be ready to offer a little real news, he was turning into the driveway of his home and easing his car into position behind Jolene's brand new Porsche.

Jeff switched off the ignition, amputating yet another commercial in mid-jingle, and took a moment to admire his wife's taste in motor transport.

The Porsche was red and sleek, just right for her in every way, and he was pleased to discover that he could look at it with approval untarnished by even a twinge of envy. Jolene deserved her toy. After all, her own residency in psychiatry, had been completed more than a year ago and she was now in a position to enjoy the rewards, both professional and financial, of private practice, even if it was as the employee of a long-established and profitable psychiatric group.

They had agreed that she would enter practice in this way, avoiding the fiscal hazards of trying to establish a practice while he was completing his own residency.

The decision was logical. For one thing, in discussing the future, they had discovered that neither of them was really ready to make a final decision about where they would settle and build their professional lives.

Jolene had a staff appointment at Northwest Regional, but it was a corporate one actually tendered to her employers. She might or might not be offered one of her own if she chose to set up her own practice. And it was obvious that a specialty, such

as the one for which Jeff was now training, would offer, at
most, only one staff position at any given hospital. His chance
of filling the one at Northwest was good, of course. He had the
inside track. But it wasn't certain, and wouldn't be until the
year-long program was completed.

Besides, both of them had admitted a vague restlessness. No
overwhelming urge to seek the "new frontiers," no irresistible
lure of the unknown. But even so, there was a tiny whisper of
curiosity, perhaps even of doubt. This city might be a
wonderful place to live and practice, rated high on most
surveys of amenities and ambiance. But, what if . . .

"Yo!"

Entering the house, Jeff's thought train was derailed by the
sight of his wife struggling abstractedly with the cork of a wine
bottle, and he found himself, not for the first time, momentarily
deprived of speech and volition by the sheer physical impact of
the woman he had married.

At thirty-one, Dr. Jolene Jagger, M.D., F.A.C.P., was a
conventionally attractive woman with long legs, perfect skin
and athletic slimness. Her slanted brown eyes and black hair,
wound into a chignon during professional hours but free now
because she knew Jeff liked it that way, added the suggestion
of the Orient. These were directly contradicted by the
somewhat overstated nose and an oddly sensual mouth,
completing a package that might appeal to any male not
intimidated by direct female assertion. She was not a person
who would ever be overlooked in a crowd.

But there was something more, as well, and though Jeff
could not have identified the quality with any kind of clarity or
accuracy, it had riveted his attention the first time he had seen
her on the opening day of the surgical residency in which she
had been enrolled before switching to psychiatry.

It was more than the simple animal grace with which she always seemed to move. More than the lively intellect and bubbling sense of humor always lurking just below the surface. More, even, than the eager and demanding sexual adventurousness he had discovered only after the tension of their first few weeks together had dissolved into a warming atmosphere of mutual trust.

She was the best friend he ever had and he'd had the good sense to recognize the magnitude of his good fortune.

All the same, she still had the power to astonish him at times, briefly curtailing his thought processes and limiting his speech to the kind of monosyllable he had uttered upon entering the room.

"Yo!"

"Yo, yourself," Jolene said, easing her hold on the wine bottle and flashing him a smile that seemed to him to change the light values of the room. "Come make yourself useful."

Wordlessly, still vibrating just a little to the resonance he always felt during their first few moments together, Jeff maneuvered the jack of the corkscrew to the neck of the bottle and applied a steady pressure that retrieved the cork without damaging it.

It was a Beaujolais, his favorite, and he noted with interest and approval the bearnaise sauce warming at the edge of the stove, and the small steaks prepared and waiting for the broiler.

Beef medallions, by God, as only Jolene seemed able to prepare them!

"Company coming?" he inquired, teasing.

"My three brothers," Jolene replied, playing up. "Also their wives and eighteen kids."

Jolene had no brothers, and, of course, there were only two places laid at the table. Jeff realized, with an extra starburst of relish, that she must have left her office early in order to set up his favorite meal for just the two of them and that she had done it because she knew he might be a little edgy after the events of his day.

Well, she had been right. As usual. And as usual, she had come up with just the right way to handle the situation.

"Young doctors," he heard himself pontificating before the seminar of his own mind, "would do well to marry a psychiatrist!"

Especially if she's just like Jolene . . .

The living room television set was turned on and tuned to the evening news, but the sound was off and he almost left it that way before remembering his earlier curiosity about the media's treatment of the world's first legally sanctioned euthanasia procedure.

Lines of sign-carrying pickets had been marching in orderly fashion across the screen. But as he watched, they suddenly broke ranks to gather in front of a building in the background, evidently attempting to block the double doorway with their bodies. Instead of concentrating on their efforts, however, the television cameraman panned left to pick up the determined approach of riot-clad police.

It seemed he had begun watching at just the right moment.

Bottle still in hand, Jeff reached out to increase the volume. But the story in progress was not the one he'd expected.

"– ized effort to halt legal abortion, and this was the scene: a determined, but non-violent effort to block ingress outside the Wichita Clinic for Women, just a few hours before the blast."

Blast? What blast?

What the hell was going on in Wichita? Jeff then recalled the news item he had heard on the radio just as he had arrived at the hospital that morning.

"But in the hours before dawn," the television reporter went on, "the non-violent context of the demonstration was literally blown to pieces by what police said was an explosive device, evidently triggered by electronic remote control rather than a simple timer, which shattered the inner and outer walls of the building and touched off a fire that demolished anything that was left.

"Because the explosion occurred at night, when the clinic was unoccupied, the only injuries reported were minor cuts and bruises sustained by a police officer left on guard duty outside.

"But federal authorities, who launched an immediate investigation, said the bombing appeared to be the work of anti-abortion urban terrorists responsible for similar incidents at legal abortion clinics in Denver, Colorado, and Cincinnati, Ohio.

"No deaths or major injuries have thus far resulted from any of the bombings, but an FBI spokesman said this was –"

Chapter Five

"Genius! Absolute genius!"

Charles Parker Pennington's face was aglow, his tone almost reverent, as he cut off the sound on the big-screen television set where the image of the Wichita abortion clinic had been replaced by even greater scenes of violence and mayhem on the international news front.

Pennington had been switching back and forth between channels, trying to catch all three networks' coverage of the Wichita bombing, avid for additional details. In this hope, however, he had been largely disappointed. The film clips had all told much the same tale, with only an occasional garnish, such as a glimpse of the single police officer who had been assigned to duty outside the clinic at the time of the blast.

But there could be no doubt of the satisfaction in his voice as he turned from the screen to face the two people who had been watching with him in the sitting room of his hotel suite.

"Micah," he said, beaming at the tall man seated stiffly at the table near the window, "you're one in a million! Maybe a billion!"

He paused as if searching for words, but his audience had known him long enough to be aware that this was mere oratorical management. Charles Parker Pennington always had more words than he knew what to do with.

"Any damn fool," Pennington continued, when he judged the dramatic timing was right, "can make an explosion. But it takes real genius to do it three times now – three times, by God – without hurting a living soul!"

This elicited a tentative response from the dark-haired woman standing at the bar.

"They said a policeman was –" she began.

"Minor injuries," Pennington dismissed the objection with airy disdain. "Little nicks and cuts that could've happened while he was shaving. A week from now, he won't even remember them."

The woman, Julia Hartt, drew breath as if to speak again – perhaps to voice a personal reservation – but then held her peace. Charles was probably right, of course. Charles loved her. And he always knew best.

"Yes, of course, but that's the whole problem right there," the man at the table countered, taking over the dialogue by default. "The trouble is, they don't remember. They don't seem to learn!"

His voice was controlled and resonant, an art, he had told them, learned in homiletics during seminary training. But Father Micah Chaine had long since resigned those pastoral and teaching duties assigned him by Mother Church and, while not formally unfrocked or even laicized, no longer held any priestly license or function within the Roman Catholic communion.

He remained, however, in his own eyes, both a priest and a warrior against those forces of damnation that he conceived to be abroad in the modern world. Father Chaine was a True Believer. And he could dominate by the sheer power of that belief.

At six feet, four inches, Micah Chaine was a physical presence that filled any room he chose to enter, and the granitic ridge of blue-shaven jaw, surmounted by a nose that would have drawn admiring glances from the Caesars, did nothing to soften the impression of authority.

But it was the eyes, so gray as to seem almost devoid of color, that captured and held the attention, adding to the sense of tightly bridled power. The eyes were magnetic. And quite impenetrable.

"They don't remember," Chaine continued now, directing the full, feral intensity of his gaze at Pennington, "because they can simply sweep up the rubble and put more glass in the windows and spray on some paint, and they're right back in business again. Without having learned a blessed thing!"

Pennington moved nervously to the bar and began to fumble among the glassware, his high spirits visibly evaporating.

"Now, Micah," he said, "we've been through this several times . . ."

He selected a delicate bubble from among the various shapes and sizes, and filled it with straw-colored wine from an already-opened bottle before turning again to face his companions.

The contrast between the two men could hardly have been more pronounced.

Where Chaine was tall, Pennington needed shoe inserts to reach the five feet, nine inches of height claimed on his driver's license. And where the other man was lean, Pennington's face and body still bore lingering traces of a juvenile chubbiness which, while not entirely unattractive, placed him at something of a disadvantage when faced with the overwhelming male aggression of men like Chaine. Fortunately for him, such confrontations were rare.

From earliest childhood, Charles Pennington had been surrounded by those unseen but potent perimeter defenses that old money, carefully preserved and augmented over generations, can erect around its possessors. Education at Lawrenceville and Williams College had done nothing to erode or even threaten this insulation, and Pennington might well have spent the rest of his life within its protective shell had an interest in one of his family's charities not drawn him into a militant offshoot of the anti-abortion movement.

That involvement had brought him into contact with Julia. And Father Chaine.

"You can't show support for life by killing people," he said, offering Chaine a mild smile over the rim of the wine glass. "It sends the wrong message. We've all agreed on that."

But of course, they hadn't. In fact it was a longstanding, if tacit, point of disagreement between them, and Pennington was aware that his view had prevailed thus far in large part because he provided the entire financial support for their operations. Still, he was confident this lever would always have power to move the world. It always had.

"Yesterday," he went on when Chaine didn't reply, "some lives were saved when they blocked the doors to that damned abortion mill and turned a few misguided women away. But they were arrested for doing that, and the doors would've been open again today if not for the good work you did in planting your bomb. Now the place will be out of business, at least for awhile, and the baby-killers will have something to think about."

He paused again, hoping for some reaction, but there was none. If Chaine felt anything at all, he gave no outward sign, and in the end it was Julia Hartt who broke the ensuing silence.

"I . . . think Charles is right," she said.

Chaine's eyes moved, shifting to focus on her without moving his head, and for a moment Pennington thought she might be silenced by their pallid force. But for once she seemed able to withstand the confrontation.

"We've done this three times," she continued, "and it's been successful. Three clinics destroyed and put out of operation, at least for awhile. And who knows how many lives saved. But we've been lucky."

She paused for breath, and Pennington was hard pressed to resist the urge to take her into his arms. He knew what it cost her to stand up to Chaine, or to anyone in authority for that matter. She was a gentle person by nature; it was one of the aspects of her character that he most admired. Yet in defense of a deeply held conviction, she could be a tigress. And this was the quality that he loved.

"No one's been hurt," she went on, "and we haven't been caught. But things are changing."

"That picture –" Chaine said, ready at last to enter the conversation.

But Julia hadn't finished.

"This time there was a surveillance camera," she said, cutting the priest off for a moment, "one we didn't know about, installed after the other explosions. All right, the picture it got wasn't good. The changes you'd made in your face before you walked into the clinic did work. All right. But all the same, they spotted you."

"Let them!"

Chaine stood up, instantly dominating the room with an aura of animal power and conviction.

"They identified the bottled-water man as an impostor," he said, "and decided that it was he who delivered the bomb. Marvelous! The picture they got from their cheap little camera didn't even show my limp, never mind my face. They got an image on film. One that matches nothing in the real world. It means nothing!"

"They might have –" Pennington began.

"Stop it!" Chaine interrupted. "Just stop it. Now! If they'd spotted anything else, it would've been on the news. They didn't. It wasn't. That's all. End of story."

Pennington's expression said he wasn't satisfied, and Julia seemed ready to offer further argument, but Chaine had heard enough and acted with dispatch to end the discussion.

"Besides," he went on, moving towards the television set, "there's something else we need to talk about. Something I've already put in motion. And I think they're finally getting around to it now."

The limp Chaine had mentioned was, in fact, no more than a slight stiffness in the right leg and was barely visible in the few steps that he took to the television set to turn up the volume of the news program.

At first, it seemed to be just another account of the abortion clinic incident. Demonstrators were marching and chanting could be heard in the background.

"LIFE IS SACRED!"

"STOP THE MURDER!"

But as the camera angle widened, it was immediately apparent that this protest wasn't the one in Wichita. The building in the background was larger than the single-story structure demolished by Chaine's bomb, and the television reporter was telling a different story.

"Mercy killing," she said, emphasizing the words with unmistakable distaste, "graduated today from the realm of legal and intellectual dialect to the world of reality – and attracted its first direct threat of violence – here at Northwest Regional Medical Center. A simulated bomb was received in the mail just as the first patient was subjected to death under new legislation legalizing euthanasia procedures in this state . . ."

Chapter Six

The state's first legal euthanasia procedure had all the elements of the perfect news story. Not only was it a first of its kind, it was an issue surrounded by controversy, evidenced in the rhetorical term "mercy killing" found in every page one headline, in the news clips of the hysterical demonstrations outside the hospital, and, of course, in the bomb scare.

On the day after Mike Statton's death, Dr. Rickoff made the mistake of granting a brief interview. He answered just three questions, clearly and with honesty. The next morning he arrived at the undersized office allotted to the euthanasia service for seminar purposes to find the whole complement of residents sitting around drinking coffee and trying their best to avoid looking at a newspaper headline tacked to the bulletin board:

'THE FUTURE IS OURS!' SAYS MURDER CLINIC DOC

But if they expected fireworks from Rickoff, they were disappointed. He had spent the previous evening watching the five and ten-second video segments edited from his comments for airing on the various news shows, and the distortions had lost any shock value they might once have possessed for him.

Standing before the bulletin board he did, in fact, redden slightly and even move his right hand towards the neatly clipped bit of newsprint as if to tear it down. But instead he backed off a step, and turned to face the residents.

"Carl Jerricoe warned me," he said.

No one seemed to want to comment on that.

"Carl warned me," Rickoff repeated, "but I had to find out for myself. All right. So I found out."

He turned his head to read the headline again out of the corner of his eye. "We'll leave that up there as a reminder, just in case any other damned fool is tempted to tell any reporter the time of day!"

And that seemed to close the subject.

Public interest in the Euthanasia Center remained high for a few days, while protest demonstrations continued outside the building. But news media and demonstrators alike feed on novelty, and by midweek the hand-mikes and television trucks were gone and the lines of protest demonstrators had dwindled to a few die-hards bearing battered slogan signs.

Meanwhile, more than one hundred applications for admission to the Euthanasia Center had been received, and eleven, regarded as the most critical, were actually accepted. It was obvious that the four semi-private rooms allotted to the service were going to be inadequate to meet the need, and the hospital trustees had taken under advisement a proposal for an entire new clinical wing and were promising an early decision.

Everyone took a deep breath, and tried to get back to work. The noise and the anxiety created by the simulated explosive device faded gradually into the familiar pattern of hospital life.

Most of the applications for euthanasia were routine, easily fitted to the classic profile developed on a theoretical basis before the service was formally opened. These were patients facing certain, painful death, and with less than six months to live under optimum conditions. In these cases, it was necessary for the doctors only to confirm diagnoses, make sure of the patient's motives and consent to the procedure.

But, as in all fields, there were exceptions, and one such exception was a twenty-two-year-old man who had been in deep coma since a swimming pool accident nearly a year earlier. The case was an especially complicated one because of the superb physical condition of the patient.

John Adams Barclay had been an athlete, a diver of championship caliber considered a shoo-in for the next Olympic team, until the morning he mistimed a relatively simple half-turn and struck his head a glancing blow on the low board before entering the water.

The incident had appeared to be minor. Barclay had emerged from the pool more humiliated than hurt, ready to continue with the day's practice regimen despite a bleeding lump at the back of his head and what he said was "just a little headache." But his coach would have none of it, and by the time they reached the hospital the headache had escalated to the point of agony.

He lost consciousness during the ride to the emergency room.

". . . and has remained unconscious ever since," Sheldon York said, reading from the case history he had prepared. The three residents had been assigned in rotation to the various applicants considered for admission to the service. York would be in charge of the Barclay case under Rickoff's supervision from admission to the actual euthanasia procedure. If Barclay was admitted at all.

And that, news media nonsense notwithstanding, was the major working concern of the euthanasia service: making the decisions. Deciding who was, and wasn't, a candidate for the procedure. From the outside, from where the vast majority of the public, and even the less-informed reaches of the medical profession, were standing, the work of the euthanasists seemed mostly to be concerned with certain relatively simple bits of medical equipment – and a few carefully labeled vials of venom. Push the valve. Watch the monitors. Sign the certificates. Nothing to it.

"To cause a death," Hyman Rickoff had lectured on their first day as euthanasia residents, "is nothing! Sub-moronic thugs kill people every day in back alleys, with no difficulty whatsoever. Hitler and his lunatic henchmen found means of putting death on an assembly line basis. More recently, and on a professional level, in the years before euthanasia became legal in this state, I think we all remember the case of the doctor who assembled a simple mechanical device that made it both easy and painless for the average person, without medical training, to take his or her own life. If that was all we were doing, there would be no need for a residency program. Anyone could handle the job, or you could put the little 'suicide machines' into mass production, sell them in discount drugstores on a non-prescription basis and leave the matter to individual discretion!"

He paused for a moment to let the idea sink in, and when he was sure he had their full attention, continued in a milder tone.

"The alternative to this delightful picture is the discipline that you and I are pioneering here, in this place, at this time. We're called upon to take human lives, yes. That's the nature of our specialty, the privilege and the responsibility placed in our hands by the law. But let me emphasize that word 'responsibility'.

"As physicians, you and I belong to the only segment of society permitted to commit manslaughter with relative impunity. When such a mishap does occur, the penalties we face are civil rather than criminal. It is accepted that we are not Gods, but human beings, subject to human error. And we have come to terms, both as a profession and as a society, with the result that the practice of medicine is not possible if criminal penalties are to be imposed every time a doctor makes a mistake.

"But . . . now the pressures escalate. Now it's not just manslaughter for which we're offered criminal immunity, but intentional homicide! That's right – murder. The law says we can do it. It says we have the right. But the circumstances in which it is permitted are, of necessity, strictly delineated. And we're trusted to remain within those limits."

The primary responsibility of the euthanasist, he said, was an exercise of discretion, of collecting facts and analyzing them, and then forming, testing, and re-testing conclusions based on those facts. Research, further inquiry directed to the perfection of lethal technique, there would and must be. At present, the chemical approach used in Michael Statton's case might seem the ultimate in sure and painless termination. But millenia of experience had, if nothing else, taught scientists in every field that there is always another step, another rung in the ladder.

And so, surely, with euthanasia.

The day might come, sooner, perhaps, than anyone now imagined, when the needle rudely thrust into the vein, and the mechanical shunt, might be medical museum pieces, as quaint and vaguely repulsive as the bleeder's knife and the leech bottle. Nonetheless, now and forever the first and foremost of the euthanasist's concerns must be selection of subject, a form of triage heretofore unexplored, but valid and vital to the ethical practice of their specialty.

"There is a difference," Rickoff had concluded, "between life and existence. You're called upon to define it, to refine the definition and to act upon the result."

It was a sobering preamble, and Jeff Taylor found himself

recalling it vividly as he read Sheldon York's careful workup on John Barclay, which was, in its way, hard testimony to its effectiveness. York seemed to have covered all the usual bases and added a few of his own.

"Brain scan?" Jeff inquired, looking up from the folder he had only begun to read.

"That," York nodded, "and surgical exploration to nail down the exact nature of the injury, which turned out to be a depressed fracture of the skull. They went in as soon as possible, picked out a couple of splinters, relieved any pressure exerted by the rest, and got out of there. The guy should've been blinking and stirring by the time they closed him up."

"But, he wasn't."

"No."

Jeff returned to his reading, and York got up to pour himself a cup of coffee. He took it black, without sugar, and put the cup aside after the first sip, trying without notable success to seem nonchalant. Jeff was the first person who had seen the report. York had typed it himself on a computer, unwilling to confide the work to a secretary, and the discovery of even a misplaced comma would have been devastating. But Jeff seemed oblivious to his concern, and turned the pages without comment. He finally put the report aside and smiled.

"Beautiful," he said.

Sheldon York tried not to heave a sigh of relief.

"They have no idea at all why the guy doesn't wake up?"

York shook his head. "EEGs showed near-normal sleep patterns at first. But that deteriorated pretty quickly."

"And now, nothing."

"Well . . . almost." York's tone was uncharacteristically tentative, and Jeff was instantly alert.

"Almost?"

York fidgeted. "Flatline most of the time," he said. "Yes.

In fact, when I was preparing the report I thought it was all the time, which would give us a clear, sharp-edged set of facts to work with. No real questions . . ."

"But?"

"But . . ." York picked up the coffee cup again without drinking from it. "Yesterday I looked in on the patient just to see if there'd been any change. The chart said there hadn't, and I was about to leave when I saw something, just a little blip really, on the EEG monitor."

"A blip?"

"That's all you could call it. One little irregularity, as if the machine were clearing its throat."

Jeff nodded. "So you checked the tape . . ."

"So I checked the tape and found nothing, nothing at all, for the past couple of hours."

"Uh-huh."

"Well, that was that. I was ready to pass the whole thing off, put it down to something in the machine's gizzard."

"But instead, you asked the nurses on the floor . . ." It was what he would have done, and Jeff was certain that York would have done the same.

"I asked them," York nodded, "and the first answer I got was a blank stare. The RN in charge didn't know what I was talking about, and just shrugged when I showed her the blip on the tape. She hadn't noticed anything like that, and didn't consider it significant."

"So of course you dropped it," Jeff said, teasing.

But Sheldon York had no sense of humor.

"I certainly did not!" he replied, astonished. "And a good thing, too, because my next question was the right one."

"And that was . . . ?"

"I asked her how familiar she was with the case, and discovered that it was her first day on the floor. She'd just been transferred from obstetrics, didn't know Barclay from a can of paint, and hadn't had time to talk to any of the RNs or other personnel who'd actually worked with him."

Jeff nodded again. "So you talked to them yourself," he prodded, wishing his colleague would cut to the chase, while, at the same time, resigning himself to let him tell the story in his own way in the interest of harmony in the service.

"So," York continued, "I went looking for someone actually in contact with the patient and struck pay dirt on the first try."

One of the RN's assigned to Barclay, he said, was a woman in her late twenties who was as eager to talk as he, York, was to listen. In fact, she'd been trying for weeks to get someone to pay attention to an irregularity she'd noticed in the Barclay EEGs.

"She'd seen the same thing I'd noticed," York said. "Little blips, occurring from time to time with no discernable pattern. And she'd done her damnedest to get someone interested."

"But, of course, she's just an RN."

"Exactly."

With the nurse's help, York said, he'd spent the past night digging back into the files for older EEG tapes, found plenty of others with the odd little blips in them, compared those with every standard reading known to medical science and came up empty.

"No match?"

York shook his head. "No match. Not even something I could look at and say, 'Okay, then. I was right the first time. It's just the machine'."

Jeff thought it over. "No other response from the patient?"

"No."

"What about life support?"

"Life support?"

"Sure. Maybe the irregularity has something to do with the respirator, or the –"

"No respirator."

Jeff stopped short, in mid-sentence.

"No respirator?"

"None needed," York said. "The guy's an athlete, remember, in superb physical condition. No steroid complications, no nothing. And there was no trauma to any other part of the body."

"But . . . if he's brain dead . . ."

York shook his head emphatically. "That's the whole problem, right there, Jeff." he said. "No brain activity, but autonomic system's up and running at optimum efficiency as usual, thank you. As I said in the first place, the guy should be awake."

Here was the situation for which Rickoff had been trying to prepare them, the "almost" that is the secret bogey of every doctor.

"Have you – ?" Jeff began.

But the question and the thought behind it vanished before it was fully formed, blown away by the furious arrival in the seminar room of the third euthanasia resident.

He was hardly recognizable.

In most circumstances, except when most deeply engrossed in a professional problem, Dr. William Dane Skelton was a living monument to personal adjustment. Smiling, affable, and relaxed as a pound of liver, he exuded a kind of laid back equanimity that most people found well-nigh irresistible. A soother of egos and a calmer of waters, Bill Skelton was an ever ready collection point for lost kittens and perplexed patients, an island of sanity in every scene of chaos.

He was in a white-knuckle rage.

Slamming through the door of the surgical lounge where his two colleagues had been having their discussion, he seemed for a moment to be weighing the relative effects of smashing the windows or ripping the plumbing from the walls. In the end, he settled for hurling a brightly illustrated supermarket tabloid newspaper down on the nearest table, and delivering himself of what was, for him, an almost unimaginable obscenity.

"Shee-yit!"

The other two doctors stood dumfounded, regarding him with surprise. Until that moment, the strongest language they'd heard him use was an occasional "darn."

But Skelton wasn't through.

"If I ever," he said in a voice loaded with uncensored passion, "if I *ever* lay my hands on the slimy little son-of-a-snake who wrote that piece, I . . . am . . . gonna . . ."

Skelton's voice broke, and the sentence trailed into nothingness as its author searched his imagination for some infliction proper to the situation. Finding none, he contented himself with hammering a fist on the four-color front page of the publication, which announced itself to the world as *The National Advocate*.

The headline was a grabber:

"108-YEAR-OLD MOM BEARS TWINS"

With it went a color photograph of "Mom," suitably decrepit, wearing a snaggle-toothed smile and holding what looked for all the world like a perfectly normal brace of babies.

The headline at the bottom of the page was equally as interesting:

"ELVIS FOUND; HAD SEX CHANGE!"

No photograph this time.

But the *piece de resistance*, so far as the doctors and the tabloid-buying public were concerned, was the color photograph, of an obviously helpless man lying on a hospital bed, clearly at the mercy of the tall, young doctor (easily identifiable by the stethoscope clinging to his neck), who stood poised and smiling with his hand on a shunt attached to the intravenous line plugged into the patient's arm.

The patient was Mike Statton.

The doctor was Jeff Taylor.

And the headline summed up their relationship in just six words:

"MERCY-KILLER DOC MURDERS MUTE MARTYR!"

Chapter Seven

At first, all Jeff could do was stare at the photograph. It didn't exist. It had to be a trick. But it wasn't. He remembered the moment vividly, the instant when he'd begun adding sodium thiopental to the Ringer's, the moment Mike Statton drifted away into his final sleep.

And yes, he supposed he had been smiling. The thought that his patient would never again have to suffer the indignity and frustration of a body that no longer served even his most basic needs was not a sad thought. And the knowledge that he had eased a fellow human being's passage through the final experience of life was not something any sane human being could regret.

But he would never be able to feel quite the same way again.

The picture had ended all that.

And there was an extra dollop of futility in the realization that he hadn't the vaguest notion of how, or by whom, the photograph had been taken.

"What . . . in . . . the . . . hell?" Sheldon York's face was pasty; the Barclay case folder had slipped from his hand and the pages lay in disorder at his feet. He didn't seem to notice. His attention was riveted on the picture of Jeff and Mike Statton, and the finger he pointed was trembling, as was his voice when he was finally able to utter his next word.

"Monstrous," he said, then lapsed into silence. No one else seemed to have anything to add. He had spoken for all of them.

A caption line just below the front-page picture referred readers to "full details, page 54." The residents opened the tabloid, and began to read.

By D. W. Teeples
The National Advocate Staff Writer

Physicians at the nation's first legalized euthanasia clinic inaugurated their new service last week by killing a man who they knew could not utter a word of protest or even beg for his life.

Acting as paid agents of his family, resident physician, Dr. Jeffrey Taylor, and Chief Euthanasist, Dr. Hyman Rickoff, injected wealthy pharmacist Michael Statton first with sodium thiopental, a barbiturate that produces unconsciousness, and then with the chemicals pancuronium bromide and potassium chloride – a combination sometimes known as the "Venom of Hippocrates" – to complete the procedure.

Statton died in his sleep, without a murmur.

But even had he been awake, Michael Statton could not have uttered a word in his own defense.

The disease for which he had been under treatment at Northwest Regional Medical Center (the hospital that also shelters the Euthanasia Center) had long since robbed Statton first, of the ability to move his body, and finally, of the power of speech.

Mute, helpless and legally at the mercy of a family doubtlessly appalled by the medical profession's inroads on what had once been a considerable fortune . . .

The story filled most of the page, leaving room only for more photographs – black and white this time, but no less appalling for their lack of color – apparently taken inside the room where the euthanasia procedure had been carried out. And the text left no doubt that its author had somehow been privy to all that occurred there.

Putting aside the purple pejoratives of tabloid prose, Jeff found himself almost admiring the accuracy with which certain bits of dialogue had been reported.

He recognized almost every word, and found he was prepared to admit the probable fidelity of the rest. Whoever he was, however he had obtained his information, D. W. Teeples had invented nothing and misquoted no one in his story. But that didn't make the article accurate. Or fair.

Teeples, if that was his real name, hadn't made the slightest effort at objectivity. From beginning to end, his screed took the position that doctors and family were co-conspirators against the life of Mike Statton, devoid of human compassion and motivated entirely by greed.

He wondered briefly if the hospital's lawyers could make something of that, but discarded the notion after the first moment. No way. A scandal sheet like that would employ ranks of legal eagles to make sure that even the most biased mishandling of fact fell short of outright libel. And anyway, the basic damage had been done.

From this moment forward, he and the other two residents at the Euthanasia Center (not to mention every other member of the hospital staff, from the ladies of the women's auxiliary to the kindly, old furnace attendant) would be under suspicion, and, he suspected, under heavy surveillance. Northwest Regional Medical Center didn't allow leaks. From now on, everyone in the shop would have someone looking over his or her shoulder.

*   *   *

And that was just what happened.

Less than an hour after the first copy of *The National Advocate* made its appearance, the regional representative of a nationally known security firm was seen entering the office of the hospital's chief administrator. Before sunset, the hospital's regular guard force had been "augmented" by grim-faced men in military-press uniforms, who checked identification badges and documents not only of those arriving or departing the premises, but of those moving between floors or between services, as well.

The staff grumbled and growled, and members of the regular guard force made no secret of their discomfiture. But it was all low key, and subsided into silence after the first few days. Everyone had seen the tabloid story, and understood the reasons for the sudden strictures.

But that didn't stop the rumor mill.

Within a week, Jeff found himself drawn aside and informed, in strictest confidence, of course, that security personnel had begun performing background checks on every member of the euthanasia staff (true), that if nothing turned up there, the investigation would be widened to include every single employee of the hospital (false; the suggestion had been made, but the expense was deemed insupportable), that some of the more recently hired orderlies, nurses and clerks were in fact undercover security officers (true), and that the Federal Bureau of Investigation had been drawn into the case because of the bomb threat (false; it was the Postal Inspectors).

He did his best to concentrate on the work at hand, turning a deaf ear to the whispers, and in the end this strategy seemed to have the desired effect. The sensation gradually died and the new security system became an accepted part of life. Most of the staff fell back into familiar patterns and routines, allowing the basic human need for order in life to block out any sense of being under scrutiny.

But there were exceptions.

Chapter Eight

Nurse Gertrude Nordstrum's personal life was in chaos, and she loved it.

She had been lying for weeks, steadily and with increasing conviction, to friends, acquaintances and co-workers, and more recently, to personnel administrators and security investigators.

For awhile, she had tried to set ground rules. She didn't lie to herself or to David. But the terrible article in *The National Advocate* had erased even that small reservation. From the moment she'd seen the byline "D. W. Teeples," she'd decided to ignore the truth, deluding not only herself but also the man she loved.

It was a question of emotional survival.

For most of her life, until David Wallace had come into it, Trudy Nordstrum had resigned herself to the existence of a neglected and frustrated demi-virgin. Even during the first high school burst of hormonal agitation, her basic shyness and social inexperience had relegated her to the sidelines, with only a vague memory of sweaty groping and probing to mark the technical passing of maidenhood.

In college, and on into professional life, there had been little or no improvement.

The few men willing or able to penetrate the facade of icy reserve with which she held the world at bay had, for the most part, been married and looking for their third or fourth divorce, or single and looking for a quick fling. In desperation, she had once even considered the possibility of a lesbian affair, rejecting the notion only because the mental images it inspired seemed both grotesque and undignified. Of late years, therefore, she had simply made a conscious decision to avoid painful experience by closing the door on the whole spectrum of human sexuality, and even affection.

The effort had been largely successful and, in fact, had even become something of a professional asset. The time, energy and passion that might otherwise have been channeled into erotic or familial activities was now available for her work at the hospital. And it had paid off, making her, by turns, Head Nurse of the hospital's highly rated Trauma Center, Nurse Manager of the Intensive Care Unit, and finally, perhaps looking for new worlds to conquer, a highly reliable nurse/anesthetist, and then nurse/manager, for the Medical Center's entire surgical/postoperative floor, in charge of both classified and certificated personnel.

Her predecessor in this position had been known as "The Dragon," but no one ever considered applying such a term to Trudy Nordstrum. Instead, she knew she was, by general consent, referred to as "The Ice Maiden," and she told herself that this was a compliment, a tribute to her efficiency and to the cool even-handedness with which she applied herself to the job.

She also told herself she was happy, and in a sense it might even have been true. Until she met David Wallace.

It had happened in the coffee shop just down Zonal Street from the hospital's main entrance, where she usually stopped for a snack after coming off shift. She was working nights at the time, and David had been seated at the counter, staring, as if hypnotized, at what she immediately recognized as one of the hospital's standard employment applications. A neglected stack of pancakes stood cold on a plate beside him.

Later, Trudy would tell herself that she might very well have offered to help anyone, man or woman, whom she found so obviously stumped by a simple work form. It was no more than her duty as a human being.

But in the secret place where she lived with herself, Trudy knew it was a lie.

What she'd seen that morning was a young man with eyes of the most startling and electric blue she'd ever encountered, framed by dark lashes so long that she would have thought them false had they appeared on a woman. His generous mouth seemed to conceal a boyish grin somewhere in its corners, and his not-quite-wavy hair was becomingly barbered.

But mostly, it was the eyes.

They were beautiful, and it was the perfectly uncomplicated urge to go on looking at them for as long as possible that brought Trudy to break what amounted to a lifelong regimen of social repression.

"Perhaps . . ." she ventured, hardly able to believe it was her own voice coming from her lips. "Perhaps I could . . . help you with that?"

The blue eyes blinked, then turned their full power upon her.

For a moment Trudy truly thought she might faint, like some languishing heroine in a Victorian novel. The color was even deeper than she had thought. Violet, really, with tiny flecks of fire. She wanted to turn around and leave the restaurant. But the first words he spoke, and the clear ingenuousness of the smile that went with them, seemed a surety of gentle diffidence as all-pervading as her own.

"If you would," he said, "I would be so grateful. I really don't know what to write in some of these spaces . . . and I need a job. Really."

Trudy came to the counter and saw that the only spaces actually completed on the entire paper were those reserved for name and date of birth (David Wallace; 9/20/59). She suggested they switch to one of the booths. He moved at once to comply, forgetting the plate of pancakes, and went back to fetch them with clumsy haste when Trudy mentioned the omission.

They exchanged names in formal awkwardness, and set to work.

He was so willing, even eager, to accept any of her suggestions, that Trudy felt confident the employment application could be completed without difficulty – and found herself unutterably depressed by the thought. When they were done with the form, she would lose him. When they were done, the blue eyes would go away.

Forever . . .

Once they settled in the booth, however, she began to suspect that the problems might be more numerous and convoluted than she had imagined. At first, he was hesitant about filling in his social security number. Then he recited it rapidly, but corrected himself, changing a least two of the digits while she was writing it into the allotted space.

"If you've got the card with you," she prompted, "it might be best to check it against the form. Just to avoid errors."

But he said he'd left the card in his other wallet at home, and they went on to such matters as his place of birth, and nationality: New York City and American – quick answers, uttered without hesitation. Nor was there any question about his present residence (a hotel not far from the hospital) or next-of-kin: None.

"None at all?"

David Wallace shook his head.

"No parents," he said. "I grew up in a series of foster homes. No living family at all, far as I know."

Trudy still couldn't believe it. "No wife? No –"

"– no nothing. No."

The blue eyes were clouded, now. Behind them, Trudy was sure she could see a lifetime of loneliness and frustration. Hard to believe that such an outstandingly attractive man hadn't attracted a wife, or wives, by the time he was in his thirties. The possibility that he might be gay crossed her mind, but was dismissed out of hand. He just couldn't be gay. He mustn't be.

"Well," she said carefully, moving on to what seemed safer territory, "that brings us to the job history."

"Uh . . . yes."

David Wallace shifted uncomfortably in the booth and glanced out the window. Trudy waited, ballpoint poised, for him to offer information about his last employer. But he said nothing more, and in the lengthening silence, Trudy at last permitted herself to do some delayed mental arithmetic.

This beautiful man was neither stupid nor illiterate, so if he needed someone to help him fill out a simple job application, there had to be some other reasons, and the time to find out about them was right now. Immediately. Before she started manufacturing any more fantasies.

"David," she said, amazed at her own presumption in using his first name, but instinctively avoiding the more formal address. "David, we don't know each other, but if we're going to –"

"I'm on the run."

The bleak simplicity of his words and the sincerity of their tone amputated her thought in mid-sentence, and a moment later she again fell under the spell of his blue eyes in which she now saw the tiny silver pinpoints of suppressed terror.

"The police in Salt Lake City want me for murder," he said. "I didn't do it – I swear I didn't – but I was seen in the neighborhood and when I found out they were looking for me, I just . . . ran."

Trudy sat silent, waiting for him to go on. After a moment, he continued.

"My first name really is David," he said, "and my middle one's Wallace. So I, like, told you mostly the truth. Just not all of it. I don't want to lie to you. But if . . ."

"Wallace," Trudy said when his voice trailed into silence. "Your name is David Wallace and you were born in New York."

She looked down at the application form, and then back into the blue eyes.

"You were born and raised on your family's farm," she went on. "But they're all dead, now. That's why you don't have any past employers to list on the application. And you hurt yourself trying to run the farm alone. You got out of the hospital in Pennsylvania, I think we'll make it – I know a lot of hospitals back in Pennsylvania – which explains why you don't look much like a farm worker."

David Wallace was shaking his head. "Miss Nordstrum . . . Trudy," he said, "I can't let you do this!"

She favored him with a wicked grin she hadn't known was in her. "Just how do you plan to stop me?"

"If we're caught, you'd be an accessory. You could even wind up in prison."

It was true. Somewhere deep inside her, a tiny simulacrum of Trudy Nordstrum was running around in circles, screaming. She was being a fool. This man, attractive though he might be, was someone she'd known for less than a half hour, to whom she owed nothing and from whom she could expect no kind of reward. The police said he was a murderer. They might be right. Or he might be a confidence trickster with designs on her savings account. He might be a sex maniac, or a sadist, or almost anything else. The only intelligent thing to do was to pick up her purse, walk out the door, and forget she had ever come in here this morning. Anything else would be ridiculous . . . no, insane!

But she looked deep into the blue, blue eyes. And was lost.

* * *

An hour later, Trudy Nordstrum drove back to the hospital, stopped outside the administrative office, and waited while "David Wallace" filed the employment application.

Then she offered to drive him to his hotel, but he explained that he'd spent the last of his money on the plate of pancakes he'd forgotten to eat and had checked out.

So she offered to lend him some money. And when he said he couldn't take it, she insisted he come home with her. She told him he could sleep on the couch in her living room.

But he didn't.

Chapter Nine

The occasional irregularities noted in John Barclay's EEGs continued to worry the doctors of the Euthanasia Center. And their concerns were the ones that counted, now.

Barclay's family had abandoned hope. Had he been the average deep-coma patient, dependent on life support systems for respiration and perhaps for heart rhythm as well, they were frank to say that they would have ordered the hospital to "pull the plug" at least a month earlier. Their wonderful, Olympic athlete son was gone. What remained was merely a hollow, albeit expensive, shell, existing somewhere below the threshold of true life. They wished to remember him as he had been, not as he would be after months, perhaps years, of waste and atrophy on a hospital bed.

In this case, however, their hopelessness was actually beside the point. There was no "plug" waiting to be pulled. The superlative condition of John Barclay's body at the time of his injury had rendered life-support (except for the minimal efforts of feeding and cleaning) irrelevant. He was breathing on his own, and his heart continued to tick along like a Patek Philippe. If that body was going to die, someone was going to have to kill it.

So the decision was in the hands of the euthanasists, who made no secret of wishing it were somewhere else.

"For my first case," Sheldon York mourned, "I had to get one that would cross the eyes of a Wall Street tax lawyer."

Bill Skelton grinned owlishly at him. "Well, now," he said, "there are lawyers and there are lawyers . . ."

York's face went blank for a moment, then he returned the grin. "Sorry," he said. "Sometimes I forget your wife's an attorney."

"And a tax specialist at that," Skelton nodded equably, "which enables her to support me in a style which I find very comfortable indeed."

"You and your damned BMW," Jeff said in mock disgust. "Lording it over us peons just because you're married to a rich shyster."

"Sir, you are speaking of the shyster that I love!"

It was 9:00 p.m. and they were in the bowels of the hospital, wrestling with Wolverine, an application run on the hospital's mainframe. The system was supposed to be the font of all wisdom on all subjects medical, from diagnosis to the billing of patients, and it had been specially designed nearly a decade earlier to meet the requirements of Northwest Regional.

In any event, it had remained one of a kind, made obsolete by technical advances even before it was fully operational. The hospital continued to use it because it represented a mind-boggling capital investment, and because it did, in fact, perform the work for which it had been intended.

Wolverine had one main drawback, so far as the personnel who used it for diagnostic assistance and therapeutic suggestion were concerned. Like many expert systems, it required that the user have knowledge of both the subject and computerized database search techniques before he or she could access any information. Unfortunately, most of the doctors had not undergone the required training.

Adding to the unfriendliness of the software's user interface was the fact that the mainframe's terminals were unreliable: sticky keys and screens that often blacked out for no apparent reason were typical. Consequently, there were fewer terminals available than were required. The only one assigned to the Euthanasia Center had been taken away for repairs shortly before noon. By 6:00 p.m. neither it nor any kind of replacement hardware had appeared, so the doctors had descended to the basement of the hospital to use one of the terminals located in computer center.

"I feel like a burglar sneaking down here to tap into the hospital's records for some nefarious purpose," Sheldon York said over his shoulder as he entered some numbers and watched the screen. "Hmm. 'Bad Command.' Damn! Either my access code isn't working or I've got one of the numbers wrong."

"Here, try mine. 'NRMC-732/EU.JO'," said Jeff, not as anxious about maintaining security as he was to get started.

"If we were sneaking, we'd be in a nice, comfortable room on the other side of town overlooking the Sound, maybe, hacking into the system with our own little computer, a telephone line and a modem. That's how it's done. I've seen it on TV," said Bill Skelton.

York snorted his disgust. "If we were, I bet we'd be in by now."

"What's the problem?" Jeff wanted to know.

"Not sure," York said, as he tried to figure out what was happening on the screen. "But your access code doesn't seem to be doing the trick either. Maybe the damned terminal's broken, like ours."

"Can't be," Skelton said. "It was the only one up and running when we got here."

Jeff blinked and touched York on the shoulder. "Well, maybe that's the problem, Shel."

"What do you mean?"

"That's why you can't get in with the access code.

Someone else was probably already in and didn't bother to log off when he was done."

"Huh?"

"It happened to me once. I tried to get in, and couldn't. So I asked for help, but no one else could seem to get in, either."

"And what happened?"

"A candy-striper," Jeff said, grimacing ruefully.

"Candy-striper?"

"One of the volunteers the nurses are supposed to lead around by the hand. She wandered by, saw what we were doing, and suggested we ask the computer about its status."

"You're kidding," York said, as he punched the query into Wolverine and was rewarded by the information that a program called D-701 was already up and running on that workstation. He sighed and leaned back in the operator's chair, considerably deflated.

"First thing I should've checked, of course," he said. "Very first thing!"

"Well, now we know," Bill Skelton said. "So what do we do? Shut the program down and go back to square one?"

"Uh . . . that's probably not a good idea," Jeff said.

The other two residents looked at him.

"That's what I did," he said, "that time I found out about this, and it turned out I'd dumped a couple of hours work by some poor bastard who'd just been called away on an emergency and left his program running. Hadn't even saved it."

Skelton shook his head "The guy must've been ready to kill you when he got back."

"Worse. He was very patient and understanding. Just sat down and went to work again."

"And left you to feel guilty as hell about it for about the next thirty years."

Jeff shrugged. "How do you think I happened to remember it just now?"

They helped Sheldon York gather his papers and move to the next terminal, which was dark. York switched it on, tried his access code once again, and, after a few tries, finally found the database they needed.

"Alright! Not only does my own access code work, but we are exactly where we want to be," he said triumphantly.

"Okay, then," Bill Skelton said, holding the list of questions they'd come up with in discussing York's case. "Okay, number one: let's see a list of all the coma cases handled by Northwest for . . . oh . . . the past ten years."

"That's a good place to start," Jeff teased, "since we've had the computer for only a decade."

"Now just a minute," Skelton said in mock defence. "They might've entered earlier records."

"In a perfect world," Jeff answered. "However, this world is not so perfect and that would have been a huge and very expensive task."

"You're probably right about that, Jeff," York said as he defined his parameters. "So let's start, as Bill suggested, with cases occurring over the last decade. If we don't find anything, we'll try to go back further. You never know, we might be living in a more perfect world than we think."

After two refusals on technical grounds ("Syntax Error," "Null Program"), the computer finally came up with the requested data. It was a longer list than they had expected, but it could be narrowed down further.

In the next half hour the doctors were able to discover that their coma patient was unique in several ways, at least insofar as Northwest Regional Medical Center was concerned. For one thing, he wasn't on life support. They'd known that was unusual, but assumed there had been similar cases.

There hadn't. And the little irregularities in his EEG remained a puzzle.

Wolverine was capable of analyzing and filing any EEG or EKG digitally, and, therefore, of matching the pattern to any others on record that were alike, or even similar, within adjustable parameters. The system was reputed to be accurate within about a seven percent error margin, and when a match was found, all records concerning it would be available at the touch of the command key. Only no true match or reasonable similarity was in Wolverine's records.

"Son of a bitch," Bill Skelton said, frowning ferociously at the "File Not Found" message on the screen.

"Well . . . hell," was Jeff's contribution.

Sheldon York shook his head. "I can't believe it," he said. "I simply cannot believe that John Barclay's case is as different as all that from any other case that's come in here."

"It probably isn't," Jeff agreed. "But records of any similar cases must be over ten years old."

"And I've already searched for cases over ten years old. So you're right – if they do exist, they have not been entered into the database."

"You told us so," Skelton conceded.

"I told you so," Jeff repeated with a quick wink. "I guess our world really is not so perfect after all."

"Still, there is some consolation in knowing that there may have been cases like this one before – lots of them, for all we know – where you get occasional flickers like this."

"And maybe not."

"And maybe not."

Bill Skelton stood up and stretched.

"The hell of it," Sheldon York said, still intent on the problem, "is that nobody keeps records of mechanical errors."

"Screw-ups in the machine," Jeff nodded. "Sure. If they

did, we could come at the problem from the other side; maybe eliminate this . . . whatever it is . . . by matching it to a known glitch pattern."

"Which would give us a clear 'go'," Bill Skelton finished. "Only, no one does. So we can't. The hell with it, friends. Ma Skelton's little boy's goin' home."

Jeff stood up and yawned. "Terrific idea," he said. "Come on, Shel. Make it unanimous. Stay down here long enough and this beast'll eat you."

York started to tell them he would be along in a moment or two, but thought better of it, quit the application, and switched off the screen. He was still convinced that there was something they'd missed. Something duly digitized and recorded in one of the byways of the computer brain that would yield the information they needed, if only one could find one's way to the proper storage shelf. But they weren't going to find it tonight.

He followed his two colleagues out the door and down the corridor to the elevators. It didn't cross his mind, or those of the other two residents, that no one had ever returned to work on the program they'd interrupted when they first arrived in the computer bay.

*　*　*

For several minutes after the doctors' departure, nothing happened in the room.

Three hours remained before the first crew of maintenance and monitoring personnel would report to begin their shift; the overnight troubleshooter had disappeared in the next-to-last economy wave, and had never been replaced. The section seemed to get along well enough without him.

Like any hospital, Northwest Regional operated on a twenty-four-hour basis. All functions of the computer were, and had to be, on call at all times. But overnight was down time for most research and similar activities, with staff reduced to a minimum. Only the simplest and most routine of programs would be running, and inputs would be limited to regular patient monitoring and medication records.Even with the new security system inaugurated after the bomb scare, and the threatening letters that continued to arrive regularly, only janitors visited the computer bay after midnight.

Which solved a major problem for David Wallace Teeples of *The National Advocate.*

From the first, even before his carefully contrived coffee shop encounter with Nurse Trudy Nordstrum, Teeples had been sure the hospital's computer system held the key to his coverage of the Euthanasia Center's activities. Talking to other hospital employees, and even hiding a voice-operated tape recorder in the procedure room, as he had done in order to assure himself of an accurate record of the final moments of Mike Statton's life, were all very well in their way. But they couldn't offer the background detail, particularly the names and addresses of relatives, suitable for personal or telephone interview, that were bound to be readily available in the official hospital records.

There was a time when those files would have been nearly inviolate. Records committed to paper and locked away in filing cabinets can be found and examined, certainly, by anyone with a lot of nerve and a little knowledge of locksmithing. But that kind of snooping is inherently dangerous in that it requires the snooper's actual presence in the place where the records are kept, making him vulnerable to the chance visitor, or even to ambush, if the violation of security is discovered by someone with sense enough to keep quiet about it and set a trap for the intruder.

Computer records, however, were a whole different ball game.

In the beginning, Teeples had hoped to use the computer's dial-in numbers to get into the records from some location well removed from the medical center's premises. For that, he knew he would need an access code of someone in a position of trust that would carry with it a fairly high security clearance. But the method he'd used to get himself physically inside the hospital had been considerably more effective than he'd expected, and the very totality of its success had complicated the situation, causing him to deviate from his original plan. He couldn't set up a computer and modem in his living room. That was no longer an option; he wasn't living alone.

Scouting the hospital and observing its personnel for a few days before beginning his actual penetration effort, Teeples had marked Trudy Nordstrum as an easy target and tailored his approach to suit the environment.

As Dave Wallace, innocent man-on-the-run, he'd projected an aura of helpless vulnerability calculated to appeal strongly to a lonely woman approaching middle age. It was a ploy he'd used before, and expected to use again. Its basic appeal was sexual. But even if the target turned out to be totally sublimated, she could usually be counted upon to mistake her natural urges for maternal instinct, and follow his concealed scenario anyway.

Trudy, however, was most certainly not sublimated, and he'd found himself first a bit shocked and then physically intrigued by the totality of passion that had been unlocked during their first night together. It was like nothing he'd encountered before, and the intensity hadn't become diminished with the passage of time. She was the greatest lay he'd ever had – eager, inventive, and utterly committed. From his first response of elation and self-congratulation at finding pleasure in what might have been the onerous chore of keeping Trudy happy while pursuing his main objective with the Euthanasia Center, he'd long since graduated to a more complicated condition in which he found that he actually cared about her opinion of him. He felt real apprehension with regard to the inevitable moment when his true identity and purpose would be revealed.

It was a new experience for him, and an oddly unsettling one – even more so when, in the wake of his first illustrated story in *The Advocate*, he prepared himself to face a storm of accusation and recrimination that never materialized.

He was sure she knew.

Copies of *The Advocate*, with his byline prominently displayed, were all over the Medical Center. And even if, through some miracle, she'd failed to read it there and make the obvious connection between "D. W. Teeples" and "David Wallace", he'd found a copy of the tabloid neatly folded and buried deep in the kitchen trash basket at the apartment where he'd been living ever since their first night together. She knew.

But if he found himself reluctant to broach the subject of his identity, Trudy seemed fanatically devoted to its avoidance. Twice in the past few weeks when their casual conversations had drifted to subjects even peripherally akin to newspaper work or concealed identities, she'd acted at once to change the course of thought by abruptly unzipping his trousers or unbuttoning her blouse to bury his face between the truly formidable amplitude of her breasts.

It always worked, partly because he wanted it to and partly, he had to admit, because it probably would have been effective in any case. Sex had been a major force in his life ever since the unforgettable evening of his fourteenth birthday, when a precocious girl cousin had introduced him to its more basic techniques and pleasures. In the years that had passed since then, his interest had never faltered. And even if it had, a round or two with Trudy would have rekindled it. Or, more accurately, set it on –

"– stop it!"

The sound of his own voice, echoing through the near-total silence of the computer bay, brought David Wallace Teeples back to the real world from the haze of reverie into which he had fallen after the euthanasia residents' departure. He shook himself and stood erect, wincing a little at the cramping induced by his long crouch behind the memory-storage bank, where he'd had a clear and unobserved view of the doctors' movements as they'd retrieved the John Barclay file and attempted to match it with other records.

Using Trudy's access code, he'd been unable to obtain clearance for the records he wanted. But Jeff Taylor's code would serve nicely, and he had heard it clearly when the doctor had given it to York.

He'd found the key to the safe. Now was the time to use it, before anything else went wrong. "Come on, Teeples," he said in an almost coaxing tone. "Come on. Just another few minutes. Just a bit longer, and we can go home . . ."

To Trudy.

He hadn't said it aloud. But the words were there, hanging in the air as he sat down at the terminal and punched in the new access code.

To Trudy.

As expected, the new code got him past the security blocks, and into the full database. This was it. What he'd come for. The whole nine yards. Print out the Barclay file and get out of here. Go.

To Trudy . . .

Chapter Ten

The EEG monitor wired to John Barclay's scalp recorded another one of the puzzling little "blip" irregularities, and nurse Trudy Nordstrum found herself yanked abruptly back into the real world of the Intensive Care Unit. She resented the intrusion as she noted the incident and marked the tape to be sure it was seen by the attending physician when he arrived for morning rounds.

It was the first time, so far as she knew, that anyone had been nearby when one of the brain blips had erupted. The doctors wanted a quick check of all vital signs as soon as possible after the blip made its appearance, and she moved to take those readings now. Her actions were trained and efficient. The readings were exact. But her heart really wasn't in the effort, and a moment or two later she would have been hard pressed to assess the significance of the numbers she had recorded. The blip had thrust itself into a thought sequence that Trudy found far more stimulating than the mundane milieu of the medical center.

In the world that was most real for her, Trudy had been in bed with David. He was kissing her lips, moving down her neck to just above her collar bone, moving down towards her breasts –

"– the euthanasia ward?"

Trudy blinked and forced herself to focus on her immediate surroundings. Someone had entered the room, and was asking her something. The charge nurse.

"I'm sorry," Trudy said. "I must've been drifting off. What did you say?"

"I asked if it was true that we were going to shift Barclay to the euthanasia ward."

"Oh."

"Well, are we?"

Trudy shook her head. "Can't seem to make up their minds," she said. "It seems to depend on the EEG readings."

The charge nurse digested this, and abruptly changed the subject. "You look like death warmed over," she declared. "Being in charge of the ICU is one thing, but working at it twenty-four hours a day is something else entirely. Don't you ever sleep?"

The words "not with David around" were on the tip of her tongue, but Trudy stifled the urge to utter them and switched the conversation back to the original subject.

"Did you see the irregularity on the Barclay EEG?" she inquired.

"The irregularity?"

Trudy waited for her to recall the instructions she knew were taped to the monitor on the ICU's central station, and endured the flutter of apologies that came when she finally remembered. Vitals were, of course, constantly monitored at the central station. The nurse in charge would be able to retrieve the data, and the numbers would, without a doubt, match the readings she had taken in person.

"After I . . . read the instructions," the charge nurse said with difficulty, the pink flush of embarrassment still visible on her cheeks, "I began to look for anything that seemed out of the ordinary. But . . . I guess I must have gotten distracted . . ."

Trudy looked at the nurse with eyes that suspected her of lying, and the humiliated woman, realizing that anything else she might say would incriminate her further, asked Trudy to excuse her for a moment. She quickly bowed out of the room.

As the nurse's figure disappeared from the door frame, Trudy suddenly felt ashamed of her behavior towards the poor woman. No one could be expected to be totally alert at this time of morning, no matter what the regulations stipulated. Besides, if you wanted to go strictly by the written rules, what was she, Trudy, doing here in the room anyway?

"Hiding from myself."

The answer was immediate and uncensored, but it took a moment for Trudy to grasp the fact that she had actually spoken the words aloud. And when that realization came, she was further mortified to find herself glancing in the direction of the coma patient. Was he really unconscious? Had he heard . . . ?

Furious at the repeated, if momentary, failure of control, Trudy forced herself to complete one more scan of the various monitors. When the charge nurse returned, somewhat more composed, Trudy attempted to apologize, but no words came to her. She settled for an apologetic nod as she said good night and left the room.

Ridiculous! It was ridiculous to say a thing like that aloud, and ridiculous to be afraid that a poor soul like John Barclay had heard it, and most of all, ridiculous for a head nurse to be prowling around in the middle of the graveyard shift, upsetting the charge nurse and interfering with the routines, all because she wasn't able to deal with her personal life. She could no longer keep it from herself. The thing with David was totally out of hand.

Trudy's conscience forced her to face the facts. She was there, meddling and meandering, because it kept her from thinking about what she knew she should do – or should have done long before – about David. He was using her, deliberately taking advantage of her, personally and sexually and professionally and every other way possible, just to get a story for a cheap, sleazy supermarket tabloid. And she was helping him. Knowingly.

She had seen the story in *The Advocate* and had checked with her cousin, who worked for the San Francisco police, who told her that no one like David was wanted for anything like the kind of trouble he said he was in. Then she searched into his part of the closet and his drawer in the bedroom and found his driver's license – the real one, for David Wallace Teeples – taped under the bottom.

She had known who he was all this time, and still hadn't told anyone. She hadn't confronted David with it, either, and knew that she had no intention of doing so. Yet, she didn't really understand her own motivation. Was it just because of the sex? Because it was so much better than it ever was with anyone else (though God knows she hadn't much for comparison). Maybe it was just that. She'd already admitted to herself that she couldn't even imagine how she was going to live when he finally dropped her. And she felt certain that he would, just as soon as there was no more story for him there at the hospital. Yes, maybe it was the sex and nothing more.

"But what if it's something more?" Gertrude asked herself, in an attempt to challenge the wisdom of her conscience. But as quickly as the question came forward, she put the thought away, telling herself that she was just a fool, a silly old maid going through the last surge of hormonal sexuality before the change of life, and mistaking it for what the romance novel writers call Grand Passion.

"But . . . what if it really was something more?" The question came up again. Now she didn't know which part of her brain was addressing which, whether she was being honest or whether she was trying desperately to kid herself. What if the tenderness that she had sometimes seen in the way he treated her, the empathy and human contact, were something more than a projection of her own needs and fantasies? What if that were real? What if David felt it, too? What if –

"Oomph! Sorry!"

Rounding a corner, Trudy had come into violent contact with a young man whom she recognized as one of the interns currently on rotation in the ICU. He had been carrying an armful of charts, and now they were scattered across the floor of the corridor, dropped in his effort to save them both from what might have been a nasty fall.

"My –"

"– fault!"

Mutual embarrassment, intensified by the simultaneous eruption of apology, kept them silent as Trudy helped the young man reassemble his load.

"Thanks . . . uh . . . have a nice day!" he flung over his shoulder as he hurried away.

Trudy didn't bother to reply. But the encounter had been beneficial, all the same; it provided a much-needed break in the circular pattern her mental arithmetic had been taking of late.

The truth could be faced, she told herself as she emerged from the staff entrance and headed towards her parked car. But so could the awful truth.

"I'm not going to tell anyone." She was speaking her thoughts aloud again, but this time deliberately, in the free pre-dawn world where all things are possible and all thoughts thinkable.

"I am going to shut up about it and forget about it because that's what I want to do. And to hell with everything else."

* * *

"Give strength and skill to those who minister to the sick, and preserve them from falling into the error of using that God-given proficiency to the breaking of Thy commandment. Grant that, perceiving how frail and uncertain our mortal life is, they may apply their hearts to that heavenly wisdom which leadeth to eternal life through our Lord and Savior, Jesus Christ, Amen."

His prayer completed, Father Micah Chaine took a deep breath and closed the tissue paper wrapping around his latest message to the staff of Northwest Regional Medical Center.

Selah.

God's will be done.

Candles burned at either side of the altar improvised upon the breakfast bar in the Tulsa motel room, their flickering light the only illumination as Chaine completed sanctification of the medium he'd chosen for this expression of Divine Purpose. His hands – consecrated hands, he reminded himself – moved deftly, enclosing the little bundle in its cardboard box, to which he then affixed a label neatly inscribed with the name and home address of the Chairman of the Board of Trustees of Northwest Regional Medical Center.

There! It was ready.

The doctor in charge of the murder clinic might ignore a warning, even so plain a warning as he had offered with his mock bomb. But surely this new message wouldn't be lost on the trustees. Especially their chief, at whose particular phobia (as identified through hours of probing into newspaper and public library files) he had directed it. They must understand that he was serious, that he would brook no further delay or disobedience.

God, aye, even the God of Moses and Joshua, will not be not mocked! In His hand was the Sword of Wrath. Let the perpetrators of evil take warning and turn aside from the way of iniquity and blood-sin. God grant that it be so! If not . . .

"Oh Lord God of Sabaoth," he began, whispering once more to the close and holy silence, his hands folded above the sealed package, "stretch forth, we pray Thee, Thine almighty arm to strengthen and protect the righteous in Thy faith. Give them a clear sense of their duty, support them in the day of battle, and grant them wisdom to see and to do Thy will, honoring Thee above all else, and forsaking . . ."

*　*　*

". . . all other considerations." Dr. Rickoff was saying to his three residents, who digested the words silently and with various degrees of acceptance.

Northwest Regional's own in-house coma committee had already considered John Barclay's case, and pronounced it hopeless. That had been a preliminary step. But the situation was unusual in that mere withdrawal of life-support would not result in death; in this case, there was no life support. Withdrawal of food or water would, of course, yield such a result. But instead, the problem had been passed along to the euthanasists. And this was the session in which their decision was to be made.

Rickoff had been covering the well-known and oft-revisited territory of the differences between actual "life" and mere "existence," with its implications for their chosen specialty. They'd heard it all before. But this time Rickoff seemed intent on making them look coldly and dispassionately on one of the more subtle shadings, as defined by the second patient submitted for their procedures.

"A case already known to be terminal," Rickoff told them, "is one where, in effect, a lot of your preliminary work has already been done for you. Oh, you're required to re-check, naturally. But in fact, you're confronted not with a question of ultimate prognosis, but simply of the time, place and manner in which the patient's life will end."

Sheldon York shifted uncomfortably in his chair. The Euthanasia Center seminar room was an invitation to claustrophobia in the best of circumstances, and this morning it seemed to him that the walls were actually a bit closer together than they had been, the atmosphere a degree or two more stifling. Still, Rickoff and the others seemed to be waiting for him to make some positive contribution to the morning's discussion. He was the doctor directly assigned to the patient now under discussion, and therefore bore the prime responsibility. He could accept that. And he knew the conclusion he'd reached was the only one logically tenable under the circumstances. But that didn't make the final decision any easier.

"The Barclay case," he said, setting the folder with his accumulated notes on the undersized conference table as he launched into his presentation, "touches the borderline between those who are, and are not, properly within the sphere of euthanasia. Here we have a patient who is not on the verge of death, who is, in fact, quite capable of living for decades, given proper care. He isn't on life support. This isn't a case where it's possible simply to 'pull the plug', as the popular press would have it. Instead, if John Barclay's physical existence is to be terminated, that termination will certainly require positive, specific action on the part of some other person. Someone will have to carry out a euthanasic procedure, and be prepared thereafter to defend that action. This is the responsibility we've been asked to assume."

In the next few minutes, York detailed a brief history of Barclay's trauma, the measures taken for its reduction, the subsequent coma and the efforts made to reverse it.

"Response," he said, "has been virtually nil."

"Virtually?" Rickoff interjected the word to offer York a graceful transition to the matter that had to be discussed before any decision could be made.

"There have been occasional anomalies in the EEG readings," York said, accepting the gesture with a nod of thanks while flipping through the case records. "These readings," he said, bringing out the EEG tapes they had all seen before, "show what appear to be occasional, and apparently unrelated, bursts of mental activity."

Rickoff didn't bother to look at the tapes. "You checked the monitor, of course?"

"And completely replaced the equipment, in order to be sure it wasn't simply a mechanical problem of some kind," York nodded.

"And these . . . blips . . . continued after the substitution?"

"Yes."

"Then of course you attempted to match the pattern to those observed in other, similar cases?"

"And even those that weren't so similar," Jeff said, breaking into the dialogue. "In fact, the three of us spent a good bit of one night hammering on a computer terminal trying to find something even vaguely similar."

"Without result," Rickoff said, not bothering to make it sound like a question.

"Without result," York agreed.

Rickoff waited for him to continue, but it was Bill Skelton

who spoke next.

"So now," he said, "we're back to square one. The blips aren't consistent. Sometimes a whole day passes without one, sometimes you get two or three in an hour. They don't seem to mean anything in particular. No special wave pattern –"

"– and no apparent echo in the rest of the vital signs," York concluded. "We lucked out on that early this morning."

"Yeah," Jeff said. "Seems that Gertrude Nordstrum was there, right in Barclay's room for some reason, when one of the anomalies occurred. Give her credit, she was right on top of it like a tiger. Made personal, eyeball observation of the patient immediately afterward."

"But it only confirmed what we got from the machines," York said, "which was nothing. No heart flutter, no change in blood pressure or respiration."

"Zip," Bill Skelton concluded.

Rickoff picked up the top page of York's notes and glanced at it, though he had read the whole package through, more than once, before coming to the seminar room.

"Very well, then," he said when he was through, and the notes were intact once more. "Very well. So the occasional brain-sparking is nothing. Just the final static of a blown switchboard. This is the conclusion you've reached?"

York looked at the other two residents. They looked back at him. "Yes," he said. "That's it."

"Good," Rickoff said. "That's my conclusion, too. But it still leaves us with one step yet to be taken. The final step of making a recommendation to the family and being prepared to live with it afterwards."

This time, none of the residents seemed to want to talk.

The decision to end a life is irrevocable; keep the patient alive and you retain options. Terminate him, and your choices are nil. It can make the option of delay seem highly attractive.

But there are drawbacks. For one thing, it means probable financial ruin for the patient's family. Bills of two thousand dollars per day and more are common, even in the smallest hospitals, and they can escalate steeply in cases where prolonged care is required at an institution such as Northwest Regional.

Even more destructive, however, are the emotional effects of procrastination. Hope is like many pain-killing drugs: beneficial if used briefly and in moderation, a blight when over-employed. The doctor who permits a patient's family to hope for a loved one's recovery when it's extremely unlikely assumes a dreadful responsibility. And the price will inevitably be extracted, if not by the disappointed family, then surely by the person he sees in the mirror.

Sheldon York took a deep breath. "I think we should accept John Barclay as a candidate for euthanasia," he said. "And I say that I am prepared to tell the family of that decision myself."

Rickoff looked at the two other residents, making sure they looked straight at him as they indicated their personal concurrence. "All right, then." he said. "Good. I agree. And I will go with you to talk to the family."

York smiled, but it was a meager effort, steeped in melancholy.

"Cheer up, doctors," Rickoff said. "I can assure you, this part of the job doesn't get easier. And, if it does, then it's time for you to quit."

* * *

John Barclay's parents were fully prepared for the news that their son had been accepted as a euthanasia patient. They were religious people, but not fanatical, which helped them to accept their son's imminent death and give final consent to the procedure.

Before the end of the day, the comatose patient had been moved from the third floor Intensive Care Unit to the first floor quarters, which were still in the process of being refurbished for the Euthanasia Center. Rickoff had given his consent and blessing to the parents' request that they be allowed to spend a final night at their son's bedside.

Sheldon York was appalled. "It's sadistic!" he protested when he heard what Rickoff had authorized. "They'll go through hell in there with him."

Rickoff sighed. "And they'd be perfectly happy at home?"

"No, but . . ."

"They need to be there," Rickoff said. "They need to remember, later, that they were with him all the way to the end."

York still didn't agree, and might have pressed the argument, but the family had already assembled in the procedure room and was settling down for the night. He looked at them – mother, father and younger brother – and expelled the breath he'd drawn to speak to them. He closed the door and turned, wordless, to face Rickoff.

"We'll go home," Rickoff said. "And they'll stay here."

And that was that.

After their departure, the room and the corridor outside remained quiet for a long time.

Then the patient's father stood up, came to the bed, and took his son's hand in his own.

"I love you," he said. "I loved you the moment you were born – I was right there in the delivery room – and I loved you every minute while you were growing up, even the times I had to punish you for something. And I love you more at this moment than ever before."

"I don't want you to go. I want you to stay. But . . . you're already gone, and I'm not going to turn your body, which was so strong and beautiful, into a living tombstone for a dead man."

He paused, and his own fingers tightened on the motionless ones in his grasp.

"Good-bye, my son."

He sat down again beside his wife on a couch that had been moved into the room for their convenience, and silence descended once again.

The Barclays' Episcopal clergyman had visited them regularly at the hospital during the weeks prior to the euthanasia decision, but had firmly declined to join them in their final vigil.

"I am opposed to this," he explained. "I understand your reasons and the doctors', but I cannot be any part of such an act. It's wrong. It's murder."

The Barclays had thanked him and watched his departure without argument. But they had brought an old prayer book, not the bloodless and sterile modern version, to the hospital with them, and after a moment or two the patient's mother, Wilma Barclay, opened it to a page near the middle, and began to read:

"O Father of Mercies, and God of all comfort, our only hope in time of need; we fly unto Thee for succor in behalf of this Thy servant, here lying in great weakness of body. Look graciously upon him, O Lord . . ."

It was a prayer for the dying, when all hope of recovery has been abandoned. She read it through to the end, closing her eyes after the "Amen," and allowed the book to fall into her lap. For a moment it lay there while the others in the room sat mute.

Then the father picked the book up and turned to a prayer for the despondent:

"Comfort, we beseech Thee, most gracious God, these Thy servants, cast down and faint of heart amidst the sorrows and difficulties of the world . . ."

But John Barclay's brother was not reconciled, and would not be comforted. As soon as his father had finished the prayer for comfort, he seized the book and flipped to the back, where he found words to suit his own mood:

"Merciful God, giver of life and health; bless, we pray Thee, Thy servant John and those who administer to him of Thy healing gifts, that he may be restored to health of body and of mind . . ."

Halfway through the brief paragraph, George Barclay raised his bowed head and seemed ready to object. He held his peace until the prayer was done. But then he shook his head.

"Rick," he said. "I understand. I do. Really. But you've got to let go. Praying for Johnny's recovery isn't going to –"

"I don't care!"

Richard Barclay was two years younger than his brother and an inch taller, but they had often been mistaken for twins. Coming to his feet now, he towered over his parents. They were reminded, as always, of the remarkable similarities between their two sons as he paced restlessly to the door and back to where they were seated.

"I don't care," he repeated. "You've accepted John's death. I haven't. I can't and I won't and I don't agree to any of this."

"The doctors –"

"To hell with the doctors! Johnny's alive in there, Dad. He's alive!"

"Physically, yes. But there's no mental activity."

"How do you know?"

"The . . . monitors. The EEG."

"The EEG doesn't tell the whole story!"

"What do you mean?"

"It's supposed to measure electrical activity in the brain. But it's inexact because it can only see what gets to the surface. The sensors are up there, on the scalp, not deep in the brain where something may be happening that we don't know about."

"That's not true!"

"How do you know? How can you be so certain? Because the doctors say so? They're just people. Human beings, like us. They know what their machines tell them, but they're no closer to what's really happening, deep down in Johnny's brain, than we are."

George Barclay started to reply, to point out that two different hospital committees, the coma committee and the euthanasia committee, had considered the case and had come to the same conclusion. But he let the moment pass with the argument unspoken.

Richard was in pain. This was his own way of dealing with it.

"Richard . . ."

Wilma Barclay, who had remained silent throughout the exchange until now, looked up at her son and tried to smile.

"Please," she said. "Sit down. Just . . . be with us, now."

Richard Barclay looked at her and then at his brother's body, motionless on the bed, and sat down again in silence.

No more words were spoken in the room for a long time.

At hourly intervals, a nurse came in to check the patient's condition. She didn't speak to the family, nor they to her, but at 2:00 a.m. she noticed that George Barclay had fallen into an exhausted sleep and, with his wife's assistance, spread a blanket over him.

Richard Barclay had left the room a few minutes earlier to get a cup of coffee from the automatic dispenser and hadn't yet returned.

Before leaving the room, the nurse glanced inquiringly at Wilma Barclay, who gave a small nod, then turned out the room's overhead lights, leaving only the dim illumination from the half-open door to the corridor and the instrument lights over John Barclay's bed.

Wilma Barclay gave her a final nod of thanks and then allowed herself to lean back against the headrest of the chair she had moved to her elder son's bedside.

"Good-bye," she whispered to the semi-darkness.

The man on the bed didn't respond.

Wilma Barclay closed her eyes, not inviting sleep but hoping at least for armistice in the war going on inside her, the conflict between frustration at the leaden passage of minutes and the torture of knowing that they were the final fractions of her son's life.

Good-bye.

She had said the word, but it was like talking to a statue. The release hadn't come. John was still there, still in the bed beside her, no matter what the doctors said, and never mind logic or dignity or even her own survival.

Good-bye. In an hour or two they would come with their needles and their learning and their comfort, but she would wake up tomorrow with the knowledge that her child was gone, forever and irrevocably, and that nothing could ever –

"Mama?"

Wilma Barclay froze.

The voice had come from the bed beside her, and she knew because she was a rational human being and psychologically sophisticated that it wasn't real. The subconscious is a powerful force; it can take emotions and turn them into sound. What she'd heard was her own forlorn hopes, transmuted and amplified.

But it had sounded so very much like Johnny's real voice.

She could not avoid turning her head to look at him.

"Mama, what time is it? I'm real hungry . . ."

Recalling the moment later, hospital employees would tell interviewers that Wilma Barclay's scream – a wild melange of joy and terror and triumph and overwhelming gratitude to the Almighty – was clearly audible in obstetrics, three floors above.

Chapter Eleven

The scream continued to echo for several days.

Recovery of any long-term coma patient would have aroused interest among the news media; it was the kind of uplifting story dear to the hearts of editors surfeited on meanness and tragedy. But when it was discovered that John Barclay had regained consciousness, not just in his mother's arms but literally at the gate to eternity, the sensation was immediate and durable.

"What was your reaction, doctor, to the news that one of your patients had recovered?"

Hyman Rickoff blinked. "Pardon . . . ?"

"I mean," the television interviewer pursued, "were you pleased or otherwise?"

"I still . . . don't . . ."

"Dr. Rickoff, you are the physician in charge of the nation's very first legal euthanasia program. Had John Barclay remained in coma for another two or three hours, you or one of your trainees would have taken his life. Instead, the patient is alive, awake and functioning."

"Yes."

"Well, then . . . are you glad that it happened?"

Rickoff's control was remarkable.

"I am a doctor," he said evenly, his features still expressive only of mild puzzlement. "A physician. For me, as for any other doctor, recovery of the patient is a paramount goal."

"Yet, you and the others –"

Rickoff's expression had changed, now. "The others," he said, breaking in with a voice made of ice crystals, "are not, as you would have it, 'trainees' of any kind, but licensed doctors of medicine, like myself, who have elected to specialize in the field of euthanasia."

The interviewer pounced on the word. "That means 'mercy killing', doesn't it?"

"No."

The interviewer registered surprise. It was probably genuine. "No?"

"No," Rickoff said, launching into one of his favorite lecture modes. "Euthanasia is from the Greek 'eu', a prefix denoting ease or facility, and 'thanatos', which means death. In English, it's a word used to denote painless and peaceful death. Nothing more."

"And that is . . . what you do?"

"Yes."

"You kill people."

Rickoff hesitated and seemed about to deliver a lightning-bolt of response, but evidently changed his mind at the last moment. "I am a physician," he said gravely, "and I have specialized training in anesthesiology."

"Yes, but –"

"In addition," Rickoff continued, effectively deflecting any attempt at interruption, "I've had extensive training, and have conducted my own research, in the field of pain and analgesia." He smiled gently, turning from the interviewer to gaze directly into the lens of the camera, as if into the eyes of those watching their television sets at home. "My field," he said, making the words quiet and distinct, "is pain and its relief. Euthanasia, therefore, is simply the logical extension of that interest."

"You . . . kill people!"

The interviewer, realizing that he had somehow lost control of the interview, moved to regain command. But if he had hoped to startle Rickoff into denial or, better, into a defensive attitude, he was disappointed.

"People die," the senior euthanasist nodded, his face grave once more. "This is a fact of life and the central reality of every physician's life. If a doctor lives long enough, he will lose every single patient to his ancient adversary."

"You –"

"My colleagues and I help our patients to meet death with dignity," Rickoff went on, seemingly oblivious. "We ease the pain of transition and, in doing so, annul most of the fears that have surrounded the final phase of life throughout the ages."

"Yesterday, you and your colleges almost killed a man who could, and did, recover!"

Rickoff had paused for breath, and the interviewer had hurled himself into the breach with what he obviously considered an ultimate weapon. But Rickoff was neither surprised nor flustered.

"Yesterday," he said in the same even tone as before, "a young man recovered the hold on life that had almost slipped through his fingers."

"And how do you feel about that?"

"Elated and thankful."

The interviewer's expression said he didn't believe a word of it, and his next question reinforced the impression.

"Yet you almost killed him. Doesn't it frighten you, just a little, to have come so close to making such a tragic error?"

"Of course!"

It wasn't the answer he had expected, and for a moment the interviewer's astonishment was clearly visible. But he recovered. "You . . . admit it was a mistake?" he asked, smoothly pursuing what he obviously saw as a major chink in Rickoff's armor.

"Certainly," Rickoff said.

"Well, then . . . ?"

Rickoff didn't reply, and there was a moment of dead air before the interviewer realized he would have to finish his question or forget about it.

"I mean," he said, "doesn't it seem to you that this might be a good time to reconsider the whole question of . . . uh . . . euthanasia?"

Rickoff looked blank, and after a brief moment the interviewer decided to go on.

"Many people consider your specialty to be nothing more nor less than murder," he said. "Certainly that's what it would have been if you'd taken John Barclay's life."

Rickoff shook his head. "The decision to accept Mr. Barclay as a patient at the Euthanasia Center was made on the basis of the very best medical evidence and opinion available, re-tested and concurred upon by every responsible physician involved in the case."

"But it was wrong."

Rickoff sighed, just audibly.

"My dear young sir," he said, "I really must apologize. I'm afraid what we have here is a clear case of mistaken identity."

"Identity?"

"Yes, certainly."

"I . . . don't . . ."

"Obviously. So let me explain. I'm a doctor. So are my associates. All of us, doctors – not gods!"

"Gods?"

"That's the word. Yes. You see, if we were gods, maybe we'd go around healing people right and left and prolonging human life indefinitely and never making any mistakes. But we can't do that."

The interviewer opened his mouth to interrupt, but Rickoff went right on talking. "Human beings make mistakes," he said. "And there's no doctor alive who hasn't made his share. Nobody likes it, and everybody does his best to guard against it. But all the same, mistakes are made sometimes they can be corrected, and sometimes they can't."

"John Barclay . . ."

"John Barclay was one of the times we got the chance to correct the error. When that happens, you thank Providence for the opportunity, and make the correction. And make up your mind to try twice as hard – refine your data more thoroughly, re-think your basic criteria, sharpen your perceptions – in an effort to keep from repeating the error."

"And when it can't be corrected?"

"Then you feel dreadful, and you want to go hide somewhere and you don't much like to look at yourself in the mirror for awhile. And then you make up your mind to try twice as hard –"

"And that's all?"

"What would you have? Hara-kiri? Vows at a monastery?"

"Well, perhaps at least a little humility. A little –"

Jeff Taylor pressed a button on the remote control and the television screen instantly imploded into a tiny, fading dot at its center.

"Shit," he said under his breath.

His wife, who had been watching from the kitchen while decanting a well-chilled bottle of white wine into two frosted glasses, considered keeping her mouth shut but discarded the notion as cowardly and unproductive. She'd endured an hour or two of moody silence from her usually affable mate, and had formed the professional opinion that it was time for a change.

For both their sakes.

"Oh, I don't know," she said, putting the bottle back in the refrigerator and carrying the glasses into the living room. "I missed the first part of the interview, but from what I did see, I'd say our friend was a little more than holding his own in there."

"'Mercy killing,'" Jeff brooded.

Jolene grinned wickedly at him.

"You use the words yourself."

"I do not!"

"Not now, no. But a year ago, before the bill was passed by the legislature and before you ever thought about going into it as a specialty."

"That was then. This is now."

"And you're missing the point."

"What point?"

"That Dr. Rickoff had a first-rate platform for presenting his view of euthanasia, and he used it like a master despite the very best efforts of that oily little television twerp."

Jeff thought it over.

"Well," he said finally, taking a sip of the wine, "I do have to say he looked a hell of a lot better today than he did the day the Center was opened."

Jolene smiled. "He's a smart man, and he learns," she said. "He went into that first interview like a lamb to the slaughter. This time, he was ready."

Jeff took another reflective sip. The wine was good. Just the thing for this time of day. On a day like this one. Thank God for Jolene.

"How come," he said, "its always you, explaining things for me? Patting my head and making it better?"

"Hey, I'm a shrink!"

Jeff couldn't help laughing. He knew how Jolene hated that

term. "And I'm a professional murderer, at least to hear that TV creep tell it," he said. "So does that mean I come home and offer you a cyanide pill?"

"Jeff, come on!" But she was laughing, too, and the subject changed without either of them having to make a conscious decision to do so.

"Anyway," Jeff said after a brief silence during which they simply enjoyed each other and the hillside view, "anyway, that problem's in the past, now. Week-old news. And so far, nobody in television-land has found out about the Chief Trustee's little birthday package."

"What birthday package?"

"The bomb."

"Bomb!" Jolene froze, the wine glass an inch from her lip, and Jeff cursed himself silently. Of course she hadn't heard about it yet. No one had heard, outside the closed circle of hospital and police, and this was no way to tell her. No matter. The can of worms was wide-open now.

"Look," he began, "it was no big deal."

Jolene didn't reply, but her eyes called him a liar.

"Really! Let me take it from the top."

*　*　*

Security measures imposed after the arrival of the ersatz bomb in Dr. Rickoff's mail might not have stopped a tabloid reporter from somehow infiltrating the hospital, but they seemed, at first, to be fully effective so far as potentially dangerous packages were concerned. No more arrived at the hospital.

But the next thrust was directed at an unprotected flank.

James Emory Broadbent, former lieutenant-general in the United States Army and chief trustee of Northwest Regional, was a man both popular and respected, and his birthday parties were famous. Presents arrived from all quarters, and it was almost by chance that the shoe box-sized cardboard mailing container with the Tulsa postmark wasn't unwrapped as soon as it arrived on the day before the general's annual soiree.

"I was about to cut the tape," the general's eldest granddaughter told police later, "when I remembered something about a similar package that had been sent to the hospital . . ."

Members of the bomb squad, hurriedly but quietly summoned to the home, complimented her on her presence of mind. They spent nearly an hour examining the package – first with the help of a bomb-sniffing dog, and then with a metal detector – before moving it in a container tub to the back lawn of the general's home, where a senior bomb defuser went to work on the package with a pole-mounted knife.

The transparent wrapping tape went first. Then the top of the package was cut away. And when neither of these operations produced any kind of reaction, one member of the squad finally set a stepladder at some distance from the suspect parcel and took a look at it with powerful Navy binoculars. His reaction was immediate.

"Shit . . . bird!" he said.

Assured by the first observer that the contents of the package were non-explosive, other members of the squad, and finally the general himself, pressed forward to examine the contents. The knife that had cut through the top of the package had also torn a great rent in the tissue paper that encased the central object. It was a large rat, draped in a loincloth and nailed to a cross of wood. It had died in agony.

Beneath the obscene crucifix was a note, hand-lettered like the one in the earlier package.

"Thou Shalt Do No Murder," it said. "The Wages of Sin is Death!"

* * *

Jeff stopped talking, and for a moment the room was silent. "You see?" he said finally. "No big hoo-hoo."

But Jolene wasn't ready to agree. Gradually, as her husband spoke, her initial reaction had given way to professional concern, only slightly tinctured with revulsion.

"They . . . think it was the same person who sent the fake bomb?"

"Oh, yeah. Same kind of package. Same lettering – block letters, made with a ruler. Same ceiling walker."

Jolene nodded absently, her eyes shuttered.

"Sick, huh?"

Another nod.

"But not really dangerous," Jeff went on. "A police psychologist said this kind of thing is all the outlet the sender really needs. We'll keep an eye on the mail, of course, and report any suspicious arrivals. But he says there's probably no real danger."

Jolene's eyes re-focused and she seemed about to speak, perhaps to dispute the psychologist's reassurances. But the moment passed as Jeff waved a dismissing hand.

"All in the past," he said. "Over and done with. The general wasn't impressed. The other trustees weren't intimidated. The news people didn't find out. And that's that. End of problem. That problem, anyway. Now we've got a new one in the form of our next candidate. The good news is that this guy can talk. Tell us what he wants to do and why he wants to do it."

"So that makes it easier?"

"Not really."

The applicant's name was Duane Tanner, and at their first meeting, Jeff had found himself totally unable to accept the notion that he was a candidate for euthanasia. Tanner was a darkly handsome man in his late thirties, somewhat underweight, and apparently in good health.

"But he's got AIDS," Jeff explained.

Jolene nodded, switching effortlessly to what Jeff thought of as her "professional mode," complete with neutral expression and attentive attitude. Everything but the notebook and tape recorder.

"No doubt about the diagnosis?"

Jeff shook his head. "None at all, though of course we insisted on another complete examination."

"Uh-huh."

"But that was just pro forma. He's got it, all right, and not just the HIV virus. This is the real thing, complete with pneumonia, which almost did him in a month or two back."

Jolene allowed her puzzlement to show. "I thought you said he looked healthy."

"He did. That's the problem."

At present, Jeff explained, Duane Tanner's disease seemed to be in remission. "He's getting AZT," he said, "and that could be the reason for the remission. Or it could just happen. It does in some cases."

"And he wants to die?"

"No! Of course not. No more than anyone does. But he knows the disappearance of symptoms is only temporary, and he's seen what AIDS can do – has done – to others."

Jolene nodded slowly, her eyes clouded. "He wants to avoid that."

"Sure. And who can blame him? Death's scary. It's dark out there, it lasts a long time, and you don't get to take much of anything with you –"

"– except, maybe, a little dignity."

Jeff sipped his wine again, and directed his gaze out the window.

"A little dignity," he agreed somberly. "Yes. That. And maybe, with luck, a sense of having called your own shots right up to the end."

"So, you're going to accept him?"

"Not necessarily."

Everybody's initial reaction on seeing Tanner, Jeff said, was to reject the whole idea of euthanasia. He simply did not look or act like a dying man; he was too self-assured, too obviously still enjoying life. And Tanner himself readily admitted reservations about the euthanasia process.

"He had it all worked out," Jeff said. "He would go right on living a normal, active life – he's a stockbroker, junior partner in one of the smaller firms – and then do the job on himself when the disease became active again."

Jolene thought it over. "He's . . . not married?"

Jeff shook his head. "Not any more. He was, though, for about eight years, and has two kids. A boy and a girl. And no, he's not gay, if that's what you wanted to know. What happened was that he was in a car accident a few years ago and came out with a ruptured spleen and liver lacerations. Almost bled to death, but they got him to a hospital in time and he came through the surgical procedure, no sweat. But he needed about twenty units of whole blood –"

"– which probably contained the virus."

"Which most likely contained the virus."

Jolene thought it over.

"The way he got it," she said, "you'd think that alone might make him kind of wary of the medical profession."

"You'd think so, yes. But he doesn't seem to hold any kind of grudge."

"All right. That's good. But it's not really why I was asking about his family." Jolene's wine glass was still almost full, but she set it aside on an end table. "I wanted to know about that because they're the ones who could really be hurt by any outright suicide."

"He thought of that," Jeff said. "And he talked to a lawyer, who looked over his insurance policies. Sure enough, he upgraded everything a couple of years ago, and there's a two-year suicide clause. The kids are his beneficiaries, and they'd get nothing but the premiums he's already paid if he kills himself in the next four months."

"Which is more time than he probably has."

"Right."

"But . . . wouldn't the same thing apply if he dies as a result of a euthanasia process?"

Jeff shook his head. "The people who wrote the law thought of that. You know, there's actually an anti-suicide law on the books in this state. But they specifically exempted euthanasia patients from any such penalties, criminal or civil."

"I see."

Jolene's eyes still seemed to be focused on some point in the far distance, and Jeff didn't try to call her back. He loved to see her pick at a problem in her mind. As often as not, she would come up with an angle or an approach that he'd missed. It was only one of the reasons he enjoyed talking to her. But a good one.

"Well," she said at length, "that's good to know, of course. But it's not really why I asked about the family."

"No?"

"No," she sighed. "Maybe it's just a professional reaction, but I was really wondering about how much of an emotional burden he might be inflicting on someone by . . . taking matters into his own hands."

"Oh, right. But he'd figured that one out, too."

"Figured it out?"

"Yep. And you've got to give the guy credit, his idea was pretty slick."

Jolene was back from whatever far place she'd gone to, and was leaning back on the couch, looking at him again.

"Tell me."

"Well, I guess this must have been after the first time he talked to the lawyer. Before we came into the picture. See, he's got this neat little mountain cabin way back in the boonies, and to beat the suicide clause he was going to go up there with a quart or two of Old Friskabout and some charcoal briquettes."

Jolene's expression said she didn't understand.

"The idea was," Jeff went on, "that he would drink enough of the booze that an autopsy would decide he was drunk. And when he'd burned all the regular wood in the fireplace, then he would pile the charcoal on the fire –"

"– and be found dead a day or so later."

"Right! Because the charcoal would eat up all the oxygen in the place, and he would just kind of go to sleep and never wake up."

Jolene shook her head in an eclectic combination of admiration and rejection. "Such ingenuity, just for a way to die."

Jeff nodded. "Anyway, before he could put the plan into operation, he saw a newspaper story about the Center and went to the phone book to look up the number of his friendly, neighborhood euthanasists."

"Jeff!"

Jeff downed the rest of his wine in a single swallow, set the glass down firmly, and stood up.

"Okay," he said. "Sure. No joking matter. But I don't know what else to do with it right now, because every time I think I know how I am going to vote on this guy's case, I think again about John Barclay."

Jolene held her silence, waiting for him to go on.

"We looked at it from every angle. We performed all the tests, checked it against a computer profile and got every second opinion in the book. And we were wrong."

"Dr. Rickoff –"

"Dr. Rickoff has learned to handle a media interview like nobody's business, and I agree with every word he said. Of course doctors make mistakes, and of course they're human and all you can do is your best."

"Exactly!"

"But all of that," he said, wandering behind the couch and placing his hands on either side of her neck, "means less than nothing when you've got to make the next decision about the next case."

His hands began to wander, and Jolene closed her eyes. The wine glass was still half full, but she had lost interest in it.

"Next case," she echoed.

"Next case."

There was a moment of silence, filled with activity.

"Why, doctor," she said then, in mock astonishment. "Doctor . . . what on earth do you think you're doing?"

"Well," he said, "I'd kind of hoped it might be called 'foreplay'."

And it was.

Chapter Twelve

Jeff's mood was buoyant as he arrived at the hospital the following day, even though he hadn't yet come to any definite conclusion regarding the Tanner case. But he was, for the moment, at peace with himself, and confident in his ability to make a final decision that day. And that, as his wife was fond of saying, was considerably better than a hit in the eye with a sharp stick.

He would handle it.

And then he saw the front page of *The National Advocate*.

Bill Skelton had just push-pinned the garish page to the cork bulletin board in the seminar room, and was glowering at his handiwork when Jeff came through the door.

Again, the supermarket rag offered both a picture and a headline:

"'MURDER CLINIC' TRIES TO KILL RECOVERING ATHLETE"

As before, the photograph showed a patient, helpless on a hospital bed. But this time, instead of a doctor bending over him, readers were invited to examine the anguish of a mother about to be bereft of her eldest son. Jeff's fist clenched almost reflexively. He felt like smashing it into the bulletin board.

"How?" Bill Skelton whispered. "How in the . . . hell . . . could anyone take a picture like that? How?"

But Jeff's approach was slightly different. "How the hell," he asked, speaking like Skelton to the world in general, "could anyone bring himself to publish a picture like that, no matter how he got it?"

No answer had been expected. But the two residents were still standing there in silence, as if waiting for a reply, when Rickoff entered. He glanced at the bulletin board, allowed himself a brief souring of expression, then moved briskly away to seat himself at the head of the table.

"Where's York?" he wanted to know.

"Probably getting drunk," Skelton growled. "And if I can't think of something better to do, I'll likely join him."

Rickoff snorted derisively, obviously reluctant to broach the subject of the tabloid article.

But Skelton would not be denied. "D. W. Teeples," he said. "Teeples! Shitty name. So why can't our wonderful security force put a face to it?"

Jeff had been wondering about that, too.

"Got to be someone inside here. Working here," he said. "Got to be. So why hasn't the son of a bitch been found?"

Rickoff shrugged, abandoning any hope of maintaining a professional tone. "Because the son of a bitch is a smart son of a bitch, that's why," he said. "And because he's a professional at what he's doing, be it ever so shitty, or he wouldn't be working for the biggest of the scumbag sheets. Whereas we, gentlemen, are amateurs at dealing with bastards like him."

He paused, letting the words sink in. "So now," he continued, when he was sure they'd really heard him, "may I suggest that we get down to the real business at hand?"

Reluctantly, the two younger men seated themselves at the table and opened the duplicate record jackets they'd brought with them. Before their deliberations could begin, however, the door to the seminar room burst open again and a somewhat astonishing Sheldon York entered.

His hair was disarranged, and there was a swelling cut at the corner of his mouth. His nose showed signs of recently stanched bleeding, and the knuckles of his right hand were swollen and discolored.

Rickoff looked him up and down and then looked away with a small sigh. "Sit down, Doctor York," he said, placing a slight ironic emphasis on the title. "Or, better still, get some ice from the machine and wrap it around your hand."

York looked at him stonily. His right eye seemed to be swelling shut; he had the beginnings of a truly impressive black eye.

"Sorry I'm late," he said in a carefully controlled tone. "And my hand is just fine, thank you. Shall we begin?"

Bill Skelton laughed. And then, one by one, the rest joined in, Sheldon York included, as the morning's tensions gradually reduced themselves to their true proportions.

"All right, then, Sugar Ray," Skelton said when the hilarity finally began to subside. "Who'd you coldcock?"

Sheldon York drew himself up to his full 5'5" and tried to assume a supercilious air. "It's all very well," he said, "for the news media to insist on their rights for free expression. But those rights are not exclusive, after all."

Jeff eyed the swelling fist. "So, you expressed yourself."

"Right on his nose!"

The doctors relaxed, and waited for York to fill them in.

What it amounted to, he said, was a leak somewhere in the Euthanasia Center. Rickoff and others associated with the hospital had been careful from the beginning not to identify any of the residents with any specific patient. But someone had connected York to the Barclay case, and a television crew had been waiting for him outside his home. The moment he opened his front door to leave, the scrum was there, shoving microphones in his face, blinding him with camera flashes and attacking him with a barrage of rhetorical questions.

"They didn't force me to do or say anything, really." York said. "I could have simply ignored them or said 'no comment' or something. I could have just gotten in my car and left."

"But you didn't," Rickoff said.

"No."

Instead, acting on the apparently mistaken assumption that he was a free individual and, as such, entitled to the same privacy and human consideration guaranteed any citizen under the constitution, York had tried to remonstrate with the assorted media minions. And it had been an eye-opener. Accustomed to the semi-civilized tactics employed by news crews when under scrutiny of their peers in such locations as the entrance to a hospital or a public auditorium, he was quite unprepared for the full-scale assault strategy employed by television crews or paparazzi when they think there's no one around to see and remember.

In short order, Sheldon York had found himself first, trying to defend himself against questions roughly comparable to "Have you stopped selling narcotics to minors?" and then taunted with such epithets as "Medical Hit Man," "Poison Pusher," and "Doctor Death."

It was a standard media performance, and in fact relatively restrained in tone (one reporter on the scene was fresh from acting school, and therefore not yet fully trained in such modern journalistic techniques as the out-of-context sound byte, or the computer-looped response). But York took it personally and, when the opportunity arose, attempted to force the talent to swallow his microphone.

In this he was unsuccessful. But the haymaker he managed

to land on the point of that tormentor's nose was faithfully recorded on telefilm, complete with accompanying sound effects. It would, in the fullness of time, become a major exhibit in the newsman's damage suit, while tapes of the several blows inflicted on York by members of the crew a few moments earlier would, of course, be unaccountably lost.

"And then," York said in conclusion, "I found out it was all a case of mistaken identity."

The doctors looked perplexed.

"Huh?" Bill Skelton ventured.

"Indeed," York nodded. "My reaction precisely, when I found out they thought I was also the euthanasia resident assigned to Mr. Duane Tanner!"

And that was a real stopper.

Hospitals are, by nature and by law, notably reluctant to divulge the identities of their patients. Close relatives and friends learn quickly that they must be on a list of legitimately "interested" parties before they will receive the time of day from an admitting clerk or floor nurse, and reporters seeking condition reports on ailing politicians and celebrities are routinely advised to seek information from the patient's attending physician. But all this was a kindergarten lark by comparison to the security surrounding the identity of patients admitted or about to be admitted to the Euthanasia Center.

The media circus generated by the Center's first two patients had left doctors and staff tight-lipped to a degree that would have aroused admiration in a KGB colonel, and Sheldon York's chagrin was shared by the other three doctors.

"Jesus . . ." Bill Skelton began.

"Christ," Jeff Taylor added.

"Almighty!" Hyman Rickoff concluded reverently.

Coming as it did on the heels of *The National Advocate* photograph and story, the news that the name (and perhaps the address and background data) of a prospective patient had become public property even before they decided to admit him was almost too much for the doctors to digest at a single sitting. They sat in silence for several moments, trying to deal with alternate waves of rage and frustration.

Rickoff sighed. "I'd almost rather deal with our friend who mails the fake bombs and dead rodents," he said. "At least you know where you stand with him!"

Sheldon York was instantly alert. "We've . . . heard from him again?"

Rickoff shook his head. "No," he said. "What I meant was, people like that, they're all bluff. They threaten, but the bombs are always fake. They never really do anything."

"Who told you that?"

"My wife. She watches a lot of television."

Jeff laughed, but Bill Skelton was still preoccupied with the breach in security. "This guy," he said, "this Teeples character, has absolutely got to be found. And he's got to go!"

"Teeples?"

"Sure! It's obvious he's the leak. The one who's getting into our confidential files."

But Jeff shook his head. "Teeples didn't give Duane Tanner's name to the TV crew," he said.

"Why not?" Skelton wanted to know.

Jeff shrugged. "Wouldn't make sense," he said. "If Teeples knew the name, he'd want to keep the information to himself, to use it in his own story."

"Maybe he sold it to them," Sheldon York suggested.

"Maybe. But I don't think so." Jeff got up and wandered around the table to take another look at the tabloid article on the bulletin board. "Teeples," he said, "has a lot of ego. Twice now, he's come up with pictures that could not – repeat, could not – have been taken by someone from the outside."

"And quotes," Skelton nodded.

"Quotes?"

"The story he wrote about Barclay," Skelton said, "included quotations, absolutely accurate quotations, not only from things that were said in my presence, but things that the family said while they were with the patient that night. From the hours before he . . . woke up."

Jeff nodded.

"Ego," he said. "He's got us chasing our tails, and he knows it. So, whatever he's doing and however he's doing it, you can be sure he's not going to share it with anyone."

Hyman Rickoff snorted and stirred. "Wonderful," he said. "Wonderful. Beautiful! So now, instead of one leak to one reporter, we've got two. That really makes my day."

And that was the final word.

Nothing more remained to be said on the subject of security violations or the news media, and after another minute or two of silent brooding, the doctors' natural resiliency asserted itself. They turned to more important matters.

"Duane Tanner," Rickoff said, moving to the blackboard to inscribe the patient's name, birth date, sex and ethnic background. "Duane Tanner," he said, reading from the workup sheet in his hand. "Mid-thirties. Divorced. Successful. Essentially a loner. Heterosexual; apparently contracted AIDS through a blood transfusion."

Tanner's illness, Rickoff continued his recapitulation, had first manifested itself about three years after the transfusions, when he noticed that he was losing weight.

"And at the time," Rickoff said, "he was actually pleased. He'd been trying to lose a few pounds for years. Associates noticed, and complimented him. But then he began to be short of breath . . ."

The doctor Tanner finally consulted had made a tentative

diagnosis of pneumonia. Chest examination showed decreased breath sounds, and arterial blood gases demonstrated hypoxemia. Chest X-ray showed some haziness on both sides, starting at the center of the lungs and spreading outward. The complete blood count showed decreased white blood cells with decreased lymphocytes, as well. But the gradual loss of weight, which must necessarily have preceded the pneumonia, seemed suspicious.

"Tanner's doctor sent him to a small proprietary hospital, where they put him in a private room, hit him with antibiotics, performed appropriate lab studies, and saw to it that he got oxygen by nasal cannula, which made him feel a little better. The chest X-rays kept getting worse, though, and the shortness of breath increased. So Tanner's doctor, finally beginning to suspect they were in deep trouble, transferred the patient to Northwest Regional and called Paul Greathouse."

Dr. Paul Greathouse was a pulmonologist with a reputation of being able to interact well with the very ill, and he justified it in the Tanner case, first gaining the patient's confidence by being totally open with him, then doing all in his power to keep him comfortable while tests were being made.

"He suspected AIDS from the first," Rickoff said. "Tanner went into the ICU on a ventilator, and Greathouse performed a bronchoscopy to help remove secretions and perhaps give him a firm diagnosis."

The bronchoscopy would indeed give them a definitive answer. Greathouse and Dr. Brian Crabtree, another pulmonologist called into consultation, removed the secretions, took brush biopsies, then sat down to analyze all their data.

"Their diagnosis," Rickoff said, "was pneumocystis carinii pneumonia. And AIDS. His blood had tested positive for the

HIV virus, and all other tests confirmed the condition as active."

The patient was informed. And he seemed to take it well. His first question, of course, had been about how he could have contracted the disease. This was explained. And then he wanted to know how long he could expect to live. The doctors had told him they didn't know – sometimes the onset of the disease was followed by a period of remission as it seemed to be in his case. Clinically, he seemed to improve at once. eventually, he was weaned from the ventilator and even gained a little weight. At length, he was able to leave the hospital and return home.

"A month later, he was back. He'd begun to lose weight again, and had developed an abscess where he'd cut himself shaving. This problem was corrected, and he left the hospital once again. There were no more episodes for a month or two. But by this time, his thoughts had turned first to suicide . . . and then to what some parts of the medical profession and the more restrained elements of the press now referred to as "physician-assisted termination."

Rickoff's presentation was at an end, but there was no immediate comment as the doctors took a moment or two for final assessment.

Jeff had made his own decision within minutes of reading through the data that Rickoff had just presented in capsule form. Not included in the presentation was the fact that Tanner had discussed his condition with a psychiatrist and even with the hospital chaplain, though he said he wasn't a religious person.

He wanted to die in two days, as soon as he was sure his estate was in order and that all legal bases had been covered.

Bill Skelton, who was the resident specifically assigned to the case, voiced a slightly different concern: "I asked him if he'd told his two kids yet," he said. "And he said he hadn't."

Tanner's reasons were good ones.

"He said they were too young to understand all the factors involved," Skelton related, "and, he didn't want to put them through the countdown when he actually undergoes the procedure."

"But, later they'll . . ."

Skelton shook his head. "Got that angle covered too," he said. "After he approached us, he wrote letters to each of them, to be opened and read when their mother was sure they were old enough to understand the situation and what he'd decided to do."

Rickoff sighed. "A grown-up," he said. "A real, live, responsible adult."

"Rare breed," Jeff agreed.

"And getting scarcer."

The doctors thought their own thoughts in silence for a moment, each sure he had already come to his own decision and that it was the right one. But still they hesitated. Gun shy after the experience with John Barclay, they found that they wanted a final, face-to-face interview with Tanner before actually admitting him to the Euthanasia Center. And Rickoff agreed. "All right, then," he said. "Tomorrow. Here. Ten a.m."

The doctors nodded without further comment, and Sheldon York pulled out an electronic memo pad to make a note. They left the room in silence, each preoccupied with his own thoughts but still unable to resist a final glance in the direction of the bulletin board, where the words "Murder Clinic" burned blood red into the morning.

* * *

Four minutes after their departure, the bright blue gaze of a man in the whites of a hospital orderly kindled briefly at the sight of the push-pinned tabloid page. But he looked away at once, suppressing the vestige of a smile, as he began to clean the floor.

He left the door open, and after a quick glance to make sure he would be unobserved, reached under the conference table to touch the voice-operated tape recorder he'd planted there. He removed the used tape, and substituted a blank. No one disturbed him. He completed his work in less than three minutes, and departed with the tape in his pocket, sparing himself one final peek at the tabloid headline.

"MURDER CLINIC"

He liked it. And it sold papers. The story was beginning to take on a life of its own.

Chapter Thirteen

Charlie was waiting for them when they entered the gully. He'd been in country only a month, but that was long enough to recognize the sound of an AK-47 and try to take cover the moment he heard it.

Only there wasn't any cover. Charlie'd planned the ambush well.

The pioneering platoon was strung out along the trail en route to what was supposed to be a secure hamlet. With weapons slung over their shoulders, everybody's arms were free to carry tools and supplies. They depended on the point and flankers to give them a little warning. But it hadn't worked that way, and by the time the first round was fired, both ends of the enfilade were closed. He dropped the roll of primacord he'd been carrying and had his hand on the bolt of the M-16 when the sledgehammer hit his right knee. He went down headfirst.

Christ!

They told you that mostly you didn't feel any pain for a moment or two after you were hit, but it was bullshit. He screamed without even knowing his mouth was open. All the same, he was able to roll over and get the weapon pointed in what seemed like a useful position and even got off a burst. It must have been on automatic, though he didn't remember switching from the semi. Then the world blew up around him.

"God dammit!"

Father Micah Chaine woke with an echo of blasphemy in his ears, knowing he'd screamed the words and glad he was alone. No one to hear. No one but . . .

"God."

The single syllable, uttered quietly this time and of his own volition, made the sterile impersonality of the motel room real again and completed his trip back to the world from country. For the thousandth time. Or the millionth. Or the ten millionth.

Even before he was released from the army's hospitals and finished with the doctors, squads of them who'd tried to repair the damage to his leg, he'd lost track of the number of times he'd had that dream about the Cong ambush, and the feelings of helpless fear and frustration he'd taken with him into unconsciousness when the mortar round caught him.

"Because ye have set at naught all my counsel and would have none of my reproof, I will also laugh at your calamity; I will mock when your fear cometh . . ."

Cora.

He stood up, chilled by the dew of sweat that covered his body, and felt ashamed of it.

Cora.

A headshrinker back at Winter General, smarter than the other doctors and willing to listen instead of talk, had called the turn. Made him see that the dream was just a part of the fear. All his life, he'd been afraid. In country, sure, who wasn't scared, in country? But before, too, all the way back to when he was a little boy.

Cora.

In the church his mother took him to every day before she went to work, there was a great stained glass window crafted into an eye. God's eye. Watching him. Seeing everything. Even in the dark, even right inside his mind. He was evil. He knew he was. He had evil thoughts and he did evil things, and the Great Eye was always there, and he was afraid.

Cora.

Later, of course, they moved away and he didn't go to that church any more, and he knew it was just glass with sunlight shining through it. Inanimate. Not God's eye at all. But that didn't make it go away. The Eye was still there . . . even when he . . .

Cora.

. . . even when . . .

Cora

. . . even when he . . .

Cora.

"Enough!"

Once again, a thought had become sound without any conscious volition on his part. He looked at his wrist watch, reading the luminous numbers in the dark, and realized there would be no sleep for him in any of the hours still to be lived through before dawn.

Cora.

"O God, merciful and compassionate, who art ever ready to hear the prayers of those who put their trust in Thee; graciously hearken to us who call upon Thee, and grant us Thy help in this our need, through Jesus Christ our Lord."

Chaine paused, waiting.

"Amen."

Cora.

All right, then. It wasn't going to go away. Might as well let it do its own thing. Take its own course.

Cora.

She had been there, living right next door, when he came home on holiday after midwinter examinations, his third year in the seminary. She wasn't Catholic and didn't seem to understand. Or maybe she knew but didn't care what was involved. And in a very little while, he didn't care either.

Cora Halstead was short, chubby and blonde, and he'd never been particularly attracted to short, chubby blondes. But Cora changed all that. She was relaxed and natural and the corners of her mouth turned up in what seemed to be a kind of secret amusement at the world. He quickly discovered that this was more than a mere chance arrangement of features. Cora had a quick mind and a sense of the grotesque far livelier than his own, and in short order he'd decided he wasn't really called to become a priest after all.

"Almighty God, look mercifully upon the world which Thou hast redeemed by the blood of Thy dear Son, and incline the hearts of many to dedicate themselves to the sacred ministry of Thy Church . . ."

His mother had hysterics when he told her. Her dearest wish, for which, it seemed, she'd prayed daily since the day of his birth, was that he enter the priesthood. The news that he now had another vision for his life's work, one that didn't include celibacy in any form, only seemed to move her to new peaks of frenzy.

Even Cora seemed somewhat taken aback. "Look, Mickey," she said, "let's not get all ahead of ourselves, here. Maybe your mama knows what she's talking about."

Cora loved him. She said she did, and he saw no reason not to believe her. But marriage, well, that was something else again. "Maybe we should take this one step at a time . . ."

Micah's world tilted. In all the careful, church-centered context of his upbringing, he'd never had reason to question the ironbound link between love and marriage. Love was what happened between a man and a woman. Marriage was what they did about it. Dimly, he was aware that not everyone lived by this rule. In his own neighborhood, he knew of one man and woman who were living together without marriage, and several people who had been divorced and remarried. But all this was, quite simply, sin. He tried to explain it to Cora, quoting from St. Paul's first letter to the Corinthians:

". . . for it is better to marry than to burn with passion . . ."

Which made Cora laugh. "Well, Mickey," she said, "it sure sounds like he was talking about us, for sure!" But it didn't budge her an inch. It wasn't, she insisted, that she didn't love him. She loved him a lot. And it wasn't that she didn't think he loved her. She knew he did. "Marriage, though, that's something else, you know?" she said. "I mean, it's like your mother says, something that's going to make a difference the whole rest of your life!"

And that's the way things stood when the summer ended and Micah went, with great reluctance and only on Cora's promise of daily letters, back to the seminary, where he was quick to lay the whole problem before his proctor, Father Maartins.

Father Maartins took it calmly. "Do you imagine," he asked, without a trace of surprise or excitement in the stolid, slightly Dutch-accented cadence of his everyday speech, "that you're the first postulant to feel the stirrings of the body?"

Micah insisted it was more than that. He was really in love, really committed to the secular world and to Cora.

Father Maartins nodded. "And the girl? Cora?"

Micah hesitated, wanting to say she was as determined as he, but was unable to lie to his proctor. "She . . . has doubts."

"Ah."

In the end, Micah assured himself that he was, and would remain, serious about Cora, though he promised Father Maartins that he would pray for guidance. But as the days passed, Cora's letters, arriving almost daily as promised, referred less and less to their relationship. None contained words of love. As he read each letter, Micah felt the intensity of the previous summer of love and passion slowly diminishing until it became something like a dream, a fantasy of his own creation.

He awoke one morning to the realization that he could no longer clearly recall her face. He quickly retrieved Cora's photograph which he had carefully concealed in the ticking of his bed, and was amazed to discover that it showed him an ordinarily pretty young woman not markedly different from many others he had known.

Cora . . .

And so the summer glow faded, and the affair might have ended in that press of scholarship that prepares men to be the priests of Mother Church, had it not been for Cora's father and the letter he sent just two months after Micah's return to classes. He said his daughter was pregnant and that she didn't want Micah to know. He said he was sure Micah would want to "do the right thing."

He was right.

An hour after he received the letter, Micah Chaine was on a bus, and in seven hours, even before letting his mother know he was back, he was at Cora's home. But he was too late.

Cora's father opened the door, and one look at the man's face froze Micah in his tracks. The older man couldn't look the younger in the eye.

"I'm sorry," he began, speaking to the floor of the porch. "Sorry. I tried to –"

"Cora! What's happened?"

"Micah, you've got to understand, she was –"

"Where is she?" Micah was ready to shake the man. But before he could move, Cora herself appeared at the head of the stairs behind her father's back.

"Cora!"

"Mickey."

She came down the steps slowly and he pushed through the door to meet her, ready to touch her and reassure her that he still loved her and everything would be all right, even though he wasn't at all sure of these things himself. Instead of moving to meet him however, Cora turned toward the kitchen and Micah felt her father's hand on his arm.

"You can talk to her in a minute, Micah," he said. "Right now, we need to talk."

Micah hesitated for a moment, then followed him into the parlor.

"I think you should go back to school now."

Micah looked at him as though he'd suddenly lost his mind.

"The baby," he said. "We need to –"

"There is no baby." Suddenly the room was very still. Micah forced himself to take a breath, and then another, as he waited for the other man to go on.

Cora's father minced no words. Cora had decided to have an abortion, and it had been performed the previous day. It was over. Nothing to be done about it. Nothing at all.

"I don't believe you."

Micah knew that Cora's father wasn't lying, but he didn't want to believe that Cora could be capable of such a thing.

"It's murder," he said, when the older man didn't respond to his challenge. "It's murder, and I know Cora would never kill anyone. Ever. Least of all her own child!"

"It wasn't a child."

Micah turned to find Cora standing behind him.

"It wasn't a child," she repeated. "Not yet. It hadn't breathed, hadn't moved, it –"

"It was a human being, endowed with a soul!"

"It was only –"

"No!" It was a single word, the last he would utter in that house, and it burst from his throat as a shout of pure anguish. And denial.

But the silence that followed was louder.

Micah couldn't bear to be for another moment in that place, and if the front door had been shut he might well have smashed through it.

He had fathered a child. A boy. Or a girl. He would never know which. He, Micah Chaine, had fathered a child. And now it was dead.

"Thou shalt do no murder."

Outside the house the crisp air of autumn seemed to shimmer, and it seemed to Micah that he could actually see the words of the commandment branded upon the sky and the earth.

"Thou shalt do no murder."

But murder had been done. By Cora, yes. By her, and by her parents who'd stood by and let it happen. And by the doctor.

And by God.

God had let it happen. God had made it happen, because didn't God make everything happen? Wasn't that what they'd been drilling into him in church since before he could remember, and now in seminary?

God had done it . . . God!

His own home, his mother's home, was next door, but he didn't go there. She would tell him it was for the best, and that would be a lie. Like all the other lies she had told him over the years. And he couldn't return to the seminary, where they would lie to him, too.

He wanted to go away, and it took him less than a second to think of one place where no one was likely to look for him. For three years, since entering seminary, postulant Micah Chaine had been draft-exempt.

"Good-bye seminary, hello country!"

Standing alone in the darkness of his motel room, Micah heard himself say the words aloud and noted their mocking tone.

Well . . .

He could afford to feel some amusement at himself now, after all the years that had passed. All the lessons learned.

He had never seen Cora again, and he didn't want to, though he had heard from his mother, during one of her visits after he was released from the hospital and returned to seminary, that Cora had married and was now the mother of two children. They would be grown by now, those children. Or almost so. As his son or daughter would have been.

"Thou shalt do no murder."

Well and good.

But . . . was it murder to prevent a known murderer from taking more lives? And was there any sure way of stopping a murderer, short of taking his life?

Charles Pennington and Julia Hartt would never understand. The few times he'd tried to explain his own beliefs to them, they'd looked at him as though he had suddenly started speaking in tongues. Babbling. With them, this was all some kind of childish game, something you did to make the grown-ups notice you and listen to what you were saying.

He had gone along with them, let them think whatever they wished, so long as they provided the transportation, the mule work and financing he needed. They had their priorities. He had his.

But now the rules were changing, and now it wasn't enough simply to warn and frighten and hope this would deter. Things like that were a bandage, a patch. Not really effective in the long run, because in the long run what you had to do if you were really serious about fighting sin, especially the big sins like murder, was to take the sin upon yourself. As the Lord had done.

"I will give you the keys to the kingdom of heaven, and whatsoever you bind on earth shall be bound in heaven, and whatsoever you lose on earth shall be lost in heaven."

He could bear the sin. He could do that because he could repent it and be absolved, while the sinner who died by his hand and by his sin would be prevented forever from sinning anew.

"Thou shalt do no murder."

Yes. But he was a priest, the good shepherd.

"The good shepherd lays down his life for the sheep."

Yes. It was so.

Cora. The baby. The abortion. The army. Country. And returning to seminary, and parish work, and being fired for "conduct likely to bring discredit upon the church and to your calling," and all the rest of it. God had brought him to this place and to this time. God had brought him to this decision.

"MURDER CLINIC"

A shaft of light from the street, seeping through a crack between the shade and the window frame, fell upon the bold-faced headline of the supermarket tabloid he'd brought home the day before. His warnings had been ignored. The murderers were undeterred. They would continue to sin, to damn their own souls and those of their victims, unless stopped by force.

Very well. God's will be done.

It was time.

Chapter Fourteen

"Obviously, some specific deadline must be selected, and I believe it should be next Tuesday," Duane Tanner declared in a tone of quiet determination. "As shortly after dawn as possible." He stopped talking and sat waiting for the doctors' reactions.

Unable to come to any definite conclusion on the basis of the clinical information at their disposal, the chief and residents of the Euthanasia Center had decided to discuss their reservations with the patient himself. But the interview wasn't going quite as expected. Tanner was one of a kind. Unique. Self-possessed and almost clinically objective about himself and his situation, he seemed to confound any possible stereotype of the euthanasia candidate. But the euthanasists weren't entirely convinced. He was just a little bit too good to be true.

"No regrets?" Jeff inquired, hoping to stimulate a more familiar response. "No . . . bitterness about the situation?"

Tanner laughed. "You've got to be kidding!"

It broke the tension, and for a moment the doctors permitted themselves to relax with the patient. But they still wanted to hear his answer.

"Bitter?" Tanner said when the moment had passed. "I'm bitter as hell! And as for regrets, how would you feel?"

That was more like it. They sat still and waited for him to go on.

"Sometimes," he said, "I wake up in the middle of the night and want to set fire to the damned apartment house, or bomb the hospital where I got the blood, or just run naked into the streets, screaming."

Rickoff nodded. "But you don't do any of those things," he said. "Instead, you come here and tell us the exact date on which you wish your life to end."

"Like hell I do!" Tanner turned his head slightly to face Rickoff. "I am a perfectly normal human being, and that means I basically want to stay alive. Especially so, since my symptoms are in remission."

He paused and Bill Skelton interjected a brief confirmation.

"CD4 lymphocyte count normal," he said. "Chest clear. No fever. No shortness of breath."

"And a healthy appetite," Tanner confirmed. "I had a breakfast of fruit and an English muffin, and it went down just fine. Not even indigestion."

"But . . . ?" Rickoff prodded.

"But the food tastes a little bit funny, probably because of the drugs I'm taking, the AZT. And no matter how much I eat, I don't seem to gain any weight, so I know all this is temporary, that one day I'll wake up and it will all be changed. And yes, I regret the living hell out of that."

The sincerity in his voice was beyond doubting. The doctors waited for him to continue.

"But there's nothing I can do about it," he said. "And one of the things I learned when I was a very small boy was not to argue with the weather."

Jeff couldn't repress a grin of recognition. His own grandfather had used just the same words in warning him not to match his own will against the immutable.

"I've had good luck in a lot of ways," Tanner continued. "Lucky about the line of work I chose – that I liked it and was good at it – and lucky to have an ex-wife who's been willing to let me be a part of my childrens' lives." His expression darkened for a moment. "That's what really hurts. Knowing I won't be around to see them grow up. I really hate that. Worse than just the idea of dying itself, I mean. Everybody dies. You make peace with that as a part of growing up. But the kids . . ." His voice trailed into silence. Some kind of response seemed to be indicated, and Rickoff offered it.

"Indeed, yes," he said. "But . . . forgive me, sir. I'm sure the other doctors are as impressed as I am with your attitude. But really, that's the whole nature of the problem we face in your particular case."

Tanner seemed genuinely surprised. "Problem?"

"Yes. The fact is Mr. Tanner, that you are a little bit too good to be true."

Tanner shook his head. "I'm sorry?"

"Either you are the most totally adult, mature and self-controlled human being who ever lived," Jeff said, "or the best actor any of us have ever seen."

Tanner thought it over in silence for a moment, and then offered a wry smile. "Thank you," he said. "Thank you for giving me what amounts to a professional compliment."

"Professional?"

"Yes. I'm not an actor. Not exactly, anyway. But any salesman, particularly in a line like stocks and bonds, learns quickly to project a bland and unflappable exterior or find another line of work." He eased back in his chair. "After a while," he said, "I guess it gets to be second nature. I was doing that kind of number here with you. Not deliberately. But doing it, all the same. If I gave the wrong impression, I apologize. I was just trying to cope in my own way." Tanner seemed to have run out of words.

After a quick glance around the table to see if the residents had any further questions, Rickoff decided to conclude the discussion by telling the patient that they would make a decision before the end of the day. But just as he drew a breath to speak, Tanner continued his discourse, this time in a tone of quiet intensity that riveted the doctors' attention.

"I want to quit now, while I'm ahead," he said. "Sometime, maybe tomorrow, or maybe even before the sun goes down today, the disease will come back. I'll have pneumonia again and will be suffocating, or have some kind of cancer." His features twisted, and he looked away. "I haven't had much experience with hospitals, or even with being sick anytime in my life, except for that time after the accident and I couldn't take it!"

"You –"

"Please!" Tanner held up a restraining hand. "Please don't tell me that other people go through these things and it's not as bad as I think. They're not me. I'm not them."

He gave himself a minute to reestablish control, and when he spoke again his face and his voice were those of the Duane Tanner known to his brokerage customers. But the doctors knew who was really speaking.

"I'm going to make my exit with dignity," he said. "I can do it here, with your assistance. Or I can do it elsewhere. But I'm going to do it. I will not pity myself. And I will not . . . be . . . pitied!" He stood up, nodded once at Rickoff, and abruptly left the room.

But something of him seemed to linger, and the doctors sat for a moment in silence, savoring it while waiting for someone to say aloud what they were all thinking.

"Convinced me," Jeff said when it became clear that no one else was going to speak.

"And me," Sheldon York agreed.

Bill Skelton didn't bother to vote, but instead looked at Rickoff, who was still staring at the space Tanner had occupied.

"Hell of a man," he said at length.

And the decision was made.

Chapter Fifteen

". . . with your assistance. Or I can do it elsewhere. But I'm going to do it."

Tanner's words, pouring hot and intense from the living room stereo, combined with staccato bursts of his own typing, kept David Wallace Teeples from hearing the front door of the apartment when it opened.

"I will not pity myself."

He was almost done. Earlier, on his way back to the apartment, he'd treated himself to a preview, skipping back and forth on the cassette he'd retrieved from the seminar room shortly after the staff had adjourned. It was beautiful, and he hoped he would be equal to the task of conveying, even to an audience of supermarket morons, the intense emotion contained in the doomed man's valedictory.

"And I will not . . . be . . . pitied!"

Teeples transcribed the final syllables and reached out to stop the tape. "Terrific," he breathed, letting his eyes scan the words again.

"Yes, isn't it?"

Trudy.

Teeples froze, his hand still extended in mid-air. For a moment he was busy assessing damage, wondering just how much she'd heard and how much crap she might be willing to swallow in explanation. But the three words she had spoken told him it was no use. She'd heard. So she knew, even if she hadn't known before. Which he doubted.

"Trudy," he said finally, turning to face her. "Home sort of early, aren't you?"

Her face didn't change.

Teeples stirred, letting his left hand wander in the direction of the tape deck. Time to get the cassette out of its slot. Got to have the tape. *The Advocate's* lawyers were sudden death on that point: no tape, no quotes. And this was one story that absolutely lived on the direct quotation of the parties involved.

"Don't!"

Trudy's hand moved as if to restrain him and Teeples wondered for a moment if she would actually try to take the tape by force. He hoped not. It wasn't like Trudy and he found himself curiously reluctant to imagine any kind of physical belligerence where she was concerned. He didn't want to hurt her.

But she gave her head a little shake, and let the arm drop back to her side. "Don't . . . bother to turn it off," she said, completing the sentence in a small voice he'd never heard before. "It's nothing I didn't know already."

"Trudy . . ."

"It's all right."

Her back was ramrod straight as she removed her coat and turned away to hang it in the closet, but Teeples could not help noticing the dejection of her shoulders and the almost invisible tremor of her throat.

Jesus.

The tape was still in the stereo deck and he decided to leave it there. The hell with it – for the moment, anyway. Pushing his chair back from the card table where he'd set up his computer, Teeples crossed the room in two strides, but hesitated for a moment before making his next move. Trudy was still turned away from him, the starched rigidity of her hospital whites were somehow forbidding as she adjusted the coat on its hanger.

He wanted to say something. Words that would make her smile at him or laugh or even cry. Anything other than this quiet acceptance. No words came.

Trudy moved back from the closet and closed the door. Before she could turn to face him, Teeples' hands moved to grasp her shoulders, holding her firmly in place. Her muscles tensed, and he thought she might resist. But she did not, and they stood that way for a moment, facing the closet door with his head close to hers but not in contact, until her frangibility dissolved and she allowed herself to be drawn into his arms.

"The way it started," he said then, "was that I picked you out and stalked you like a tiger. I told you a tale I thought would get sympathy and then moved in on you because I wanted to get into the hospital, and that was the easiest way." The starkness of the words was nothing he had planned, and for a moment he thought Trudy might break away to turn on him. But she didn't move.

"My name is David Wallace Teeples," he said, "and I started out a few years ago with a Columbia degree in journalism and a bottom-rung job at a pretty fair newspaper, the *San Francisco Chronicle.* I did okay on a couple of stories and got a couple of merit raises, and everyone told me what a big future I had with the paper. And it was bullshit, Trudy. Absolute, unmitigated bullshit of the richest, most fragrant kind!"

Trudy remained silent.

"Seeing your byline on the front page of a major newspaper is nice. But it doesn't buy any extra groceries or make the down payment on one of the really great places there are to live in a town like San Francisco. That's for the blow-dry kids from television news, or the guys from Harvard Business School who wind up being publishers without knowing squat about news."

Trudy turned her head to look at him, but still did not speak.

"Some guys react by accepting the situation and making the best of it," he went on. "And some go into public relations, where the money's better even if you have to smile a lot at people you don't like. And some go into television, where you write the lines for an on-camera guy who usually doesn't understand what he's saying. I thought of all those things."

"You could have been the one on camera. You're –"

"I thought of it," he acknowledged, cutting her off. "Even working on camera. Yeah. But it just didn't feel right. And then I met a guy who'd left the *Chronicle* about the time I was getting started there. He'd quit to go to work for *The National Advocate.*"

Trudy's shoulders stiffened again at the name of the tabloid. Teeples felt it happen, and decided to wait it out. After a moment she relaxed again.

"I looked at the paper, there on the supermarket rack," he said, "and I tell you, it turned me off." Teeples took a deep breath and went on. "But I was into kind of a financial jam. Needed money pretty badly right then, and *The Advocate* guy offered to pay a lot more than I was making at the *Chronicle*. My first story was a huge . . . success, I guess you could say. It was about a country-western singer . . ."

He hesitated and looked into Trudy's eyes.

After a moment, during which he debated whether or not there was any point in continuing his story, Teeples cleared his throat and went on. "It wasn't a bad story, really. Just a little marijuana jam he'd gotten into when he was a kid. A long time back. Nothing the average person would even think about."

Trudy nodded, slowly. "I remember," she said. "And I know who you're talking about."

"Nelson Bayes," Teeples acknowledged.

This time Trudy turned to face him, and he did not try to stop her.

"Nelson Bayes," she said quietly, not accusing but merely stating facts as she recalled them, "was destroyed by the story. He'd always been a straight arrow, so far as the public knew . . ."

"Lectured to high school kids," Teeples said, taking up the story. "Told them to live clean, like him. Even wrote articles for magazines about it – or signed his name to the ones his public relations people knocked out. So when the shit hit the fan, it all landed on him."

Trudy's eyes were huge. You could fall into them, Teeples thought, and never hit bottom.

"And he killed himself."

"And . . . he killed himself."

Trudy shook her head suddenly and tried to turn away. But this time Teeples wouldn't let her, holding on and forcing her to look at him.

"Trudy," he said, making the words as clear and distinct as possible, "I didn't kill him. No more than the doctors in the Euthanasia Center –"

"Damn it!"

Trudy broke free of his grasp, but instead of moving away from him she simply took two steps backward and leaned against the wall, pressing her face to the cool plaster and trying to control the tears that seemed on the verge of bursting.

It was too much. She'd never been good at lying to herself, and this didn't seem like a good time or place to start. The fact that her David was writing stories for a tabloid newspaper was no great revelation. From the first, she'd been able to pick gaping holes in that silly story about how he was wanted by the police. And though she hadn't wanted to admit it to herself, she'd been at least ninety percent sure about his real identity from the moment she'd seen the first "MURDER CLINIC" headline in *The Advocate*. The reasons he'd given might or might not be true. In fact, she suspected they were entirely genuine. But in the balance they made no real difference, because deep in the central essence that was Gertrude Nordstrum, a decision had already been made. Before she ever heard the taped voices, before his explanations, even before the first doubts had elbowed their way into her consciousness, she had known exactly how she felt and exactly what she would do about anything that tried to come between her and the man who had moved into her apartment, her bed and her life.

"Trudy –"

"Shut up." Turning from the wall, she opened her arms and then clamped them hard around his back as he moved close to her and pressed his lips against her neck. She felt the familiar lift, the shortening breath and the crinkling of her nipples. It might be a lie. It might be a lie and a fraud and a deception that would leave her alone and empty. But not today.

Chapter Sixteen

"'MURDER CLINIC' WILL EXECUTE AIDS PATIENT"

This time, no one bothered to post the headline on the bulletin board. The hospital's new security force had lost no time in plugging the leak to the local television station. A talkative clerk in administration had been summarily discharged with a warning not to seek further employment in the health care field and the incident appeared to be closed. But the search for reporter D. W. Teeples of *The National Advocate* seemed to be getting nowhere. And now he had another story.

Everyone seemed to have a copy of the latest issue of the supermarket tabloid as soon as it appeared on the racks, including Duane Tanner, who had been admitted to the Euthanasia Center the day it was published. A copy lay on the night table beside his bed, but no one inside the hospital seemed to want to talk about it. No such reluctance seemed to apply, however, to the crowd of demonstrators that formed around the side entrance to the hospital.

Most had arrived before noon, bearing hand-inscribed signs calling on the hospital to "STOP THE MURDER," and on the patients to "ABANDON HOPE ALL YE WHO ENTER HERE," and, presumably, on the Almighty to "SEND THE HIRED KILLERS TO HELL."

Jeff Taylor heard the chanting ("STOP THE KILLING! STOP THE MURDER! STOP! STOP! STOP!") while on morning rounds with Rickoff and Bill Skelton, and decided Sheldon York must have been psychic to have called in sick.

Expansion of the Euthanasia Center, authorized by the hospital administration only two weeks earlier, had given them an even dozen beds, eleven of which were presently occupied by euthanasia candidates in the various stages of need. But the protestors seemed to be interested in only one, and no one had to ask who it might be.

"Guess I've got a cheering section," Duane Tanner said when the doctors entered his room.

The other bed should have been occupied by a cancer patient from an upstate farming community, but it was vacant and Rickoff glanced questioningly at the empty bed.

"Choking fit," Tanner explained. "Something blocking the airway. Couldn't seem to do much about it here, so they moved him . . . somewhere."

The euthanasia chief nodded, and Jeff, who was assigned to the case, scribbled a note to check the situation out as soon as they had talked to Tanner.

"You're bright enough this morning," Rickoff observed, noting the tabloid on the bedstand.

"And famous," Tanner agreed.

"Yes."

Rickoff picked up Tanner's chart and made a show of checking it in an effort to avoid discussing the newspaper story or the demonstration on the hospital grounds.

But Tanner wouldn't play. "If you haven't read the story," he said, "I think you ought to. This guy Teeples, whoever he is, may be a pain but you've got to admit, his quotes are absolutely accurate."

Rickoff put down the chart and fixed his gaze on the patient.

"Am I to understand that you enjoy this kind of thing?" he demanded.

Tanner shook his head, but couldn't repress a grin. "I'm just as happy about it," he said, "as you seem to be, believe me. But all the same, you've got to give credit where credit's due."

"Like hell we do."

Bill Skelton had been quiet until then, deferring to the patient and to the senior physician. But the idea of giving D. W. Teeples anything but the back of his hand was more than he could stomach.

"I'll give the sonofabitch credit," he said darkly, "if I'm ever lucky enough to get my hands on him."

Rickoff stiffened. "Doctor Skelton," he began, placing enough emphasis on the professional title to convey his message.

"Oh, come on!" Tanner said.

Rickoff, prevented from completing whatever he'd intended to say to his resident, favored Tanner with a barely concealed glare. But the patient wasn't impressed.

"Please, doctors," he said, "let's give each other a break, all right? I guess if I were in your shoes, I'd be angry, too. And that pack of yahoos outside there – that's what I'm hearing, now, isn't it? People whooping it up because someone with AIDS wants to make a dignified exit? – would put anyone on edge."

"Amen to that," Jeff interjected.

"But if you didn't expect every bit of this," Tanner went on after a nod in Jeff's direction, "then you've got a lot less imagination than I'd have credited you with."

For a moment, Rickoff seemed ready to argue. But then he shrugged, yielding the point.

"What we'd hoped," he said in a tone of carefully suppressed fury, "was that *The National* goddamned *Advocate* would give us a little rest, and that their reporter had . . . had . . ." He paused, seeming to struggle for words.

". . . contracted terminal halitosis?" Tanner supplied.

He was smiling, and after a moment even Rickoff was forced to join in.

"All right then," he said, "though I was going to propose chronic hemorrhoids."

That gave everyone a chance to laugh, and cleared the air for more practical subjects.

Tanner said he had checked the almanac, and dawn would be at 6:35 a.m. the following day. "I'd like to see it," he said, "but that's all."

Rickoff looked at the residents, who returned the look noncommittally. "All right," he said, "we'll be here to watch it with you."

* * *

"STOP! STOP! STOP!"

Charles Pennington said something and Micah Chaine saw his lips move, but the sound was swallowed up in the hullabaloo of chanting. He shook his head and leaned closer, pointing at his ear.

"I said, I think I remember some of these people from Wichita . . . and Tulsa," Pennington repeated, his lips only a few inches from Chaine's ear.

Chaine's features reassembled themselves briefly in what might have been intended as a smile of agreement, and his head bobbed. "Some of the same signs, too," he said. And it was so.

"STOP THE MURDER!" had been popular at Tulsa, as had "LIFE IS SACRED!" "DOCTORS OF DEATH!" was the one that had first made its appearance at Wichita. Just before the explosion.

Julia stood beside Pennington, touching his arm and shivering a bit despite the warmth of the early morning sun. Oblivious to the exchange between the two men, she watched the protest demonstration with fascination, her whole body seeming to vibrate to the rhythm of the chanting.

"STOP! STOP! STOP!"

Pennington glanced at her, and registered mild alarm at the pallor of her face. Julia had been unusually silent of late, lost at times in her own thoughts and not willing to discuss them when he roused her. It worried him. More and more, as the days and weeks slipped by, he found himself depending on her affection and basic good sense. Especially when dealing with Chaine who, it seemed to him, was becoming increasingly erratic and subject to random enthusiasms.

Such as this excursion.

Coming on the heels of the Wichita explosion, the Tulsa bombing was to have been their last "tactical deployment" – to use Chaine's terminology – for a while. Security surrounding the abortion clinics had been tightened to an almost impenetrable degree and, in any case, it seemed to Pennington that any message they might have hoped to deliver had long since been accepted, studied and digested. He felt that they had reached the point of diminishing returns.

Micah Chaine, however, was still a ready font of ideas and targets. Of course he couldn't afford to purchase necessary explosives or move them around the country without Pennington's backing, and that gave Pennington an effective counter in any critical deliberations. But it was one he was reluctant to use, in part because, in most cases, he had always tried to avoid using the power of his family's financial position, and, more particularly in this case, because he was becoming less and less certain of its effectiveness where Father Micah Chaine was concerned.

The demolitions expert was no fool, and while he had never broached the subject, Pennington had, from the first, been grimly aware that his personal involvement in the bombings gave Chaine a most potent weapon against him, if he chose to use it. Micah Chaine was dangerous. He'd known that from their first meeting. The man moved in an aura of violence, and sometimes Pennington thought he could actually detect an odor of ferocity emanating from him. It was frightening, but he had told himself it was also necessary; it went with the territory.

He had set out to find someone knowledgeable about explosives and committed enough to employ that expertise in support of a movement dedicated to the sanctity of life. It was a demanding set of criteria and, since he couldn't exactly place an advertisement in the "Want Ads," finding a man to fit it while retaining personal anonymity had taken more than a year. Chaine had surfaced just as he was about to abandon hope. So he had gone ahead, suppressing personal aversion and apprehensions in order to escalate protest in a way that he considered most effective, while fully aware that he had perhaps activated a different kind of time bomb whose clock face he could not read.

It was a gamble. Thus far it had been successful, but there was always . . .

"Listen to them," Chaine said, derailing Pennington's thoughts. "Listen to the fools!"

Pennington listened.

But the words, as such, had long since ceased to make any impression on his consciousness. Only the beat was familiar, a tom-tom from the dawn of history still able to stir the blood. He looked assessingly at the priest, whose attention appeared to be utterly fixed upon the chanters.

"They spend all day doing that," Chaine said in a voice audible only to his companion, "and then go home at night and tell themselves they've accomplished something and made things better." He paused, still regarding the chanters with apparent fascination. "What a crock."

Neither the words nor the sentiment were new. Micah Chaine had said as much and more on other occasions when confronted by orthodox protest techniques. He had no tolerance for them, no confidence in their effectiveness, no respect for those involved in them. Direct action – deterrence by fear – was the only solution he would ever trust, and Charles Pennington was scarcely more flexible.

But there were differences all the same. From the beginning, Pennington had realized that, for his colleague, there were no rules, no limits, no barriers of any kind. Father Micah Chaine could appreciate the world only in black and white. No grays at all. Right was right and wrong was wrong. And for the punishment of wrongdoers, no limits could be assigned.

"Anything for the friends . . . anything to the enemies of Almighty God!" That was the slogan that had been on the priest's lips at their first meeting and Pennington knew it would never change. He had lived with it and he hoped to continue doing so.

Lately however, he had begun to detect a fraying of the fist-tight control that he had always sensed at the core of Chaine's character. The feral gleam that lived deep in the man's eyes and never entirely extinguished, even in his most peaceful moments, seemed always at the forefront now, ready to burst forth in a paroxysm of ungovernable outrage. This was a man ridden by furies and Pennington harbored no delusions of immunity. From the beginning, he had been aware that Micah Chaine might turn on him at any moment.

"Excuse me, I'm afraid I need to come through here."

A young man in spotless hospital whites was trying to edge through the crowd outside the door. Pennington regarded him with wonder. Since the resumption of active demonstrations outside the side entrance to the medical center, members of the staff had been using other routes. This one must be new. Or crazy.

"You work in there?"

One of the loudest chanters, a woman, challenged the newcomer. But the smile he offered in return was surely the most disarming she had ever faced, reinforced by eyes whose deep blue innocence seemed to penetrate her very core. Whatever else she had intended to say was lost in their depths, and she found herself moving aside to clear his path to the door.

Pennington watched in fascination. Still smiling, the young man strode almost casually across the forecourt and up three broad steps to where the main party of protestors was gathered.

"Don't worry," he said, speaking directly to the woman who had first spoken to him, "I'm not one of the doctors, or even a technician. I just mop the floors."

"Yet you are responsible!"

One of Chaine's own chief rules of conduct was invisibility. He never spoke to demonstrators. Never chanted. Never carried a sign, lest his face become familiar to the police or other authorities. And now he had broken the rule himself.

"You are responsible," he repeated, addressing the incoming employee in a voice that defied the distance between them. "The . . . doctors . . . murder people in that temple of transgression! And if you work in there, even mopping floors, you abet their evil, and are as guilty as any of them!"

The blue eyes fastened briefly on Chaine's face, as if memorizing it, but then wandered downward, zeroing in on the newspaper he held crumpled in his fist.

"Oh, now I understand," he said, smiling even more brightly than before. "You've been reading the *New York Times* again – or is that the *Wall Street Journal* you've got there?"

Chaine blinked, taken aback, and then looked down at his copy of *The National Advocate*.

Someone laughed. Others in the crowd joined and by the time the ripple of amusement subsided, the smiling one had vanished inside the doors of the hospital.

But Chaine had not laughed. Or smiled. Or moved. His face was blue-white and suddenly Pennington was certain that the time had come to cut himself and Julia free.

"Micah . . ." he began, turning to place a hand on the priest's arm, but Chaine seemed not to hear.

"I've seen enough," he declared, turning away abruptly. He moved in the direction of the parking lot and Pennington noted how careful he was to disguise his limp. He thought for a moment of simply standing still and letting the bomb-maker walk away. He and Julia could drive their rented car from here to the airport and disappear before Chaine ever suspected that they were leaving. It was an attractive thought and he allowed himself to toy with it for a long moment. But by the time Chaine had reached the parking lot, he was tamely following in the priest's wake, trailed by Julia.

Behind them, the chanting started again.

"Last night," Chaine said when the other two were once more within earshot, "you wanted me to tell you why I wanted to come here today."

Pennington did not reply.

"So now," Chaine prodded, "do you still need to ask?"

Pennington started to say he did not, but instead stood silent, realizing suddenly that he really might not fully understand Chaine's motives for bringing them to this particular city at this particular time. He waited for Chaine to go on.

"Doctors . . ." Chaine uttered the word in a hoarse and venomous whisper and followed it with several other words in the same deadly tone, but a sudden swelling of sound from the crowd behind them drowned the rest of the sentence, and Pennington shook his head.

"Sorry," he said. "I didn't . . ."

Chaine opened the driver's side door to his own rented vehicle, a shiny new Lincoln, and hooked himself into the seat, favoring his damaged leg.

"Never mind for now," he said. "I'll see both of you tonight. We'll talk then."

He closed the door without waiting for a reply, started the engine, and a moment later Pennington and the girl were alone in the lot, staring, for no reason either could have identified, at the space where the car had been. An onshore wind had sprung up shortly after dawn. They were cold, but for a long time, they did not move.

Chapter Seventeen

Jeff Taylor and Bill Skelton each had one euthanasia procedure scheduled for the morning, and Sheldon York had another set for early afternoon. The workday of the hospital continued and the tabloid story was, if not forgotten, at least momentarily set to one side while the doctors attended to more pressing matters.

At noon, Jeff thought of phoning Jolene to see if they could meet for lunch. Montagna's was a waterfront seafood shack not far from the hospital, where the simple, rustic atmosphere belied the most delicious prawn sauce either of them had ever tasted. For entertainment, there were open windows that allowed access to importunate gulls and brown pelicans who would perform a limited bag of tricks in the obvious hope of being fed. Jolene was never able to resist.

But earlier that morning Rickoff had handed him two new candidate files, with the suggestion that both be ready for seminar on the following day. He knew he should be in his office, punching numbers into his telephone and asking questions.

Besides . . .

Yes, indeed. Jeff took a deep breath and allowed his shoulders the momentary luxury of a sag. No use dodging it, and no use trying to deny it, either. The fact was, that even while performing the morning's euthanasia procedure, he had

been preoccupied, unable to drag his mind away from the
Tanner case and the complication of feelings it seemed to
arouse in everyone involved. Even in the elevator en route to
his office, Jeff fancied he could hear the chanting, the deep,
drum-beat of the demonstrators, outside the building. It was not
conducive to coherent thought, but he did his best.

He entered the windowless cell, seated himself at the desk,
opened the topmost of the files Rickoff had given him, and did
his best to concentrate. It was uphill work. The chanting
continued to intrude. He knew the sound wasn't real, that he
was too far away and insulated by too many layers of glass
and concrete.

Still, the beat was there, telegraphing its message to his
fingers and manipulating them in cadence as he tried to
concentrate, moving on to his right foot and setting it in
motion. He tried to prevail through sheer willpower, but
irritation was a powerful distraction.

At length, however, he managed to force his mind to absorb
the meaning of the words and numbers on the reports and
charts before him. He had digested the first case and was at
work on the second when a new sound began to intrude and he
retreated from the file to discover that the protest beat had won
out after all. The rubber eraser of the pencil in his right hand
was bouncing in time with the shouts of "STOP! STOP!
STOP!" Jeff took a deep breath.

"Damn."

That single-syllable word alone spoke his frustration. Vastly
irritated, he glanced at his watch and was pleased to discover
that the afternoon wasn't a total loss after all. Despite
everything, he'd managed a full hour of concentration. Not too
shoddy. And, as happened to him more often than not, putting
his main concern on hold had produced, if not a solution, then at
least the beginning of an approach.

Jeff picked up the phone to call his wife. The lunch hour had passed, but dinner would be just as fine.

＊　＊　＊

Dinner at Montagna's was an unexpected treat for the Taylors, as it was for their guests, the Skeltons. Both couples had originally zeroed in on the waterfront restaurant as a convenient spot for lunch and found themselves intrigued by the relaxed atmosphere and excellent food. But dinner was an altogether different experience. And it was a delight.

Panhandling birds that had strutted attendance on their luncheons were joined, now, by friends and relatives. There was occasional noisy competition for preferred spots at the windows, and the two men made great show of tossing scraps just over the heads of the beggars, to watch them scramble and flap in pursuit. Nothing ever landed in the water. The birds always managed to get it first.

It was an ebullient kind of meal, filled with the sounds of cracking lobster shells, conversation and laughter, even though everyone at the table understood its deeper purpose. In addition to lifting their spirits, Jeff and Jolene had invited the Skeltons to dinner in the hope of sharing thoughts on the Tanner case. And the subject finally arrived along with the after-dinner brandies and liqueurs.

"He's my patient," Bill Skelton said, not bothering with preamble, "and that worries me . . . not because I can't take the responsibility, but because for the first time in my life, I find myself not wanting to."

His words fell into a well of total silence, seeming to echo in a void that he finally decided was in need of filling.

"Christ . . . I can't believe I said that."

Jeff grinned. "Well, don't feel too badly, my friend," he said, "because all the time you were talking, I was sitting here thinking how very damned glad I was that Duane Tanner was your patient and not mine."

Skelton smiled back in acknowledgment and gratitude, but his wife favored him with a puzzled frown.

"'Scuse me," she said, "but I think I missed a turn somewhere. You want to run through that again, ole buddy?"

"Sure," he said. "Which word didn't you understand?"

Arlene Skelton, who rated the title "Doctor" in her own right since she held a Doctor of Law degree from Harvard, pretended to take offense and flipped a recently vacated oyster shell in his direction. It missed and a seagull snagged it as it flew through the window.

"Part of the trouble with the Tanner case," Skelton continued when the general laughter had subsided, "is that it comes too darn close after the mistake that almost got made on John Barclay."

The other three sobered at once, remembering.

"Nobody, but nobody, wants to end the life of anyone who's not really a proper candidate for our procedures."

"And Duane Tanner's not?"

Bill Skelton shook his head emphatically. "That's the hell of it," he said. "Duane Tanner definitely is a proper candidate."

"Diagnosis and prognosis confirmed?" Jolene pursued.

"Beyond the shadow of a doubt," Skelton nodded. "Tanner's symptoms are in remission. I'm sure Jeff must have told you that much. But it's bound to change for the worse. It always does, with AIDS. And when that happens, the man will die. It's inevitable."

"And it will happen soon," Jeff added. "Checking the history of such cases, we know he's already pushing the limits. The relapse can't be more than a week or two away, if it hasn't already happened while we've been sitting here."

"When it does occur," Skelton continued, "the process 'will be painful, prolonged and undignified,' as Tanner said himself. Under those circumstances, surely there can be no possible doubt that he's a proper candidate for euthanasia, both under the laws of this state and the canons of ethics we accepted when we began this course of training."

He paused, not at a loss for words, but thinking about them.

"And yet . . ." Jeff prodded.

"And yet," Skelton nodded, moving on to the next step in the cycle of logic that had occupied him for the past several days, "he has this attitude – this absolutely fantastic adjustment to his situation."

"And that makes it hard to . . ."

"Hard to help him die, yes," Jeff supplied, hoping to clear the air by accentuating the negative. "Bill's got the same problem, here, that I do. The same one all of us in the euthanasia service are going to have to face, sooner or later, if we're going to remain in the field."

"Which is . . . ?"

"That no matter how much care we take, or how dedicated we become, this is still a branch of medical practice which means that we can, and will, make mistakes."

"Like John Barclay, you mean," Arlene Skelton said.

But Jeff shook his head. "Like Barclay," he said, "but not like him, too. The Tanner case is as different from Barclay's as it can get."

"They both cost you sleep," Jolene reminded.

"And cost you sleep, too, putting up with my moaning and groaning," Jeff grimaced at her. "Yes, but look at the differences. You know, the Barclay case was almost routine, in a way."

"Routine!" Arlene was frankly astonished. But Jeff simply nodded.

"Routine," he said, "because it was the kind of case that's been coming up, over and over again, for years now, at every major medical center all over the world."

Arlene blinked, still lost.

"Barclay," her husband took up the explanation, "was your basic pull-the-plug coma. Someone who's alive but not alive, requiring a personal decision by his family . . . and a purely medical decision by the doctors in charge."

"But he wasn't on life support."

"No. That's the single difference between his case and that of most coma cases. The only life support he required was nourishment, water and enough movement to prevent bed sores."

"If he'd needed a respirator or heart stimulator or any other life-support device," Jeff said, "the case would never have come to the Euthanasia Center at all. Life-support decisions are made every day by hospital committees especially appointed for the job. If they say it's hopeless, and the family agrees, the plug gets pulled, and that's that."

"But your Mr. Tanner's different."

"Different from Barclay because he's conscious, coherent and well able to make his own decisions," Skelton said. "Different from other euthanasia candidates in that he's not asking us not to relieve him of existing hopeless pain and indignity, but to make sure he never has to face these things at all."

Arlene thought for a moment and then shook her head. "Sorry," she said, "but wasn't that the whole idea of euthanasia – to prevent hopeless pain and indignity?"

"Yes, but –" Skelton stopped in mid-sentence, gazing blankly at his wife.

Jolene laughed. "Way to go, Arlene!"

And after a moment, Bill and Jeff joined in.

"Talk about standing too close to the trees." Bill Skelton gave his wife a quick hug, and turned to Jeff with a bland smile.

"Next case," he said.

Chapter Eighteen

". . . call them 'Doctor,' and after awhile they start thinking they're Almighty God!"

Father Micah Chaine was wound up and well launched into his theme. Charles Pennington and Julia Hartt sat still and listened with increasing anxiety. They had seen him in manic mode before, but ever since their visit to the Euthanasia Center that afternoon he had seemed on the verge of outright explosion, unable to sit still for more than a moment.

"It's the abortion clinics all over again," he went on, striding up and down the motel bed-sitting room. "Only more out in the open. More naked!"

"Micah –" Pennington tried to interrupt.

But Chaine seemed not to hear him. "Someone's got a problem," he went on. "Someone's looking for answers. So he goes to a doctor, and, of course, the doctor's got all the answers. Oh, yes! And they make it all so believable, right down to the secret language and handshake!"

Chaine strode to the refrigerator, his limp minimized almost to nonexistence by the power of his preoccupation, and pulled out a can of Black Bull malt liquor without offering one to Pennington or Julia. He popped it open, took a deep swallow, and resumed his harangue as if there had been no intermission.

"So now the doctor is God. The Ancient of Days. At the clinic, he tells the poor ignorant little girl how easy it is to 'get unpregnant.' Wonderful! Marvelous! And does he tell her that the child she carries within her is a human being, an immortal soul? Does he warn her that while she's letting this thing be done to her, they are, both of them, committing murder, a mortal sin?"

Chaine took another swallow of the fortified brew, and Pennington clamped his jaw, resisting the temptation to interrupt. That one term, "mortal sin," literally begged for further discussion. Was it possible that Father Micah Chaine had never admitted to himself that he placed himself at risk of the same sin – murder – whenever he planted one of his bombs, or even mailed a simulated device or dead animal to someone? Despite his best intentions, someone could have been around when the bomb went off, or have had a heart attack from seeing the contents of one of the packages. No sense trying to talk to Micah, though, when he was like this. Reason would have to wait until he finally ran down.

"And it's no different at Northwest Unholy Regional," Chaine went on. "One doctor tells a person he's going to die. Another one, another member of the club, says yes, that's how it is. And then they hand him over to the Murder Clinic!"

"Oh, Micah!" Julia Hartt surprised herself and the others in the room by breaking into Chaine's discourse, and for a moment she seemed ready to retreat once more into silence. Pennington found himself hoping she would, at least until Chaine had gotten a little more of the anger out of his system. But with the priest obviously waiting for her to proceed, she was compelled to continue.

"I don't mean to interrupt," she apologized, "and maybe it's really not worth mentioning. But I really hate those words."

"What words?" Chaine demanded. "'Murder Clinic?' You don't like the sound of that?"

"No."

Julia leaned fractionally closer to Pennington as if for supportive warmth. "I mean, yes. I mean, words like 'Murder Clinic.' They're just for cheap, trashy supermarket papers like *The National Advocate*."

"They're true!"

"They're . . . sick."

Even Pennington was regarding her with perplexity now, and Julia wished heartily that she had kept her mouth shut. But she hadn't, and now she felt compelled to go on.

"They're like calling a religion a 'cult,' or a banker a 'shylock'," she said. "Or . . . calling us 'terrorists'."

The word stung, and she could feel a minute stirring as Pennington digested it. But Chaine never turned a hair.

"If the word's right," he said, looking straight at her, "why not use it?"

"Why not."

The silence was long, as though the three people in the room were engaged in some contest, daring each other to create the next sound, and it might have gone on longer, had the phone not rung.

Chaine looked at it, hesitated for a fraction of a second, and then picked it up.

"Yes?"

Someone on the other end seemed to have a lot to say. He stood silent, listening, and then ended the conversation with characteristic suddenness.

"All right," he said. "I'll be there before five." He hung up without waiting for a reply.

Pennington was immediately wary. "That call . . .?"

Chaine looked wordlessly at him, his hand still on the telephone receiver.

For a moment Pennington returned the stare, willing Chaine to answer the question he had not asked. But after a moment it was too much. He looked away, first at Julia and then out the window.

"An old friend of mine lives here in town," Chaine said, ready to talk now that no question of dominance was involved. "I talked to him yesterday, just after I got in. He's agreed to furnish some . . . supplies I asked him for."

Julia's eyes widened.

"But . . ." Pennington began.

"But what?"

"But we haven't talked. Nothing's been decided."

Chaine turned away. "Yes," he said. "It has."

Pennington opened his mouth, but closed it a moment later, staring wordlessly at the other man's back.

"We're going to do the Murder Clinic," Chaine said, gazing out the window at the parking lot a floor below. "I already figured out how to get the stuff in there, but –"

"No!"

Suddenly Julia was on her feet, her eyes huge and boring into the demolitions expert's back.

"No," she said. "We're not going to do it. Not going to blow anything else up. Charles and I have talked, and we don't –"

"Now, is that a fact?"

Chaine's voice was quiet but steel-edged as he turned from the window to glare at the girl. But if she was intimidated, it did not interfere with her ability to speak.

"The abortion clinics," she said. "That's all it was about. Human life is sacred, and abortion is murder, and since they wouldn't listen any other way we wasted the buildings they were using. To slow them down. Make them think."

Chaine stood silent, waiting for her to go on. But instead it was Pennington who took up the recital.

"We understand your feelings, Micah," he said, placating but determined. "And we respect them. We really do. But this has gotten entirely out of hand. Julia and I . . . all right, maybe we should have talked it over with you instead of just between us. But it wouldn't have changed a thing. We agreed. No more bombings. Ever."

"Really."

The single word hung in the air between them, cancelling further argument or discussion.

"I'll give you one thing," Chaine continued when he was sure he would not be interrupted. "And it's this: we're not going to hit any more abortion clinics. If that's what you want, I'll go along with you. All right?"

He regarded the other two with what might have been a smile. "But I have an order for plastique and primacord and one or two other items, and a mission which I don't intend to abort – if you'll pardon the expression."

Pennington started to shake his head, but found himself momentarily frozen by the sheer arctic bleakness suddenly visible in Chaine's eyes.

"I don't know," he said, "and I don't care what either of you might have been thinking about when we started. I didn't ask you. And you didn't ask me."

"We –"

"If you had," Chaine went on, ignoring the interruption, "you'd have figured out what was really going on before now."

He paused then, offering them a chance to speak. When they didn't, he continued. "All this time, you thought you were using me and that it was all right, because I was using you right back. Fair exchange, and all that." His lips twisted into another mirthless smile. "Only, that's not how it was. Not at all." Chaine retrieved the Black Bull, which he had left on the table, and took another deep pull, savoring it before swallowing and putting the can down again. "I wasn't using you," he said, "and you weren't using me. We were all being used – all three of us – by God Almighty and His Son."

The pinpoints of fire were back in Chaine's eyes, and Pennington's heart sank. As long as the priest remained willing to talk, he thought it might be possible, eventually, to reason with him. But it was not reason he saw staring out at him from the hot core of Father Micah Chaine.

"The abortion clinics," Chaine went on, "were a training exercise. Nothing more. I didn't know it at the time, but I know it now. This has been revealed to me, as has the next step that we must take in accomplishing our mission."

He stopped talking. After a long moment, Pennington spoke in order to find out what he did not want to hear.

"What . . . mission is that, Micah?"

Chaine smiled, and picked up the malt liquor can again. "Thought you'd never ask," he said in a tone that was almost jocular. "Thought you'd never ask, Charlie. And that would have been bad, because we can't go on to the next step without a clear understanding."

Chaine swallowed the last of the Black Bull, crumpled the can in his hand and dropped it into a wastebasket.

"Our mission," he said, making the words flat and precise so that there could be no misunderstanding, "is the pure and simple saving of immortal souls. For two thousand years, priests of Mother Church have been washing away the stain of sin by granting absolution. And it works well, so long as repentance is sincere. The soul is saved from everlasting torment, and that is good."

"Yes, we know Micah –" Pennington began.

"But far better than forgiveness," Chaine went on as though no one else had spoken, "is prevention. Removal of the gun from the hand of the gunman, the knife from the hand of the assassin. This was our thinking – well, my own, at least – in destroying the abortion clinics."

He paused again, but this time no one tried to interrupt. "All that, however, was mere preparation, because the sin we averted by our methods was a sin that could be forgiven. One that could be expiated by subsequent repentance. Our true work, however, is more critical. And our methods, may necessarily be more . . . stringent."

Chaine let the final word float in the air for awhile, observing his companions as if from a distance, while they examined and digested it. He wondered how much he would have to spell out to them. They were such children.

Charles Pennington shook his head. "I'm sorry," he said.

"Sorry?"

"Yes. I'm sorry, but I'm afraid I don't understand at all. I know all this is somehow tied into the Euthanasia Center at Northwest Regional Medical Center. And I understand that you're saying that it should be our next target. But . . ."

"But what?"

"But, first of all," Julia said, picking up the discussion when Pennington seemed to falter, "we had an agreement."

Chaine looked blank.

"Don't pretend you can't remember," she said. "You can, and you do. The 'incident' at Tulsa was to have been the last of its kind. At least for awhile. You agreed to that."

"Did I?"

"You know you did."

"I agreed that Tulsa was to be the last abortion clinic we put out of business. Yes, I said that. And I meant it."

"But –"

"But he didn't say there would be no more bombs," Pennington interrupted, his eyes riveted on Chaine's face. "I wondered at the time if there wasn't something more to what you were saying. Something held back. I guess I should have asked."

"Guess you should have." Chaine paused again, waiting to see if Pennington had anything else to say, continuing with his explanation only when it was clear that he did not.

"Euthanasia," he said, "is a fancy phrase for mercy killing. The murder of a patient by a doctor. But you see, it's more than murder, a lot more."

Julia shook her head.

"I don't."

"Obviously. But you should, because what's involved here is more than murder. Far more! For murder is a sin that can be forgiven any Christian on the basis of true faith and repentance. A transgression for which there is redemption. But suicide – voluntarily taking one's own life – is by its very nature beyond the range of God's grace."

He had their attention now. They were staring at him, transfixed, seeming hardly to breathe.

"While a rational being lives," Chaine continued, "he can repent. But death closes all accounts. Suicide can't be repented and is therefore beyond forgiveness. It damns the immortal soul. It must be stopped. Must be! No matter what!"

Charles Pennington's throat was dry. He hoped Julia would not attempt to answer any of this, because that would mean he would need to interrupt. And he was not at all sure of his ability to do so. Until that moment, he had never truly identified the source of the rage that burned in Micah Chaine, never comprehended its depth and power. Now that he had, he hoped nothing of the shock and apprehension he felt was visible in his face, because he had just made a firm decision to get himself and Julia just as far away from Father Micah Chaine as possible and to make sure that the distancing was permanent.

"Our mission," Chaine continued, sure now that his audience was convinced and comprehending, "is to save immortal souls by direct and personal interposition, by taking their sins upon ourselves. Placing our own bodies and souls between them and the fire! This is the work to which we are called by Almighty God. And this is the work that will, by His Son's grace, be accomplished."

Pennington let Chaine finish his self-righteous discourse without interruption. He understood, now, what Chaine was saying. He and Julia were being intimidated into taking part in Chaine's mission, and this mission would involve violence and bloodshed. He nodded slowly. Yes, now he saw, very clearly, what Micah Chaine really wanted to do. And it confirmed nothing but the determination that had been growing in him for the past few minutes. It was definitely time to get out. He had only to figure out how.

Charles Pennington and Julia Hartt were still in the room more than an hour later when Chaine made a telephone call to assure himself ready access to the Euthanasia Center on the following day.

Chapter Nineteen

In keeping with almost every other facet of his case, the final moments of Duane Tanner's life were something entirely new in the euthanasists' experience. For one thing, the patient insisted on entering the final procedure room under his own power. And the head nurse on the service was scandalized.

"Mr. Tanner," she said, "we can't allow that. You have to be moved on a gurney, or in a wheelchair at the very least!"

"Why?"

"Because of the insurance. If anything happened to you, walking around like that –"

"Happened?"

"Yes! If you got hurt!"

Duane Tanner offered no verbal response to this. But the stare he turned on her was so laden with incredulous amusement that she finally left the room to seek advice from Dr. Rickoff, who suggested as tactfully as possible that she shut up and let the patient have his way.

"I guarantee the insurance people won't be angry," he said.

"Well, it's against policy."

"Yes."

She returned to her desk at the end of the corridor, muttering balefully, and Rickoff continued his early morning rounds, looked in on three new patients admitted to the service the previous day, and ended up finally in the processing room, where Tanner was again making waves.

"No," he was saying, "I've just had a good night's sleep, and I can't think of any reason in the world to go back to bed."

Bill Skelton was standing beside his patient in the middle of the room, and looked to Rickoff like a man who was prepared to argue the point. But the entrance of the Chief of Service momentarily postponed the confrontation, and a minute negative motion of Rickoff's head defused the situation entirely.

"Can't say I blame you," Rickoff said, crossing the room. "Always liked to take sunrises sitting up, myself. Bill, see if one of the orderlies can't scare up a chair for our patient, here."

Skelton hesitated only the briefest of moments before going off to find an orderly.

"Cigarette?" Rickoff offered when the resident was out of earshot. "Cigar?"

Tanner grinned at him. "You know," he said, "I thought of it. Really."

Rickoff nodded. "Read your case again last night," he said, "and noticed that you'd given up cigarettes two years ago, after nearly fifteen years of smoking three packs a day."

"It was really tough, too."

"I'm sure. I went through it myself about ten years ago."

Bill Skelton was back now, closely followed by an orderly pushing a big leather-upholstered desk chair that Rickoff recognized as his own. He made a mental note to bellow at his subordinate, but couldn't suppress an inner lift of amusement.

Tanner indicated that he would like the chair moved over to the window where the first pearl shades of dawn were beginning to define the skyline of the city. Northwest Regional was built on a palisade-like rise of ground not far from the harbor, and with windows facing east, like this one, that offered a panorama of lights at night. The lights were fading now and Tanner's expression was calm as he sank into the supportive softness of the well-worn padding.

"Good place to live," Tanner said, nodding toward the window. "And not the worst place in the world to die, either. I've been lucky."

Jeff had entered the room, and was looking curiously at Tanner.

The patient didn't seem to notice him. His attention remained fixed on the scene slowly taking shape outside. An early morning bus made its lonely way along a wide street a few blocks away, stopping to pick up a knot of passengers who were just visible in the nebulous illumination.

Tanner was Bill Skelton's patient, and Jeff made no move to interfere or assist as his fellow resident moved the I.V. stands to the far side of the room beside Tanner's chair. But Marty Bernard, the legal representative of the hospital, stirred restlessly as Skelton pumped up a vein in Tanner's arm and inserted the needle.

Bernard glanced questioningly at the vital-sign monitors not yet attached to Tanner's body. Jeff noticed his concern and leaned over to reassure him.

"No need for them right now," he said. "Patient's conscious and coherent. They'll use them to close the file when the procedure's completed. Until then . . ." He let his voice sink into silence, and Bernard seemed satisfied.

"I know we've been over this quite a few times before," Bill Skelton began, as he launched into the legally required formula that he now knew by heart, "but at this point, I'm required to ask you certain questions. Okay?"

Tanner nodded, his attention still fixed on the activity outside the window. A construction crane had come to life atop the skeleton framework of a high-rise structure nearly a mile away.

"Do you believe," Skelton said, "that your present condition is not likely to improve, and that the condition for which you are under treatment is not curable?"

"I do."

"And are you also aware of the fatal nature of the procedure about to be performed upon you?"

"Yes I am."

"And do you consent to it of your own free will?"

Tanner tore his gaze away from the window long enough to smile reassuringly at Skelton.

"I do," he said. "Yes."

Skelton glanced at Bernard, who tendered his usual nod of affirmation. "Very well, then," Skelton said.

He shifted to place his hand on the plunger that would add sodium thiopental to the Ringer's already running into Tanner's vein, and was surprised when the patient moved suddenly to intercept him.

"Please," Tanner said, "would you . . . let me?"

Skelton hesitated for the barest moment, shooting a quick glance in Bernard's direction. But he knew the answer even before receiving another nod from the legal observer. The euthanasia law had been written with considerable foresight. It permitted physicians to "assist" individuals in terminating their own lives, as well as authorizing more conventional euthanasic procedures.

Skelton took a step to place himself in the direct sight of his patient, who was still gazing out the window. "There could be a problem," he said.

Tanner seemed puzzled, but did not speak.

"The first plunger," Skelton indicated the one in his hand, forcing Tanner to look at it and at the tube connecting it to the I.V. line, "the first plunger adds a drug to make you drowsy."

Tanner nodded his understanding, and waited for Skelton to continue.

"In normal circumstances," the resident went on, "I'd wait for you to go to sleep before taking the next step."

Skelton was pointing at the shunts for pancuronium bromide and potassium chloride, and Tanner looked at them noncommittally, for a moment.

"All right, then," he said at length. "I see the point. But . . . would it at least be okay if I gave myself the sleepy-juice?"

Skelton couldn't repress an admiring grin. "You pay the bill," he said, "you call the shots."

Tanner smiled his thanks, took the thiopental plunger into his hand and returned to contemplating the awakening city.

Street lights began to wink out, and the few illuminated signs were almost unnoticeable now. The sky was a rose pink on the eastern horizon. Jeff also noted that it was, for once, clear. Most west coast dawns are invisible, hidden behind an overcast sky, but this time an offshore breeze must have been blowing – from the desert, perhaps – pushing clouds, haze and smog out to sea, and offering Tanner a final illustration of the earth's radiant beauty.

"I'm grateful to all of you," the patient said, still looking out the window. "You've done your jobs, sure, and that's only right. But you also went out of your way to help me in a situation where I could, I guess, have helped myself – but not without leaving an awful mess."

He paused for a moment, waiting. Outside the window, a single shaft of orange-red brilliance burst over the silhouette of a block of row-houses at the top of a far hill. Dawn had come.

"Good-bye," Duane Tanner said. "And . . . bless you all."

His thumb depressed the sodium thiopental plunger, mixing the sedative with the Ringer's. He set the plunger down carefully on the arm of the leather chair, and leaned back with a final smile for Bill Skelton. His eyes closed. A moment later, he relaxed into deep sleep.

Skelton waited a moment, to be sure, and then simply moved the chair and patient back in range of the EEG, EKG and other monitors. Together, avoiding any exchange of glances, the three doctors attached the leads, checked the monitors to see that they were functioning, and stepped away.

The EEG showed Tanner in deep sleep, but Skelton made a point of rolling back an eyelid to be absolutely sure. Then he opened the shunts for the lethal substances.

A moment or two later, it was over.

For awhile, nobody moved.

Even Marty Bernard seemed frozen in place, unable to shake off the sense of calm completion that had filled the room during Duane Tanner's final moments. It was nothing they hadn't experienced before, in other situations, but it was somehow stronger and more pervasive than any of them could remember. It was a remarkable legacy, and they savored it, together and separately in the privacy of their own minds, as long as possible. Gradually, however, it faded, and by the time the full light of morning filled the room, it was gone, the last sparks extinguished by the almost subliminal drumbeat of the protestors' chanting outside the building.

"Peculiar," Hyman Rickoff said, breaking the silence at last. "I didn't hear that . . . noise . . . until now. How long do you think it's been going on?"

No one seemed to know. Bill Skelton bent to remove the I.V. needle from the arm of the body.

"Do you think he heard it?" he asked no one in particular.

Jeff shook his head. "I'm sure he didn't, Bill. I didn't myself until Dr. Rickoff mentioned it just now."

"I think it just started," Marty Bernard said. "A minute ago, I mean." He looked at Tanner's body and then looked away. "He didn't hear. No."

"I hope not."

Nothing else was said until morgue attendants, summoned just before the procedure began, arrived to take charge of the remains. They moved Tanner's body from the chair to a gurney, glancing curiously at the doctors, who did not bother to explain, and departed without comment.

"You know . . ." Bill Skelton ventured when they were gone. He faltered then, ready to lapse into silence if anyone cared to interrupt. But no one did, and he went on.

"You know, seeing Tanner's face – I mean, the way he was just before he lost consciousness . . ."

Hyman Rickoff nodded. "I know," he said.

"We all do," Jeff added.

"Yes, well, what I was wondering," Skelton continued, "I mean, it seemed to me that, along with considering other lethal drugs or sedatives, or even other means of terminating life . . . well, wouldn't it be within the purview of the specialty to give some attention to, uh, what you might call 'amenities'?"

Rickoff had been standing at the window, marking the progress of the sunlight across the face of the city, but he turned now to face the two residents.

"Go on," he said.

Skelton swallowed self-consciously, but continued in a determined tone. "Duane Tanner wanted to die," he said, "and he came to us for help in doing it. He had good reasons. But all the same, he loved life and he loved this world, so he wanted to leave it on a high note, taking a final look at something he truly enjoyed."

"The sunrise, yes."

"The sunrise," Skelton agreed. "But look, what if the sky'd been overcast this morning?"

"Or raining," Jeff added.

"If the weather hadn't cooperated," Skelton said, "Duane Tanner would have had to settle for second best. I think he would have done it with grace. In the little time we had to get acquainted, he impressed me as a man who could handle disappointments better than most."

Rickoff nodded. "Continue."

"Dr. Rickoff," Skelton said, rushing on, "Tanner also wanted to die sitting up. In a chair. Not necessarily the one I stole from your office . . ."

Rickoff grimaced, but did not interrupt.

". . . but a chair, instead of a bed. And I could understand that, too."

Again Rickoff nodded.

"Beds can be frightening," he said. "Especially in a hospital."

"And especially in a euthanasia center," Jeff said. "Yes, sitting up gave Tanner a little more sense of being in control, at least to that extent."

"And so did the other thing – doing his own thiopental injection," Rickoff contributed.

"Right."

"So he got all those things, those amenities," Skelton continued. "And because of it, his death was an experience that even people like us, who deal with the end of life every day, could go through it with him and come out on the other side with a feeling of having been, in one way or another, enriched."

Rickoff leaned back against the window, shifting not quite consciously into a mood of seminar.

"Go on, Doctor," he said to Skelton. "You've got an idea, and I think we all need to hear it."

"All right." Skelton glanced at Jeff, who gave him an encouraging look but remained silent. "All right. This room is the place we have set aside for our procedures. This is where we help patients end their lives. But look at it!"

The other two doctors looked around the room.

"A rose by any other name," Skelton said. "Call it anything you want, it's still a hospital room, with all the modern technological accoutrements. Familiar to us, but pretty scary for the patients. Does it have to be this way?"

"The monitors," Rickoff said, "and the I.V. stand with the shunts –"

"– are necessary, sure. But they don't have to dominate the room. And the bed. Okay, in a lot of cases it really does have to be a bed; they're too sick for anything else. But still, does it have to be such a 'hospital' kind of bed?"

Jeff smiled, beginning to understand where Skelton was going.

"Over in the maternity wing," he said, "the birthing center's beds are designed to look pretty much like the kind of bed the mother-to-be is accustomed to at home."

"Right. The entire room is designed so as not to be as frightening as the conventional labor room," Rickoff broke in, entering into the spirit of Skelton's disquisition. "All right. The room needs work, no argument. What else?"

"The sunrise," Skelton began.

"Can't do a thing about it," Rickoff replied in what might have been a jocular tone. "Weather's not my responsibility."

"It could be."

Rickoff paused, completely off balance, and even Jeff found himself at a loss.

"What?"

"The sun and sky aren't always going to oblige," Skelton replied, enlarging on his theme. "What if Tanner wanted to see a full moon through the limbs of an apple tree. Or the desert at sunset?"

"He'd have been out of luck."

"As it is now, yes. But not necessarily. Look, the world has come a long way in providing vicarious experiences. For example, my father-in-law, who doesn't have a fireplace in his New York apartment, once spent a whole evening listening to music he liked while he gazed into a nice, comforting fire."

Jeff shook his head, completely lost.

"Where was he?"

"In his apartment. The fire was on television – it was a videotape a couple of hours long with no story line or actors, just the fire itself. And it was complete with sound effects – the crackling and hissing of the fire and the occasional thump when another log was added."

"Just . . . a fire?"

"Just a fire. I later found out there are others. Snow falling outside a window – I guess you'd want that one if you'd moved to the tropics. And another one that shows the ocean from a sailboat, for people who aren't near an ocean but would like to sail, or maybe for people who used to sail but don't anymore."

Rickoff nodded, intrigued. "So if the sky had been overcast this morning –"

"– it needn't have kept Tanner from watching his sunrise, if we'd had a tape of it and a really good television set.

"And music!" Jeff's eyes were bright with discovery, obviously attuned to Skelton's idea.

"And music," Skelton agreed. "Look, ideally you could offer a patient the chance to leave the world surrounded by his favorite sights, sounds –"

"and even smells," Rickoff concluded, nodding vigorously. "Yes! There are scratch-and-sniff books for children, why not recorded scents for our patients?"

The three doctors paused, wordless, looking at each other with pleased anticipation. Here was a first step in what each knew might eventually be a whole new direction for their speciality.

Then Jeff looked at his watch.

"Oh, Christ!"

"Patient?" Rickoff inquired.

"Down in the lobby – for the past ten minutes!" He rushed out the door and headed for the stairwell instead of waiting for the elevator.

Chapter Twenty

The patient's name was Robin Lynn Utley, and if he had been kept waiting, he did not seem to mind.

Jeff arrived in the lobby out of breath from his stairstep descent and was irritated with himself for having lost track of time. The only person in the public part of the lobby was a tall man carrying a leather briefcase who stood with his back toward the stairwell and elevator bank, studying one of the hospital floor plans displayed on the wall for the convenience of visitors.

"Mr. Utley?"

The tall man – at closer range, Jeff judged him to be several inches over six feet – turned to face him with a smile.

"Quite a road map," he commented, extending his hand. "You're . . . Dr. Taylor?"

"Jeff Taylor. Yes."

"And I'm Robin Utley. I think I talked to your . . . what . . . secretary?"

"Receptionist," Jeff nodded, with a small grin. "You have to be the head nurse or an administrator to rate a secretary."

Utley nodded. "Receptionist. Anyway, I'm sorry that I asked to see you at this ungodly hour, but my own schedule . . ."

"Not ungodly for doctors, Mr. Utley . . ."

"Call me Robin. Please."

"Robin."

Looking at the man, Jeff couldn't help thinking that he had never in his life met anyone who less fitted a name like "Robin." In addition to being tall, Utley seemed to have the kind of physical power that only comic book superheroes possessed – pure energy that could be held in check with nothing less than fortified steel wires. This impression was only enhanced and emphasized by the blue-shaven hardness of his jaw line. The charcoal pinstripe business suit was well cut and perfectly fitted, but Jeff had the impression that the wearer might be accustomed to more restrictive attire. A uniform, perhaps – or conversely, the studded leathers of an outlaw biker. He did not look at all like a candidate for euthanasia.

"Your case records . . ." Jeff prompted, half expecting to hear the man say he had come to make inquiries for a friend or relative.

But Utley had come on his own behalf.

"The paperwork will be along any day, if its not here already," he replied. "As I told your . . . uh . . . receptionist. It's coming from my doctor. In Wichita."

Jeff nodded. "In general," he said, "we like to have a chance to review the medical records before beginning our own file on a prospective patient."

Utley nodded. "Sensible."

"Yes. But failing that, perhaps we might talk for a few minutes?"

"All the time in the world." Utley turned to follow Jeff, but then hesitated. "Pardon me . . ."

"Yes?"

"I . . . uh . . . well, one of the things I'd like to do today, I mean if it's permitted, is to get a firsthand look at your facilities here. Would that be alright?"

Now it was Jeff's turn to hesitate. He found himself taking a long second look at Robin Utley and wondering if he might be both more and less than he seemed. Northwest Regional's revitalized security section had warned all personnel to beware of people seeking admission as patients for reasons unrelated to health problems. Nonexistence or unavailability of health records, the security chief had advised them, was one of the telltales of an attempted penetration.

Teeples.

D. W. Teeples, *The National Advocate* reporter. Was it possible that he was talking to D. W. Teeples right now?

No.

Somehow, it just didn't fit. Logically, Jeff was aware that a newspaper writer – especially one working undercover for a national scandal sheet – would not necessarily match any specific physical or personality profile. But all the same, he was sure this was not *The National Advocate's* man. Whatever it was those hard-looking, slightly oversized hands might do for a living, it didn't involve punching keys on a typewriter. Or a computer. And the briefcase didn't quite fit, either. Besides, would even the dumbest undercover reporter simply walk in and request a guided tour?

"Let's start on the second floor," Jeff said, leading the way.

* * *

Four more beds – two semi-private rooms – had been turned over recently to the Euthanasia Center by a wary, but approachable, administration, and Jeff was surprised to see that two of these had already been filled. York and Skelton had been busy.

"The patients' rooms," he said, easing himself into the role of guide and lecturer, "are kept separate from the Center itself, in the interest of efficiency and economy." And because it's going to be a while before we can raise enough money to set up shop in a building of our own, he added silently, thinking of the architectural rendering Hyman Rickoff had shown the residents on the day they took up their duties. As it was, the hospital's administrators were anxious to make no major physical changes in case it was later decided that the euthanasia service, still regarded by some as a rather questionable experiment, had failed to find its proper venue.

Robin Utley seemed only mildly interested in the patients and the arrangements made for their comfort during their brief sojourn at the Euthanasia Center, and Jeff allowed himself a mental sigh of relief. A reporter, he told himself, would surely have tried to find out the patients' names, perhaps even attempted to talk to them, in order to print some distorted version of their stories. But Utley asked no questions, responding only with noncommittal nods to explanations of the various measures taken and devices seen in operation. There was, however, a subtle change in the visitor's attitude when they moved down the corridor and around a corner into the operational area.

As before, Utley asked few questions and offered only innocuous comments. But Jeff could sense a growing restlessness behind the man's facade of composure, and Utley hesitated momentarily in mid-stride when they entered the room where Duane Tanner's life had so recently come to an end. No trace of that event remained. But there could be no doubt of the room's purpose.

"This," Jeff said, trying not to belabor the obvious, "is

where final euthanasia procedures are carried out." He stopped talking to allow Utley a moment of assessment.

Remembering Skelton's suggestions, he found his own perception of the room had changed. Where once he had thought it almost cluttered and unprofessional compared to a surgical operating room, he now found himself looking at it through the eyes of a prospective patient and feeling just a bit appalled. A hospital was a hospital, of course, and every one of the various monitors and bits of mechanical paraphernalia were there for a purpose. But if he were a patient, especially one who had perhaps been subjected to a long and miserable parade of similar chambers marking the progress of a fatal disorder, how would he feel about such surroundings? And how would he react to the thought of taking his final departure amid them?

"This is the room where you . . . die?"

The unadorned bluntness of Utley's question brought Jeff back abruptly to the reality of the room he had been about to reconfigure in his mind.

"Yes," he said carefully, all his original suspicions re-aroused, "this is where our final procedures take place."

Utley nodded, but offered no further comment.

"That's really about all there is to see," Jeff said, suddenly anxious to be out of the room. "Our conference room is on this floor. Perhaps we should use it now, to discuss your own . . . situation."

Surprisingly, that caused Utley to smile.

"Why, of course, Doc," he said equably, turning back to the door. "Let's do talk about that."

Outside the procedure room he paused, and then fell into step alongside Jeff when he turned left down the corridor. A trace of the smile remained at the corners of his mouth, and Jeff was bemused to find himself resenting the expression. Like most physicians, Jeff hated being called "Doc," and was somehow not quite comfortable when walking beside the man. Strange. And irritating.

Before they reached their destination, however, he had unraveled at least a part of the puzzle. Walking with Robin Utley was not comfortable because his gait was curiously stiff and uneven. Jeff suspected an old back injury or perhaps an impaired limb, its defect sternly compensated. Perhaps the case history would explain. If he ever saw it.

Seated across the table from Jeff in the seminar room, Utley responded with apparent ease and candor to the standard questions.

He stated his name, spelled it without having to be prompted, added a birth date that made him forty-three years of age, and declared that he was "almost" seventy-six inches tall. His weight was something of a surprise. Utley said he tipped the beam at one hundred and ninety, about ten pounds more than was apparent even to the practiced eye, and Jeff speculated that most of it would be hard muscle. Robin Utley didn't seem to run much to fat.

"So far," he commented, looking up from the yellow legal tablet on which he was taking notes, "I must say you appear to be in excellent health."

Utley's expression did not change, and he did not reply.

All right. Let's do it the hard way.

"Mr. Utley," he said, reverting to the formal address to underline his need for a direct answer, "in the absence of actual medical records what I'm trying to determine is your reason for seeking admission to the Euthanasia Center." He stopped talking, hoping to force an answer, but for a moment Utley did not reply. In fact, he did not seem to even hear him.

Utley's eyes were opaque, seemingly focused on some other time or place, and as seconds ticked away, Jeff began to wonder if he might be dealing here with an epileptic subject to petit mal attacks. But then Utley came to life, shaking his head as if to clear it of reverie, and flashed Jeff another of his peculiar half-smiles.

"Huntington's chorea," he said quietly.

Oh.

"You know," Utley continued. "The disease that killed Woody Guthrie, the folk singer. You inherit it . . ."

"Yes."

Jeff realized he had been staring, and forced his eyes away from Utley's face and down to the paper, where he watched his right hand write the name of the disease.

"I knew my father had it, of course," Utley said, as if anticipating Jeff's next questions. "And one of my sisters, older than me, is just a kind of a vegetable now. You have to move her from place to place, and she doesn't know you're doing it. Nothing there at all."

Jeff nodded.

"And you, yourself?"

"Early symptoms," Utley nodded. "Lapses of memory now and then. Nothing serious, you understand, nothing that would mean anything at all by itself. But I'm beginning to have trouble walking normally. I mean, I find that I have to concentrate on it . . ."

Jeff nodded again, mildly irritated with himself. He'd noticed the oddity of the man's gait. Why hadn't he attributed it to illness? And why did he still have trouble getting his mind to accept the explanation?

". . . and sometimes my tongue seems to get tangled over easy words. You'll get all the details when my file gets here. And, as I said – or, did I tell you? – my doctor sent it days ago. I'm surprised it isn't here already. Perhaps it'll be in this morning's mail."

Jeff was convinced that Utley's file wouldn't contain any conclusive evidence of his disease. Certainly the few symptoms he had mentioned weren't evidence, in and of themselves. But even if he did have Huntington's chorea, it didn't necessarily qualify him for admission. In fact, considering certain of the more obscure provisions of the law under which the Center operated, Jeff was fairly sure the application would be rejected.

"Is there a . . . ah . . . restroom near here?"

Jeff had been preoccupied, trying to remember the exact wording of the euthanasia statute, and Utley's question recalled him to the real world.

"Why, yes," he said, looking up from the tablet. "Just two doors down. To the left."

"Do I need a key or something?"

"No. It's always open."

"Good." Utley clambered to his feet. "Sorry to interrupt, but that's another thing's been happening lately. I'm actually starting to have 'accidents' if I don't deal with physical needs, like a full bladder, right away. I feel like some kind of overgrown infant."

He turned and left the room without further ado, allowing Jeff to return to his previous line of thought.

One thing, at least, seemed obvious. He would be unable to give Utley any kind of answer today. The key information – all the things that the hospital's lawyers would want to know – was simply not available. Things could be expedited, of course, if they had the fax number of the medical center that was supposed to be sending his file. Perhaps Hutley had it somewhere in his briefcase.

Jeff's thoughts brought him to sudden awareness that Utley had taken the briefcase with him to the washroom. Yes, there was something very peculiar about Utley.

* * *

Utley's business in the restroom took less than a minute, but that was almost too long. The package he had smuggled past the loose lobby security in the false side of his briefcase fit neatly on the high lavatory shelf, looking, as designed, like the other extra bundles of paper towels. But there was no lock on the door to the corridor, and someone entered the room just as he was stepping down from the lavatory shelf. It was all right, though. The elderly intruder didn't seem to notice anything amiss, and Utley managed to pick up his briefcase and depart without making eye contact.

Hurrying, he almost ran into an orderly who had just begun to mop the floor, and skidded on the wet surface, almost falling when his right knee gave way. The orderly moved to steady him at just the right moment.

"Whoa . . . sorry."

Utley winced, recovering his balance, but then turned the grimace into something resembling a smile.

"Don't be, son," he said. "Not your fault. It'd have been okay if it wasn't for this gimpy leg picked up in 'Nam."

* * *

He came back to the seminar room, but was unable to furnish a fax number and readily agreed to leave his telephone number and return when his tardy medical records finally arrived. A moment later, he was gone, saying he would find his own way to the door.

Jeff watched him go with some reluctance, still unable to identify the factor that caused him to be uneasy about this particular patient. But he had other things to think about, other patients to tend.

The tablet with the notes he had made on "Robin Lynn Utley" was still in his hand, but his mind was on other matters by the time he left the seminar room to begin morning rounds.

*　*　*

Jeff had been gone about two minutes when the orderly who had kept Utley from falling entered the seminar room and removed a cassette from the tape recorder hidden under the table. He dropped it into his pocket, inserted a fresh one, and snapped it into place.

Then he returned to his duties, humming a little tune.

Chapter Twenty-One

"You said it would be the last. You promised!" Gertrude Nordstrum's eyes were wide, and tears were only a word or two away.

David Wallace Teeples looked at her and found himself unable to decide whether to take her in his arms or simply tell her to shut up. Either action, he suspected, would break the floodgates. And if that happened, he knew he might as well abandon all hope of getting back to the hospital for the final hour of computer snooping he'd been planning ever since his first quick survey of the Utley interview tape.

Love.

Damn it!

Love.

But that's what it was. No room for doubt. After days of procrastinating, he was finally ready to admit the obvious. Actually use the word. Look at the facts and face them squarely. For the first time in his life, David Wallace Teeples actually cared about the feelings and future of another human being. And, as he'd always suspected it might be, it was a mess.

"It's just this one, final time."

"You promised you wouldn't."

"Trudy . . ."

She turned away, and after a moment's hesitation he crossed the room and put his arms around her, first drawing her close enough to touch her ear with his lips, and then raising his hands to cup her breasts. She stiffened momentarily and then, with the small sound of a cornered animal, relaxed against him, placing her own hands over his and twining their fingers.

"David," she said in a near whisper. "Damn you, David."

Teeples nodded, barely moving his head.

"Damn me," he agreed.

"You did promise."

"Yes . . ."

The silence between them grew and Teeples felt himself reacting physically to her presence. If tears had been likely to disarrange his plans for the evening, he knew acting upon the urge he now felt would mean a sure postponement. They would be all over each other, avid and ravenous, in a moment. But Trudy would still be here when he returned.

And tonight might be his last chance to visit the computer room. Coming in from outside the hospital to use a private terminal and telephone were no longer a possibility with the new security systems in place. And using any of the open terminals in the hospital was too risky – someone would be sure to wonder what business an orderly could have prowling around in the computer's data banks.

No. He had to get back to the computer floor itself. It had to be tonight. He had promised Trudy to drop his series of articles about the Euthanasia Center and, despite the sulfurous and threatening response of *The National Advocate* editors on being told the news, it was, for once, a promise he fully intended to keep.

Love, damn it . . .

"I'll be back in a couple of hours" he said, breaking away with a final squeeze and a quick kiss at the nape of the neck.

"Don't go."

She hadn't turned to face him, and her voice was so small

as to be almost inaudible. But there was great power and pleading in it, and for a moment it was almost enough. He didn't want to go.

"Please."

But the Utley story was just too good to miss. Huntington's chorea. Would the doctors take the life of a man who almost certainly did have years to live? Damn it, he had to see what else the computer could tell him. He would quit, pack it in, as soon as he had that. But not until. One more time.

Trudy would simply have to understand.

*   *   *

Teeples entered the hospital through the emergency ward, speaking to no one and going directly to the locker room in the basement where he put on the orderly's whites for what he expected would be the last time.

Trudy was right, of course. No sense hanging around after this. The story was dying, no matter who got snuffed from now on. But it still made sense to milk it just one more time. The Huntington's story might not sell as many copies as the one about the guy with AIDS, but if he could find a good impact word or phrase something with the easy identification of "Murder Clinic" for the editors to hang their headline on, it would be worth the effort.

And getting into the computer room was really no sweat, anyway. For one thing, it was practically deserted at night. Located a floor below the present offices of the Euthanasia Center, the bay containing the bank of specialized terminals, usually manned by the hospital's own computer experts, needed only occasional attention during what were called "off-peak" hours. The accounting office, for instance, made no demands on the computer at this time of night, nor did the various secretarial or advance planning sections. Attending physicians' requests for information were minimal. In most cases they would have been long gone from the premises before sunset and the main data inputs and outputs would relate to the intensive care and emergency services. Ongoing computer maintenance was, of course, a daytime function, and traffic arriving by telephone would be turned away automatically unless top priority codes were entered.

He expected to have the premises to himself, and he was not disappointed. Using his own pass key to open the main door, and dragging a broom and bucket for stage-dressing on the off chance that he might be challenged, Teeples snapped on the overhead lights in the terminal area and stood perfectly still, waiting for any sound of reaction.

But none was forthcoming, and he moved immediately to the bank of terminals. All the screens were on. That had jarred him on his first visit to the room, but now he knew it meant nothing. Turning off a terminal made no sense – it took too long to log in and navigate through the maze of commands and directories to get into Wolverine's main menu. Easier, and even cheaper he'd been told, to keep it open at all times.

But of course, that didn't mean he could use the terminal. It would tell him nothing until the entry command and the right access code were punched in. He attended to these tasks immediately, then settled himself in the spring-backed chair.

Unlike modern desktop equipment, the hospital's obsolete mainframe was command-driven, and it had taken Teeples some time to get used to the system. After making a selection from the main menu, he could tap any one of twenty-one specific keys to search out a word or idea, or, he could make a direct request for the records of one specific patient, which was what Teeples did as soon as his access was confirmed.

But he hadn't expected the night's work would be as easy as all that. And it wasn't.

The computer didn't recognize the name "Robin Lynn Utley." Or "Uttlee." Or "Uttley." Or any of the other variations with which Teeples tried to burgle the machine's memory banks.

It was frustrating. Listening to the tape earlier, Teeples had been elated to hear Utley spell out his own name for Dr. Taylor. That should have simplified his work, offering him a direct approach to whatever personal and/or medical information the hospital might possess. In fact, he'd really hoped to get a look at the whole case history a few hours before the doctors at the Euthanasia Center saw it. If the patient's records had come in the morning mail, in the normal order of things, they would have been punched into the computer before the end of the workday. Only, nothing was coming up.

The name was in there, some damn where, but the computer wasn't going to volunteer it. He made one final effort, entering the name "Udderly" as a wild guess, and was rewarded with the expected "File Not Found."

Horse shit. All right. In setting the search parameters, he had specified names which had been entered during the past week. Perhaps, despite some of the dialogue on the interview tape, Utley's case had somehow been entered months earlier, when he was first diagnosed. Who knew what kind of back-and-forth there had been before the man actually came to the hospital in person?

Teeples re-structured his search order, removing the time limit, and told the machine to take another look.

Hot damn! Seven hits on the name "Utley". That was more like it. Unable to think of any better way to identify the file he was seeking, Teeples simply began at the top of the list, calling up each set of records in turn and rejecting those that, for one reason or another, could not be his man.

It took him over half an hour. And at the end, he had exactly what he'd had to begin with – nothing. Of the seven Northwest Regional files for "Utley," not one was the man whose records he was seeking.

"Bite my shorts," Teeples growled.

Dismissing the patient name reference, he tried accessing, first, the Euthanasia Center database, and then the admissions list for the past week. No such patient. Not even close.

"Crap."

But wait a minute. This particular patient hadn't actually been admitted as yet. So he was only an applicant for admission. All right, then. There had to be such a list.

But if there was, the reference was so cleverly cloaked that he was unable to find it. Methodically, Teeples plodded through the arcane array of data headings associated with the Euthanasia Center. There were 132 of them. He went through each heading twice, item by item. Nothing.

"Balls."

Teeples drew a deep breath and forced himself to relax against the meager support of the secretarial chair provided for computer operators. His back hurt and his forearms hurt and he wished he were home. With Trudy.

"Double balls."

His voice seemed to echo in the room and he closed his eyes, trying to imagine where he had gone wrong. The patient was real enough. He had the evidence of the voice on tape for that, plus the memory of the man's physical presence, emerging from the men's room. Big, raw-boned mother. All right, then. If he'd seen the bastard, and the tape recorder had heard him, why the fuck didn't the computer have him?

Was it possible that the doctors in the Euthanasia Center had taken to keeping things in their –

Wait! Yes. Oh, yes!

Whatever else the Northwest Regional Medical Center might or might not be, it was surely as hell one of the most painstakingly documented environments on the face of the earth. No way was a patient – potential or otherwise – going to enter its portals and walk back out again without a full record, including name, age, social security number, and, probably, bank balance. He knew the business office spent immense sums each month for credit checks on patients. So there must have been one on the Huntington's chorea patient – however he spelled his damned name.

Teeples switched to the admissions database and entered the first command to begin a name search, but aborted the effort almost at once. He'd been down that road once, and there was no reason to think the master name file didn't contain everything from admissions, as well as from every other part of the hospital.

Try a different angle. Try only the files accessed during the past two days.

Carefully, using simple trial-and-error methods to cope with the unfamiliar search structure of the computer's software, Teeples finally managed to access the records for the past two days . . . and was rewarded with a partial explanation of his earlier lack of success.

The name "Robin Lynn Utley" was there, all right, entered at 08:32 hours the previous morning. But it would not appear in the regular patient database – or anywhere else in the hospital's record system for that matter – because of the asterisks entered on either side of the name. Teeples had seen the notation before, and recognized it. Security. For some reason, the hospital's security staff had temporarily assumed control of all data concerning Robin Lynn Utley, which meant no access to it without the special security code. That meant he was out of luck.

A first-rate hacker, familiar with the system and sure of what he hoped to find, might pick his way through or around the codes. But it was beyond Teeple's limited expertise. The night's work was a bust. A total waste of effort.

He paused a moment for control, resisting the urge to slam his fist down on the keyboard.

Ridiculous! The first thing he should have expected was a tightening of security measures on records of patients under consideration by the Euthanasia Center. Surely it would be among the first steps taken. And it had been.

All right, then. Enough! Time to go home and tell Trudy she was going to get her wish. No more screwing around with the computers, no more stories about the Euthanasia Center. No more –

Wait!

Teeples stayed his hand just as he was about to enter the code to quit for the night. The bastards had made the admissions records secure, and from that he could assume the rest of the regular patient data would be equally unavailable to him from now on. But what about the microfiche?

It was an older system, due for early replacement by a laser scan, which could break down any document digitally, and then reassemble it on command. Letters, photographs, X-rays, magnetic images, anything, could be scanned by the laser and then played back by the computer.

Only it wasn't available yet. Just a week ago, one of the computer-bangers, whom he'd cultivated for obvious professional reasons, had told him the hospital was waiting for a Ford Foundation grant to pay for the new gadget. Until then, they were still limping along with microfilm, reducing photographs and correspondence to minuscule size and then printing them on microfiche, which had to be searched for and found and then projected on a screen by a separate (and distinctly inferior) computer system. It was obsolete, cumbersome, and a pain in the ass. But he was willing to bet that the security hotshots hadn't bothered to set up any kind of restrictions on its use.

Hopeful once more, and already beginning to congratulate himself on finding an information source that would drive the hospital security staff right up the wall, Teeples stood up and moved across the room to the microfiche system, dragging the secretarial chair behind him.

It was a stand-alone system, and he was not surprised to discover that no access codes were required to enter it. Probably no one had ever considered the possibility of intrusion since it could not be reached by other terminals in the building, or by telephone from outside.

Holding his breath, Teeples checked the menu for its filing system and found it virtually made-to-order for his requirements. The microfiche filing system was probably archaic beyond belief, but access was possible by a marvelous selection of methods. You could call up a set of records by patient name, by case number, by Social Security Number, by symptom, by ailment or by day. And the most recent entry under that heading was the day that had ended just two hours earlier – he looked at his wristwatch to be absolutely sure.

Okay. Right. Now we call up the film for the final day.

"Gotcha!"

According to the day register, the very last thing the microfiche operator had done on the previous afternoon was to photograph and enter the records of one Robin Lynn Utley.

Grinning widely, Teeples called up the microfiche, flipped to the beginning of the medical record, and had just enough time to wonder why the photograph of the patient didn't match his memory of the man, when the room around him shuddered to a crash on the floor directly above.

The microfiche image died.

Earthquake?

Lights in the computer room flickered, burned brightly for a moment, and then went out.

"Jesus Christ!"

Already on his feet, Teeples moved at once toward the door to the computer bay, remembering something he'd heard about doorways being the safest place to be in an earthquake. He was quick, but not quick enough to reach it before a second concussion – much louder than the first one had been – knocked him from his feet and opened the ceiling to fiery ruin.

The room fell on him.

Teeples lost consciousness for a moment, and recovered to find himself pinned to the floor. Something heavy was on his back, trapping him against the cold of the linoleum floor tiles. He struggled briefly, but realized at once that it was useless. He would be there until someone came to rescue him.

Trudy.

She would worry, and that was bad. Thinking about her, he almost smiled as he imagined what she would have to say when he got home.

And then he saw the first flicker of fire.

It was on the floor above, feeding on what he identified by smell as a natural gas leak. But it was heavy, and if he could smell it, the gas must be pouring down!

Teeples screamed.

But only once.

* * *

It was 3:30 a.m. and David still hadn't come home. Trudy sat up in bed, book in hand, but her eyes could not focus on the words in front of her. She knew something had happened to David. She could feel it.

The possibility that he might have left her had crossed her mind, but only for a fleeting moment. No, he had not – he could not – have left her. She knew that he had feelings for her that were real, though he had never verbally expressed them to her. And besides, she reasoned, if he wanted to leave her, he wouldn't have left all of his belongings in the apartment, least of all his computer and precious tapes. No. David was in some kind of trouble, and Trudy knew she had to try to find him.

She got out of bed and rummaged through her night table drawer for a bus schedule. David had taken her car, despite mild protest on Trudy's part, and she didn't have enough cash on hand for a cab. She suspected that at that early hour the buses would run infrequently, and she was not surprised, upon finding the schedule, that she had just missed one bus and the next one would not arrive for another half hour.

Within minutes, Trudy was dressed in her nurse's uniform. Anyone seeing her at the hospital would not even question her early arrival. She had done that several times in the past, before she had met David.

David. She looked at her watch. Twenty-five minutes before bus time. She began to feel anxious. A quick cup of tea might be relaxing and pass the time, she thought, but then quickly forgot the idea as her eyes fell on the telephone on the nightstand.

Against her better judgment, her first call was to the computer room at Northwest Regional Hospital. She let the phone ring twice and hung up. She dialed again and hung up, this time after only one ring. It was their code, and they agreed that she would never call David at the hospital unless it was an absolute emergency. But emergency or not, she could no longer bear the suspense. She dialed one last time and let the phone ring. And ring.

Her next call was to the police station.

"Yes, uh . . . hello. My name is Gertrude Nordstrum," she ventured, not knowing exactly how to begin. "I . . . uh . . . I wonder if there have been any car accidents reported in the last three or four hours."

"Well, yes ma'am," a station operator said. "Several, in fact. That's not unusual in a city this size. Is there something I can help you with?"

"Well, my . . . friend borrowed my car several hours ago and he hasn't returned. I'm beginning to worry . . ."

"What sort of car was he driving?" the operator said, her voice now sounding flat, as though she had heard the same story, and had asked the same question, a thousand times before.

"A burgundy, 1993 Volkswagen Jetta," Trudy said, suddenly feeling foolish.

"Hold the line, please."

Trudy heard the operator typing the information into a computer as she spoke, and knew it would be only a matter of seconds before the details, if there were any, would appear on the screen.

"Jetta . . . 1993 . . . no . . ." the operator said distractedly as she read the screen. "No ma'am," she repeated, this time speaking directly into the mouthpiece of her headset. "No 1993's. There was one accident involving a *1994* Jetta," she added, emphasizing the year of the car so as to avoid worry.

Trudy's heart began to pound, nevertheless. Anybody could have made a mistake entering the year of the car.

"And it occurred much earlier last evening. Eight forty five," the operator added.

Trudy closed her eyes. Thank God, she said to herself, her heart still pounding in her chest. Then a new thought occurred to her.

"Is it possible that an officer who files an accident report could mistake the *model* of the car?" she asked, a renewed sense of fear now detectable in her voice.

"It's not likely, ma'am," the operator said reassuringly, "unless the car was rendered unrecognizable for some reason."

Unrecognizable! The thought of all of the horrible possibilities that could make a car unrecognizable sickened Trudy. No. God, no. That was just too unlikely, too improbable, too imposs –

"Perhaps you could give me his destination, if you know it," the operator said, breaking into Trudy's private nightmare. "I can search the computer reports by vicinity."

Trudy was instantly sobered by the request and forced to think quickly for an answer that would not divulge David's real whereabouts.

"I'm not certain," she began, stalling for time, "but he may have gone back to his office. It's near Northwest Regional Hospital," she lied.

"All right, just a moment." The operator punched the keyboard again and waited for the information to appear on the screen. "Is his office *at* the hospital?" she asked while scrolling through the on-screen information.

Trudy was caught off-guard. "What? No. No it isn't. Why do you ask?" She was puzzled. Why on earth would the operator have asked that?

"I ask because, although there are no car accidents

reported in that vicinity, there are quite a few cars that have been damaged at the Northwest Regional Hospital. In the parking lot."

"What do you mean? Is something going on at the hospital?" Trudy asked urgently, eyes now wide with panic.

"Oh yes, ma'am," the operator said. "There was a fire or an explosion of some sort that occurred there earlier this morning. Both the police and fire departments are out there at this moment."

The operator waited for a response from the caller.

"Hello ma'am?" she inquired. "Are you there?"

But within seconds she heard the familiar click of a disconnected phone and the inevitable lonely sound of the dial tone that followed.

Chapter Twenty-Two

The sirens had fallen silent by the time Jeff and Jolene Taylor arrived in the parking lot outside Northwest Regional Medical Center. The walls of the wing that had contained the Euthanasia Center were still brightly illuminated by searchlights brought in by the fire department, and the Taylors had almost been turned away as sightseers before Jeff could get a police officer to look at his hospital identification.

Once inside the line they were little better off. No one seemed to know exactly what had happened or what was going on, and answers to Jeff's questions, when fire or police personnel deigned to respond at all, were abrupt and unenlightening.

Black streaks above the first-floor windows and entranceway gave convincing evidence of fire, however. Shards of window glass that littered the parking lot more than a hundred yards from the building clearly indicated that an explosion had played some part in the incident.

"They . . . think it was some kind of bomb."

The words had come from behind them. Jeff and Jolene turned to see Hyman Rickoff standing there, regarding the damaged building with haggard concentration. He had evidently dressed in haste, pulling on a windbreaker over a tee shirt. Now his hands were filthy, the jacket was smudged, and there were smears of black soot on his forehead and right cheek.

"Good God!"

Jeff's vocal reaction to his appearance seemed momentarily to take Rickoff by surprise. He followed the direction of Jeff's gaze, noticed the condition of his hands, and stared at them for a long moment before dropping them to his sides.

"After," he said. "It was after the . . . whatever. They called me. I came down. Went inside."

"What . . . ?"

"Two explosions," Rickoff continued. "That much we know for certain. First a minor one, probably in the heating duct of the men's room on the first floor, and then, right after it, a second one, much bigger. Oxygen bottles, stored down the hall."

Jeff nodded distractedly, trying to connect the events. "And there was a fire."

"Yes. A natural gas line broke. And with the oxygen . . ."

Rickoff started to add something else, but was distracted by a sudden flurry of activity at the entrance way. The double doors, now glassless, burst open and two men in yellow firefighters' turnouts appeared, struggling with some heavy object.

It was totally black, almost too big to fit through the doors, and something was still burning inside it, shooting occasional tendrils of flame from slots in its side. Finally they managed to get it outside, where they unceremoniously tipped it on its side and let it slide down the front steps.

Jeff recognized it as the familiar lineaments of the oversized steel desk that was manned during daylight hours by the Euthanasia Center's receptionist. For an instant, he found himself trying to estimate how long it would take to refinish and re-stock the drawers. The poor woman couldn't be expected to function properly until that was done.

Then he caught himself, and glanced at Jolene with what might have been a self-deprecating smile. Shock. Dear God, he hadn't been anywhere near the building when the explosions occurred, but he was in shock anyway, worrying about minutiae. He silently chastised himself, and made a deliberate effort to exercise some professional detachment.

"Was anyone . . . ?" His voice trailed off with the question only half formed.

"No," Rickoff said. "We don't think so." He nodded in the direction of a burly, soot-faced man, whose helmet proclaimed him a battalion chief.

"That's the head man," Rickoff said, "and he tells me the steel fire doors in parts of the building nearest the initial explosion all lowered and closed automatically."

"But I thought –"

"So did I," Rickoff agreed. "But it seems that here on the west coast, the systems can be triggered by a sudden shock, like an earthquake, as well as by heat."

"For earthquakes," Jolene nodded. "Of course. And the explosion was enough to activate the system. Yes."

"But you said there was a second explosion." Jeff pursued.

"There was. Two more, really. You have to count the sudden ignition of the natural gas."

"But by then the doors were down? All closed?"

"No. The second explosion," a voice from outside their circle broke in, "actually caught the doors with about five inches to go before they made contact with the floor. And jammed them there."

The speaker was a man in civilian clothes, whom Jeff recalled seeing deep in conversation with the fire battalion chief a minute or so earlier.

"But it was enough," he continued, "to shield the rest of the hospital and the patients from major injury or damage."

As the stranger moved nearer, the doctors could see that he wore a small badge pinned to the breast of his poplin jacket identifying him as a Fire Marshal Investigator.

"Is one of you Dr. Rickoff?"

"I'm Rickoff."

The Fire Marshal Investigator didn't offer to shake hands, but glanced questioningly at Jeff and Jolene.

"This is Dr. Taylor, a member of my staff," Rickoff said. "And his wife, Dr. Jolene Jagger Taylor."

The man with the badge bobbed his head.

"Kessel," he said. "Harry Kessel. The badge says Fire Department, but I actually work for the police. I'm an arson investigator."

Kessel looked to the right and left, as though seeking some private place. Finding none, he turned back to Rickoff. "There are some things I need to tell you," he said bluntly, "and some questions I need to ask."

Rickoff read his thoughts. "It's too far to go back to our cars," he said, "and there's nowhere else handy." He looked directly at Kessel. "And there is nothing you could tell me or ask me that I wouldn't want the Taylors to hear."

Kessel still hesitated, darting glances at Jeff and Jolene. But Rickoff didn't seem disposed to move, and at length, he acquiesced.

"Dr. Rickoff," Kessel said in a tone somehow more formal than before, "I'm told, now, that the Medical Center's mainframe computer system was seriously damaged and went off-line at the time of the initial explosion."

Rickoff did not reply. He hadn't been thinking about computers.

"At first," Kessel went on, "we assumed that this was merely because of the impact. That a few adjustments would get things going again. But we've now discovered that the central core of the computer, the mainframe bay, is located right under the offices of the Euthanasia Center, in the basement."

Rickoff nodded but remained silent, unable to guess where the fire investigator might be headed.

"The second explosion," Kessel went on, "the one from the oxygen bottles that broke the natural gas line, also broke through the floor of the building. Not enough to endanger the structure. But –"

"Oh, shit."

Rickoff finally broke his silence, and Kessel paused long enough to allow him to digest the full dimensions of the situation. Damage to the central processing units of a system such as the one at Northwest Regional was one of the recurrent nightmares of the computer age. True, much of the data would probably be retrievable, if not from the hospital's own memory banks, then from the newspaper mainframe across town with which the Medical Center shared off-peak time, twinning its records against just such a disaster as this. But that didn't mean the hospital itself could go back on-line at once.

"They'll have to make some kind of arrangements to hook the undamaged portion of the Medical Center's system into the mainframe at the newspaper," Rickoff said, "and then get some temporary units working."

"But it will take time," Kessel said. "Right now, it's my guess that your hospital is going to be back to the quill-pen-and-paper age for at least a day or two."

"Medication, scheduling, even routine instructions from the attending staff," Jeff said, thinking aloud. "All of that. And more. In the computer."

"And therefore unavailable," Rickoff groaned.

"They'll have to re-schedule just about everything," Jolene said. "Not just the elective procedures, even the things that can't wait."

"The things that can't wait are going to have to," Rickoff said. "But the re-scheduling has got to start right now." He looked back at Kessel. "The Medical Center administrator and the Chiefs of Medicine and Surgery, have they been –"

"– already notified," Kessel interrupted, "and already on the scene. In fact, they were called before you were, Doctor. They're in the main offices, over on the other side of the building and, I imagine, already at work on all the problems you've brought up."

"Good." Rickoff glanced at the ruins of the Euthanasia Center then forced himself to turn away.

"Very well," he said, shaking himself as if from a nightmare. "Perhaps we'd better go along then and see if we can be of any assistance."

Kessel made a motion to speak, but was distracted by the battalion chief, who came up behind him and placed a summoning hand on his shoulder. The two men moved away, the chief speaking quietly but at some length to the investigator. Kessel listened to all that the older man had to say, his head bent to catch every word amid the noise and confusion, and then nodded abruptly.

"All right," the doctors heard him say. "That's how it'll be."

Kessel turned back to them. The expression on his face told them that something had changed, and not for the better.

"Was there anyone working anywhere in the Euthanasia Center tonight?" he asked.

Rickoff shook his head decisively. "No."

"You're sure?"

"Not in the Center itself. If you're referring to the rooms actually occupied by patients –"

Kessel dismissed this with a quick negative gesture. "I know about the patients. That they're not actually moved to the Euthanasia Center until they . . ."

He seemed to have trouble with the idea of the Euthanasia Center's function, and Jeff found himself able to sympathize. He was himself still wary of discussing his work with people outside the medical profession. You could never be sure how someone would react.

"They stay in the regular rooms assigned to our service, just across the corridor," Jeff supplied, "until they're ready to undergo our procedures. Yes. That's right."

Kessel had been expecting Rickoff to answer, and Jeff could tell he was on the verge of suggesting that he shut up. But after a moment he went on, speaking now to all three of them.

"In that case," Kessel said, "do any of you know of any reason that anyone might have been working in the Euthanasia Center after midnight?" He paused, but there was no response. "Someone catching up on reports? Finishing last-minute details?"

Rickoff's eyes narrowed slightly. "I don't think so," he said in a voice carefully purged of emotion. "But as to that, I don't think any of us could be absolutely certain. The medical staff's not large, as I'm sure you're aware. The Center is very new. I can't think of any good reason for anyone to have to come in during the night. But still . . ."

"Someone might?"

"It's . . . possible," Rickoff said carefully, waiting for Kessel to say what was on his mind.

"All right," Kessel said, ready now to end the suspense. "What Battalion Chief Williams was telling me a minute ago was that he'd confirmed something his men had suspected ever since they broke into that computer bay in the basement." He paused, as though searching for the easiest way to phrase what the doctors now expected to be unpleasant news.

"There was a bad smell," he said.

Rickoff closed his eyes, and Jeff found that he was very grateful for the sudden, reassuring pressure of his wife's fingers on his arm.

"There's a body," Kessel said. "Somebody burned to death down there, somebody working on the computer. That's why I was so anxious to find out if any of your people might have been working late."

Kessel looked at the three doctors, each of whom felt a renewed sense of shock and horror as they dealt with the possibility that the unfortunate soul was someone they knew.

"Anyway," he continued awkwardly, "I'm sorry to have to deliver the bad news. We obviously won't be able to positively identify the body for a while."

Rickoff nodded his head thoughtfully.

"I'll continue to work on the case," Kessel continued, "but not as the officer in charge. The coroner and the homicide squad will be in charge of the case from now on."

* * *

As Kessel turned to walk away from the doctors toward his vehicle, he saw a woman standing close by whom he had not noticed before. She was in nurse's uniform and stood staring at what probably had once been her place of employment.

Had she heard what he had just told the doctors? He started to approach her for questioning, but decided that this woman could not have much to add to the investigation. She seemed very distraught – he could now see tears streaming down her cheeks, though she stared, unblinking, at the building in front of her – and he hated trying to ask serious questions to people who were clearly not in the right frame of mind to answer coherently. Fires were devastating, and this woman was obviously devastated. She looked like the kind of woman who, with her daily routine now disrupted, would not know what to do with herself, who might, in fact, fall apart. He wondered how long it would be before she would collect herself again.

Kessel continued on to his car, unlocked the door and eased himself into the seat, still thinking about the nurse. He looked through his windshield to where she was still standing, and watched her as she searched her purse for something. A tissue, probably, thought Kessel. No . . . keys.

The woman started toward a section of the parking lot closest to the building, the area reserved for doctors, department heads and some of the administrative personnel.

Something wasn't quite right, Kessel thought, as he tried to analyze the situation. When he had first noticed the nurse, she was standing clear across the parking lot from where the evacuated hospital personnel and patients were now gathered. If she had been working in the hospital at the time of the explosion, why would she have walked from where the other evacuees were, past her car, only to stand near where he and the doctors had been? And if she hadn't been working earlier, and had just arrived at the hospital to report for work, what was her car doing in the parking lot, covered with bits of glass and debris from an explosion that occurred a couple of hours earlier? Kessel decided to question the woman, as disoriented as she might be.

She was just getting into her car as he approached it. He noted the name on the plate affixed to the post in front of her parking space: "G. W. Nordstrum." Well if she was G.W. Nordstrum, she didn't seem to notice or care about the condition of her car, Kessel thought, as he knocked lightly on her window.

"Y . . . yes?" Trudy said, unrolling the window only a few inches.

"Are you G. W. Nordstrum?" Kessel asked.

"Yes, I am," Trudy answered, trying to sound as though everything were normal.

"I'm Detective Harry Kessel," he said, flashing his badge at her. "Mind if I ask you a few questions?"

"Well," Trudy began, feeling a sense of sheer terror well up inside her. "You can ask me anything you'd like. I'm not so sure that I can be of any help."

Kessel was direct. "Did you just get off shift?"

Trudy panicked. She had no idea where he would go with his questions, what sort of information he was looking for.

"Why do you ask?" she questioned back, stalling him a moment so she could have a few seconds to think.

"Because that's my job," Kessel said flatly, now suspicious of something, but not knowing exactly what.

"I did . . . yes. I just finished my shift," she answered, finally realizing that she was sitting in a car that had been parked for a number of hours now. "Please excuse me a moment," she added as she reached into her glove box for some tissues and wiped her eyes and cheeks.

"Can you tell me where you were and what time it was,

when the explosion occurred?" Kessel continued, somewhat impatiently, familiar with just about every stalling technique imaginable.

Trudy now realized that anything she would say could be checked with other personnel, with records, from just about any angle. And had she been on shift, she most certainly would have known what the time was when the bomb went off. Kessel was setting her up. She was trapped.

"Look, Mr. Castle. I actually worked a double shift and I am very tired, and obviously upset about this whole event. Would it be all right if I went home to get some sleep? I'd be happy to talk to you tomorrow or some other time, really."

"Sure, Ms. Nordstrum. Here's my card. Be sure you call me before I call you. And notice, that's Kessel," he added, pointing to the card he had just handed her through the small opening in her window.

Trudy put the man's card in her purse and flashed the detective an appreciative, but worried smile as she rolled up the window and backed out of her parking space. She looked through her rear view mirror and saw Kessel taking down a few notes on a small, palm-sized note pad. Her license plate number? What could he do with that, she worried, as she drove out of the lot and onto the main road.

Trudy was now in a state of panic. No, she had nothing to do with the bomb, or fire or whatever it was. But she knew David . . . David! She burst into tears, not knowing how to handle all of her emotions and fears at once. David. David was dead! What would she do without him? She could not imagine going back to the loneliness she had lived before she had met David. And how could she continue working at the hospital in such a state? She would be grieving, mourning. And over what? Over the death of some unknown orderly who had died while mopping floors in the computer room?

She tried to contain herself as she continued driving, and suddenly realized that she had no idea of where she was going. She had nowhere to go. She couldn't go home; the apartment would seem so dark, so empty without . . .

Her thoughts then turned to Kessel. Did he really think she had something to do with the bomb? God! *Could* there have been any connection between what David was doing and the bomb? No. She dismissed the thought entirely. It was ridiculous.

But Kessel would quickly discover that the man who would not be showing up for work at the hospital was the same man who would not be showing up for work at *The National Advocate*. And then her relationship with David would be discovered, somehow, some way. Someone might remember having seen her drop David off at the hospital's front entrance and wait for him when he went in to file his employment application. Dr. Taylor had once come into the lounge where she and David had just stolen a few kisses; she didn't know what Taylor had seen, but he seemed to indicate by his crass comment that he had seen more than she had hoped. Yes, she would be exposed. She would be the woman who knew, even helped, the man who wrote those horrible articles for *The National Advocate*. She would be destroyed. Her career would come crashing down, everything she had worked so hard to attain.

She gripped the steering wheel harder as she found herself almost blinded with tears. She would have to pull over to the roadside to pull herself together. At this hour of the morning trucks seemed to be everywhere, their drivers trying to get in or get out of town before sunrise and the accompanying rush hour traffic. Trudy looked into her rear view mirror to see if it was safe to pull over. No. There was a transport truck too close to her. The driver would have difficulty slowing down.

She pressed on the gas pedal to increase the distance between them and put on the indicator to signal her intent to pull over. The truck driver seemed not to notice the blinker and pulled up again, close to her bumper, headlights glaring through the back window of her car.

It was beginning to rain, and fat raindrops splattered against her windshield. With her eyes still teary, Trudy's ability to see was getting increasingly difficult. She turned on her windshield wipers and again tried to increase the distance between her car and the truck. She attempted, at the same time, to wipe her eyes with the back of her hand. Looking again in her rear view mirror, she could see, much clearer now, that the truck had fallen behind. But what she didn't realize was that the truck was actually slowing to a stop. Unlike Trudy, its driver had noticed the flashing light and the barricade lowering in front of the railway tracks which intersected the road ahead. Trudy had been worrying too much about what was behind her, and, in doing so, had not noticed the passenger train in front of her. Until it was too late.

* * *

Could she have known by some other means, the police station operator who had answered Trudy's call earlier that morning would have found it ironic that the next accident reported did involve a burgundy, 1993 Volkswagen Jetta. Only the officer filing the report was not able to identify the year and model of the car.

Chapter Twenty-Three

"A crispy critter!"

The edges of Father Micah Chaine's mouth quirked upward in what might have been a smile as he snapped off the television set, and Charles Pennington found himself momentarily empty of words. The air in the room seemed suddenly too thick for breathing, and he wanted to run away.

"A crispy critter," Chaine echoed the phrase, obviously relishing the taste. "They found a body, and we did it, Charlie, my son! We did it! You and I . . . and, of course, little sister here!"

The words etched themselves into Pennington's consciousness, altering the world and his place in it for all time. But they could not be denied.

Standing beside him, Julia Hartt seemed for a brief moment ready to voice some kind of protest. Her eyes were wide, and her mouth actually opened as if to emit the words. But in the end, she remained silent, standing as if rooted to the floor.

The speechlessness of his companions did not phase Chaine, and if he saw any need for further discussion, he gave no sign. Clad only in undershorts and tee shirt, he was still brushing the sleep from his eyes as he limped, more deeply than usual, Pennington noted, across the room to the wet bar.

Chaine had been asleep when the other two arrived at his door. It had taken them several minutes to wake him and get him to turn on the television. The 24-hour news channel had had its camera crew and reporter on the scene of the explosion within minutes of its occurence, and Pennington, unable to sleep, had seen live coverage of the immediate aftermath.

Since their last conversation, Pennington had known that he could not stop Chaine from carrying out his plans to bomb the Euthanasia Center, and had wanted desperately to step out of Chaine's life, to have nothing more to do with him. But he was afraid, and he knew he could not really escape Chaine. By getting the priest to see what he had done, to witness, along with the rest of the nation, the devastation and the human death that his fanaticism had caused, he had hoped that Chaine would come around. He might even feel horror-stricken at the aftermath of his Almighty mission and repent, maybe give it up altogether. Then he, Pennington, and Julia could leave him. In peace.

But it didn't work out that way. Chaine seemed to revel in the discovery that his actions did, finally, cause the death of another human being. In fact, he wanted to celebrate his accomplishment. Shortly after greeting Pennington and Julia at the door and turning on the television set, Chaine went to the miniature refrigerator and emerged with a bottle of *Moet et Chandon* in one hand and chilled glasses in the other.

"Party time!" he declared.

Pennington's breathing stopped. He had known Micah Chaine for nearly two years, and had thought he was beyond being surprised by him. Their mutual support of a life-affirming cause had been the initial point of contact; frustration with the glacial slowness of progress in achieving its goals had forged a closer bond. They had worked together, and had accepted the risks inherent in the steps they believed to be necessary to fulfil those goals. No one was perfect, no human being flawless. Gradually, with the passage of weeks and months, he had been forced to face the wild and unpredictable side of the man to whom he had entrusted implementation of actions he believed to be morally defensible, even though extra-legal.

If they could not achieve their ends by means of simple reason and example, then they would achieve them by fear. Governments, after all, did no less. The rule of law survived only by the fear of retribution. Laws were obeyed only when they had teeth – real penalties for real transgression – and then only so long as the courts were willing to invoke those punitive powers.

Very well.

Now the transgressors would feel the weight of justice. But what had happened at the hospital – the taking of a human life – was as much a travesty as the Vietnam general's insistence that "it was necessary to destroy the village in order to save it." Crazy! And now Chaine actually expected him to toast the murder.

"Who was it, Charlie?"

Pennington blinked, mentally forcing himself back into the motel room where Chaine had just finished filling the three glasses and was now asking him something.

"Who'd we get?"

Automatically, without consciously willing it, Pennington found himself crossing the room to the bar, and accepting two of the glasses from Chaine's hands.

"Get?" he said.

"The bomb," Chaine prodded, his voice rising to the pseudo-patient range of an adult addressing a child. "We put a bomb in the hospital. It went off. Someone got killed. So . . . who?"

Pennington tried to reply, but found himself unable to frame any logical response. For some reason, the question seemed to make no sense.

"They don't know yet," Julia answered for him.

"One of the doctors?"

"Maybe."

"I hope it was one of the doctors."

Pennington had carried the two glasses back to where Julia was standing, but instead of handing one to her he turned again to face the bar and stood staring at the man who had made him an accessory to murder.

"Not that it really matters," Chaine went on. "Here's to our own crispy critter, whoever he or she may be!" He raised his own glass to his lips, apparently oblivious to the lack of reciprocation by the other two.

"I'm going to . . . call the police."

For a moment, Pennington couldn't be sure he had actually uttered the words aloud. Micah Chaine did not react, and it occurred to him that he might have voiced them only in his mind. Ever since the first television news report of the death in the bombing of the Euthanasia Clinic, events had taken on a somewhat dreamlike quality. If he now picked up the telephone and dialed 911, would the police answer or would he simply wake up with the moon shining through his window as it had when he was a small boy?

"You'll die first, Charlie."

Chaine wasn't looking in his direction. In fact, he seemed totally preoccupied with re-filling the champagne flute he had just drained. But there was no doubt that he had heard Pennington's words, and was replying to them. This was no dream. This was real.

"You'll die," Chaine repeated, "before you ever get that telephone off the hook, Charlie-boy."

The telephone was beside the bed on Pennington's side of the room, and Chaine had made no overt move in his direction, but he knew the bomb-maker's threat was no idle one.

"Micah . . ."

"Micah, what?" Chaine came out from behind the bar, the re-filled glass in his hand.

"You used to be a priest!"

Chaine shook his head.

"Not used to be, Charlie-boy," he said. "Not used to be. I *am* a priest. That's how it is, you know. Unless they defrock you, or laicize you, once ordained, you remain a priest all your life long."

He grinned crookedly and put down the champagne glass to hold out his hands for Pennington's inspection.

"These hands," he declared, "are sanctified. They can bless. And, Charlie, they can also smite the enemies of Almighty God!" Chaine turned his hands palms-up, palms-down, and then dropped them back to his sides.

"We destroy the flesh," he said in a tone of quiet certitude, "in order to save the soul. In this, we are the servants of His will."

Pennington shook his head.

"I . . . we . . . never agreed to countenance murder," he insisted. "The taking of a human life, no! We . . ."

Pennington's voice faded. His lungs seemed suddenly unable to contain enough air to complete another sentence. For a moment, he and Chaine stood facing each other in silence.

And then Chaine laughed.

"Funny," he chortled. "Oh, you are funny, Charlie-boy."

Pennington didn't reply.

"'Never agreed to countenance murder.' Who talks like that? Or, more to the point, who thinks like that, Charlie? We're in this together. All three of us. To the end!"

"Micah, stop!"

Since entering the room, Julia Hartt had spoken only once. But Pennington's thunderstruck silence seemed finally to compel her to say for him the words she had expected him to say for himself.

"Stop what?" Chaine said, shifting his focus to concentrate his gaze on her. "What would you have me to stop?"

"Stop gloating over the death of a human being," Julia said. "Stop trying to justify the worst thing that's ever happened to any of us."

For a moment, Chaine seemed ready to laugh again. He smiled wide and something wild danced in the recesses of his eyes. But then it was gone, replaced by a peculiar blankness. "Nobody's gloating," he said in a voice that was almost a whisper. "No one is gloating, and no one is trying to justify anything, little sister."

"You –"

"I am the Lord's man, on the Lord's work, and for that I need no justification."

"You murdered somebody!"

"I saved an immortal soul!" Chaine picked up the champagne flute again, raised it to his lips and swallowed half its contents without seeming to interrupt the flow of his thoughts.

"Murder," he continued in a voice bleakly innocent of all feeling or sympathy, "is the deliberate taking of human life, and it has been a real possibility in every move we – any of us – made, from the very first. If you don't understand that much, there's no point in further discussion."

Pennington shook his head. "We were trying to save lives, not take them."

"Save lives, yes," Chaine nodded. "Save lives, by putting the fear of God into the hearts and souls of the life-takers.

And – come on, Charlie, you know all this – the only way to do that is by violence."

"Violence!"

Pennington's face was pale now, and he noticed suddenly that his hands were damp and clammy. The rest of the sentence stuck in his throat, and he could not seem to finish it.

"Violence," Julia took up the rebuttal. "Violence, yes. But against property. Against things, not against people. We don't take human life. Or even animal life for that matter. We –"

"Bullshit!" The rest of Julia's thought was amputated by Chaine's crude interjection, and there was no longer a trace of amusement or any other human emotion in his expression. It was neutral, almost detached, as he described for them the true dimensions of the world into which they had blundered.

"What drives me crazy, sometimes," he said, "is hypocrites like the two of you." He paused a moment to let the words sink in, and then went on. "You think there's more than one kind of violence, that you can decide what kind of crockery is and ain't going to get broken. And when it doesn't work that way, you act as though someone had broken some kind of rule!"

Chaine surveyed his partners and then shifted his focus from them to some other place where he was alone.

"There are no rules," he declared. "That's the first thing to know. No rules! Not when it comes to saving a human soul. No rules and no limits to the violence because some people respond only to direct, physical force!"

He filled his glass again.

"The trouble with violence," he said, "is that it is so very damned violent. That's a ridiculous sentence, of course. But true. Oh, yes, Lord! And once it starts, it can't ever stop, because, see, you've always got to escalate!"

Pennington's mouth opened again, and again no sound emerged. Chaine seemed not to notice.

"You think I was gloating, when I called the victim who burned to death at the hospital a 'crispy critter'?" Chaine snorted. "Believe me, I do not – *do not* – gloat over the taking of a human life. But here it was necessary. Necessary to set free a soul, return it to its maker, to save other souls. Crispy critter? That was a mere husk of flesh. Nothing!" Chaine shook his head. "You start with a firecracker," he said, "and everybody jumps the first time one goes off. But not the second time. So the second time you shoot a bullet, close to them so they can hear it go by. And then, when they get used to that, you let them see the fire." He was now sipping delicately at the champagne. "But the hell of it is," he went on, "is that they can become accustomed to the fire. Yes, even the fire, until it's a fire that burns their own tender, personal, irreplaceable backsides! And even *then*, some people still don't get the point."

Chaine shook his head, looked once again at Pennington, and then shifted his gaze to Julia.

"People like you," he said. "Both of you." Abruptly, he turned and strode back behind the bar, setting the bottle and the glass down on it and bending to retrieve something from the bottom shelf.

"So when it happens," he continued, "when someone just doesn't seem to see what's real and what's not, well, then, sometimes what's needed is a therapeutic dose of reality!"

Chaine stood up again and let the other two see what was in his hands. It was a double-barrelled shotgun, sawed off about a foot from the firing chamber.

"This little toy," he told them conversationally, "is loaded with triple-ought buck. That is, each of the shells contains a dozen thirty-eight-caliber balls of steel."

He paused to let them think about it while he thumbed the hammers back, ready to fire.

"Standing together, the way you are," he said, "I'd only have to fire one chamber. That alone would knock the both of you halfway through that wall behind you."

Julia was standing as if rooted to the floor and Pennington risked the first stirring of a move to shield her. But he froze again at a slight indication of tension in Chaine's trigger finger.

"And, funny thing, you know, nobody would even come to find out what had happened, because no one ever does anything about just one noise, even if they think it's a gunshot. They don't want to think that's what it is, so they just simply don't believe it!"

"Micah, listen. This is crazy!"

Chaine snorted. "You're right about that," he nodded, keeping the muzzle of the shotgun pointed at a spot between the two frozen frames of his former partners. "Yeah. It's crazy. But I'm not the crazy one."

"You –"

"Crazy. That's the word for people who can tell themselves that things are the way they want them to be, and then really believe it. I don't do that. What I do, I see things just exactly the way they really are, and I never, *ever* try to tell myself they're some other way just because I might like that better."

"You try to change them."

"I try to change them."

"Then you –"

"But I don't try to change them just by thinking about them. I change them, with God as my help and guide, by really doing something! By making a real difference, as we did this time, blowing up that hospital's murder clinic. Yes, and by killing some poor, deluded fool inside!"

"But Micah, killing doesn't . . . accomplish anything! And it's mortal sin. You said so yourself!"

Chaine's features contorted. His eyes closed momentarily as if in a transport of rage or pain, and Pennington felt a fleeting rush of adrenaline as he readied himself to take advantage of the lapse. But the moment passed and the chance was lost forever.

"Mortal sin," Chaine repeated as he nodded slowly. "Mortal sin. Yes, but on my soul, not that of some deluded doctor. Christ died to make of Himself a blood-covering for all our sins. Can I, who am sent by Him, do less?"

His eyes were blazing, now, and any impulse his listeners might have had to reply or reason with him was consumed in their fire.

Chaine laughed suddenly. "Poor Charlie-boy," he said, shaking his head in a burlesque of sympathy. "And poor little sister-girl. Never thought it through. Never saw where it had to go. Right? Right! Well, not to worry. Father Micah's here. And he's going to do the thinking for all of us from now on!"

Chaine moved suddenly to close the distance between himself and the other two. The barrels of the shotgun came to rest just under Julia's chin, and when she tried to retreat, Chaine stopped her with an extra prod of the weapon.

"You stand right still, now, little sister," he said. "And Charlie-boy, you do like I tell you." He glanced in the direction of the closet. "Over there," he said, "over there is my suitcase. You go pick it up, Charlie, and take it to the bed and put it down there. Then stand still till I tell you what to do next."

For a moment it seemed possible that Pennington would refuse. His fingers trembled with the urgency of his desire to fasten them about Chaine's throat, and every nerve of his body tensed to spring at the other man. But the sawed-off shotgun did not waver, and, in the end, reason was stronger than rage. Pennington left Julia's side, crossed the room, picked up the suitcase and moved it to the bed.

"Attaboy! You're doing just swell, Charlie."

Pennington stood waiting, his eyes on Julia.

"Open up that side pocket," Chaine ordered. "The one nearest to you. That's it! Now, there's an address book over on the bureau. Pick it up . . . right . . . and put it in that pocket. Close the pocket again. Good! Now turn the suitcase on its side, and open it up."

Pennington did as he was told, and stood transfixed.

"Pretty, aren't they?"

The interior of the overnight bag was lined with foam rubber, carefully molded and hollowed to contain the casings for what Pennington recognized as a dozen of the neatly machined bombs that Chaine favored for his work.

"The address book," Chaine said, "is a little something I picked up from an old friend in the medical supply business, and it's got the home address of every one of those doctors over at the mercy-killing clinic."

Chaine smiled again.

"Now, I wonder," he said, "if you can guess what I've taken it into my head to do with that."

Chapter Twenty-Four

It was still dark when Jeff and Jolene Taylor finally forced themselves to leave for home.

Earlier, a coroner's crew had arrived to claim the human remains found in the deep rubble of the computer room, and the doctors had finally been given permission to enter the building with an escort to ensure they did not satisfy the natural impulse to touch and examine.

"It'll be a week before the crime-lab crew gets done with this thing," one of the escort officers had explained. "They'll go over it with a fine-toothed comb, and put a lot of stuff in little plastic baggies and take it back home and look at it through microscopes."

"And then?" Shel York inquired.

The policeman grinned. "And then," he said, "one of the dicks will talk to a street snitch who will tell him who's been buying stuff to make bombs lately. They'll look him up and find the stuff in his closet . . . and he'll cop a plea and be out on the street again before next Easter."

York didn't think it was funny, and neither did the policeman, and they'd walked the rest of the way to the wreckage of what had been the doctors' offices in gloomy silence, preoccupied with their own thoughts.

On arrival, it had been immediately obvious that salvage would be minimal.

York had reached for the charred corner of a color photograph, one that Jeff remembered seeing on the corner of his colleague's desk. The subjects, he recalled, were a slightly younger York and another man with a similar cast of features, both clad in soccer uniforms, and both trying to smile into the camera despite the harshness of sunlight that seemed to be shining directly into their eyes.

The policeman stayed York's hand before he could make contact with the fragment. "Not 'til the lab boys get through. Right, Doc?"

York shook his head. "Sorry. You just now told us, of course. Not thinking really well, I guess."

The officer nodded without rancor. "That's why they sent me along."

The situation in Jeff's cubbyhole was marginally better. The fire that had blackened the walls of York's office had not reached there before firemen brought it under control. But glass was gone from the windows, and water from the high-pressure hoses had turned most of the paper back in the scene.

Jeff had looked the mess over from the doorway, and had decided not to bother going inside. "Hell with it," he said. "let's go."

Jolene had been waiting outside when they emerged from the shattered and deformed doorway of the clinic, and was pleased, though not really surprised, to note that her husband's features were set in a mold of angry determination. One of the things she admired in him was the fact that his affections would always be reserved for people rather than things. Jeff would never love anything that couldn't love him back, and so while he might be irritated over the loss of records or notes or even treasured keepsakes, he would not mourn them.

"Let's go home," was all he said when he was within earshot, and nothing more was said until they were inside their car, headed for home. And even then, words were few.

Behind the wheel, Jeff was trying to frame a proposal that he was sure Jolene would resist. He wanted her to get out of town. Perhaps she could visit her mother or maybe take a week or two skiing in Vail or Aspen. Anything that would get her out of what had suddenly, to his mind, taken on the more threatening aspects of a combat zone.

On her side of the car, arms wrapped around herself to ward off a chill that had nothing to do with ambient temperature, Jolene was already at least one step ahead of her husband. She knew what he wanted her to do. And was determined not to do it.

"No," she said, breaking the silence when she decided it had gone on long enough.

Jeff glanced at her.

"No what?"

"No. I am not going to go visit my maiden aunt or take a cruise to Acapulco – unless you'd like to come with me."

"Jolene –"

"Je ne cède pas!"

It was almost the only French she knew, and Jolene used the phrase only when it was really no use trying to reason with her.

Keeping his eyes on the road, Jeff girded himself mentally for battle, marshaling phrases and arguments he knew were unanswerable in their logic. This one time she must see reason. He had gone into the euthanasia residency with his eyes open, knowing there would be fierce opposition and fully aware that it might become physically abusive. Even the possibility of deadly force had been considered. And accepted. No forward step in history had ever been taken without opposition; sometime, someplace, the battle would be joined. Why not here and now?

But that was for himself. Not Jolene.

Somehow, the possibility that his actions might endanger those about him – in particular, his wife – had simply never occurred to him until tonight.

"Everything's changed," he said.

Jolene smiled. She enjoyed talking to her husband, especially at times like this, when whole chapters of exposition could be skipped as redundant. Their thoughts and perceptions would run in parallel, even though diverging in conclusion.

"I work with potentially dangerous people all the time," she said. "I'm careful where I put my feet. I stay away from dark alleys, and I do not accept rides from strangers."

"They wouldn't be aiming at you."

"No. They'd be aiming at you. And I'm no more willing to let you face that alone than you would be if it were the other way around."

Jeff fell silent for a moment, as he negotiated a left turn. His lips were compressed in a way Jolene recognized; Jeff was about to turn stubborn.

Well, he could be as mulish as he pleased. She was staying.

"The . . . person . . . they found in the computer room . . ." Jeff began when the corner had been turned and the street was free before them, "he's dead. But he's not one of the doctors, and all the regular personnel of the Euthanasia Center are accounted for."

"That's good."

Jeff nodded curtly. "Good, yes," he agreed, "because otherwise that would be a friend of ours – a professional acquaintance, anyway – dead back there. And that would hurt like hell."

He paused, but Jolene remained silent.

"So maybe it'll be a while until we find out who it was," Jeff continued. "But that's the whole point, as far as I'm concerned. Whatever it was that caused the explosion, time bomb or you-name-it, may have been aimed at the Center, or even at the doctors and other medical personnel who work there. But it didn't kill any of them."

"It still took a life."

"Of course it did! But a life selected at random. An innocent bystander."

Jolene snorted mirthlessly. "Bystander, maybe," she said, interrupting her husband's flow of thought. "But innocent? Who says?"

Jeff paused, thought it over, and conceded the point. "Comment noted. No one was authorized to be down there tonight, at least as far as we know. So whoever it was, was at the wrong place at the wrong time and for the wrong reason. But –"

"– but trespassing, even in a high-security computer zone, is still not a crime punishable by death. Right? Right. Got it! So now tell me, husband of mine, how that buys me a ticket to nowhere?"

Jeff took a deep breath, and when he spoke, no trace of humor remained in his voice.

"The bomber didn't address his package to any specific person. This time the address label was marked 'To Whom It May Concern.' He or she – terrorists come in both genders, last I heard – may not even have intended to kill anyone. But he didn't intend not to kill anyone, either."

"So what happened was still murder."

Jeff nodded. "Still murder," he agreed. "But random murder, like the guy who climbed up on the tower in Texas and just fired on anyone in range. Or people who put poison in medicines at the supermarket."

Jolene shook her head. "Sorry," she said. "I don't understand your point."

"There isn't any."

"Uh . . . pardon me?"

"There isn't any point to the killings, Jo-Jo. They're non-selective. Illogical. So no, there's no way to predict the next target. Or even pick out a group of probables."

Jolene considered this. She could see where Jeff was going, now. But that didn't mean she was ready to follow.

"Okay," she said. "All right. Let's say that's true. So, why don't we both go away? Together. Before anything else happens?"

Jeff risked another look at his wife, and felt a powerful temptation to agree with her. But the impulse lasted for only a moment.

"Can't."

Jolene nodded. "I know."

"Uh, no, you don't."

"Hey . . . !"

Abruptly, Jeff removed his foot from the accelerator and applied it sparingly to the brake. The car slowed and eased to a stop at the side of the street.

"Look, Jo-Jo, this isn't the time to tell you this, or even bring it up, but I think maybe I've got to."

His tone was hesitant, and Jolene felt a familiar urge to lighten the mood by making a joke. But she stifled the impulse.

"You know how I feel about the Center. The work we do there. I think it's right and I think it's necessary in an age where human existence – not life, but mere existence – can be prolonged almost indefinitely."

Jolene nodded. They had talked of almost nothing else during the weeks before Jeff made his decision to apply for one of the first euthanasia residencies. She knew his commitment to the principle was complete. But from the first she had been aware of her husband's personal doubts and reservations about his own place in such a program, and his emotional ability to sustain a career that involved taking lives rather than trying to sustain them.

"The only thing," Jeff continued, "that keeps me from handing Rickoff my resignation right now, today, is the thought that some son of a bitch somewhere is going to think he scared me off."

Jolene sighed inwardly and fought back the impulse to hug her husband. As a psychiatrist, she knew that would be the wrong thing to do. It would be something he would resent and subconsciously identify as "mothering", perhaps even to the point of allowing it to influence the decision-making process. And that, she knew, had been the death of more marriages than alcoholism and philandering combined. But as his wife, the impulse remained strong, so she decided to smother it beneath the weight of practicality.

"All right," she said, "fair enough. Table the question of the residency for a moment. There's no rush. But what does all that have to do with sending me off to hide under someone's bed while my husband stands around with a target pinned to his chest?"

Jeff, who had been expecting, and dreading, a very different reaction, allowed himself a deep sigh of relief. He eased the stick shift into park, set the brake, and turned off the engine.

"You know," he said, turning to his wife and taking her into his arms, "I think I could really get to like this thing of being married to you."

Jolene relaxed, easing herself into a more comfortable position, and rested her forehead against his neck.

"Well," she breathed, "they do say its a warm way to spend the winter . . ."

* * *

For Sheldon York, however, warmth was as elusive as sleep.

Returning home, he had slumped down into a leather easy chair, telling himself it was just for a moment. He would sit quietly in the darkness of the early morning hours and bring his thoughts into order. Then he would go to bed.

But the chair was comfortable, and the thought of going alone into the spartan reaches of the half-furnished bedroom was not attractive enough to bring him back to his feet. Physical exhaustion rode his shoulders and placed an intolerable weight on his eyelids, but somewhere in a well-fortified corner of his mind a hungry ferret of fear ran frantically back and forth, nipping at the edges of drowsiness and ripping the blanket of sleep each time it tried to cover him.

Shel York was afraid.

Not of death. Death was an old professional acquaintance, a one-time adversary turned colleague and co-worker. Death was as natural a part of life as birth, as necessary as the turning of the earth and as emotionally acceptable as time. But if death itself held no terrors, the same could hardly be said for the process of dying.

He'd once heard a well-known comedian say that he didn't mind dying, but just didn't want to be around when it happened. Sheldon York hadn't laughed. Instead, he nodded a solemn accord.

Doctors who wished to survive in their profession developed, by necessity, a certain emotional distance from the sufferings of their patients, because to do otherwise was to court personal destruction. Death could be both peaceful and dignified. But it could also be unutterably painful and prolonged, and it was this aspect of euthanasia – the easing of pain and the maintenance of human dignity – that had attracted him to the residency when it was first offered.

Now everything was changed. Different. And frightening. No dignity had been left to the man who died in the computer room, no moment of preparation, no compassionate medication.

Quick. Yes, it had been quick. That much could be said for what had happened. The man had not burned to death like some medieval witch at the stake. The detective who had questioned him, and the fireman, had both been emphatic on that point. The initial explosion had swallowed the oxygen in the room at a single inspiration, leaving the victim unconscious. He might have known when the room came down, but it seemed unlikely. In any case, he had not been forced to smell the charring of his own flesh.

For such small mercies, York could hear his grandfather saying, let us be truly thankful.

But it was an evasion.

Someone, somewhere, had meant to send death and destruction among those who worked at and for the Euthanasia Clinic at Northwest Regional Medical Center, and if the target hadn't been selected by name, it had certainly been picked by position.

God!

Sheldon York's eyes had been almost shut, but now they popped open and he sprang to his feet at the impulse of a sudden adrenal rush.

What –?

Terrified, unwilling to take a single step from the oddly comforting eminence of the leather chair, he stood like a statue, listening to the not-yet-familiar whisperings of the house where he had lived during the brief opening weeks of his residency. His grandfather's house had been like this one. Sparsely furnished. Teeming with echoes. But it had not terrified him, and in all the years he had spent there as a boy, as an adolescent and as a young man, never had it allowed him to imagine bogeys in the night.

York forced the air from his lungs, and re-inflated them gradually in a ritual that had always banished night-shivers of the past.

There. Better. A minor after-frisson rippled the skin along his spine, but the short-circuit spark of fear that had roused him was gone. He almost smiled at the light afterglow of perspiration that covered his arms and upper body before he stopped to wonder what had caused it to happen. He had not been dreaming. And there was no television to produce an artificial stimulus.

A sound.

Yes. There had been a sound. Something not usual to the quiet street. A passing car? No. A car. But not passing. A car . . . pulling into the driveway below.

York's rented dwelling was in an older part of the city where houses were built on a plan popular in the 1930's, with garages that were part of the basement of the house. His own garage door was equipped with an automatic opener, and with characteristic neatness, he made a habit of parking his nondescript leased sedan inside, closing the garage door behind him and entering the living quarters of the house via the basement stairway.

The sound that had roused him, he realized, had been made by another car pulling into the driveway between the street and the garage. And something else . . . a door. He had heard a car door open. But he had not heard it close.

York was on the point of moving to the front windows to check the accuracy of his sonic reconstructions when speculation turned moot with the ringing of the front doorbell.

The police. York took a deep breath, and resisted the impulse to pretend he wasn't home. The police – and it could hardly be anyone else – could not possibly have come to his door at this hour to bring good news. And he was really not up to any more of the other kind.

But the bell could not be ignored. With a mental sigh of apprehension, York forced himself to cross the living room and undo the two deadbolt locks on his front door.

The door was seldom used, and it resisted his first effort, forcing him to bend for a second pull, which left him physically as well as mentally off-balance when he discovered that the caller was not a police officer after all.

It was the euthanasia candidate he had seen touring the center with Jeff Taylor the day before. Utley? Yes. Utley. But now the man was pointing a sawed-off shotgun at York's head and smiling wolfishly.

"Guess who's coming to breakfast?" he asked.

Chapter Twenty-Five

Chaine offered no explanation as he ushered the doctor out the door and into the darkness.

Silently, without protest, and moving in a kind of fog as though standing somewhere outside himself and watching his actions with astonishment, York accompanied his pre-dawn visitor down the front steps to the car parked in his driveway. He stood waiting while the trunk was unlocked to disclose the form of a young woman curled up among suitcases, boxes, cans and a peculiar assortment of tools, her hands bound behind her.

"Come on, Julia," Chaine said, prodding her. "Climb out of there and stand up."

The woman sat up awkwardly, trying to comply. She swung her legs over the edge and tried to stand up, but she had to lean forward to balance, and once out of the trunk, her legs were unequal to their task. She slumped sideways against the trunk lid and struck the side of her head. She moaned, and York could see that her mouth was taped.

"Please . . . !" he ventured, reaching automatically toward the tape, to remove it.

Chaine smashed the barrel of the shotgun down across York's extended forearm, releasing a sheet of white pain that brought the doctor to his knees. He might also have screamed, but the barrel of the weapon was back between his eyes before he could draw breath.

"'Bridle thy tongue and thy hand, lest it betray you unto death,'" Chaine said. "Not holy writ, Doctor, but worth remembering, all the same."

The menace of the shotgun never wavered.

"The tape stays," Chaine said. "And you keep your mouth shut."

York nursed his arm and stood up again, waiting quietly for orders.

"Here." Chaine reached into his pocket and drew forth a roll of one-inch white adhesive tape. He handed it to York. "Around her neck."

York hesitated, trying to understand what Chaine wanted him to do.

"Wrap the tape," Chaine said in a neutral tone that served only to emphasize the menace of the shotgun, "around her neck. Now!"

York moved to comply, abandoning all effort to understand, or even believe, the events transpiring around him. None of this was real. It couldn't be.

"All right. Good," Chaine said when two turns of tape had been applied. He moved a step closer, bringing the twin muzzles of the shotgun into direct contact with the woman's neck.

"Now wrap some tape around the barrel of the scatter-gun. No! Don't try to move the barrel out of position while you're doing it! Just wrap it. That's it. So there's no way the muzzle can be pointing at anything but the neck."

York complied as well as he could, finally beginning to comprehend what the other man had in mind.

"Now," Chaine said, "wind the tape another turn around the pretty lady's neck. Right . . . okay. That's enough!"

Grinning, Chaine stood for a moment as if inviting York to admire the result of his efforts. Then he nodded suddenly in the direction of the still-gaping trunk.

"In you go, Doctor," he said cheerfully, indicating that York was to take the place formerly occupied by the woman, "and make yourself comfortable. We're going for a little ride."

* * *

The trip took nearly an hour, and York experienced it as a series of painful and unrelenting jolts and bounces in the blackness of the car's trunk. Periodically, the car would stop, and Chaine would open the trunk to retrieve a few tools and other items which York could not identify. But at last the car came to a final stop and Chaine opened the trunk lid to release its prisoner.

"All right," he said, "everybody inside – and then we talk!"

York did his best to get out of the trunk under his own power, but his muscles were cramped, and in the end he needed help from his captor to bring himself back to his feet.

The world was still in darkness and they were at the beach, parked in the driveway of a house with no visible neighbors. York could smell the sea and hear the waves coming ashore.

Chaine moved quickly to retrieve a suitcase that had shared the trunk space, and then gestured to indicate that the doctor was to precede him down a gravel path to the door.

York led the way, and wondered for the first time if any of his neighbors might have been witness to what had happened outside his home. He concluded that it wasn't likely. When was the last time he had looked out his own window at this time of morning?

"So here's the way it's going to be," Chaine said when they were inside and the front door had been locked behind them. "From now on, what I say is what you do. Got it?"

York turned to face his kidnapper.

The front part of his mind – the part that moved his hands and feet and fed him – might have been temporarily dysfunctional due to shock. But the back part, where problems were solved and major decisions considered, was untouched. That part of Sheldon York had already concluded that the man he knew as "Robin Utley" was the author of the bomb that had destroyed the Euthanasia Center and claimed the life of whoever had been working in the computer bay. The man was a killer. He was not sane. And he would not hesitate to kill again.

"The way I've got the shotgun tied to this pretty lady's neck," Chaine said, breaking into York's thoughts, "means there is just absolutely no way she could possibly live through any heroic idea you might get about jumping me, even if I were half asleep. Do we agree about that, Doctor?"

York nodded, but didn't speak.

"Good," Chaine said. "Very good indeed. Now, sit down in that chair."

When York was seated in the hard wooden chair, Chaine moved cautiously, never releasing his hold on the shotgun, to a table where he deposited the suitcase he had taken from the trunk. He laid it on its side and snapped open the locks.

"More tape in there," he said to Julia. "Get it out and go to work on the doctor. Move slowly. I'm a little nervous, and you wouldn't want me to get the trembles, now would you?"

Julia hesitated, glancing at York as if for confirmation of the order. But York made no sign, and, after a moment, she opened the suitcase, brought out another roll of tape and moved slowly to York's side.

"Nice," Chaine said approvingly. "That's very good, little sister. Now start with the arms. Tape his wrists to the arms of the chair. Then his elbows."

Julia did as she was told without resistance, and Chaine seemed confident enough of her compliance to begin talking. He spoke as though presenting a lecture to an unseen audience, with only occasional monitoring glances to make sure the work was going as intended.

"The first and most important thing to know about me," he said, "is that my name is not Robin Utley. I got that out of the telephone book just before I made the appointment to get inside your little corpse factory."

York's head and shoulders were still free, and no effort had been made to tape his mouth, but he could think of no reply.

"My real name," the gunman continued, "is Chaine. Micah Chaine. Or, more properly, Father Micah Chaine. You've probably never heard it before. But you'll remember it for the rest of your life . . . what little there's going to be of it."

That final phrase seemed to strike Chaine as humorous. He laughed suddenly and loudly, causing Julia to shy away from him in a sudden spasm of terror.

"Freeze!"

The laughter was gone as quickly as it had come, and Chaine's tone turned icy cold.

" 'The foolish shall not stand in thy sight,' " he quoted. "No, indeed, little sister. They shall fall down!"

Chaine's lips had come away from his teeth and they remained in a bare grimace as he spoke slowly and condescendingly to the woman.

"Understand this, Julia. This shotgun is cocked, the trigger's got a featherweight pull, my finger's on it, and it's tied to your neck."

Julia stood perfectly still, looking at him with eyes from

which all hope had vanished. She seemed to York to be teetering on the edge of collapse, but Chaine did not appear to notice. Or care.

"Just a little tug, you see," he went on, "just the tiniest movement of a finger, and you cease to exist!"

Julia made no effort to respond to what Chaine had said, if she had heard him at all. But Chaine did not wait for acknowledgment and continued his soliloquy.

"Keep taping," he said. "Now . . . where was I? Oh, yes. Of course. This will probably interest you, missy. Riding over to the doctor's house – I know it wasn't too comfortable back there where you were – but do you remember we made a few stops along the way? And every time, I came back and got something out of the trunk, and then after awhile we moved on? Certainly the good doctor will remember."

Julia's mouth was still taped, and the expression in her eyes was no longer readable, but she managed a motion of the head that might have been interpreted as a nod.

"Sure you do," Chaine said. "Of course. So you can make the doctor, here, understand I'm not exaggerating in any way when I tell him about the things that are going to be happening later today."

Even the paralysis of hopelessness that York could feel tightening its coils about him with each turn of the tape was not powerful enough to suppress the sudden lightning-flash of mortal terror sparked by Chaine's words. In that instant, he understood the enormity of Chaine's plan. The bombing of the Euthanasia Center was not enough; the paraphernalia he had seen in the trunk of Chaine's car was proof positive that he had not limited himself to a single target.

He had made more bombs, and he had planted them, one by one, along his route. That he had been able to find his way to York's house was evidence enough that he had somehow obtained the home addresses of all the doctors employed at the Euthanasia Center.

"Mass . . . murder!"

Shel York's mouth was still free, and he used it. But not to shout or scream the words, as he might have done at some other time. He knew he would not be heard outside the house itself, and he was well aware that no argument of whatever kind would be sufficient to turn Chaine from his course. But he couldn't help repeating the words.

"Mass murder," he said, looking at Chaine as if studying an alien life-form. "You think killing all of us will make a difference."

Chaine shook his head and favored him with another of the wolfish smirks.

"Mass murder," he said. "Rather an odd choice of words for someone in your position, don't you think . . . Doctor? I mean, considering the fact that you've killed so many more people than I?"

He let York think about that for a moment, and then went on.

"As to what kind of difference killing a few of you is going to make, though, I'll have to grant you, that's what might be called a whole different ball game!"

He shot a glance at Julia, who had stopped taping York to the chair while listening to him. She looked away, and bent to continue the work.

"As to that, about it making a difference, I guess I've got a 'yes' for you. And a 'no,' too. First, yes. I think killing doctors can make a difference – to you! You'll be dead, and dead is different, let me tell you."

He took a deep breath and his attention seemed to turn inward, focusing on some elusive landmark in his own core.

"'I have been forgotten as dead out of mind, I have been as a perishing vessel,'" he quoted. "And no, I don't think it will

stop you, people like you, anyhow, from playing God
Almighty. From deciding you've a right to decide who dies
and who lives. But that's where you're stupid. All of you. You
go to sleep, believing this is some kind of one-shot deal. That
I'm some kind of aberration, one that won't be repeated. And
that's just where you, all of you, miss the boat! Because my
name is Legion!"

Julia had finished immobilizing York's arms and upper
body. Chaine took time out to show her how he wanted the
doctor's ankles secured to the legs of the chair, and to get
another roll of tape. Then he went on as if there had been no
interruption.

"I'll walk away from this," he said, not bothering to conceal
his satisfaction. "The people I met there at your little snuff-
shop might be able to describe me to the police, even if one of
them should live through the morning, which I surely do not
expect. But, chances are, the descriptions will leave a lot to be
desired. And even if I'm arrested, and tried, and executed, do
you really think the Lord's will can be frustrated?"

Chaine's eyes closed, as if he were in a kind of ecstasy.
"Another will come," he whispered. "And another. And
another. Forever!"

His eyes opened, and he turned to Julia with a smile that held
no hint of warmth. "You can see that, can't you, little sister?"

The smile widened. "You see?" he said, glancing back at
York. "See how she understands it? Not even a quiver. And she
really thinks I am going to kill her, too."

Chaine looked back at Julia and shook his head.

"Don't be stupid. You are worth a million dollars to me – to
the cause of righteous retribution – but only if you're alive.
Remember? That's what I told your fancy playmate it would
cost him to get you back in one piece, and that's just how much
he is going to pay me."

Julia shook her head as Chaine ripped the tape from her mouth.

"He hasn't got that kind of money," she said.

But Chaine just went on smiling.

"No, but he can get it. Old Father Micah's been around Charlie-boy enough to know that he may not have the money himself. Not now. But he can drop the dimes – make a phone call to dear old daddy – and the only question would be, does he want to pick the money up or have it delivered?"

Chaine smiled again at Julia, and she looked away, seeming to concentrate on the task before her.

"Money," Chaine repeated, turning his gaze back to Sheldon York. "That's the key. The key to the Lord's triumph! Little sister, here, can't talk because if she did, she and her boyfriend would be in jail so long they'd forget what daylight looks like. And Charlie-boy knows it, too. And he also knows that if he did open his mouth, he'd spend the rest of his life looking over his shoulder. For me."

York had been struggling with himself, trying to remain silent. But finally the pressure was more than he could resist.

"It won't work," he said tightly.

Chaine seemed interested. "What won't?"

"Any of it – starting with the ransom, and going on to everything else."

Chaine nodded. "Keep coming," he said. "Why not?"

"Because no matter what you've seen or what you think you know, the world doesn't really work that way. It's not that simple."

"Uh-huh . . ."

"You think if you keep this up, eventually people will be too frightened, of you, and the others like you, to abide by decisions they have made. Decisions based on free and rational thought, not touched by fear and superstition."

Chaine laughed, a real laugh this time, and despite his suspicion that the words he was saying might be the last he would ever be permitted to utter into the world, York allowed himself to pause and listen. There was something in the laughter that reminded him somehow of a trip he had taken with his grandfather when he was a little boy. Yes. That was it. They had gone camping in the mountains. There was wildlife there, and the night hours had been filled with its voices. Chaine's laughter reminded him of that night. Cavemen had produced such noises, sounds that weren't tame. And would never be.

"Rational!"

The laughter had ended, but Chaine's voice retained its feral intensity as he spat the word in York's face.

"Free and rational choice!" Chaine reached out to flick a forefinger against the end of York's nose. Not hard enough to do damage, but enough to cause momentary pain and to demonstrate total contempt.

"You crawling little slime," he said. "What would you know about being free?" He shook his head in simulated wonderment. "Free!"

Chaine nudged Julia with the end of the shotgun that remained taped to her neck, forcing her to move away from York. The doctor was totally immobilized now, except for his head.

Using the shotgun like an animal-handler's loop, Chaine forced Julia to kneel on the floor opposite York in a position that kept her out of reach of the doctor and under control, while affording him left-handed access.

"Free," Chaine said almost conversationally, "is not what you are . . . Doctor. It's what I am!"

He flicked the end of York's nose a second time. "Free is arranging to take the lives of every one of the life-takers at that Satan-spawned charnel house of yours. All of them!"

He turned to Julia and flashed his teeth at her.

"And free," he continued, "is making sure you see and remember what I do to this one." He nodded at York, inviting her attention. "So you can tell your boyfriend, after he buys you back from me."

He stood up, switching the shotgun to his left hand and moving to tower over the helpless pair.

"And free," he said, "is the difference between standing here, where I am, and sitting there where you are, while someone does things like this to you!"

In a single motion, without the slightest impairment of his own balance, Chaine's foot snaked out to move behind the leg of York's chair, flipping it upward and to the right.

York's world tilted suddenly to the left, as the floor rushed up to strike him a blinding blow in the temple. He screamed – and Chaine laughed again.

"Go ahead, Doctor," he invited. "Purge your soul. Let it all out! No one's going to hear you outside this room. And I want little sister, here, to have some really interesting memories to share with her boyfriend!"

His foot drew back, and York's sight cleared in time to see it coming toward the center of his face as if in slow motion, blotting out the entire world of light and joy and hope.

Chapter Twenty-Six

Like the sudden snapping of an over-stressed wire, the final moment of her nightmare brought Jolene Taylor upright in bed, eyes open, searching the room for the awfulness that had seemed ready to swallow her only a moment earlier. Breath was trapped in her lungs, and she felt a momentary urge to expel it in a shriek of pure animal terror. But Jeff was there beside her, sprawled on his side in the bonelessness of total inertia, and she forced herself to forego the needed release of emotion.

Damn!

Slowly, carefully, Jolene tested the limits of the self-denial that had been one of the hardest parts of her psychiatric training. She had been reared in the warm, loving and almost totally permissive environment of a father and mother who valued her as a person rather than as an extension of themselves. Learning to repress emotion in the interest of professional attitude had not come naturally to her. It had been learned at the cost of constant, disciplined practice. But learned it had been. And if it had proved a useful adjunct of professional life, it had turned out to be pure gold in making the multitude of adjustments necessary to even the happiest of marital relationships.

And now it came into play again, first prompting her to take the time to be sure that the last quivering remnants of nightmare were banished, then helping her to move deliberately and soundlessly from the bed.

It was early morning and Jolene could see a thin strip of bright sky between the closed bedroom curtains. She knew that she needed more sleep, but there would be no more sleep for her.

She was up for the day, despite the fact that she had slept for less than two hours.

Snatching a robe from the closet, Jolene made her way downstairs and into the kitchen.

Coffee!

Real coffee, not decaffeinated and not instant. Jolene Taylor had never been an especially self-indulgent person. But good coffee was, in her view, more a necessity of life than any kind of luxury. And the best kind she'd ever had was made from the wonderful Mexican beans available to her through a carefully nurtured friendship with the proprietor of an all-night convenience store whose mother sent them from the Yucatan.

She reached eagerly into the freezer compartment where her special blend was kept. Damn! The sack was empty. Of course it was; she had used up the last grounds the day before, making a mental note to re-stock on the way home. But there had been a hang-up in her schedule. She had been late returning home – and then that awfulness at the Euthanasia Center.

Reluctantly, Jolene ran tap water into the teakettle, set it on the stove, checked the gas burner to see that it ignited properly, and turned toward the shelf where the "emergency" jar of freeze-dried instant was hidden. But she halted with a hand half-extended in mid-air. The instant beverage would be guaranteed to produce total wakefulness, but her whole system rebelled at the thought. It was too early in the morning, and there had been too many bad dreams last night. For times such as these, the only proper medication was made from good Mexican beans, fresh ground and brewed with sweet spring water.

Returning to the bedroom, Jolene moved swiftly to the closet and divested herself of robe and nightgown. She selected a skirt and blouse at random in order to avoid turning on a light that might disturb her still-sleeping husband. Panties were an afterthought, almost set aside in the interest of haste. She wriggled her feet into loafers without the bother of socks, and congratulated herself on being able to snag her jacket and purse in a single open-handed grab as she fled silently from the room.

The store was only four blocks away, and Jolene frequently walked the distance for pleasure, but this morning's errand seemed clearly to call for motor transport, and the keys to her own car were already in her hand as she came out the front door.

In the driveway, however, there was a small problem.

Instead of parking their cars in the garage, the Taylors used the space for storage and parked the vehicles outside. They were standing now, in tandem, with Jolene's elegant red Porsche parked ahead of her husband's aging Plymouth.

Suppressing mild frustration, Jolene set her purse briefly on the roof of the older car while she fumbled with her key ring. Two different keys were needed: one to open the door and the other to unlock its ignition. As usual, they hid themselves from her amid the welter of office, house, safe-deposit, bicycle padlock and assorted other keys required for life in any modern city.

Aha!

Finding the two she needed, Jolene opened the car door, slid into the driver's seat, thrust the other key into the ignition, turned it . . . and groaned inwardly.

Teakettle!

She had left the damned teakettle on the burner, and it was

the whistling kind that would be screaming at any moment, startling Jeff awake. She would have to go back and turn it off.

* * *

To make sure his victims were well settled into their seats when his bombs went off, Micah Chaine had fitted the triggers with five-second delay fuses. And Jolene moved fast. Turning off the ignition did nothing to interrupt or halt the sequence leading to detonation, but it did allow her to just get out of the car before the explosion.

She was in mid-stride, a step away from the vehicle, when the device exploded, hurling her halfway across the front yard and annihilating consciousness in a single hammer-blow of incredible power and fury.

Chapter Twenty-Seven

The concussive force of the blast that dismantled his automobile shattered the windows of Jeff Taylor's bedroom and brought him wide awake with no sense of transition from sleep – and no doubt about the nature of the disturbance.

A bomb.

A bomb had exploded outside his home. A bomb like the one that had devastated the clinic . . .

Shards of glass from the ruined window were strewn across the bedroom carpeting and furniture, and he quickly turned to his wife to make sure she was all right. But her side of the bed was empty.

Jolene! Dear God – Jolene!

He had slept in the nude as usual, and a major effort of will was required to keep himself from running naked across the floor and down the stairs.

Jolene!

He grabbed the sheet and blanket and threw them on the floor between the bed and the closet, covering the bits of glass that lay there. He quickly pulled on trousers and a sweater, while thrusting his feet into soft shoes.

Jolene!

He was on the stairs, descending in a series of lunatic bounds, when it finally occurred to him to shout his wife's name aloud.

"Jolene!"

There was no answer to his call, and he did not repeat it. The sound of his voice shocked him, breaking into a peculiar sense of unreality that had begun to form in his mind, and dispelling once and for all any suspicion that this was any kind of nightmare. This was real.

But the name echoed in his mind as he crossed the living room – noting without surprise that it, too, was littered with window glass – and tore open the front door.

Jolene!

Outside, the bright cloudness sky made a mockery of the scene on his front lawn.

To his left lay the remains of his car, a twisted and flaming metallic ruin. The fire seemed to be centered upon the fuel tank, which appeared to have burst open, providentially eliminating the danger of a secondary explosion. The doors were gone, and the wreckage lay on its right side.

To his right lay . . . Jolene.

Clamping his jaw against the shrieking panic that boiled up from within him, Jeff crossed his lawn in two giant racing strides and knelt beside his wife, pressing his fingers to her carotid artery and forcing his mind to disregard any promptings save those of his training in medicine. She was alive. But barely.

A-B-C

Airway. Breathing. Circulation.

Finding the carotid pulse had settled the matter of circulation, at least for the moment. Quickly, he checked her mouth and nose. They were open, and he noted with passing astonishment that while the back of his wife's head seemed to be bleeding from numerous small lacerations, her face appeared to have been spared any damage – except, perhaps, for the bruise that was beginning to form on the right side of her forehead.

Forget the bruise, Doctor!

What about her breathing?

At first he thought her lungs were not functioning, but, forcing himself to hold still and observe carefully for a moment, he was able to see regular movement in the chest.

All right, then, next question.

Jolene was unconscious and her eyes were closed, so he rolled back an eyelid and was marginally relieved to note a minor adjustment in the size of the pupil. Same with the other eye, and the pupils appeared to be of equal size.

Jeff took in a deep breath and expelled it with difficulty. Fair enough, he told himself. Maybe it's a miracle.

And then he saw the blood. The front of her skirt, the part most readily visible to him, was spotless. But there was blood on the one leg he could see, and on the other one, which was folded under her at what he realized, tardily, was an unnatural angle.

Panic, never far below the surface since he had awakened, rose again to challenge control as he threw the skirt back and moved to determine the source of the red stains.

If the pelvis . . . or the abdomen . . .

But the answer was both better and worse than he might have hoped. Jolene's abdomen and pelvic area appeared to be of normal size and were not distended with any evidence of internal hemorrhage. There was also no evidence of vaginal bleeding. Instead, the blood seemed to be coming entirely from the right thigh, where the flesh was torn by what appeared to be a compound fracture of the femur. Not arterial. No pulsation or spurting.

Jeff's hand descended at once on the pressure-point above the wound.

"Anything I can do?"

A man he had never seen before stood in the street, wearing a robe and an expression of apprehensive concern.

Neighbor.

"Call nine-one-one," Jeff said, looking away from Jolene long enough to be sure the man understood what he was saying. "Nine-one-one. Tell them there's been an explosion, and make sure they send paramedics."

The man nodded. "Explosion," he repeated. "Paramedics."

"Right now!"

The man needed no further urging. Barefoot, he ran back across the street to where someone was evidently waiting to open the door for him. He would do as he was told.

Jeff turned back to Jolene and saw with satisfaction that his hand pressure had evidently slowed the bleeding to a trickle. He checked the carotid again. Strong and steady. Breathing regular. Airway open.

"Its going to be okay," he told her, not aware that he was speaking the words aloud. "Its going to be okay . . . going to be okay!"

* * *

Jolene still hadn't recovered consciousness by the time the paramedics arrived. But Jeff had been successful in controlling the external bleeding by hand pressure alone and he was content to stand aside as the emergency medical technicians started an I.V. with Ringer's. They strapped his wife's limp body to a heavy back board intended to minimize any possible spinal trauma en route to the hospital after encasing her in the Military Anti-Shock Trousers. The paramedics inflated the MAST suit to control the bleeding, loaded Jolene into their ambulance, and tried to close the back door in Jeff's face.

"No way," he said, seizing the handle.

"Sorry," the paramedic said, tugging at the door. "We don't carry passengers. Law against it. Anyway, you'd only be –"

The sudden, unannounced concentration of effort with which Jeff ripped the door from the paramedic's hands nearly hurled the man to the pavement. Jeff entered the back of the ambulance and seated himself beside his wife's gurney.

"Look, asshole –"

But the glare Jeff turned on him aborted anything the astonished man might have intended to say.

"That's 'Doctor Asshole' to you," Jeff said in a surprisingly even voice. "And this is my wife."

The paramedic opened his mouth to speak, but was given no opportunity to reply.

"One of the things I know about your operation," Jeff went on, "is that you're basically an EMT-2. No radio, so no direct contact with a qualified physician."

"We –"

"I'm a physician. And a surgeon. Now shut the door and let's move it!"

If he had shouted the words, the result might have been different. But there was no mistaking the sincerity and intensity of emotion in Jeff's voice, and the paramedic closed the door without further delay.

The driver hit the lights and siren at the corner, and swerved onto a freeway ramp for the ride across town to the Trauma Center at Northwest Regional.

For a moment after leaving the scene, the paramedic simply held onto his seat across from Jeff and braced himself against turns with the patience of long experience. But once they were on the freeway, he let go and hooked up the sphygmomanometer attached to the forward bulkhead.

Jeff eyed it critically, but was pleased with the reading. Ninety systolic. All right. Probably no serious internal injuries, then. Or, anyway, none that were going to bleed. He turned his attention to the I.V., but found the paramedic already adjusting it in accordance with the changed situation.

"Sorry to come on so strong," Jeff said, not really meaning it but ready to make amends if possible.

The paramedic gave him a lopsided grin. "Nada," he said. "And, hell, you're right. At least about the paramedic thing. We used to have the radio-links and all, but the city's going through this recession thing the hard way, and the budget was cut, and –"

"And you're back on your own," Jeff nodded. "Yeah. I know." He looked away from his wife for a moment and tried to return the man's smile.

"Anyway," he said, "I'd probably have tried to push my way in here even if you had a link working."

He offered his hand. "Jeff Taylor."

"Hank Marhaus," the paramedic's grip was firm and dry. "Nice to meet you, Doctor. I guess we – oh, shit!"

The paramedic was staring at the sphygmomanometer gauge with open consternation, and Jeff could understand why. From ninety systolic, Jolene's blood pressure had begun to drop like a stone. Already it was below 70 and descending. He pressed a finger to her throat and thought for a moment that she had no pulse at all. But it was still there, faint and racing.

"Bleeding," he said. Bleeding big time – chest, maybe. But more likely the abdomen or pelvis. Kill the center section of the MAST."

Marhaus did as he was told without question, and as soon as the area was clear both men could see what had happened.

Jolene's midsection, normally flat, was distended like the top of a microwave popcorn bag, and unyielding to the touch. She was bleeding to death before their eyes! And there was no way for anyone to go in and make any permanent repairs as long as they were in the back of a moving ambulance.

Think, Doctor!

The alternative was to gain control of the thoracic aorta . . .

"Knife!"

Jeff was already tearing at his wife's blouse, ripping it away from her chest as he turned her onto her right side, and the tone in which he spoke the order left no room for argument. Marhaus plunged a hand into his kit and brought out a scalpel. But he hesitated before handing it over.

"Not sterile," he objected. "We don't –"

Jeff seized the instrument and turned back to the gurney.

"Sterile procedure, my ass," he said in a strangled voice. "Just hang on, there! Don't let her move."

Beginning at a point just a few centimeters below Jolene's left breast, Jeff made a deep incision, laying her open from front to back, and dropped the knife.

"Rib spreader," he demanded.

Marhaus shook his head.

"Don't have one."

"Then fuck it . . ."

Bleeding from the chest was not exceptional, and that was as expected. But this wasn't the site. He had to get inside.

Lacking a spreader, Jeff took a deep breath and forced his hands into the intercostal muscle, exerting maximum effort and feeling the muscle rip in half.

Alright!

Upward pressure, now, on the superior ribs, downward on the inferior. Damn it, why did she have to be in such great shape? The ribs had to break, or he wouldn't be able to . . . ah!

"Jesus . . . Christ!" Marhaus breathed, his eyes the size of teacups. "Jeez-us!"

But Jeff was inside the rib cage now, fingers touching the lung, pushing it aside, probing for the heart itself.

Okay. We're still okay, here. Still no significant blood. But where's the . . . ?

Yes!

There it was. Still going a mile a minute, and still faint as a nun's kiss. But beating. Beating.

Showtime.

Jeff brought his knuckles to bear on the thoracic aorta and pushed, with every bit of strength he could muster.

He had closed his eyes to aid concentration while exploring inside Jolene's chest, but he opened them again now, to check the blood pressure.

If this doesn't do it . . .

But it had. Already, Jolene's reading had stabilized at sixty, and now it began to rise again almost as sharply as it had dropped. The distention of the abdomen no longer appeared to be increasing.

"My God," Marhaus said, and then fell silent.

A moment later, the ambulance pulled into the emergency driveway at Northwest Regional.

*   *   *

The Trauma Center doctors didn't know Jeff, and were aghast when they saw that his hands were inside the patient's chest. But Marhaus identified him as a physician, and after a moment they quieted down, listened to his explanation, and agreed that it might be best for him to keep his hands where they were while they dealt more directly with the problem.

Jolene was moved into one of the emergency operating rooms, and the trauma team went to work. Jeff was content to be a silent spectator, moving only when told to do so, and finally removed his cramped fingers from his wife's chest cavity when it was safe.

He felt drained and crushed by mortal fear for Jolene. He also felt . . . exhilarated.

Chapter Twenty-Eight

Three hours later Jolene was out of the operating room and in stable condition. Still not out of danger, still not conscious, and still under observation for injuries as yet undiscovered. But alive. Wonderfully, miraculously, unbelievably alive. And one of the reasons for this, Jeff reminded himself as he stood waiting for permission to enter the room where a specialist team was attaching an imposing array of monitors and I.V. tubes to her body, was that her husband had once been a surgeon.

Once?

Jeff lifted his maimed left hand to the strong morning light now pouring through the windows of the waiting room outside Northwest Regional's Intensive Care Unit and flexed the three fingers that still worked. The other two remained, as ever, cramped inward and inert. But he'd completely forgotten about them, forgotten their uselessness and forgotten the feeling of inadequacy they gave him when it had come to fighting for Jolene's life. And try as he might, he couldn't remember whether or not they had been a hindrance when he'd gone into her chest. Help or hindrance, one thing at least was certain: he'd gotten the job done. With that hand, in that condition. It may not have been as quickly or even as expertly as he might have liked, but Jolene was alive, and this repulsive, frustrating, sixty-percent-instrument of a hand had had one hell of a lot to do with it.

For the first time in more than a year, Jeff found himself looking at his left hand with real interest, evaluating its potential on an objective scale no longer directly connected to the past, or even to himself personally, but to the practice of medicine in general, and surgery in particular. Maybe it was time for a second look. Maybe –

"Dr. Taylor?"

A rasping voice broke into Jeff's reverie and he turned abruptly to see a man he knew he ought to recognize, accompanied by Bill Skelton.

"Harry Kessel," the man re-introduced himself, and Jeff remembered at once. This was the arson detective he and Jolene had met outside the wreckage of the Euthanasia Center. The policeman who wore a fire department badge – the one he'd talked to in what now seemed like another century. Another life.

Kessel's face was streaked with soot now in a way it hadn't been at their earlier encounter and, connecting it with the condition of his voice, Jeff was beginning to wonder if the man might spend his whole life breathing smoke.

"Sorry to hear about your wife," the detective ventured.

It was a social form, one the man probably had to go through several times every day, and Jeff accepted it as such. He nodded, and waited to see why the arson investigator and Bill Skelton had come to see him.

But Kessel's next words seemed more personal than professional. "I . . . turned off your teakettle," he said.

Jeff looked at him.

"We got there, to your house, maybe fifteen minutes after you left in the ambulance," Kessel explained. "We would have gotten there sooner, only whoever called in to make the first report forgot to say it was a bomb – or maybe didn't know it. But the fire department people clued in as soon as they arrived.

Anyway, when I got there, the front door was open and the teakettle was calling."

It made sense, of course. Kessel was part of the investigative team that would be notified of any bombing or suspected bombing. And, of course, he'd left the front door standing wide open.

"I closed the door and made sure it was locked after I left," Kessel continued. He fumbled in his pocket and came up with a familiar-looking set of keys.

"Had to search the house," Kessel said, almost apologetically. "Would of had to, even if it wasn't for the open door and the screaming teakettle. Bombing, see, you can't tell what you're going to find in the neighborhood. Anything, believe me. Anyway, I saw these and figured there was no sense locking you out just because you were in a hurry when you left."

It was a surprisingly thoughtful gesture and Jeff accepted his key ring while trying to think of a proper way to express gratitude. His social upbringing hadn't covered anything remotely like this. But Harry Kessel was still talking.

"We went to the other houses," he said. "Soon as we made the connection at your place."

This time Jeff was completely lost. "What houses?"

"The other doctors," Kessel nodded, as if it were the most obvious thing in the world. "One explosion down at the mercy-killing clinic . . ."

Jeff cringed inwardly at the terminology, noting a slight narrowing of the eyes that indicated a similar reaction on Bill Skelton's part, but neither doctor interrupted.

". . . and another one at your place. Coincidence? Not likely. So of course we went to have a look-see."

"And a damned good thing," Bill Skelton nodded somberly. "There was a bomb hooked to my ignition, just like the one that –"

He stopped suddenly, realizing where the sentence was going, and Kessel took over again.

"One bomb, yeah, at the Skelton place," he agreed. "And another on the car your boss drives."

"Someone tried to kill Dr. Rickoff?" Jeff was surprised to discover that he was still capable of outrage. But the notion of trying to kill Hyman Rickoff seemed somehow grotesque, beyond even the limits of the incredibly strange and violent world into which the events of the past six hours had propelled him. It added a nightmare-like quality to the already ephemeral outlines of the familiar universe, setting him somehow at a distance. Fire and bombs and murder! What had he to do with any of that? His function was to heal – or, at any rate, to preserve human dignity and hold pain at bay. Let the violent bear the violent away.

"But we couldn't find Shel York," Skelton said, bringing Jeff abruptly back to the cold reality of the waiting room.

"Find him?"

"We went there last," Kessel said. "No special reason. It was just the place farthest from the hospital."

Skelton took up the narrative, "We arrived at the same time as the first fire trucks. The house was on fire. Upstairs and down."

"Was he . . . ?"

Skelton shook his head. "No."

"I went inside with a breather," Kessel said, "even before the fire was out. Wanted to have a look. Be sure in my own mind. No. But what I did find was almost worse, in a way."

Jeff waited for him to go on.

"What I found was – nothing. No signs of violence, no evidence of break-in, no bomb in the car and no Dr. Sheldon York."

There was a finality in the words and in his voice that halted conversation for a moment. Then Jeff cleared his throat.

"The fire –" he began.

"– was arson," Kessel said.

"You're sure?"

"Oh, no doubt about that! Gasoline, for God's sake, and a little gag with the gas stove and, I think, the telephone."

The two doctors looked blank, so Kessel filled them in.

"Turn on the stove burners," he said, "but make sure the gas doesn't get lit. Close up the house nice and tight. Go away. Give yourself maybe ten, fifteen minutes and then go make a phone call to the house. The ringing makes a spark, and one hell of an explosion occurs!"

"But the gasoline?"

"Just to be sure, I'd guess. Or because whoever it was that set the fire wanted a really big blaze. Hell, maybe he just likes fires!"

"Lord," Bill Skelton breathed. "Poor Shel!"

But Kessel shook his head.

"I told you, your friend wasn't in there. In fact, I'd probably be looking for an insurance torch or someone like that if it hadn't been for the bombs in the other doctors' cars and the ones in Tulsa and Wichita."

That got both doctors' attention.

"Tulsa?" Jeff asked. "Wichita?"

Kessel nodded, and looked curiously at Skelton. "I guess I didn't get to that yet."

"No, you didn't," Skelton said, inquiringly.

The detective sighed, catching a dim reflection of himself in the waiting room window and wiping ineffectually at his smudged forehead.

"Meant to," he muttered in lieu of apology, "but we've been sort of busy."

The doctors waited for him to go on, and in a moment he was ready to oblige them.

"There wasn't anything left of whatever it was that went off at the hospital last night," he said, "and hardly anything – of what we found, anyway – in what was left of your car."

Jeff winced inwardly at the reminder, but managed to avoid giving any outward sign.

"Anyway, where we got lucky was being quick enough to get to the other doctors before they got up and around this morning."

Skelton nodded readily. "You saved our lives," he agreed. "And, if I didn't say so earlier, thanks."

"Well, yeah. Sure," Kessel said, as though this aspect of the matter were new to him. "But the thing is, we found the bombs themselves. Intact. And that was a big plus."

This was new territory for both doctors. They waited for the detective to go on.

"See, guys who make bombs are like people who make anything," Kessel said. "They find a way to do something that seems to work and they stick to it. At least, until they run out of one kind of material and have to use something else, or someone shows them a better way to do the job."

"Okay," Skelton said. "But you already knew the same guy had rigged all of our cars."

Kessel almost smiled. "Sure we did," he replied. "But what we didn't know until we got a good look at those car bombs was that they, and the bombing at the hospital, were the work of the same nutcase who blew up abortion clinics in Wichita and Tulsa."

Skelton was fascinated. "How'd you make the connection?" he wanted to know.

"The computer," Kessel said. "We've developed a classification system, a kind of a code, like the one the FBI set up for fingerprints. When you have information about a person or an event, you can key in a few details and see if the computer can match it with anything or anyone already in the system."

"So when you found the bombs," Jeff said, following the investigator's logic, "you coded it into the computer –"

"– and out came the bombings at the abortion clinics."

"Nothing else?"

Kessel started to shake his head, but hesitated. "Uh, well, kind of yes and no," he said. "The computer came up with those two positive hits – no doubt about them – but there were some others."

"Others?"

Kessel nodded.

"Ones where the materials were a little different, but the technique was the same. And a couple where the descriptions matched."

That brought both doctors to full attention.

"You've got a description of the bomber?" Skelton asked, fascinated.

Kessel blinked, and then rubbed his eyes. "I could use a little sleep," he declared. "Getting punchy. Can't remember who I've told what. The perpetrator, yeah . . . or, anyhow, a probable. From your boss, Dr. Rickoff. Dumb of me. Thought you'd know. But, of course . . ."

Jeff's features, normally animated a moment earlier, were now drained of all expression. But his voice was hoarse with controlled tension.

"Who?" he demanded.

"Robin Utley," Kessel said. "That was the name Dr. Rickoff said he gave when he –"

"The patient we saw yesterday?"

"Yes."

Jeff accepted the information without further comment, but Bill Skelton remained curious.

"Why him? In particular, I mean."

"How'd we pick him out?"

"Yeah."

"Opportunity."

Suddenly Kessel seemed to feel the weight of the hours he had spent on his feet. He glanced around the waiting area, and Skelton, correctly interpreting the situation, nodded in the direction of a line of lounge chairs facing the outside windows. Kessel sat down and allowed his head to fall back. "Opportunity," he repeated, staring now at the ceiling, "and background."

He glanced at Jeff, who was staring through the glass into the ICU.

"What do you mean by 'background'?" Skelton prompted.

"The file, or lack of it," Kessel said. "The one here at the hospital was destroyed, along with just about everything else in the Euthanasia Center. But it turned out your boss had taken a copy home in his briefcase. So I had one of the guys try to check it out . . ."

"Try?"

"That's all you could call it. Nothing there. I mean, at all. Everything the guy said about himself – adress, phone numbers, medical records from Wichita – was bogus. The guy absolutely couldn't have been intending to come back, because by then you'd have known he was a phony. So –"

"– so," Skelton took up the sentence, "the only other reason he could have had for representing himself as a possible candidate of euthanasia would have been to get inside and plant the bomb."

Kessel nodded. "Right. And nice going, there."

Skelton shook his head. "Maybe not."

Kessel looked askance.

"He could have had other reasons," Jeff said now, while still staring into the ICU as if willing himself on the other side of the window glass.

Skelton and Kessel waited for him to go on.

"Maybe 'Utley' was a reporter," Jeff said.

"A reporter?" Kessel was incredulous.

Skelton nodded. "Could be."

"For a few weeks, now," Jeff took up the explanation again, "a scandal sheet – the kind they sell to idiots in supermarkets – has been running a series of articles about the clinic."

Kessel didn't buy it. "They make up nine-tenths of everything they print," he said, "and everybody knows it. 'Elvis Alive On Mars'!"

But Jeff remained firm. "Much as I'd like to agree with you," he said, "I'll have to admit, and so will Dr. Skelton, that no matter how vicious, biased and generally unfair the stories in *The National Advocate* were, the basic facts were absolutely accurate."

Kessel turned his head and regarded both doctors with renewed interest. "Tell me," he said.

"The stories had long stretches of dialogue – I mean, really long – that were as though the writer had been right there in the room with us."

"Only, of course, he wasn't."

"Of course not," Jeff agreed. "And there were even pictures that just absolutely could not have been faked."

"The guy was there. On the premises," Skelton confirmed.

"Only, neither one of you saw him."

"Right."

Kessel looked thoughtful and took a deep lungful of air, exhaling it slowly through puffed cheeks. "Okay," he said, at length.

"What do you mean by 'okay'? Do you think that Utley might have written those articles?"

"No." The detective pulled himself to his feet with obvious reluctance, and took another deep breath before going on. "Utley wasn't a reporter," he said. "Or, anyway, not the one who wrote those stories for *The Advocate.*"

"Why not?"

"Because you never saw him before he walked into your clinic and said he wanted to die."

Skelton thought this over and decided the detective was probably right. "Hmm . . . you've got a point, there. And Utley was quite the imposing figure. I'm sure we'd remember seeing him if he had been in the hospital before we actually met him as 'Robin Utley.' Hell. Back to square one."

But Kessel didn't see it that way. "Not exactly," he replied. "Not exactly. See, Utley was your bomber. That's the only way it fits. But no one ever told me about any reporter before."

Skelton shrugged. "So?"

"So," Kessel echoed, "we still got a body, the one we found down there in the computer room, that still doesn't have a name. Only now I think I know who might be able to give it one!" He shook his head in mock disgust. "And just when I was thinking about catching a couple of zees," he sighed.

Nonetheless, the idea seemed to give him new life and energy, and a moment or two later the detective was gone, pursuing his new line of thought down the corridor and around the corner in the direction of the elevators, leaving the doctors to their own devices.

Jeff Taylor watched him go in silence, then turned back to stare again at the doors of the ICU. Skelton, for want of better occupation, waited with him.

Their thoughts were elsewhere, however, and, at length, Skelton voiced one of his own.

"I don't give a damn," he declared, "whether the dead guy was the tabloid reporter or someone else. All I want . . . I just want them to find the guy – Robin Utley, or whoever – who put that bomb in your car."

Jeff shook his head. "No," he said.

Skelton turned to look at his friend, certain he'd misheard Jeff's response. But there was no mistake.

"No," Jeff repeated. "I don't want Kessel to find the guy. Not Kessel. And not anyone else."

"But –"

"He's mine," Jeff said. "Personally."

Chapter Twenty-Nine

Bill Skelton realized, of course, that Jeff was still in shock. Seeing Jolene so near death and under such circumstances would have done it to anyone, and he certainly understood the underlying sentiment. If it had been Arlene . . . . But there had been something in Jeff's voice, a quiet determination that did not fit into the profile of temporary rage.

Jeff's declaration of personal vendetta had ended the conversation for the time being, and, a few moments later, he was told he could enter the ICU. Skelton did not follow.

One of the surgeons from the Trauma Center had waited to talk to Jeff, and what he had to say was both private and frightening.

"What you did in the ambulance," he said, wasting no time on preliminaries, "was just exactly right. It saved her life, and if the circumstances were different, I guess I'd suggest you write a little monograph about it. I have to tell you, Doctor, even knowing your background, everyone in the unit was really impressed as hell."

Jeff did not seem to hear. His attention was fixed on his wife's vital signs, on the regularity of her breathing, the quiet pulse visible just below her jaw. And on her continued unconsciousness. He glanced away for a moment to check the EEG monitor. It showed minor beta and delta activity. But no alpha at all.

"Yes," the Trauma Center surgeon said, noting the direction of Jeff's interest. "That's what's worrying us, too."

Jeff looked back at Jolene again, then turned his attention to the other surgeon.

"Her vitals are good," the man was saying. "Better than we could have hoped. She's a fine, strong lady, and she came through the multiple procedures without a bobble."

Jeff moved his head impatiently. "Let's hear it," he said. His gaze was direct and demanding; he was clearly in no mood for amenities.

The trauma specialist took a deep breath, and wished, probably not for the first time, that someone else could handle this part of his work.

"She's in a coma," he said. "Not just unconscious due to shock. Maybe a concussion, who knows?"

"Edema?"

"No. We thought of that, of course."

"But . . ."

"But no evidence of blockage, no elevation in intracranial pressure, no edema, and the head CT is normal –certainly nothing there to drain."

Jeff nodded slowly, digesting the information. He looked again at the EEG monitor, then back at the trauma surgeon. "Prognosis?"

The trauma man shook his head. "Too early –"

But Jeff wasn't having any. "Too early, my ass!"

All the hours of accumulated rage and frustration were concentrated in the gaze he turned on the other man, and he struggled with less than total success to keep his voice even as he spoke.

"You keep your professional compliments for the golf course, and you keep your bedside manner for the paying customers."

The trauma surgeon moved back a step involuntarily, but kept his mouth shut.

"What you give me," Jeff continued, "is the truth. The bottom line. And right now!"

Jeff had not made any threatening gestures, but the other doctor would always have the impression of a man walking the sharpened edge of violence. And in this he was entirely correct.

"We don't know a hell of a lot about long-term coma," the trauma man said. "You know that. One of your own patients . . ."

He was waffling again, skittering away from the hard words. But a fleeting glance at Jeff's face put him back on track.

"The EEG doesn't look good," he said. "We'll have a neurosurgeon – best gourd-cracker on this coast, matter of fact – in here in about an hour to take a look. But he's already seen a printout. And he thinks she's beginning to look like . . . long term."

"Get a second opinion."

The other doctor nodded. "Of course."

He waited for Jeff to say something else, ask another question or make another suggestion. But the silence lengthened into a minute, and the first minute into two, and after awhile he simply went away.

* * *

Two hours later, the RN assigned to Jolene's unit got tired of seeing a man standing up at the bedside of a motionless patient. Getting no response to her repeated suggestions that she might bring a chair into the room for him, she got an orderly to help her move one of the recliners in from the lounge. She placed it behind Jeff, and left the room. Later, when she went in to check her patient, she saw with some satisfaction that he was sitting on the lounge chair. But he remained oblivious to her presence in the room. Keep that up, she thought, and there'll be a hospital bed in your future, too, Doctor. But she had better sense than to say the words aloud.

* * *

Jolene was still unconscious and Jeff was still at her bedside, when Bill Skelton returned to the ICU nearly four hours later. He had brought Hyman Rickoff with him, and the older man wasted neither time nor words.

"Doctor," he said, "we need your help. Now."

For a moment, it seemed that Jeff might not respond. He had aged at least ten years in as many hours, Bill Skelton told himself without much surprise, and there was something almost fragile about the angle of his head and shoulders. But Rickoff was in the doorway to the private room, his stance intentionally impatient and demanding. Jeff responded, slowly looking over his shoulder at the Chief of Service and shaking himself as if from a deep sleep.

"I –"

"The administrator's office has made some new space for us, over in the west wing. The part they were going to start remodeling next week," Rickoff said, still disregarding Jeff's disorientation. "The patients will be moved," he continued, "and Dr. Skelton and I have been going through what's left of our former quarters."

Jeff was on his feet. He scanned his wife's various monitors one last time, kissed his finger and touched it to her lips to avoid disturbing any of the sensors, and followed the other two doctors from the room.

The next few hours were simple drudgery, calculated to short-circuit logical thought, and for that Jeff would always be grateful.

Most of the desks in the Euthanasia Center had been of metal, and their contents were in various states of disrepair. Offices farthest removed from the bomb site and, therefore, farthest from the fire had fared best. In many cases, their papers were largely intact, as were contents of similarly located filing cabinets. But those closer to the center of violence had been less fortunate, and one of these was the space formerly assigned to Hyman Rickoff.

"It might not have been quite so bad," the euthanasia chief speculated, surveying the ruins, "if I hadn't been such a damned show-off."

Jeff understood, and surprised himself by feeling a pang of sympathy. One of the few luxuries Dr. Rickoff had allowed himself in what was otherwise a rather spartan lifestyle had been the furnishings of his office. No hospital-issue, Rickoff's desk had been a glowing cherrywood antique he told them had once been the property of President James Madison, and even the filing cabinets had been specially made for him of matching wood. All gone, now. The fire had been particularly intense in the vicinity of the service chief's office, and Rickoff was careful to avert his eyes from the remains.

"Not even the brass fittings," Bill Skelton commented, shaking his head.

Rickoff did not reply, but led the way down the hall to the office that had been Sheldon York's.

York's office had been a little farther from the blast, and his furniture was of steel. But the damage seemed only marginally less severe. What was left was combed through by a police forensic team, put to the task by Kessel, hoping to find some clue to the missing doctor's whereabouts. Had he been paying rent on another apartment somewhere? A storage space? A cottage? But they had found nothing useful, and York's colleagues were hardly more successful.

Three intact files were found in the back of the lowest drawer of York's one steel filing cabinet. But they pertained to patients already processed by the Euthanasia Center, and had evidently been intended for storage.

"Be in the computer, anyway," Skelton said and then stopped short, remembering. "Oh . . . Jeez!"

Rickoff, however, favored him with a smile that was almost benign. "With files," he said, "I don't think we've got a problem."

That got the other two doctors' attention.

"The time-share," Rickoff prompted. "You know, our mainframe computer's hooked in with the mainframe of the newspaper . . ."

Bill Skelton nodded, but slowly, and Jeff wasn't sure he remembered at all. But Rickoff continued as if they did.

"In order to function," he went on, "each of the time-sharers would need perhaps fifty percent more random access memory than we actually have. But by using each others' excess capacity when one is at peak usage and the other is not, we can get along with what we've got."

Skelton started to object, but Rickoff was ahead of him.

"What we had, before the bombing," he acknowledged, "and will have again."

"But . . . how does that help us now?"

"In order to carry part of their load when necessary, we had to have most of their database in our own permanent memory."

"And they –"

"– have most of ours," Rickoff nodded with the air of a pleased pedagogue. "Right. Already, our workstations are mostly hooked into their mainframe. We lost most of yesterday's input and part of the input from the day before. But the rest is in good shape."

Subtly, without seeming to do so, Rickoff had used the two residents' absorption in his computer dissertation to steer them out of the charred wreckage of the Euthanasia Center and down the hall to the surgical lounge, where coffee was available.

As soon as the doctors had finished triage of their office furniture and equipment, deciding what was immediately usable, what required renovation, and what was due for permanent retirement, hospital orderlies and a special crew hired from an office-moving firm took over the dirty and discouraging work of evacuation and transportation.

Patients from the Euthanasia Center were already in new beds consigned to the new quarters, and most routines would be back in effect by nightfall. In this sense, the bombing had been an incident, not an ending. But in a larger sense, the bombing would always be an emotional watershed for the Center and for the medical staff employed there. They had accepted their assignments with open eyes, in full awareness of the powerful emotions, both positive and negative, evoked by their choice of occupation. No one seemed to be neutral on the subject of euthanasia, and the organized protests outside the doors of the clinic had come as no surprise. Actual violence – and murder – were something else, however.

"My best advice," Dr. Rickoff said when he and the other two doctors had poured coffee into plastic cups and taken their first, tentative sips, "is to go home, get some sleep, and come back here tomorrow, ready for work. I'm sure that none of us had more than a couple of hours sleep last night."

Two pairs of eyes focused on him, waiting to see if he would turn the advice into an order. But no competent executive ever gives an order he thinks might be disobeyed, and Hyman Rickoff was, by no means, a fool.

"On the other hand," he said, swallowing another mouthful of the dark and potent beverage, "I don't recall anyone taking my unprofessional advice about anything. So make your own decisions. And let it be on your own silly heads." He flipped the still half-filled cup into a wastebasket and strode out the door, leaving the two younger men alone.

Skelton watched him go, and felt a strong impulse to follow. The thought of sleep was more than attractive. Doctors learn various strategies for sleepless survival during internship, and usually refine these techniques during their years of residency. But euthanasia, while emotionally and professionally demanding, was a most forgiving specialty in terms of sleep. He wanted to lie down and close his eyes, but one look at Jeff was enough to change his mind.

Jeff was already on his feet, ready to return to the ICU. If he was weary or in pain, the only visible sign was a slight tremor in the fingers of his right hand, and a tightness of the mouth that left no doubt of the violence and ferocity still lurking just beneath the calm exterior.

"You could come to my place," Skelton began. "There's a spare room. Bed all made up. We could –"

"Thanks, no."

Skelton didn't urge the point. Let the man work out his pain and frustration in his own way. But Jeff's unvented rage still troubled him.

"About the . . . bomber . . ." Skelton began.

"Utley."

"Or whatever his real name is. Yeah. The police will handle him. Kessel will. The law. Right?"

"No."

Jeff moved back to the coffee urn, poured himself another cup, and moved toward the door of the lounge.

"Look . . ." Skelton began.

But Jeff wasn't listening.

"I'd value your help," he said with a calm determination that was not to be doubted, "but with it or without it, that son of a bitch is mine!"

Chapter Thirty

At the ICU, Jeff nodded in the general direction of the floor nurse and prepared to re-enter his wife's room, but was intercepted by an old friend.

Donald "Tank" Marshall had been a year ahead of him in medical school, but they had shared a room for two years and chased some of the same women. It had been a pleasant surprise to find him reigning as chief neurosurgical resident at Northwest Regional, and Jeff was glad he would be one of the doctors in charge of Jolene's case.

But now he was blocking the door.

Jeff started to move around him. But the bulk that had earned Marshall his nickname as a college football player simply shifted to a new position where he was still in the way.

"How long have you been on your feet?" Marshall wanted to know.

"Tank, damn it!"

"How long?"

Jeff stepped back and estimated his chances of moving his friend by main force. Maybe with a bulldozer.

"Since early this morning," he replied.

"Bullshit."

Tank Marshall stepped forward, circling Jeff's shoulders with one bear-like arm, and proceeded to the nurse's station, compelling him to turn and walk or be dragged. Jeff walked.

"She's unconscious," Marshall said, "and has been that way since she got here. It's likely that she's going to stay that way, for a little while, anyhow."

"Comas –"

"– are comas. Just that. We understand some things about them, don't understand most, though, like every coma since we started calling them that."

Marshall reached over the counter and picked Jolene's chart from the rack, flipping back its cover and shoving it under Jeff's nose.

Doctor Tilgheman just got done checking her out from top to bottom. He says another thirty-six hours, minimum. That's minimum, bro. Another thirty-six before we'll know anything at all."

"But –"

"– but, hell!" Marshall put the chart back in its place and positioned himself directly in front of Jeff. "If you want to sit in there with her for the next thirty-six hours," he said in a suddenly gentle voice, "I can't stop you, and I'm not going to try. But it's not going to do a thing for your wife. And it'll make you a walking dead man when she may need you the most."

He waited for the words to sink in, and then went on. "You were always a stubborn mother," he said, "and I don't see any signs of change. But if you want to be some real help to the lady you're smart enough to know what you've got to do for her. And for yourself."

* * *

In the parking lot with Skelton ten minutes later, Jeff fumbled automatically for the keys to his own car, and then remembered what the car had looked like the last time he'd seen it.

He turned to Bill Skelton. "Bum a ride with you?" he asked.

Skelton was almost offended. "No way," he said, turning to lead the way to his own car. "I thought I'd just let you find your way home on the bus."

* * *

The ride back to Jeff's house took twice as long as the ambulance trip in the opposite direction, but the two doctors passed most of the time in silence, each occupied with his own thoughts.

Skelton's were largely icons of concern for his friend. There was nothing either of them could do for Jolene now. Jeff's improvised surgical intervention in the ambulance had saved her life. What happened from now on was in the hands of the Almighty and the neurosurgeons, not necessarily in that order. But Jeff was tearing himself apart, Skelton thought. If Kessel, with the entire resources of the police and fire departments behind him, was unable to find and deal with the maniac responsible for the bombings, what possible chance would there be for a couple of doctors? He included himself in the equation because, as the situation had developed, he could not imagine abandoning Jeff to his own devices until the crisis was resolved, one way or another. If nothing else, Jeff was going to need someone to keep him from going off the deep end when he finally had to face the fact that he wasn't going to be dealing with the bomber on any kind of personal basis.

"If you're thinking about playing nursemaid," Jeff said, somehow knowing exactly what his friend was thinking, "just forget it!"

His tone was neutral, and Skelton glanced away from the road long enough to try and read his expression. But it told him nothing.

"Nursemaid, no," Skelton responded, maneuvering through freeway traffic to the off ramp. "Friend, yes."

Jeff nodded. "Okay."

But the conversation wasn't really ended, and Jeff picked it up again as soon as they were moving at a slower pace through the network of city streets.

"I know you think I've been seeing too many Arnold Schwarzenegger movies," he said, "and if I was looking at it from your angle, I'd probably think the same thing."

Skelton had no argument with that and continued to drive the car in silence.

"Also, I'm aware that I'm in shock, with a lot of adrenaline running through my system," Jeff went on. "But with all that, I know one other thing, too. If I don't find the guy myself and kill him, I don't think I'll be able to go on living with Jolene.

"Jeff, you've lost it, buddy."

"Hear me out, Bill, please." Jeff's tone was quiet and measured, rather than pleading, and it silenced whatever

Skelton had been about to say. "I've found out a lot of things about myself in the past few hours, and one of them is that casting myself in the role of a civilized man, let alone a healer, may be the century's most gruesome case of mistaken identity."

"You're a doctor. Doctors are healers. You –"

"I kill people! Day in, day out. It's what I do."

"Legally. Painlessly. In order to spare them –"

"I kill people," Jeff interrupted. "Right! And now I'm going to kill one more person."

"You're –"

"I'm going to make sure that that crazy son of a bitch who's already killed at least one person we know about, and tried to kill several others, doesn't kill anyone else. No more. No less."

"But it's got to be you."

"Me."

Skelton forced himself to keep his eyes on the road, while inflating his lungs with the moral imperative of telling his friend he would like to talk to him again when he became more rational. But it was no use, and he knew it. Maybe from another angle.

"Okay, then," he said, pretending for the moment to concede Jeff's moral right to execute another human being without trial. "Okay, so you'd be doing society a favor. But if they catch you at it, baby, I surely do hope you understand that they will probably not elect you to national office."

Jeff favored him with the pale specter of a grin. "They would hang me by the balls."

Skelton shrugged. "Long as you know . . ."

Another silence grew between them and lasted until Skelton finally turned into Jeff's street, pulled over to the curb and parked in front of his house.

The wreckage of the car had already been removed, probably by the police crime lab crew, Skelton speculated, but the scorched grass and concrete were ghastly reminders of the tragedy that would otherwise seem unreal.

Jeff stared at the evidence for a long moment, then averted his eyes. He made no move to get out of the car, though, and Skelton was content for the moment to have him remain where he was. He had one more arrow poised in his bow, and this seemed as good a time as any to let it go.

"So, tell me then," he said, forcing himself to relax against the seat cushions, "just exactly what you intend to do. How do you think you are going to go about all this?"

Jeff attention was still focused on the effort of not looking at the spot where his car had exploded.

"All this?" he said finally.

"All this," Skelton nodded. "The detective work. Making positive identification of the bomber, tracking him down, and then putting yourself into a position to do unto him before he gets a chance to do unto you."

To this, Jeff did not reply, and Skelton experienced a heady, if momentary, sense of relief. Reality was beginning to intrude.

"Jeff," he said, pursuing the apparent opening, "face it. As detectives, you and I are pretty damned good doctors. In our own field, we're the authorities. And in euthanasia, we are going to be the very first people ever board-qualified in a brand new specialty. So, hooray for us, and to hell with anyone who doesn't like it."

Jeff turned to look at him, but his expression said nothing and he remained silent.

"But pro is pro, and amateur is amateur," Skelton continued, "so the first thing we've got to admit is that in the business of criminal catching, we are the amateurs and guys like Kessel are the professionals. It's their bag, not ours. Okay?"

Still unresponsive, Jeff looked steadily at his friend. Skelton shifted in his seat, unsure as to whether he was getting through or merely wasting his words, and decided he could lose nothing by continuing his lecture.

"You can slice it any way you want to and you can hype yourself with all the great television detective stories you want, where the priest or the private eye or the police commissioner's wife or some other amateur catches the bad guys while the poor dumb cop is still fumbling around trying to find his notebook. But it's nonsense, Jeff, just as it would be if Kessel were to come into the hospital and correct a diagnosis or assist in a heart transplant."

Jeff heard him out without interrupting, and when Skelton was finally out of words he still didn't speak. Yet there was a sense of acceptance, of weary yielding in the posture of his shoulders as he turned to let himself out of the car, and Skelton followed him into the house with a growing sense of encouragement. At least he was listening. Acceptance, he told himself, was probably just a step away.

But that was before they heard the telephone tape.

*   *   *

They almost missed it.

Skelton's thought, once Jeff had checked the house over and performed whatever minor housekeeping chores needed doing, was to bring him along to his own home, at least long enough to sleep. And he was on the point of suggesting this when he heard the man's recorded voice, coming from the bedroom where the Taylor's telephone answering machine was kept.

". . . don't know me," said the man, sounding utterly persuasive, "but my name is Charles Pennington. I got your home address and telephone number from a list that was made up by the man who put a bomb in your car."

Skelton's eyes widened and he started to speak, but Jeff held up one hand to restrain him while he pressed a button with the other, causing the machine to save, rather than erase, the message after it had played through.

"I tell you this," the caller continued, "and I ask you not to pass it on to the police, because I need your help and I think you need mine. For both of us, it's a matter of life and death . . ."

* * *

Detective Harry Kessel was also thinking about matters of life and death. Nurse Gertrude W. Nordstrum had been alive earlier that morning and now she was dead. Just . . . gone. Like that.

Kessel leaned back in his chair, his eyes half-focused on the stack of cassette tapes sitting desk amidst the papers, file folders and other office paraphrenalia. A lap-top computer, still in its case, leaned against the wall beside the office door. There was almost no point in checking out the files saved on the hard drive. He knew what he'd find. And he knew what he'd hear if he listened to the tapes.

He shook his head. What a tragedy. And he may not have been alerted to it, especially so soon after it had happened, if the emergency crew that had dealt with the remains of Nordstrum's car hadn't found her purse, and his card in it, crushed and pulverized amongst the wreckage.

He had just left the doctors at the hospital when he got the call from his office, and shortly after obtaining Nordstrum's purse, he went to her apartment in the hope of finding an address book or some personal letters which might bear in them the names of family members. He somehow felt that it was his responsibility to notify them. Not that he felt responsible for her death in any way, but because he was probably the last person to see her alive. And he had given her cause to be upset. Or greater cause, anyway, as he had quickly discovered.

David Wallace Teeples, the *National Advocate* reporter who had written the scandalous articles about the Euthanasia Center, had been living with Nordstrum. His things were all over the place, and, since no effort had been made to conceal the tapes or the computer, Nordstrum was well aware of who he was and what he was doing.

Still, Kessel felt sorry for the woman and had mixed feelings of pity and indignation. She had been used – at first, anyway. That much was clear. Teeples obviously used her so that he could infiltrate the hospital, and she let him, even after she knew of his doings. Surely she hadn't known what he was up to from the start. But she had been roped in. It was pathetic, really. She must have been a very lonely woman, Kessel thought. And now she was dead.

So was Teeples. Kessel had suspected, from the moment the doctors had told him about the articles in the *National Advocate*, that the body found in the rubble of the computer room at the hospital was that of the reporter. When he had returned from Nordstrum's apartment, he made a call to the *Advocate's* editor. Teeples had told his editor that he was on to another "doozie" and that he'd be by before noon that day. When Teeples didn't show up, the editor began to panic. The paper was soon going to press, and Teeples' stuff was definitely going on the front page. It wasn't like Teeples to do that. He did have some loyalties.

Kessel got up and poured himself another cup of coffee before picking up the phone to call Rickoff. He wondered just how much more bad news the man could take and then smiled at the grotesque irony in those words. Bad news. The good news was that the bad news wouldn't be forthcoming in the *National Advocate.*

Chapter Thirty-One

Winter had come to the beachfront, but the house was heavily insulated and equipped with an automatic forced-air heating system. It was a year-round dwelling only superficially similar to the scattered summer-only beach cottages, with which it shared a pallid and windy seascape just a little too far outside the city for daily commuting. Its owners were in Europe, treating themselves in retirement to the trip for which there had never been enough time during their working lives, secure in the knowledge that their stateside home was cared for by a professional house-sitter. He was a former security guard, no less, whom they had contacted through a newspaper advertisement.

The name he had given them and the references he offered were equally bogus. But his expressions of admiration for the vacationers' property were entirely sincere. Micah Chaine loved the house at least as much as its errant owners, though for very different reasons; it was secluded, equipped and under the scrutiny of no one. A perfect, private prison.

A number of hours had passed since York had lost consciousness. Chaine had kept himself busy by, first, taping Julia to another of the kitchen chairs, and then by watching television in the hope of catching some news about the successful detonation of his car bombs. He was elated when he'd learned that at least one bomb had gone off, and that one person had been critically injured, even though the victim's name could not be mentioned until family members had been notified.

Julia had been staring wide-eyed, at the television screen. The camera crew had arrived before the police could remove the wreckage of the car, and, while they hadn't been able to get footage of the victim, they had focused on the pool of blood that marked the spot where the body had lain. It was then that Julia had begun to scream.

"Go ahead," Chaine had said to her, as she drew breath for yet another throat-bursting effort. "Go to it, little sister! Scream as much as you want, as loud as you want, for as long as you want! No one to hear you but old Father Micah, and he won't mind, seeing we're alone here."

Chaine had removed the shotgun and tape from her neck after she had been securely taped and strapped into the kitchen chair. She and York sat facing each other in the beach-view living room and Julia's screaming had finally roused York out of his unconscious state.

Chaine had then noticed York stirring. "Welcome back, Doctor," he said, reaching into his suitcase. "You missed some interesting television news. That's okay, though. We can always create a little of our own."

Julia had closed her eyes, and then clenched them tight, when Chaine produced a pair of pliers and strolled across the room toward Sheldon York.

But York had surprised both Chaine and himself by emitting only the softest and most restrained of grunts when the pliers closed on the bridge of his nose, and Chaine, who had hoped by that means to compel the doctor to open his mouth, was forced to exert pressure on York's jaw muscles at the same time in order to accomplish his purpose. And even when the makeshift dentist's blocks were in place and the pliers had begun their work on York's teeth, it was Julia's screams which, once again, had filled the room.

Chaine had nodded appreciatively. "That's the way!" he said. "Way to please the Lord, sister!"

York had continued to resist. For awhile. The blocks inserted between his jaws had prevented him from closing his mouth against the vandalism of the pliers. But his head was free to turn and move, and Chaine had been visibly annoyed when it proved necessary to bend York's head so far backward as to be in danger of breaking his neck before he could obtain the necessary leverage.

"You can make the pain stop any time, you know," Chaine said, pausing for a moment before going to work in earnest. "All you have to do to save the body from agony and the soul from hell is to call upon Our Savior to forgive you. Just that." He offered York a gentle smile. "Is that really so much to ask?"

The euthanasist had closed his eyes and concentrated the whole force of his will on resisting the urge to capitulate. With all his heart, he wanted to give in. To say anything, to do anything, to avoid the pain.

"Go to hell," he said.

Chaine sighed deeply, and moved the pliers again in the direction of the euthanasist's mouth. "It's you who is going to hell."

This time, York screamed.

* * *

Shortly before sunset, Chaine called a temporary halt.

"Don't go 'way, now," he said amicably, putting down his tools on the coffee table. "I won't be long. Just time enough to make up a little coffee and maybe a sandwich for the lady and me."

He spared a glance for York, who hung motionless, now, in the bindings that attached him to his chair.

"I'd offer you a little hospitality, too," he said in a burlesque of solicitude. "But, the way I see it right now, that would be just plain wasteful. I'm sure you understand, don't you, Doctor?"

He grasped York's hair and raised his mutilated head, squinting into the physician's face with real concern until he was sure the man was still breathing, and then allowed the chin to fall against the chest once more.

Chaine turned his attention to Julia.

She was conscious, sitting bolt-upright in her chair. But she no longer seemed aware of his presence, and he felt an obscure irritation, a sense almost of personal betrayal. He had done his best for her. All through the day, he had spared no effort to see that she remained physically comfortable, able to see and to remember all that occurred. Able to deliver a faithful account to Pennington, to assure that prime idiot's continued silence and future compliance with any orders that he, Chaine, might care to give.

Northwest Regional would not be his last operation. Beyond the immediate horizon, a whole world stretched before him, rich with promise for a man of determination and a tame millionaire on the string.

Julia, however, was not cooperating.

She stopped screaming over an hour earlier, ceasing suddenly and at peak volume. No dwindling. No gradual weakening of the voice. She had simply quit.

At first, he had thought it might be a sudden, stress-induced upwelling of logic and self control. Screaming was ineffective; it obviously gave him pleasure, so she had simply decided to give her lungs a rest. That made sense, and Chaine had not yet entirely rejected the idea. But the passage of time had given rise to doubt.

Julia's eyes were open and she had not averted them from the scene before her. But she seemed oblivious to her surroundings, and he noted, tardily, that saliva was seeping from the corners of her mouth. Her chin was covered and glistening with drool, and she offered no reaction when he picked up a paper towel and moved to wipe it away.

Chaine grunted. "Want to play possum, do we?"

The kitchen chair he had been using was beside the one occupied by Sheldon York. He drew it close to Julia's and reached out to wipe her chin again.

"Want to drool for Father Micah? Okay. Suits me." He finished dabbing, set the towel aside, and smiled at her. "You know, little sister," he said, "the one thing I always noticed about you was that little strain of prudery that seemed to be worked into you, even though you were sleeping with Charlie-boy."

Julia did not respond, but Chaine went on talking to her as though it were a two-way exchange.

"Always the little lady," he nodded ruminatively. "And always just the littlest bit nervous about being around me. " He touched her face again, but Julia did not move. "So, what I think," he continued, moving his hand to stroke the motionless cheek, "is that I just might get a little bit of a rise out of you if I was to do something like this . . ."

Julia's lower legs were secured to the legs of the chair. She was wearing no hose, and the full skirt offered only momentary resistance when Chaine lifted the hem and placed his hand on her knee.

"Let's see," he said, "how far you want to let me go."

Unhurriedly, barely in contact with the skin, Chaine moved his hand along Julia's inner thigh until his fingers rested against the barrier of her panties. He let them rest there for a moment, and then intruded a finger under the elastic.

"That all right?" he inquired. "You like that? Want me to go on?"

Julia sat like a statue, unmoving except for the regular rhythm of respiration.

"Good," Chaine said, "that's very good, indeed. All right, then. Let's get down to business."

With some difficulty, drawing the crotch of the panties aside, Chaine moved his finger to her labia and there halted. The entrance to Julia's body was closed – not clenched against him, but totally arid. He withdrew his hand and replaced the skirt.

"Hell and damnation," he said, drawing a deep breath through clenched teeth while shaking his head. "Nobody, nobody anywhere, has got that kind of control." Chaine leaned back in his chair, surveying the motionless woman with disgust. He stood up, moving his chair back to a neutral position between the two prisoners.

"Now what in the blue-eyed world," he demanded, "am I going to do with a thing like that?"

* * *

Chaine was still mentally wrestling with the problem half an hour later, when he pulled his car up to a telephone booth at a service station about a mile from the beach cottage. But he was nearly five minutes early, and he used the time to move all uncertainties to the background of his mind before making contact with Pennington, who answered, and began talking, on the first ring.

"I've got the money," he said. "All of it, right here. Is Julia all right?"

Chaine leaned the weight of his body against the side of the booth.

"Julia's fine," he said. "But she's anxious to get back to you, of course. I hope you've got a pencil or something right there in your hand because I don't want to say any of this more than once."

Pennington asked him to wait a moment, but Chaine paid no attention. All things considered, he couldn't imagine Pennington being dumb enough – or brave enough, for that matter – to bring the police into their relationship. But it never paid to take chances. Unless police procedures and telephone equipment had changed a lot in the last year or so, he knew it would take them a minimum of three minutes to run any kind of trace. Two minutes, therefore, was the maximum length for any telephone contact, and there could be no more than two consecutive calls from the same part of town.

"First, make sure that all of the money fits neatly into one suitcase. Got it?"

There was a pause. Chaine waited for Pennington to answer. Was someone listening on the line? The police? Signalling answers or writing them out for him?

"Uh . . . yes. All right."

"All right what?"

"The money. Yes, it will all go into one suitcase. Yes!"

"Uh-huh."

Chaine listened critically to Pennington's responses, thought things over, and decided there was no cause for alarm. The little wimp was just frightened and jittery. As usual.

"Then put it in there," he said, "carry it out to your car and put it in the trunk. Drive south down the Coast Highway, *not* the Interstate, to a little town called Moon Harbor. You think you can find that?"

"I . . . yes. Moon Harbor. I'll get a map."

"You do that, my son."

Chaine paused again, checked his watch and glanced up and down the roadway. But traffic was minimal, and there were no suspicious looking pedestrians, slow-moving cars or hovering helicopters.

"So, then, in Moon Harbor, down on the water, there's a little joint called Captain Jack's."

"Captain . . . ?"

"Captain Jack's You can't miss it. Or if you're blind, just ask someone. Everybody knows the place. It's the only restaurant in town."

"Captain Jack's."

"Captain Jack's. You be there at eight o'clock sharp. Park a block away. Leave the suitcase with the money in the trunk, and walk back to the bar with the keys in your hand."

Pennington did not reply at once, and Chaine sighed audibly, telling himself it was all the woman's fault. If she hadn't come unglued, or whatever her problem was, he wouldn't be having to get so cute about the exchange. But this way would work all right. No problem . . .

"I want to talk to Julia," Pennington said.

Chaine smiled. He had expected something like this. Even hoped for it, in order to give Pennington a little extra incentive.

"Sorry," he said. "Like to oblige you, but I can't."

"Unless you –" Pennington began. But Chaine cut him off before he could frame whatever threat he had intended. The wristwatch showed twenty seconds to go.

"Charlie-boy," he said, "you'll do exactly what I tell you,

when I tell you to do it, because you've got no choice. I told you Julia's all right, and she is perfectly safe in a nice, quiet place where no one's ever going to find her, if you don't do just exactly as I say. Do you understand that?"

"I . . ."

"Good! Once more, then. Moon Harbor. Captain Jack's. Eight o'clock."

Chaine hung up the phone with two seconds to spare.

Chapter Thirty-Two

Parked across the highway from the bar, at the top of an abandoned driveway where he could observe traffic in both directions without being seen, Chaine had spent the past half hour waiting patiently for any indication of police presence in the vicinity. But there was none.

It was a Tuesday night and business was slow at Captain Jack's, limited thus far to a few commercial fishermen and a pair of women who looked as though they might be part of the establishment's atmosphere. No threat.

He allowed himself to relax, paying only peripheral attention when one of the fishermen stumbled out of the bar, stood for awhile looking thoughtfully at the door that had just closed behind him, and then trudged away down the beach road.

Checking his watch from time to time, Chaine remained in his slumped posture until a minute or two before the hour. He finally straightened his shoulders just as a car he recognized as Pennington's rented sedan eased slowly past the shabby entrance to the restaurant and then moved on to park on the shoulder of the highway, about five hundred yards south of the parking lot.

Okay. So far, so good.

Chaine sat perfectly still, his whole attention concentrated on the scene below, as Pennington set the parking brake, turned off the head lights, got out of the car and closed the door behind him. He paused to check the lock and then cast a nervous over-the-shoulder glance at the trunk before setting off toward the bar.

That look told Chaine all he needed to know, and he permitted himself a small inward sigh. The money was there, as ordered. The rest was simply a matter of mechanics.

He started the car's engine and smiled at the woman sitting stiffly upright in the passenger seat beside him.

"There's your boyfriend," he said, putting the car in gear and steering it down the hill toward the highway. "Good ol' Charlie-boy. He'll be back here to get you soon. Be sure you tell him, now, what a good time I showed you. Hear me, sister?"

Chaine laughed uproariously as if he had come to the punch line of some joke. But Julia Hartt, silent and immobile, sat staring fixedly into the distance as the car waddled down the hill and onto the highway.

$$* \quad * \quad *$$

Inside Captain Jack's the lights were dim and customers few. No one seemed to be in charge of greeting and seating prospective diners, so Pennington stood for a moment just inside the door, allowing his eyes to become accustomed to the meager light level. The dining room seemed to be vacant except for two couples seated at widely separated tables, both at the window overlooking the beach. The only visible drinker at the bar was a man wearing a fisherman's yellow slicker, who sat slouched on a corner stool, hands cupped protectively around a mug of beer. Pennington noted that there was something odd about the way the man was holding his drink; two of the fingers on the left hand didn't seem to fit properly around the glass, but were somehow cramped against the palm. Occupational injury, perhaps.

But, where was . . . ?

"Hey, there!"

A hand clamped on his shoulder, fingers biting hard into the muscles.

"Good to see you. Right on time," Micah Chaine declared, smiling with his teeth. "'Preciate it! So, now, what do you say we find us a table?"

Pennington started to protest, but Chaine had already taken the first step into the bar, leading them both to a corner table. There was no cocktail waitress, but the bartender ambled over to take their order, and they sat in silence while he brought the two scotch and waters that Chaine ordered, collected the bill and ambled back to his station beside the cash register. The solitary beer drinker seemed oblivious.

Chaine downed his drink in a single swallow and grinned again at Pennington.

"You've got the money," he said, making it a statement rather than a question.

Pennington started to reply, but couldn't think of anything to say.

"And you left it in the trunk of your car, as we agreed?"

"I did . . . yes. In the trunk."

"And now you've got the keys . . ."

Pennington's Adam's apple bobbed, as though he were about to speak, but instead he merely goggled uncomprehendingly at the ex-priest.

"The keys," Chaine prompted, "give them to me."

"What?"

"The keys to your car," Chaine repeated. "I want them." He held out his hand.

"But . . ."

Chaine decided to be patient. He could afford that much. "What's going to happen, here," he explained, "is that we're going to do some trading. Dig it?"

Pennington could not. So he went on.

"You're going to give me your car keys," he said in the tone of a man addressing a backward child, "and then I'm going to give you mine."

Pennington's brow furrowed. "But you –"

Chaine took a deep breath. "Charlie-boy," he said. "Listen closely, and try to follow what I'm saying. You parked your car down the highway from here, is that right?"

"Uh . . . yes."

"And you've got the money, all of it, in a suitcase that's locked up, now, in the car's trunk."

Pennington nodded.

"Then – follow me through, here – what we need to do, you and I, is to trade car keys," Chaine, continued, "because my car is parked out there, too. On the other side of the road, pointing in the other direction."

Pennington brightened, as he began to understand. "And Julia?"

"Is there. In my car. Waiting for you."

Pennington's hand went into the pocket of his coat and came out with a pair of keys on a rental company's ring. But he hesitated before handing them over to Chaine.

"The trunk," he said, concern suddenly visible again between his brows. "You haven't . . . I mean, you didn't . . . put Julia . . . in the . . . ?"

Chaine laughed, but silently.

"No," he said. "I didn't put her in the trunk."

"She's –"

"– sitting right there," Chaine nodded, "in the front seat. Waiting for you to come drive her away."

Pennington considered this for a moment and seemed about to raise some other objection. But Chaine silenced it by opening his fist and offering him the set of car keys that had been concealed there.

With only a moment's hesitation, Pennington put his own keys on the table.

Chaine picked them up and placed his set in Pennington's open hand. "A fair trade is not robbery, according to all the law books," he declared.

Pennington looked at the keys, and then seemed to think of something else.

"How do I know she's really there?" he demanded.

Chaine favored him with an odd smile. "Good question," he admitted. "And, come to think of it, how do I know that the money's really out there in the trunk of your car?"

Pennington thought about that.

"Well," he ventured, "I guess you don't. I guess neither of us knows . . . really."

But that wasn't the answer Chaine wanted to hear.

"Horse shit Charlie-boy," he said, the teeth bared again, but the rest of the face not smiling. "Horse shit!"

Chaine's hand snaked out and grasped Pennington by the collar of his coat, pulling the younger man's head sideways and down almost to the table top.

"You can trust me that little sister's out there, waiting for you," he said, bringing his own face down to a point less than an inch from Pennington's, "because I never lie. Never! I always do just exactly what I say I will." He eased his hold, but Pennington did not try to move. "And I can trust you," he said, "for the same reason."

Chaine released Pennington, and sat back to let him think about the seriousness of his words.

"You brought the money," he said after a moment, in a more reasonable tone, "because you knew I would surely as God's vengeance kill your woman if you didn't."

Pennington slowly lifted himself to an upright position, never taking his eyes off Chaine. He was beginning to get the idea, Chaine thought. He could see it in his face and see him beginning to pick up on the implications.

"And because you can see that," Chaine went on, "you can see, too, exactly why you are never going to open your silly mouth to the police, to your family, to your head-shrinker, or to anybody, ever. You don't talk about me or anything we've ever done together. Or anything you might think that I'm doing, from now on."

He looked directly at Pennington and, no longer smiling, made sure that his one-time friend and co-conspirator saw and comprehended the bleakness that had always lived behind the face he showed to the world.

"Your woman," he said quietly, "and then your father. And then your mother. And after them your two sisters, and your brother. And their families. And then, when they're all attended to, but not a moment before, you."

Pennington's emotions were plain in his face. He was no longer making any effort to conceal them. He was afraid, in a deep and terrible way that few human beings ever experience.

"I've saved you for last," Chaine explained, "to make sure that you knew what happened to all the others. And why. Call it a little foretaste of damnation right here on earth!"

And then the smile was back.

"But, say now," he said, standing up suddenly and dropping a dollar tip on the table, "this is no time to be talking about bad things! No reason for us to sit around here thinking about death. You've got better things to do! Right? Sure you do! And I'm late for evening prayer!"

Chaine picked up Pennington's untouched drink, downed it, and strode across the room in the direction of the door, not looking back.

*   *   *

Outside, the air seemed cooler than he remembered, but he attributed that to the rage that had filled him, suddenly, and without warning, during the final exchange with Pennington.

It worried him. A little.

One of his chief weapons in dealing with the world had always been an ability to control and suppress his own emotions while arousing them in others. Selected emotions like fear or anger, even those leading to friendship on those few occasions when it would serve him best. But something had changed. Something that had happened in the last few hours had opened a door – perhaps unlocked a cage – somewhere deep inside Micah Chaine, and he was honest enough with himself to be able to identify the event and evaluate its probable consequences.

Sheldon York had provided the key.

The death he had given Sheldon York was different, different in quality and different in meaning, from any previous event in his life. It had changed him. Made him . . . larger. In the beginning, it had all been for Julia's benefit. To give her something to remember. Something to tell Charlie-boy to make sure he kept his mouth shut and remained properly obedient and available when and if Father Micah Chaine should ever need his help, or his money, in the future.

But along the way something else had taken over, and before he was aware of the change, it had taken him farther inside himself – and outside, as well – than he had ever expected to go. Too far, entirely, for Julia. It might be a long time before she was in any shape to tell her lover anything about the events she had witnessed. And in that respect, the whole operation had to be considered a failure.

And too far, perhaps, for Micah Chaine, as well.

He stumbled on the unevenness of the highway shoulder en route to Pennington's car, but caught himself and continued without breaking the cadence of his thoughts.

Something about the sounds of Sheldon York's agony, something about his total loss of dignity, had brought down a wall that must have been building up inside him since he was a child. The thrill of success and discovery he had felt during the final moments of Sheldon York's life were a phenomenon entirely different from any experience he had ever had in his life.

To deal death was nothing, really.

Any animal could do that. Any back-alley thug. But to clothe the terminal experience in such mortal pain as to save the soul, to bring such a dedicated and heedless sinner as York to full repentance, opening to him the gates of larger life and winning for him, at a single stroke, the eternal victory, was to share a moment of common perspective with the Savior Himself!

This was what the Son of God had felt, when he cleansed the lepers. When he cured the sightless. When he raised the dead! No wonder Satan had been unable to tempt Him, there in the wilderness. What had the devil to offer that could compare?

Murder. Yes, he had committed murder. Broken the

commandment. Taken the sin of York and the others upon himself. But unlike all the other times he had taken life, this time he would not confess his act as a sin. Or repent it. Or accept absolution. He had not sinned. He had acted as he did not merely to prevent the sin of another, but in fact to bring that sinner to the very throne of the Almighty.

In agony and in extremis, Sheldon York, murderer, transgressor, non-believer, had shrieked out his repentance and his acceptance of Christ as Savior, just as Chaine had told him to do. He had even repeated it, as well as he could considering the condition of his mouth, to be sure he was believed. Then the relief. The ecstasy of a human being cleansed of all transgression! It had changed the world, opened a universe of understanding to Father Micah Chaine, giving him a glimpse of glory that would be a major factor in all of his future plans.

Had anyone else ever experienced such an insight? Was this what the mercy-killers felt when they sent one of their patients? Was this what it was all about?

Chaine shook his head, intrigued by the thought and wishing, obscurely, that he could have had a few more words with Sheldon York. Perhaps next time . . .

He had reached the parked car, and he glanced up and down the highway before entering it. Down the road in the direction from which he had come, far past the entrance to Captain Jack's and almost lost in the night, he could see the car where he had left Julia. Pennington had evidently reached it. The lights were on, and now they were moving. But Chaine did not bother to watch their progress.

If he, himself, had been in Pennington's position and at the wheel of that car, by now he would have turned the vehicle around and raced down the highway hoping to knock him, Chaine, off the face of the world. But he was here. And Pennington was there. And he was in no danger.

Casually, feeling a partial relaxation of the tensions that had ridden him for the past forty-eight hours, Chaine moved around the car to the driver's side, hesitating momentarily at the trunk-lid, but resisting the urge to open it and inspect the contents of the suitcase.

Another man might have tried to short-change him, even left him staring at a suitcase full of newspaper. But not Charlie-boy. He was such a fool.

Dismissing the thought, and ready at last to think about plans for the future, Chaine unlocked the car and slid into the driver's seat, automatically closing and locking the door as he fumbled for the key that would fit the ignition.

His first intimation that he was not alone in the vehicle came when he felt the sting of the needle at the base of his neck. But he did not remain conscious long enough to feel surprised.

Chapter Thirty-Three

Consciousness returned slowly, and, at first, he could not be sure he was alive. Brilliance filled the world, drowning all colors and confusing all shapes. He thought, fleetingly, of the near-death experiences he had read about in supermarket tabloids and heard recounted on television talk shows. But it didn't fit. For one thing, he could feel himself breathing. And for another, he could blot out the brightness, at least to a degree, by shutting his eyes, and he'd never thought of the disembodied dead as having eyelids.

"Hello, there! With us again, I see . . ."

A human head entered his field of vision, upside down at the extreme upper limit, and spoke to him.

He tried to move his own head, and was gratified to discover that he could do so, although with difficulty. His skull felt oddly swollen, almost disconnected from the rest of his body, and an attempt to move his arm, to raise himself on an elbow so as to have a right-side-up view, failed entirely. The arm seemed to be attached to something. Or perhaps it was paralyzed. He couldn't be sure.

Nonplussed, and still not convinced that he was awake, Chaine relaxed and tried to decide whether he recognized the head that had spoken to him. But it had disappeared, and for a moment or two his eyes lost focus and began to close.

"No," another voice said. "Oh, no. No more sleeping for you, my friend."

A different face now entered his field of vision from the side and this time he was sure he recognized it. This was a doctor . . . Taylor . . . Jeff Taylor. Right! From the Euthanasia Center. The doctor he'd spoken to during his visit to the clinic as "Robin Utley." The doctor for whom his car bomb had been intented.

An alarm bell went off in the back of Chaine's brain. But he quickly dismissed it. Doctors weren't dangerous, he told himself. Far more worrisome was the fact that he still didn't know where he was or how he'd gotten there. In the absence of any better explanation, however, he was more and more inclined to dismiss the whole business as a dream. Not even a nightmare. Just a dream. A nightmare would at least be frightening, and he was not afraid. On the contrary, he was merely interested, which meant there was a better-than-even chance he would remember all of this when he woke up . . .

"Fading out on us again."

No source for the voice this time. No heads anywhere in sight. But a hand reached in from somewhere and tapped his cheek a time or two before fastening itself to the end of his nose and giving it a remarkably painful tweak.

"Stay with us!"

It was an order, not a suggestion, and the hand emphasized it with a second tweak.

Chaine began to lose faith in his dream theory. Dreams could be frightening at times, or even grotesque, with hideously deformed creatures pursuing him through lunatic landscapes. But never yet had he had a dream that was physically painful.

"Stop!" someone said.

No reply.

"Stop that!"

The voice was harsh and cracked and flavored with an undertone of fear. He could hardly believe it was his own. But the after-vibration of speech was there in his throat, and he found that he had to clamp his jaws against the urge to repeat the stupid words yet again. What was going on here? Chaine moved his head again and blinked his eyes rapidly in an effort to see beyond the brilliance.

"Doing better," the familiar doctor-voice said from a location close at hand but invisible to him. "Keep him interested while I get a spike into the vein."

Suddenly the first head, the one he didn't recognize, was back. But right-side-up this time, and nearer the bottom of his visual circle.

"My name's Skelton," the head said. "Bill Skelton. What's yours?"

It was such a common, offhand inquiry that Chaine began to reply before he caught himself. If they didn't know, fine. If they wanted to make an issue of it, so much the better.

But the head that had identified itself as "Bill Skelton" didn't really seem to care whether he answered or not.

"The name you gave when you came in here to plant your bomb," it said conversationally, "was 'Robin Utley.' So we can go on calling you that, if you like. Or we could make it 'Micah Chaine.' That's the one we got from Charles Pennington."

Chaine felt a sharp stinging sensation inside the elbow of his right arm, and tried to move it. But it was still paralyzed.

"We just thought perhaps you'd prefer to die under your own name," the other head said, visible once again at the left edge of the universe.

Chaine twisted his head from side to side and tried to move his shoulders in an effort to obtain a better view of the more familiar head, perhaps to determine whether or not it was connected to a body. If it wasn't, then this was surely a dream. If it was . . .

"I guess it's time to bring you up to speed, now," the Bill Skelton head said, glancing away for a moment as if checking something in the near vicinity. "Let's have a little less light for a moment."

The brilliance above his head diminished suddenly, and a moment later Chaine was able to discern the outlines of several high-power lamps, arranged inside a reflector system. The peripheral array had gone dark now, and the central globes, evidently on a rheostat, were reduced to a bearable level.

He looked around him, trying to accustom his eyes to the comparative gloom.

"Better?" the Skelton voice inquired, and now Chaine was able to note that the voice and the head were, indeed, attached to a body.

All right, then. No dream. But . . . what?

He looked curiously around the room, noting its considerable size, the shadowed remoteness of the ceiling, the dark outlines of a windowed wall, darkness outside the windows in the far distance. Apparently it was still nighttime. The rest he couldn't see. His head was mobile, but the rest of him seemed to be tethered in some way. Curious now, but still unintimidated, Chaine craned his neck to look down at himself.

The view was not reassuring.

A sheet seemed to be in the way, but he was able to discern the basic outlines of his situation. He was lying on a bed, or perhaps it was a kind of table, and his body was bound to it by a number of straps, augmented at strategic points with heavy adhesive tape. Special attention had been paid to his arms.

They were taped tightly to boards that were somehow attached to the sides of the bed.

Something else about the right arm . . .

Yes. A pressure cuff was attached to his upper right arm, just above the elbow, and an I.V. was running through a needle that had been inserted into a vein. He looked away, wanting to ask a question but not willing to give his captors the satisfaction. Who did they think they were – and who did they think they were dealing with? Did they really believe they could frighten him?

"By now," the one named Skelton was saying, "I suppose you have a number of questions you might like to ask. But I don't think you're going to ask any of them, because you feel that would give us some kind of advantage."

He paused, as if expecting an answer, but Chaine remained silent, inwardly annoyed that Skelton had called his bluff.

"No matter," Skelton went on. "We want you to know about everything that has happened to you thus far, so you will not only understand what happens next, but also why it is happening."

"Suaviter . . . en . . . modo."

The voice was back in working order, crisp and distinct, and Chaine was gratified to note that there was no quaver of uncertainty. Spit in their eyes! Believe it!

But Bill Skelton only smiled.

"Fortier en re," he said equably, completing the Latin phrase. "'Gentle in manner, resolute in execution.' Oh, that's us, for sure, my bomb-making friend."

He seemed on the verge of saying something else, but shrugged and moved aside as the other doctor emerged from the shadows to take over. The one he'd recognized. Taylor.

"Earlier tonight," Jeff Taylor said, ignoring the previous exchange, "you made an appointment with Charles Pennington to trade his friend, Julia Hartt, for one million dollars in cash. The exchange was to be made at a beach restaurant called 'Captain Jack's'."

It was a statement requiring no reply, and the doctor's expression was neutral. But Chaine told himself there was something, some important fact, that he ought to remember about this person. He fixed his attention on the doctor's face, trying to penetrate the peculiar composure and wondering, though still almost academically, what might be going on behind it.

But the memory eluded him.

"You knew Pennington couldn't bring the police into this," Jeff continued, "and I think that made you a little more careless than usual. You got into his car without checking the back seat."

He waited for Chaine to assimilate this, and gave a small nod of approval when the man's face told him that he understood.

"My colleague, here, Dr. Skelton, was in the back with a syringe full of sleepy-juice."

"Enough to fell an elephant," Skelton confirmed, still faintly smiling.

Chaine turned his head to look at Skelton with renewed interest. Nerdy-looking little character. Who'd have thought he'd had it in him?

"And so," Jeff continued, "we find ourselves here. Just you . . . and us."

He had said the words as though they ought to mean something special, but Chaine couldn't imagine what it might be. He glanced around at those parts of the room available to his limited radius of sight. Nothing new, except for a few tables like his own dimly visible in the vicinity. They meant nothing to him. But he was not left in ignorance for long.

"We are in a gross anatomy laboratory, in the teaching wing of Northwest Regional Medical Center," Jeff said. "Do you know what a gross anatomy laboratory is? What is done there?"

"Should I care?"

That response drew another little smile from Skelton. But Jeff Taylor did not seem to notice.

"This," he said, "is where medical students dissect cadavers – cut up dead bodies – to learn first-hand how they are put together. It is a vital part of their education, and if that doesn't seem really important to you just now, I think that it might become so in the very near future. Because you are going to become a part of that process. Are you following me, Mr . . . Utley?"

Chaine's eyes narrowed momentarily as he took in the proportions of the threat, but his common sense still rejected the idea. It just wasn't real.

"That," Bill Skelton said, taking up the narration, "is why we went to so much trouble to keep you in one piece. Undamaged."

Chaine didn't reply, but his face said he didn't understand, and Skelton was quick to explain.

"Gross anatomy," he said, "requires whole bodies. Complete. They can't have missing limbs or be badly damaged because that would cheat the students of a chance to see how each part ought to look, how it ought to fit its surrounding parts. You see?"

Chaine did. It was clear, however, that he still didn't accept their account of events as entirely factual. Skelton's patience, however, seemed infinite.

"We could have taken you at any time after you left the restaurant," he said. "Jeff and I were both armed, and he was inside the restaurant, not ten feet from you. He could have followed you out and then killed you in the parking lot."

"But we didn't want to do that," Jeff said.

"No," Skelton agreed. "As I said, we wanted you intact because we wanted to show you something that we thought you might find interesting."

He stepped back a pace, as though inviting an audience to inspect the array of I.V. stands, tubes, plungers and shunts arranged on the right side of the table to which Chaine was tethered.

"You've shown a lot of interest in our specialty," Jeff said. "In euthanasia. So we thought you might get a little lift out of seeing just how it works. First-hand."

Chaine looked down at his arms again, then at the apparatus connected to the I.V. needle.

"Sorry about that," Jeff said in a tone that held no trace of regret. "We really have to apologize for the crudeness of the accommodations. Ordinarily, we'd have been able to offer you more sophisticated equipment and a more comfortable setting. But this was the best we could do, under the circumstances."

"That's right," Skelton said. "You see, the quarters where we usually do our work were wrecked by a bomb and all of our equipment was either damaged or destroyed. You follow me, friend?"

Jeff went over to stand beside the array of tubing and shunts connected to the IV. "This equipment," he said, "had to be taken from storage earlier today. And it will have to go back again when we're through with it."

"So, of course, we had to do without a few things. Nonessentials, as it were," Skelton said. "For instance, I'm afraid we weren't able to bring any sodium pentothal."

Jeff tapped the plastic container presently feeding slowly into Chaine's arm.

"This is a substance called D-5 lactated Ringer's," he said. "It can be used for several different things around an operating room, but in this case its job is mostly to keep that vein open so the other fluids we'll be using will enter your system readily."

"You following so far?" Skelton wanted to know.

But there was no pause for an answer.

"Normally," Jeff went on, "there would be a shunt here, connected to a syringe full of the sodium pentothal I mentioned. That's to relax the patient. Induce sleep. That way there's no pain or anxiety."

"But we knew you'd want to see it all, experience every moment," Skelton chimed in. "So you'll be awake through the whole process."

"Let me explain exactly what's going to happen," Jeff took over again, carefully monitoring his tone to guard against any hint of the rage that continued to boil just below the surface.

"As soon as you're ready – or, in this case, as soon as we decide the time is right – I'll depress this plunger."

He picked up what appeared to be an oversized hypodermic syringe and held it out to give Chaine a clear view. It was attached to a tube leading to a "Y" connector, which was, in turn, attached to the I.V. in his arm.

"This syringe," Jeff said, "contains pancuronium bromide. It's a paralyzing agent, and you will know that it's in your body, doing its work, when you stop breathing. The muscles used to draw breath will be paralyzed, unable to function. But not instantly. No. I really think it might take, oh, perhaps as much as one or two minutes. Less, if you struggle." He turned to Skelton as if for corroboration. "I think he could go for a minute anyhow, don't you?" he asked.

"Oh, yes. Maybe more."

Jeff nodded thoughtfully.

"In any case," he said, returning the pancuronium syringe to its place and picking the one that lay beside it. "In any case, it won't matter a whole lot, because here, in this syringe, is a substance that will do the job instantly."

He held the instrument up for Chaine's inspection.

"Potassium chloride. Just a little bit of this, not much at all, and your heart stops beating. Just stops. And that, as they say, is that."

He put the second syringe back beside the first and turned again to face Chaine. "Ordinarily," he went on, "we'd have you wired up to monitors of various kinds. Heart. Brain waves. Respiration. The whole nine yards. But as I said before, this procedure is kind of impromptu."

"So, no monitors," Skelton said. "When the drugs are in you, we'll just back off and wait for you to slow down and stop. And then we'll unstrap you and put you inside a container like the one on which you are resting right now."

Skelton moved aside to show him what he meant. As in most gross anatomy laboratories, the cadavers, when not actually being dissected, were kept safe and cool inside coffin-like storage tables, which would raise automatically to a convenient height for study when the lid was opened. Skelton opened the lid of one such table and raised the body up and into Chaine's field of vision to give him a clear view. The dissection process had hardly begun. The body was almost intact.

"This," he said, allowing the subject to sink out of sight again as he closed the lid, "is why we chose to demonstrate our process to you here, rather than in some other, perhaps more convenient, part of the hospital. First, because this wing is deserted at this time of night; no one is going to hear you if you make a little noise."

"And more importantly," Jeff resumed, "because getting rid of a body can be a problem, even for a doctor. But here in gross anatomy, you'll just be another teaching tool."

"No questions asked," Skelton agreed. "Kind of anonymous. But . . . you don't really mind that, do you?" He smiled fondly, and reached out to pat Chaine's cheek.

Chaine suffered himself to be patted, glanced at Jeff, looked back at Skelton and then relaxed suddenly against the restraints as he exploded into gales of laughter, filling the room with the roar and gusto of pure animal delight.

The doctors stood silent, waiting for the ebullition to run its course. But Chaine seemed to be enjoying himself. Twice, he seemed about to subside, only to lose control again as yet another tidal wave of jubilation washed over him. At last the outburst began to taper toward an end.

"You idiots!" he marveled, when his voice was under control once more. "The two of you – Jesus, lover of my soul – there you stand, showing me your toys and waiting for me to go all trembly, thinking how it would be if you were to use them on me. Lord, what a total crock!" He shook his head in mock astonishment and closed his eyes.

"You don't believe us?" Skelton inquired.

"Not in a million years!"

Skelton was intrigued. "Why not?"

Chaine took a deep breath. "Because you're like a couple of bad little boys," he said, his tone suddenly patronizingly serious. "Little kids playing doctor. Or war. Or other kid games. You can't really murder anyone. Either of you!"

Jeff was startled. "But . . . we do," he pointed out.

"Do what?"

"Kill people. Every day. That's the nature of our work, remember? We're euthanasists. We help people die."

But Chaine was already shaking his head. "You kill people, yes," he said. "But you didn't do it before it was legal in this state. Right?"

"Of course not!"

Chaine's head nodded vigorously.

"Of course not!" he echoed. "Of course not, because that would be murder and you have to be able to tell yourselves that people like you don't do things like that. You need a license to kill a human being. A judge and legal papers and the law, all saying what you do is right and proper. You need somebody's permission!"

Jeff thought it over, and then nodded solemnly.

"You think we're too civilized."

"I think you're . . . pussies!"

"I see."

For a moment, oddly jarred by Chaine's use of the vulgarism and piqued by his line of reasoning, Jeff seemed ready to pursue the argument. But the impulse faded, and instead he turned away to check the I.V. tubes and the needle in Chaine's arm.

Chaine adjusted the position of his head to watch, with genuine interest, as Bill Skelton pumped the cuff on his arm to get a blood pressure reading, took his pulse, and noted both results to memory.

"You know," Chaine said, "if you were really going through with this, you wouldn't be doing any of that."

"How so?" he inquired.

"You're keeping a record on me as though I were one of your patients, but it would be the last thing on earth you'd do if you were serious about killing me. If this were not a game, you'd just . . . do it."

"Really."

"Really! I mean, look. I had a little training in the life-taking trade once, myself, in 'Nam. And the very first thing we learned was, if you're going to kill someone, really going to make him dead, you just do it. That's the first rule. Kill the bastard! Don't talk to him first. Don't let him talk to you. Just do him! Just –"

Chaine suddenly stopped talking. A look of mischief flashed across his face, and when he resumed talking, his voice was controlled, almost smug, as though he had discovered a new angle he had not thought of until then.

"Unless, of course, you're trying to make an example of him."

Skelton nodded judiciously and then suddenly realized where the crazy man might be going.

"What are you talking about?" he demanded.

"Your buddy. Doctor York. Poor bastard had to be the one exception to the rule." Chaine looked pleased with himself. "He's dead, of course. I didn't waffle on that. It's just that I didn't kill him right away –"

Before he could continue, Jeff grabbed Chaine by the collar and jerked his head off the table.

"Where's York!" he yelled, spitting the words at him. "What did you do to him?"

"He's burning in hell, Doctor!" Chaine said, almost gleefully, oblivious to the fact that it was he who was now at the mercy of an angry man. "He's as charred as that poor son of a bitch who got caught in the explosion right here in this temple of Satan! Only they won't be able to identify him by comparing his teeth to his dental records!" Chaine laughed maniacally.

Jeff slammed Chaine's head back down on the table, cutting off Chaine's laughter with a thud.

"You fucking bastard! You sick, deranged, murdering bastard!" Still grasping the collar in his tightly-clenched fist, Jeff lifted Chaine's head and began smashing it down on the hard table again and again.

In an instant, Bill Skelton grabbed Jeff's wrist. "Jeff!" he yelled, "Stop it! Stop! You can't do this!" Panic was in his voice.

Jeff turned to him, eyes wild with hatred. "Let go, Bill! I'm going to kill the son of a bitch!"

"Yes. You are! We are! But we can't damage him! You know that! We can't let there be a hint c͏ᶠ a struggle – you *know* that!" he repeated, emphasizing it with another hard squeeze of the hand now digging into Jeff's wrist.

Jeff's breathing was heavy and fast with adrenalin. He stared hard into Chaine's face, pulling it up to within an inch of his own blood-flushed face, knuckles white with rage.

"You're right, Bill," he hissed through clenched teeth, eyes fixed on the ex-priest. "We *are* going to kill him. And you're wrong, Chaine, we aren't just going to 'do you' as you say, but we're not into setting examples, either." Jeff paused, took a deep breath, and added in a harsh whisper, "We just want to kill you and we want you to feel it as it happens."

He released his hold on Chaine's collar and let his head drop back onto the table. Stepping back, hate-filled eyes still glued on Chaine's face, now contorted in pain, Jeff inhaled and exhaled deeply, several times, in an effort to bring his breathing, and his rage, under control. Bill Skelton released his own hold on Jeff's wrist, and the two doctors stood there, speechless, breathing audibly.

Chaine's eyes were shut tight as he dealt with the throbbing pain in the back of his head. But for the breathing, all else was silent.

"Bullshit!" Chaine suddenly blurted out, eyes still tightly closed. "All the two of you are really hoping to do is to frighten me. You want to watch me beg! But it's no sale. Satis verborum. Enough of words. The action's just not in you, so let's drop the charade."

The two doctors waited for him to say something more, but Chaine seemed to have run out of words.

Jeff shook his head emphatically. "No," he said, still trying to slow his breathing. "I can see why you might think as you do, and until this morning, you'd have been right. But things have changed. And to be perfectly honest, Mister Utley, or Chaine, or whatever it is, I don't give a damn whether you beg or not."

Chaine's eyes opened and he squinted inquiringly at Jeff.

"Even when the Euthanasia Center was bombed," Jeff said, "I was perfectly content, eager even, to have the police handle the matter. That's their job. Let them do it."

He waited for Chaine to respond, but, after a moment, he went on.

"Same thing even later," he said, "when I found out that someone had burned to death in the computer center, because of your damned bomb. People are like that, Mr. Utley. Objective. Impersonal. Rational . . . until violence touches them personally. You following me?"

He had Chaine's full attention now, but still the bomb-maker did not speak. He felt, but would not acknowledge, the sensation of fear that was beginning to well up inside of him.

"That line was crossed," Jeff continued, "when you blew up my car this morning. You meant it for me, but you got my wife instead, you son of a bitch! But by some miracle, she survived. Just barely, and her life's still hanging by a very thin thread."

For the first time, the fear that Chaine could no longer ignore was visible in his eyes. Jeff saw it and realized, without surprise, that he didn't really care.

"And if she does live, she won't be quite the same person. No one could be. You've done this to her. To us. So you can well and truly believe me when I say I don't really care to hear you beg. Or cry. Or laugh. Or do anything else." He paused again, and this time there was no mistaking the dawn of full awareness and understanding in the man strapped to the dissecting table.

Chaine knew now, for certain, that this was no prank. Jeff Taylor, at least, was entirely capable of carrying the program through to its end. This was all about revenge, and Chaine, more than anyone perhaps, knew just how determined a man motivated by avengement could be.

"All I want," Jeff concluded with a quiet sincerity that annihilated any lingering doubt, "is to take your life. I want to do it with my own hands and I want to make it as painful and terrible and frightening as I can, while still keeping your body in shape for the gross anatomy students."

It was a simple, straightforward statement of purpose. Clear. Concise. Not subject to much interpretation. Chaine accepted it at face value.

"Crazy," he breathed in a voice of nails and gravel. "You're both . . . crazy!"

Jeff did not deny it, and Skelton seemed almost relieved.

"We may be crazy," he said, nodding in Chaine's direction, "but we're also alive."

Conversation was suspended then, and the doctors busied themselves with what appeared to be last minute physical arrangements.

Skelton disappeared, walked out of the range of Chaine's vision for a brief moment and returned with a sheet of clear plastic, folded flat.

"There will be some things to clean up when we're done," he said to Jeff. "Thought I'd put this down, make sure nothing spills on the floor."

Jeff nodded absently, as he checked the two syringes, the shunts and the tube leading to Chaine's arm.

The bomb-maker's eyes were almost closed now, and his features were tight with an exaltation of effort that he didn't trouble to conceal. He was straining every muscle, exerting every ounce of will, in an attempt to break just one of the straps that bound him to the table. If one went, the others would go, too. One by one, he would break them all, and take these two lunatics in his hands.

Skelton noticed what was happening and nudged Jeff.

Jeff watched for a moment, but turned back to his work without visible reaction.

"Save your strength," he advised, addressing Chaine over his shoulder as he bent to some task just outside the bomber's line of sight. "In a minute or two, you're going to want it all, just to take one more breath."

Chaine paid no attention.

Sweat burst from his forehead and upper torso as he strained against his bonds. Muscles groaned audibly and there was a distant crackling sound from the vicinity of his shoulders. But the restraints held firm while the doctors attended to last minute details.

At last all seemed to be in readiness.

Jeff picked up the two lethal syringes, unsnapped the safety clamps below their noses, and placed his thumb on the plunger of the one that held the pancuronium bromide.

"This is the injection that stops your breathing," he said, holding the syringe out to be sure that the man on the table had an unobstructed view.

Chaine made one final, maximum effort.

In panic mode now, eyes wide and breath coming in shallow gasps, he seemed to concentrate the whole force of his being on the straps across his chest. Muscles of the arms and upper torso knotted and trembled, and as Skelton watched in fascination, the fabric of Chaine's shirt burst along a seam. But the bindings held firm.

And then, as suddenly as it had begun, the paroxysm passed, leaving Chaine somehow diminished. The ego that had given peculiar life and individuality to his features seemed entirely drained from them. His eyes focused on some infinite and impersonal horizon.

"Let me go," he whispered.

"No."

"You are damning your souls, both of you, to eternal torment!"

"We'll just have to chance it."

"I am the Messenger of the Almighty!"

"You're a slimy, murdering son of a bitch who's about to get the nearest thing there is to justice in this world!"

If Chaine understood the answer, or even heard it, his face gave no sign. But the atmosphere in the vicinity of the table where he lay was filled suddenly with the unmistakable odor of terminal terror. Chaine had lost control of his anal sphincter.

"Aw . . . Jesus." Skelton stepped back a pace and turned his face away, disgusted. "Good thing I brought that plastic," he gasped. "We're going to need it."

Jeff, now with his back to Chaine, seemed hardly to notice. He was reflecting on what had transpired. The very depths of his conscience lay bare, exposed for self-examination. Perhaps by coincidence, he caught a glimpse of himself in the small mirror that hung above a sink in a darkened corner of the room. He paused.

"Will I be able to do this and then face myself the next time I look in the mirror?" he asked himself.

"Jeff, are you okay?" Skelton asked noticing Jeff's sudden change of mood.

No reply was offered.

What was once ungovernable rage had now manifested itself as calculated calmness. As a surgeon, there existed a barrier, an uncrossed, objective threshold which allowed the knife to perform its duty. Never wavering, cutting straight along the path, and resisting any show of emotion would allow him the sanctity of being focused. This, however, was a step beyond. Any further delay could produce less than the desired results. But Jeff couldn't resist. He had to speak to the pathetic man on the table.

"Now is the time for you to take a look inside yourself, Chaine. I think you are the one who needs to make atonement for your offenses."

Rather than looking at Chaine, Jeff looked through him as the first portion of the venom reached Chaine's blood vessel.

"You will never kill again. You're dead. You're fucking dead."

"No!" was the last discernable word that spewed from Micah Chaine's mouth.

He remained calm, but only for a moment. Suddenly, he felt entirely embraced by the overwhelming power of the drug. Paralysis was beginning to occur secondary to the neuromuscular blockade. Each time a breath was taken, two were lost. His mind pleaded for air, begged for it, but his body couldn't respond. He began thrashing about and the effect was accelerated as promised. Drowning. He was drowning and there was no escape. Gasping, his thoughts turned to sheer terror, easily visible in his contorted face.

A full minute had passed, and every second felt like ten as Chaine's body writhed and shook in its final, desperate moments of life. At last, his bound body heaved upward as a thickened bloody froth filled his lungs then overflowed into his mouth and nostrils. A final gurgling sound exited his throat, signaling the death of Micah Chaine.

Skelton remained in the background, saying nothing, while Jeff bolused the corpse with potassium to end any doubt. The two doctors stood for a long minute looking at Chaine's remains.

Some paperwork remained so that, by the time the gross anatomy class would arrive the next day, the body would be carefully integrated into the dissection program. In a month or two, there would be nothing for anyone to find. Ever.

Jeff urged Skelton to go home and leave him to the task of filling out the required forms. At first, Skelton refused to leave Jeff with that onerous task, especially in light of the fact that he so desperately needed sleep. But one look at Jeff's face said that he needed the time alone, not so much to think, but to busy himself with some mundane drudgery, perhaps to bring a sense of normalcy back into a day that was so very far from normal.

After they cleaned Chaine's corpse, they moved it to another table to replace the blood with a latex solution, the minimal embalming procedure required by the lab. When they finished the job, Skelton turned to look directly at Jeff. He said nothing for a moment, but remained thoughtful, exhaling slowly.

"Well, I guess that's it," he said, quietly. "It seems so anticlimactic, just walking away from this as if nothing extraordinary had just happened."

"Nothing extraordinary did happen, Bill," Jeff said, with equal solemnity. "We just did our job. We put a man out of his misery and out of ours."

Skelton smiled faintly.

"Good night, Jeff. I wish I could convince you to let me stay and help you with those tedious forms, but I know better than to argue with you at this point."

"Thanks," Jeff said, reaching out to give his companion a friendly squeeze on the shoulder. "For everything."

Jeff sat down to prepare the various files and documents required by the teaching hospital. Normally, it was a simple task. But this was not just another day, and Jeff found himself making errors in procedure and even in spelling as he struggled with the documentation. Pain and fatigue weighed at his arms and eyelids; he would have mortgaged his immortal soul for an hour of dreamless sleep. But more exasperating than the physical discomforts was the undischarged emotional pressure that caused his fingers to fumble at the typewriter keys, and the muscles of his back to shiver with a chill that had nothing at all to do with the temperature of the room. Stubbornly, fighting to focus on each individual task, he worked on.

And finally it was done. Slipping the last bogus certificate into its folder and extinguishing the office lights, Jeff forced himself into a standing posture, took a single step toward the door and stopped short, realizing he had no clear idea of where he was going. Or why. Not home, certainly. His brief visit there with Bill Skelton had been more than enough. He would go there again when he was ready. But not now.

The alternatives, however, were unattractive. At the other side of the hospital, outside the main building but still on the grounds, were the dormitories allotted to interns and unattached residents. He could, if he wished, find a bed there. Or he could check into one of the various motels in the vicinity.

Taking a deep breath to quiet the jangle of nerves that besieged him, Jeff stood still in the darkness and fought back the demons of fatigue, anxiety and emotional confusion long enough to look closely at his own needs and realized, with a sudden shock of recognition, that the answer had been staring at him all the time.

Like most happily married men, what he wanted and needed most in the world was to talk things over with his wife.

Chapter Thirty-Four

Jolene's condition seemed unchanged. She was still in a coma, and while the floor nurse made no objection when he passed her desk and walked into his wife's room, it was clear that she thought he was wasting his time.

Jeff looked at the monitors and wasn't encouraged. Heart rhythm and respiration were within normal parameters, and the computer record of the past few hours showed them unchanged during that time.

But the brain's alpha wave remained flat.

Knuckling weariness from his eyes and fighting to maintain a surface attitude of professional detachment that he knew was his only bastion against the rise of rage and panic, he forced himself to check through the whole EEG printout.

But it offered little cheer. This record, while generally discouraging with minimal beta and delta waves and a flat alpha, offered occasional and apparently random spikes of what might have been alpha activity, and he recognized at once their similarity to the occasional blips that he and the others had disregarded in the Barclay case.

Barclay had recovered. There was hope in that. But not enough to cling to. Barclay had been one in a million.

Never mind.

This was Jolene. His wife was here, beside him, in this room. He drew a chair close to the bed, sat in it, and took her hand. For awhile, it was enough merely to sit with her in silence. His eyes closed momentarily, and he thought of sleep. But too much had happened in too little time. The pressure within was greater than the pressure without, and somehow the imbalance had to be equalized. He took a deep breath, and began.

"I learned something important tonight," he said.

There was no response, of course, and he had not expected one. Yet he found that he couldn't avoid the momentary pause for reply. Though only one person was talking, this was not a monologue.

"A lunatic," he went on, "a violent, crazy man taught me more about the nature of my profession, and my own place in it, than I managed to learn in all the years of med school, internship and residency."

He shook his head in mock bewilderment. "Isn't that . . . crazy?"

Jolene's hand remained limp, but warm, in his, and the silence of the room was broken only by the sound of his own voice and an occasional metallic quaver from one of the machines. To Jeff, however, the simple act of speaking had filled the empty space with a real presence. He wasn't alone.

"We got him," he said. "Bill Skelton and I. We found the man who blew up the hospital and almost killed you. It was amazing, completely out of left field, but we got him.

Jeff paused again, glancing in the direction of the monitors as if to read in them some acknowledgment of what he now saw as a grotesque fantasy. But there was nothing.

"Instead of turning him over to the police," he went on, "Bill and I kidnapped the guy, drugged him, and brought him here. To the hospital. We strapped him to a table in the gross anatomy lab and then let him wake up. Just like something out of a Vincent Price movie." He sighed. "Talking about it now, he said, "you know, I have trouble believing it really happened. But it did. We woke him up. Told him what we were going to do, and why. Then we put an I.V. needle in his arm and performed the procedure."

A nurse passed the room, looked in for a moment, and then went her way.

Jeff didn't notice her.

"I had to do it." He paused again, as if to let the simple declarative sentence float in the air above their heads. He drew a deep breath, let it out slowly, and continued in a voice somehow less urgent than it had been in the beginning.

For just a moment, it seemed to him that Jolene's hand had tensed, that the fingers had responded to some message from the brain. But the EEG scan remained flat, except for one of the meaningless blips, and he dismissed the idea as wishful thinking.

"The most important thing I learned, the big thing, was that I am not even cut out to be a euthanasist in the first place." A wry smile played at the corners of Jeff's mouth as he relaxed in the chair, most of the day's tensions already discharged and the rest flowing quietly and clearly into oblivion as he spoke his mind.

"Euthanasia has its place," he said, nodding a little for emphasis. "The arguments that we used, protection of the patient's terminal dignity, prevention of hopeless suffering, the right of a human being to control his own life, all these are valid. I was convinced in the beginning, and I'm still convinced. I haven't changed my mind and I don't think I'm going to. But . . ."

He paused for breath, and for another over-the-shoulder peek at the monitors. They seemed unchanged.

"But it's not for me. I'm so tired of death. I've killed for the last time." He smiled at Jolene and gave her hand an extra squeeze.

"What it comes down to," he went on, "is that I finally remembered something that kind of got lost there for awhile. Hell, babe, I forgot why I decided to be a doctor in the first place!"

His face was turned away from the monitors again, so he didn't mark the sudden slight irregularity in breathing, the minor acceleration of the heart, and the tiny, but increasingly frequent, spasms of activity visible on the EEG.

"Sure, I wanted the money and the prestige and all that. Who doesn't? But we both know that's not the whole story. The knowledge that you can really make things better for someone, give them back a life, that's the Seven Cities of Cibola and the Philosopher's Stone and the Lost Continent of Atlantis! The real jackpot! The works! I just do not, and will never, get that sense of accomplishment, that sense of purpose, from practicing euthanasia."

He sighed and stretched, satisfied at last to have uttered the words aloud and listened to them and found them both true and acceptable.

"Tomorrow," he said, "I'm going to go see Rickoff and tell him. I'm going to tell him I'm out of the residency program. And more than that, I'll tell him I'm going back into surgery."

Jeff stopped talking abruptly and stared with real interest at his maimed left hand. As always, two fingers were curled into his palm. But the others were totally responsive, and he found that the memory of their strength and dexterity during the wild ambulance ride to the hospital with Jolene was as fresh as ever.

"What's been going on, here," he went on, "has been a downright disgraceful case of self-pity." He snorted in disgust. "I got hurt. Okay. And I took that as an excuse to crawl off to a little box in the corner and invite people to pat me on the head. God!

"But even though I may not deserve it, it looks like there could be a reprieve. Judging by what happened today, it seems just possible that I might be able to work around the problem. I can train the three remaining fingers to do the work of five. It might just be possible!"

Jeff thought for a moment.

"And what if it isn't possible? I guess there are no guarantees. What happened today may be a one-shot deal. I won't know until I try. But even if that's how it is, and it turns out there really are surgical procedures that are beyond me, so what? Even if I still had all ten fingers, there would be operations like that. Everyone, but everyone, has limits.

"The thing is, I'm back to square one. Home again! Back to being a Real Doctor. Gonna heal with steel!"

He permitted himself a brief retrospective grin, and the last of the stiffness left his face. He allowed his head to fall back against the cushioned back of the chair.

"Oh, babe," he said softly. "Oh, babe, it's going to be so great . . . so great . . . just as long as you're with me."

Behind him, the EEG monitor had begun to trace regular alpha and beta waves, while delta responses were less frequent – a clear pattern of deep sleep, rather than coma.

Jeff saw none of it. His eyes were closed, his face filled with the peace of decisions reached, choices made and journeys ended. He was where he wanted to be. With Jolene. The rest could wait.

The fingers of the hand he was holding curled comfortably around his own.

And then, at last, he slept.